THE DEVIL

UNLEASHED

Visit us at www.boldstrokesbooks.com

What Reviewers Say About BOLD STROKES Authors

KIM BALDWIN

"*Force of Nature* is filled with nonstop, fast paced action. Tornadoes, raging fire blazes, heroic and daring rescues…Baldwin does a fine job of describing the fast-paced scenes and inspiring the reader to keep on turning the pages." – *L-word.comLiterature*

ROSE BEECHAM

"…her characters seem fully capable of walking away from the particulars of whodunit and engaging the reader in other aspects of their lives." – *Lambda Book Report*

GEORGIA BEERS

"Beers weaves a tale of yearning, love, lust, and conflict resolution. She has constructed a believable plot, with strong characters in a charming setting." – *JustAboutWrite*

RONICA BLACK

"*Wild Abandon* tells how these two women come to realize that 'life was too precious to be ruled by…fears, by…demons.' While these two women struggle with their issues, there is some very, very hot sex. If you enjoy complex characters and passionate sex scenes, you'll love *Wild Abandon*." – *MegaScene*

GUN BROOKE

"*Course of Action* is a romance…populated with a host of captivating and amiable characters. The glimpses into the lifestyles of the rich and beautiful people are rather like guilty pleasures…a most satisfying and entertaining reading experience." – *Midwest Book Review*

CATE CULPEPPER

"…an exceptional storyteller who has taken on a very difficult subject …and turned it into a spellbinding novel. As an author, she understands well that fiction can teach us our own history." – *JustAboutWrite*

JANE FLETCHER

"*The Exile and the Sorcerer* is a mesmerizing read, a tour-de-force packed with adventure, ordeals, complex twists and turns, and the internal introspection of appealing characters." – *Midwest Book Review*

JD GLASS

"*Punk Like Me*…is different. It is engaging. It is life-affirming. Frankly, it is genius. This is a rare book in that it has a soul; one that is laid bare for all to see." – *JustAboutWrite*

GRACE LENNOX

"*Chance* is refreshing…Every nuance is powerful and succinct. *Chance* is not a novel about the music industry; it is about a woman discovering herself as she muddles through all the trappings of fame." – *Midwest Book Review*

LEE LYNCH

"Lynch, with a dozen novels to her credit dating back to the early days of Naiad Press, has earned her stripes as a writerly elder. She was contributing stories to the lesbian magazine *The Ladder* four decades ago. But this latest is sublimely in tune with the times." – *Q-Syndicate*

JLEE MEYER

"*Forever Found*…neatly combines hot sex scenes, humor, engaging characters, and an exciting story." – *MegaScene*

RADCLYFFE

"…well-plotted…lovely romance…I couldn't turn the pages fast enough!" – Ann Bannon, author of *The Beebo Brinker Chronicles*

SUSAN SMITH

"This disparate duo's lush rush of a romance - which incorporates reincarnation, a grounded transman and his peppy daughter, and the dark moods of a troubled witch - pays wonderful homage to Leslie Feinberg's classic gender-bending novel, *Stone Butch Blues*." – *Q-Syndicate*

ALI VALI

"Rich in character portrayal, *The Devil Inside* by Ali Vali is an unusual, unpredictable, and thought-provoking love story that will have the reader questioning the definition of right and wrong long after she finishes the book." – *JustAboutWrite*

THE DEVIL
UNLEASHED

by

Ali Vali

2006

THE DEVIL UNLEASHED
© 2006 BY ALI VALI. ALL RIGHTS RESERVED.

ISBN 1-933110-61-9

THIS TRADE PAPERBACK ORIGINAL IS PUBLISHED BY
BOLD STROKES BOOKS, INC.,
NEW YORK, USA

FIRST EDITION DECEMBER 2006

CREDITS
EDITORS: SHELLY THRASHER AND STACIA SEAMAN
PRODUCTION DESIGN: STACIA SEAMAN
COVER DESIGN BY SHERI (GRAPHICARTIST2020@HOTMAIL.COM)

By the Author

The Devil Inside
Carly's Sound

Acknowledgments

Thank you to Radclyffe for believing in my writing and for your continued encouragement. Your staff and the rest of the Bold Strokes family have been wonderful from the time I signed on.

This book is a sequel to *The Devil Inside*, and I wanted to thank all those who read it and enjoyed it enough to want more. That is the highest compliment you can pay a writer—wanting more.

The Devil Inside and *The Devil Unleashed* would not exist without the tireless dedication and work of my editor, Shelley Thrasher. Each word I write is important to me as an author, and Shelley treats them with the kind of respect that makes me grateful to Radclyffe for introducing us. She has been the kindest of teachers, a great sounding board, and the best when it comes to giving praise. Thank you, Shelley, for the hours you put into this and for your and Connie's friendship as well.

Thanks also to my partner for providing the inspiration I need to keep the words flowing. You have been and continue to be the muse that sparks my imagination. This past year hasn't been the easiest, and I'm sure we have some hard days yet to come, but it only strengthens our commitment to each other. Difficult or easy, each day with you is a gift I try hard never to squander.

Dedication

For C and Papi
You both instill in me the imagination to tell stories
and the courage to share them

CHAPTER ONE

"Fuck!" Merrick Runyon said, slamming the phone down. Blue, the manager of the club Emerald's, had called to tell her about the explosion that had just destroyed it. If she had to guess, mob boss Giovanni Bracato had thrown the first punch in the upcoming war. With his sons and grandson back in his possession, Giovanni wasn't wasting any time on exacting revenge.

The tall, slim African American woman leapt from the desk chair in Derby Cain Casey's home office, the clanging alarm system making her dive to the floor and start crawling. As soon as she opened the door, the wall of Cain's first-floor office erupted with gunfire. Screams rang from every corner of the house as soon as the firing began, which, judging from the spray of bullets, wasn't going to end any time soon. Outside, three of the six men stationed on the wall had to be dead for anyone to get this kind of access to the back of the house.

The gunfire seemed to be concentrated on the office and the bedrooms. With the safety of a few walls between her and the outside of the house, Merrick ran up the stairs. If something happened to Cain's family on her watch, she'd never find anyplace on earth to hide. She gripped her Glock 9 mm as she sprinted down the hall to the rooms where Hayden, Emma, and Hannah Casey had been sleeping.

"Emma," Merrick yelled as she ran.

A huge wave of relief washed over her as Hayden stepped into the hall in just a pair of jeans. She pushed the twelve-year-old to the ground and continued to the room next door, where she found Emma and five-year-old Hannah cowering in the middle of the room in front of the bed. Without thinking, she dashed in, grabbed them both by the collar, and dragged them into the hall. The windows were history and the wall looked like swiss cheese, but they were safe.

Merrick pointed at Hayden. "Stay here, I mean it."

They would be safe in the middle of the house on the second floor unless the idiots outside planned to use some sort of missile as a big finish to the colossally stupid move they had already made by opening fire on Cain's house, especially with her family at home.

From her vantage point at a window in the back of the house, Merrick could see two cars and a utility truck with the rear basket in the up position in the street. The man in the basket, holding an Uzi and what seemed like an endless supply of clips, was covering the two men who'd scaled the wall. The cars were inching forward with the back doors open, waiting for the climbers to hit the sidewalk.

Thankfully, reinforcements had arrived, and more of Cain's guards were returning fire. Merrick jerked the window open and aimed for the driver of the first car, keeping her finger on the trigger until she emptied the clip. The car drifted to the sidewalk and crashed into a vehicle parked on the street. The attackers jumped out and joined their allies in the second vehicle, but not before Cain's men took out another three of them. After Merrick rammed another clip into the gun, she shot the guy in the utility truck in the head, and the driver sped away, the basket still raised.

An almost eerie silence followed as the car raced after the truck toward town. Emma Casey sat clutching both of her children, almost in shock as she waited for Merrick to come back and tell her what was going on. She hadn't been out of town long enough to forget what the alarm from the men guarding the house meant. When the thing had gone off she had grabbed Hannah and hit the floor out of pure instinct, Cain's warnings ringing in her ears from years before.

"Mama, what's happening?" Her daughter sounded terrified, and Emma could feel her shaking from the abrupt awakening. Hannah pressed her small hands against her ears as if they hurt from all the noise.

"It's all right, Hannah. Merrick and the rest of Mom's men will make it all right," Hayden answered for her. "There's just some bad people outside, but they won't hurt us."

"Emma, get the kids dressed and ready to move."

The order came from the top of the stairs where Merrick stood. She breathed deeply, as if to center herself, as she jammed the gun back into its shoulder holster. "I have to call the cops, and I don't want you here if I can help it."

"You mean they aren't on the way after all this?"

"Before we let anyone on these grounds, I have to look around."

"Hayden, go get ready, and take Hannah with you," Emma said.

Hannah, however, clung to her.

"Please, Hannah, go with your brother and I'll be right in."

Emma and Merrick stared at each other until the door to Hayden's room clicked closed.

"Who was out there, Merrick?"

"Some idiots who're going to regret their parents ever met once I tell Cain what happened today."

Emma ran her hand through her hair and closed her eyes for a long moment. "I want to go see Cain."

"Why?" In the last few days Merrick had grown to like Cain's wife, but she was about to see what Emma was made of. Merrick was afraid her boss was about to get screwed again.

"Whatever I need to see her about is between the two of us, Merrick. It's a family matter and really none of your business."

"You're right. I work for Cain and can't pry or make decisions for her, but I'd spend the time until we get to the hospital thinking about what you're going to say. Cain's willing to give you just so many chances. Then not even the Virgin Mary will get you back where you want to be." Merrick tapped her finger against her temple. "Just some food for thought."

Pausing halfway down the stairs, she shouted back up to Emma. "Finish getting dressed and don't come out until I come get you. I've got a few things to do before we can even think about moving to the hospital, so be a little patient."

Emma watched Merrick take the rest of the steps two at a time. *She's right, Emma. You cut and run now, and it's over.* She wasn't going to run away again, but was it fair to raise children in a house where they could get killed just for sleeping in their own beds? Surprisingly, the voice in her head that asked the question sounded a lot like her mother's, and for once it didn't sound all that unreasonable. A responsible person would have been on the first flight out of town, consequences be damned.

Behind her Hayden opened the door, fully dressed and holding Hannah's hand. "You want to leave now, don't you?"

"I'm not going anywhere without you, sweetheart."

Hayden pulled back as Emma reached out. "Just so you know I won't live anywhere without Mom. I want to be with Hannah, but not at the expense of my mother."

"We don't have to talk about this now."

"Merrick's right, you know, and I hope you listen to her. If you walk away again Mom might not let you come back. If you do go, I'm staying here with her, just so you know."

Emma was stunned. "Like I said, we don't have to talk about anything right now."

"I heard you, but I just want you to know that before we get to the hospital."

Emma didn't have any idea what she would say when she visited Cain.

❖

Three dead strangers sprawled on the sidewalk, and another lolled in the front seat of the abandoned car. When Merrick snapped her fingers, two of her men removed anything that would identify them. As Cain's personal bodyguard and the head of her security forces, she had to make sure they carried out a thorough investigation before the cops arrived. She strode to the car, pushed the guy over, and jerked out his wallet before going to the passenger side and removing all the papers in the glove box.

One of her men shoved everything they found into a bag and hurried back toward the house in case the police were on a quicker schedule than they planned for. Then another pulled out a digital camera and snapped pictures of the remnants of the men's faces.

"Make copies and don't come back until I know who paid them. Whoever finds the ones who got away will get a big bonus in his paycheck this week. Now get moving." Merrick stalked to the front door.

Sirens sounded in the distance, probably responding to a dozen emergency calls from the neighbors. Merrick figured they mostly thought it was 'kind of cool to live next door to such an infamous personality—until the ugliness of Cain's life landed on their doorstep so dramatically. She shook her head and headed inside. For the rest of the day she would have to answer questions and prove she and her men had acted in self-defense. From the kitchen she made two phone calls to speed up the process.

"Muriel, I need you at the house as soon as you can get here. We have a situation, and I don't want it to get out of control. And I sure don't want the police to use it to broaden the scope of the investigation that'll begin in about two minutes."

Muriel Casey sat up in her office chair and tapped her fingers on the mahogany desk, a gift from her cousin Cain when she'd graduated from LSU Law School. "What's the situation?"

"Someone blew up Emerald's before coming over here and shooting up the back of the house."

When Merrick explained, she sounded like she was ordering lunch, but Muriel knew better. Later, Merrick would decompress over a stiff drink, but now she had to keep her head.

"Anyone hurt?" Before Merrick could answer, something else occurred to Muriel. "Wait, if you were at the house, that means Emma and the kids were with you. God, tell me there isn't a scratch on them."

"They're fine, physically anyway. I'm afraid the trauma may frighten away our little blond bird, but I don't have time to think about that. I'm going to call Agent Daniels next. We have enough trouble trying to keep the locals at bay, so maybe for once the feds will come in handy."

Muriel stopped tapping her fingers and flattened her hand on the cool wooden surface. "I'm not saying that's a bad idea, but hold off on that call. Get Emma and the kids out of there for now and over to the hospital. Cain will want to see them all as soon as possible, just for peace of mind."

"I think we should phone the feds now, Muriel. This has someone else's fingerprints all over it, since I don't believe Giovanni can be this stupid. I say we turn them in to the proper authorities and let them give us a head start on the investigation."

"I'll make the call after I talk with Cain, but only when you're out of the house. After all, Cain's the one who says you should live with your blinds open every so often, even when you should be locking the doors. Shows whoever's watching you that you aren't dirty."

On her end, Merrick twirled a paring knife between her fingers, trying to temper her desire to plunge it into someone's chest. "Do you think it's a good idea for me to leave? Won't the police wonder where I've gone? I'll look like I'm running from something."

"You'll look like you're trying to protect the people you're hired to protect. I know who we're dealing with, my friend, so I can only imagine the damage they've left behind. No one's going to blame you for trying to keep Emma and the children safe. If the police need to talk to you, they'll do it with me in the room. It's not like they won't know how to find you."

Muriel stood and buttoned her jacket. "Get moving, and I'll deal with everything. After all, that's my part of the job. Oh, make sure we have the gun permits handy, and everyone's license to carry them all the time. Having those might get me out of there before midnight."

"Call me if you need anything else."

"Merrick, that's my line."

Merrick grimaced, afraid that when Cain heard about this episode, she might want to stick a knife in her.

CHAPTER TWO

"My God. What's wrong? Is Cain okay?" Emma said when she saw the startled expression of the hospital administrator who met them and their protection in the lobby. It had never occurred to her that Cain might be in danger, since she was always the one who kept everyone safe. If someone had attacked Cain in her vulnerable state, Emma didn't know if she would be able to endure it.

"Please, Ms. Casey, I didn't mean to scare you. Everything's fine. Your partner just wanted me to escort you to her new private room." The administrator waved toward a bank of elevators.

As Emma, the children, Merrick, and Mook, Hayden's longtime bodyguard, rode to the sixth floor, Emma felt immensely better that they had a contingent of armed guards in the lobby. She imagined an assassin around every corner and jumped every time she heard a noise.

Considering all she'd been through in the last couple of months, Cain looked amazing. Being shot two weeks earlier by Agent Barney Kyle on her enemy Giovanni Bracato's order hadn't been the only thing that had taken its toll. She'd been dealing with the return of her partner Emma after a four-year absence, and the discovery of their daughter Hannah. Those emotional blows had been hard, especially since she was still grieving the murder of her sister Marie.

Now, though, there was no sign of the pallor that lingered since Agent Kyle shot her. She sat up in a chair talking to Lou, freshly showered, appearing like the Cain Casey all of them were used to dealing with. She still looked a little tired and on edge, but the strength that always seemed to pour from her was returning.

"Ah, now there's a good-looking group," Cain said, seeming surprised to see Emma.

When Cain nodded, everyone whose last name wasn't Casey left the room. Without any encouragement, Hannah ran to Cain and started climbing into her lap.

"Careful, honey. Cain's got an owie and we don't want to make it worse," Emma said. She moved to pick the little girl up but stopped when Cain shook her head brusquely.

"It's all right. Let her do what she wants. I feel better after a shower."

"Was that wise? You're still weak. And what about your sutures?"

"Don't worry. A big guy from the ward helped me since you weren't here. And they wrapped me up fairly tight before I got wet." Cain waved Emma off and opened her hand to her daughter. "How are you doing after all that excitement this afternoon, sweet girl?"

"It was scary, Mom," Hannah said, her fingers in her mouth.

"I know, sweetheart, but you're going to be all right. Nothing bad's going to happen to you, your mom, or your brother." She stroked Hannah's thick black hair and kissed her forehead. "I promise. Want something to drink?"

"Can I have a Coke?"

"What do you say, Emma, just this once?" Cain looked at her.

"Just one, Hannah, and you have to stay with Hayden the whole time." Emma helped her off Cain's lap and walked her and Hayden to the door. The sight of them following Mook down the hall made her heart hurt.

"Are you all right?" Cain asked as the door closed.

"Two carloads of men came and shot up the room where I was sleeping with our daughter and destroyed the room where you sit day after day working. Am I all right?" Emma's voice grew louder with each sentence, and Cain didn't try to stop her. "No, I'm not all right." The controlled veneer she'd put up for the sake of the children disappeared in a second as she twirled around to face Cain.

"Can I ask you something else?" Cain put up her hand this time when Emma opened her mouth. "Just be quiet and think about what I'm asking before you answer."

"What?"

"When you first met me, did you ask anyone who I was before you went out on our first date?" They had come a long way from that first night at the Erin Go Braugh, an Irish pub Cain owned in the French Quarter. That first date had blossomed into a relationship that had produced two children, but also the betrayal of Emma leaving.

"What does that have to do with anything?"

Cain stared at her and tried to appear relaxed, though she was convinced that Emma would leave her again. And this time would be the last. "It has everything to do with everything."

"I knew you were the owner of the pub and people had a million stories to tell about your women and what you did for a living. It was just all rumors, but I didn't go out and ask anyone about you specifically. Why?"

"Because I want to know if you knew me before you entered the devil's lair, Emma. No one forced you, so don't act like you think I was some saint who deceived you into a life you didn't want. Do you regret leaving the farm this time around?"

"Of course I don't regret coming back, but I love my children and want them to be safe."

"Come on, then, let's be done with it." With considerable effort Cain put her hands on the arms of the chair and pushed herself into a standing position. "Keep your place." Cain swayed a little, but didn't want any help from Emma. "I'll be keeping my feet and dignity as you tell me what you want."

"I want you—"

"But. It sounds like you wanted to end that statement with a 'but,' sweetling."

"I can't live like this. It's not you. I love you more than life, but we have to consider other people. Yes, I knew who you were before I committed to you, and I thought I could handle it, but I just want to keep us all safe. Is that wrong?"

The pain was starting to come in short aching throbs again, and it wasn't just from the wound. Cain dug deep to stay on her feet. "This time I didn't set myself up with unrealistic expectations of you, Emma, so I'm not disappointed. If you want to go, then go."

"Cain, please—"

"I won't stand in your way. You want to leave, you leave, no questions asked and no tearful farewells. But—yes, I can add those to the ends of sentences too—you won't take my children if they don't want to leave. I won't keep you from them, Emma, but that works both ways. You won't keep them from me either. I'm sure, being the only parent Hannah's ever known, she'll choose you, but if Hayden wants to stay, I won't send him away."

"Even if he could get hurt? He and Hannah could be dead right now. All that shooting—"

"Take off your blinders, Emma. You're standing here alive because my people did their jobs. You think people like Barney Kyle are going to keep you safe? Do you think I'll just hand over my kids to someone like your mother?"

"Forget my mother, and Kyle. I learned my lesson about trusting people like him. I just want us all to go somewhere until you're healthy and ready to take on what you need to, to make all this go away. You're a parent, Cain. Don't you want that for Hannah and Hayden?"

"I see it as running, and so will Bracato's men. Do you think Giovanni and his sons will show mercy until I'm ready to fight back? What you're asking will only put us in more danger. This is the life I've chosen, hard realities and all. Just because you can't take the heat, you don't have the right to use our children to try and guilt me into seeing things your way. Just get out."

As much as she wanted to stay on her feet, Cain had to either sit down or fall on the floor. "I don't have the energy to deal with all this shit and you along with it. Go back to the farm and to Mama, and tell her how she was right all along. We'll make arrangements as soon as you're settled."

"Please, Cain, we need to finish this."

"I said for you to leave. It's what you're good at, and I see it still comes naturally to you. Just tell Merrick where you're going."

"You want to know where I'll be?" Emma took a step forward.

"Of course I want to know where you'll be, since Hannah will be with you. I won't keep Hayden from you, but Hannah has a right to know me."

"Of course—"

Cain pinned Emma with a glare. "Get out. We're done."

Emma had hurt her for the last time.

CHAPTER THREE

W hat's wrong?" Hayden asked, having chased Emma into the ladies' restroom and found her leaning on one of the sinks with her head down, crying.

"Nothing, honey. Cain and I just had a painful conversation, and I'm trying to sort it out before we head back. I don't want you to worry about it."

"She gets upset sometimes, but you just have to give her time to cool off. You can't give up so easily."

"She gets upset with you?"

"Only when I run off and get picked up by some idiot. It's just a getting-upset-with-you-for-your-own-good kind of thing, as she likes to call it. There's usually a lecture, but most of the time I learn something, too. It's not all bad once the grounding part's over." He moved closer, as if he wanted to touch her, but stopped just short of that. "You just need to get to know her again, and then you'll see."

Emma ran the cold tap and washed her face before looking at Hayden. "Why do you think she's upset with me?"

"I don't know, but I'm sorry I gave you a hard time at first." He grabbed her hand. "I saw you guys today and how you made her smile. I want Mom to be happy."

"Do you want me to stay?" Emma asked as she peered into eyes so much like Cain's.

"I want you to not go. I want you to stay so Hannah will be close to us."

She shook her head, her eyes filled with tears. "No, do you want me to stay?"

"Yes. I want you to stay with Mom and me. We can't ever be a family if we're so far apart."

And that was just what Emma needed to hear.

As Emma headed back toward Cain's room, Merrick grasped her arm and stopped her. "Haven't you done enough damage for one day? You have the spine of a slug."

"I think you'd best get your hands off me and let me finish what I came here to do today." Emma pulled her arm free and continued down the hall, wiping her face as she went.

For the first time since the shooting, Emma was glad that Cain wasn't up to full strength. She walked back in as a nurse was arranging the sheets around Cain's waist on the bed, then stood silently while the woman folded the blankets neatly and wrote something on the chart. When the door clicked closed, Cain didn't even look at her, seeming tired of the whole exercise.

"Forget something?" Cain asked.

Instead of answering, Emma climbed onto the bed and straddled Cain's hips, taking care to keep her weight off Cain's injured chest. She leaned forward until her hands were at the sides of Cain's head and their faces were inches apart. "I have just one more thing to say, and then if you want, you can have one of your big goons throw me out."

"I'm listening."

Cain's smugness under pressure had always amazed Emma. They could be in the most bizarre or dangerous situation, and Cain was always cool, with that cocky little grin on her face. At that precise moment Emma could think of only one way to knock it off, and she decided to take a chance.

The kiss wasn't one of their most incendiary, but it did take Cain by surprise. Emma had always been able to wipe all thought from her mind, and this time was no exception. The feel of her lips was sweet, nice, and prompted Cain to put her hands on Emma's hips. "You were saying?"

"I want to stay here with you," Emma said when she pulled away just a little while Cain caught her breath. "I love you and don't ever want to be with anyone else as long as I live."

"What about everything else? I can't change who I am. If that's what you're asking, then in the end neither one of us will be happy."

"Everything else will take care of itself because I trust you to keep our children and me safe. I just need to know if I've got a chance here? I'm not asking for anything more than that."

Cain worked a hand up and pressed her palm to Emma's cheek. "Do you know what my greatest regret is?"

"Not letting me get fired that first night we met?"

The deep laugh almost made her melt into Cain's chest, but Emma stayed where she was.

"Not going after you when you left. My pride stole a lot of years and a lot of good memories from me."

"I'm sorry for everything. I should've come back when Hannah was born, but I thought you'd have me shot the minute I stepped foot out of the cab."

"Nah, maybe just a few warning shots to make myself feel better, but this time you brought the second greatest gift you could ever give me."

Emma closed her eyes and relished the feel of Cain's hand on her face.

"I missed a lot in Hannah's life, but so did you in Hayden's. That doesn't make us even, but it gives us something to talk about for months to come. Just one thing, Emma. If you stay, it's for good this time. It's going to take time to rebuild what we had, but you need to be here if we're going to try." Cain pinched her cheek slightly. "I can't say if this will work or not, but I'm willing to give it my best for the sake of our family."

"Don't worry. I learned from my mistakes. I need you and love you, and I'll try as hard as I can not to hurt you again."

"I don't mean to be blunt, but only time will prove that. I meant what I said. I won't go through this kind of pain again."

"I know better than to promise you any more than that. But each day after this one I'll prove to you that I'm sincere. There'll be no more pain for you or our son. If you allow Hannah and me back in, you'll never doubt my word. It's the mark of a true Casey to keep their word."

Cain laughed again and pulled Emma down far enough to kiss the tip of her nose. "And are you a true Casey?"

"I'm something better. I'm your Casey."

Across town Muriel's law office went up in bits when the second bomb of the day went off, sending pieces of debris flying in every direction and trapping two of her young associates in the rubble. It was six o'clock, and they were the only ones left in the building.

Cain had no choice but to answer those responsible, but would Emma keep her promise once she did?

Chapter Four

Without warning, Merrick opened the door and stood stock-still. She expected them to be at each other's throats, not kissing.

"We're almost done, Merrick. I'll call you when we are," Emma said with a fair amount of authority in her voice.

"I need—" Merrick started, only to be interrupted by Cain.

"Do as the lady said. This won't take long, but she's right. We need to finish." When they were alone again, Cain gazed up and into the eyes that had always fascinated her.

Emma's eyes were a vivid deep green that looked like some special power had speckled them with gold flecks. Cain had always used them to gauge how Emma was feeling. At the moment they were filled with love and adoration, a potent combination for Cain, but the depth of Emma's betrayal had cut deep. As much as her heart wanted to forget, her head screamed for her to be careful.

"I didn't mean to overstep my bounds with Merrick." Emma moved up a little and ran her fingers though Cain's hair.

"Didn't you?" The voice rumbled, and Emma could feel it where their bodies touched. "It sure sounded like you did."

"This won't work if we go about it the way we did before. I won't go back to that."

Emma began to move off her, but Cain held her to her injured chest. "What way is that, lass?"

"I won't be sent out of the room like a child or some addlepated woman who needs looking after every time the adults have to talk business. I'm either your partner or I'm not."

"Would this be a good time to remind you that just days ago you were in a deal with the feds to have my ass arrested?"

Emma didn't bolt or smart off only because Cain asked the question without anger or malice. She was more curious than anything. "If you can't forgive me, we'll never be able to trust each other again."

"Do you know what trust means to me, Emma?"

"I do know, and I'm sorry for the pile of betrayals between us." Emma brushed Cain's damp hair from her forehead, knowing the pain was making her sweat. "But I refuse to believe there's no love between us anymore. That's strong enough to build on, don't you think?"

"If life has taught me anything, it's that sometimes it doesn't matter what I think," Cain said almost to herself. "Have you ever gambled?"

"A long time ago I left everything and everyone I'd ever known to move to a place about as different from my upbringing as you could get. It was one of the greatest times of my life, but *that* gamble paled next to the one I took the night I met a rogue who stole my heart." Emma picked up one of the Cain's hands and placed it on her chest. "I take that back. I gave that gift freely. You didn't steal it. I gave myself to you because I wanted to be with you. If you believe my mother, I did so at the peril of my soul."

"And now?"

"The true sin is to keep denying the way I feel about you. Four years is a long time, but I don't think four hundred lifetimes will be enough to make me forget you."

Cain looked at their joined hands and let out a slow sigh. "I'm sitting at the high-stakes table with only a few chips left. I can throw my ante in one last time and gamble, but if I lose…the devil takes my soul. That means I survived you leaving once, Emma, but twice isn't in me."

"I know something about you, Derby Cain, that most do not."

"What's that, darling girl?"

"You're too good a gambler not to bet on a sure thing. That's what we are together, and that's what I'm fighting for here."

"You commit again and you know what that'll mean, don't you?"

"I didn't understand before, not fully anyway, but I do now."

Emma kept hold of Cain's hand with one of her own and leaned down carefully. As strong as she was, Cain was still injured. "To be a Casey wife I accept all of you, and I hold nothing back. I will love you, protect you, and be waiting in your bed every night. I will give you everything you need, but I'll expect just as much from you in return."

"Pretty words indeed."

"I want an answer, Cain."

The gold flecks did Cain in. She was crazy to trust Emma again, and if she was honest, they didn't share the same level of trust as before, but Cain loved her. That was a starting point. The rest would come later as Emma proved herself, or it would come not at all. For the moment as she gazed into Emma's green eyes, she decided to at least gamble on the possibility. "Ante up."

Emma went willingly when Cain pulled her forward. These were the lips she remembered and had dreamed about. Cain kissed her like she wanted her, which made Emma want to cry. "I love you so much," she whispered when they pulled apart.

"I love you too. God help me if you're still working for the other side, because I do believe they've finally found my greatest weakness."

"Trust me, we'll have plenty of things to worry about for the remainder of our days, but that will never be one of them." Emma pressed her lips to Cain's once again, feeling almost weightless. "Are we all right?"

"We're heading in that direction, so it's a start, but we'll have a lifetime to get it right." Cain cupped Emma's cheek before patting her on the butt. "As much as I'm enjoying this, it's time to let in the real world."

"Merrick?" Emma called down the hall. "We're ready."

Merrick buttoned her jacket and pushed off the wall. "If you don't mind, I need to talk to Cain about some pressing issues. One of the guys will walk you down to the waiting room."

"Come in and close the door, Merrick. Emma's sitting in today, so start talking," Cain ordered. She pressed the button to make the bed fold up into a sitting position, and Emma went to her side.

"I don't think that's such a great idea."

Cain's dark brows hiked over her bright blue eyes. "I see. Emma, could you step out for a moment, please?" She put up her hand, stopping the protest before it came out. "Practice some of that trust we talked about. I said for a moment, and that's what I meant."

The door clicked closed completely before Merrick smiled at it and started talking. "Some stuff's come up and we need to move fast."

"Be quiet."

Merrick whipped her head around, thinking she had heard wrong. "Excuse me?"

"I thought 'be quiet' wouldn't be as rude as 'shut up.' Either way, I want you to stop talking and listen to me." Their eyes met and Cain waited before continuing. "Tell me, Merrick, who is the head of this family?"

"You are. Why?"

"I am, so when I say something, I expect not to be questioned about it. Not in public, not in private. Do we understand each other?"

"She betrayed you once before."

"And she'll most likely make quite a few more mistakes in the future, but she'll have a future with me. She's here to stay, so you'd best be getting used to the concept. So do we understand each other?"

"I understand you perfectly, though as your friend, I hope it works out. As your employee I'll keep my eyes open in case it doesn't, and please don't be offended. Someone blew up Emerald's today, and I'm afraid it will lead us into war. If she couldn't handle you beating the crap out of your cousin, then how's she going to handle you ordering the necessary actions that are coming up?"

"If I knew the answer to every difficult question I'd rule the world, as they say."

Merrick blew out a long breath as she glanced back at the door Emma had just walked out. "Look, I know what she means to you, but don't let that blind you. I want what's best for you, but this isn't it."

"I appreciate what you're saying, but it's my choice. Emma's the mother of my children but, more importantly, she's the one woman I haven't been able to forget."

"Then I'll support you in that, but I'm going to censor what I say in front of her until we know for sure."

"Just as long as you remember what I said. I'm the head of this family, Merrick, not you." Cain held her hand up and smiled when Merrick shook it. "Thank you. Now go get her back before she comes in here and removes my spleen with a plastic spoon for making her wait. I promised her a chance, and it's the only way I'll know just how much of a chance we have."

"Everything all right?" Emma asked when she walked in and sat close to Cain.

"I'm sure it's not, but Merrick hasn't had the opportunity to break the whole thing to us yet." Cain waved toward Merrick and nodded. "What's going on?"

"This isn't funny, boss. Like I said, some fool blew up the club this afternoon."

"When exactly did this happen? Did anyone get hurt?" Cain asked.

"Just before they hit your house. Dean and Paul were in the building," Merrick answered. "They didn't make it."

"And Blue?"

"He's fine. He was getting something out of his car."

Cain took a painful deep breath and held it at the innocent-sounding answer.

"Don't worry, I have someone looking," Merrick said.

Emma put her hands up. "Could someone explain, please?"

"Blue is the manager of Emerald's, and it's just too much of a coincidence that he steps out of the building the second the place is blown to shit. There wasn't a stud left standing, but he barely has a scratch on him. We have to check him out." Merrick took a seat in the chair next to the bed and went on when Emma nodded in comprehension. "There's more."

"Of course there is. Get on with it," Cain said.

"Muriel's office was their next target after the house. I got a call just before I stepped in here. Thank God whoever's responsible is waiting until the locations aren't crowded before hitting them."

"It's a message," Cain said softly.

"What, honey?" Emma asked. Throughout the whole talk she was just happy Cain was conscious to deal with the aftermath. She wanted to help but was smart enough to know she was out of her league.

"They're sending me a message." Cain looked at Emma, wanting to gauge her reaction to the reality of the coming weeks.

"What do you mean?"

"There's no place safe for me to hide myself or my family."

Emma's hands flew to her mouth, and Cain thought she was trying to hold in the scream that wanted to come out. "What are we going to do?" The question sounded muffled.

"I won't let anything happen to you or the kids."

Locks of blond hair fell into Emma's face when she nodded. "I'm not worried about that. I asked what we're going to do."

"First you have to believe me that we'll get through this together."

"I believe you. It's just been a hell of a day."

"Hell is coming, love, but it'll take a bit of planning first."

CHAPTER FIVE

When Muriel received the call telling her what had happened to her two junior associates, she squeezed the glass she'd been holding so hard that it shattered. She was sitting in Cain's kitchen with two telephone lines going, having personally talked to everyone on her staff, from secretaries to file clerks, except for the two young attorneys.

Fortunately, the glass was the only victim of her Casey temper, and she hadn't sliced her hand open.

"Just stay home tomorrow until we regroup. The files can be re-created from the backups in the safety deposit box, so stop worrying. Call me if you hear anything else." Muriel put the phone down gently and pinched the bridge of her nose. She felt like hitting something, but now wasn't the time for a meltdown.

"Who shot and killed the men on the street?" the detective standing in Muriel's personal space asked.

"And you are?"

"I asked you a question first," he replied, a smirk firmly in place.

"And I asked you one second. What difference does it make?" She stood up and took a step closer to him, getting him to take one back. Muriel was no stranger to intimidation tactics, but she was usually the one doing the intimidating. "Either state your name or get out."

The slightly overweight man glared at her through slitted eyes before he acquiesced. "I'm Detective Newsome, and I'd like some questions answered, Muriel."

"I didn't realize we were on a first-name basis, Officer." She rifled him a glare at the familiarity, making his dull brown eyes disappear further behind his lids.

"Ms. Casey, then. Who took out the guys on the street?"

"Our security people killed these men in self-defense. I gave someone with the police department all the necessary paperwork pertaining to gun permits and carry licenses. If you've walked through the upstairs, I'm sure your keen detecting skills deduced that we did not provoke this fight."

His pen scraped along the notepad in his hand long after she finished talking. As a veteran cop he knew she could tell him precisely who had pulled the trigger, since each of the dead men had tight bullet patterns to the middle of his chest and forehead.

But this was Muriel Casey. Any information he would get out of her would be with a court order in hand. Like her infamous cousin, Muriel never volunteered anything.

"And I'm sure you know nothing about any identification these guys might or might not have been carrying?"

"If I were to send hired killers to someone's home, I'd make sure they left their wallets and credit cards at home, Officer. Of course, since we have no experience with that sort of thing, I'm only guessing. Call it pure conjecture on my part." She watched as the smile came to his lips, giving him an echo of one herself.

"Of course." He laughed. "And you probably have no idea why this happened, do you? Law-abiding citizens have crazed killers showing up at their houses all the time. It's a regular citywide epidemic, from what I hear."

"None. My cousin is a tavern owner. I have no idea why someone would want to harm her family. Maybe it was someone who thinks her beer is flat."

The feminine laughter coming from the doorway made both Muriel and Newsome turn around. Agent Shelby Daniels, wearing a conservative dark suit with a light-colored silk blouse, leaned against the door frame with her arms folded against her chest. Both members of her audience took a visual tour down her body to the black pumps, then back up again, but Shelby cared about only one perusal.

"You shouldn't stand so close to her, Detective. The lightning might take you out too when God strikes her down for telling such lies. I'm sure Muriel is way ahead of us already." Shelby pushed off and stepped into the room, stopping a couple of feet in front of a smiling Muriel.

"Ms. Casey prefers not to be addressed by her first name," Newsome said with authority. "And you are?"

"Agent Shelby Daniels, meet Detective Newsome, one of New Orleans's finest. Detective, you best be on your best behavior now. The feds have arrived, and you don't want a bad report on your job performance, do you?" Muriel said. She was clearly teasing, and Shelby brought a hand up to her mouth to cover a laugh she tried to disguise as a cough. "Now that we all know each other, to what do I owe the pleasure of your company, Agent?"

Shelby Daniels's presence wasn't a surprise since she'd become a fixture in their lives almost from the time Cain had met her trying to bug Vincent Carlotti's plane. The head of the Carlotti family, and also one of Cain's strongest allies, had wanted to throw Shelby out of the plane for the infraction, but Cain had intervened and saved her life. That encounter had evolved into innocent flirtations between Shelby and Cain until it became clear to Shelby that Cain was off-limits for a number of reasons, starting with what she did for a living. Her cousin Muriel was another story, though, and Shelby found her incredibly attractive.

"Two explosions in one day? With all the excitement how, pray tell, did you think I'd stay away? Tell me a story, Barrister Casey."

"Would you excuse us, Detective?" Muriel buttoned her jacket and started walking toward Cain's office. When Newsome attempted to follow them, two men stepped in his way and refused to move.

"I'm not finished with my questions," Newsome yelled after the two women.

A closing door with more than a few bullet holes in it was his only answer.

Shelby scanned the room with a critical eye and shivered when she thought of Cain sitting in the chair behind the desk, one of her favorite spots in the house. The amount of firepower the hit men had concentrated on the room would have cut her in two had she been sitting there.

"They did a number on this place, didn't they?" Muriel said, breaking the silence.

"Who was it?"

"I don't know, Shelby, and that's as far down that conversational road as we're going. Why are you here, really?"

"We're here to help, if we can. The city has enough problems already without a gangland war breaking out. Trust me, Muriel, my team and I just want to help catch the guys who did this. You and Cain lost people today. Don't you want someone to pay?"

Muriel pushed aside a pile of broken glass with the toe of her expensive Italian leather loafer as she appeared to think the offer over. "Ask the staff whatever you please, but I want to know if you're planning to leave any surveillance equipment behind. Granted, closed warrants will cover your ass from answering truthfully, but if you lie the trust between us will vanish. You betray Cain and me, and I'll cut you out of our lives."

"We're here only in an investigative capacity for now. How's that?" All Shelby saw for a long moment was the top of Muriel's head as she continued to stare at the ground and move around broken glass. "Who was sitting in here when hell broke loose?"

Muriel looked up at her. "What makes you think someone was?"

At the edge of the desk, almost as if Merrick had just put it down, sat a glass half filled with milk. Everything else in the room was in tatters, but the glass sat untouched. Muriel just started laughing, a heartfelt, belly-shaking sound that made Shelby join in without knowing why.

"What's so funny?" Shelby asked, as she watched long fingers wipe tears away from the sudden outbreak of humor.

"I've never compared Cain to an inanimate object, but does that glass remind you of her? The room is totally destroyed, but no one touched this." Muriel picked up the glass of milk and set it down next to her. "All my life I envied her the ability to just walk through the chaos and end up just like this—untouched and whole. Cain's mother, my aunt Therese, used to say it was because she was touched by the angels."

"As a wise man told me on a plane ride one night, Counselor, Cain was the reason Agent Barney Kyle's hair was so gray. She was graced with more than her share of Irish luck, I swear. That was very true, though your comparison would've been more accurate had it been a glass of beer."

"Nah, Irish whiskey is her favorite, but I've never known her to turn her nose up at a good brew. As much as I enjoy your company,

Agent Daniels, I really must get back to my duties." Muriel's fingers touched Shelby's elbow as she passed by her on the way out the door. "Have a good day."

"Could I maybe buy you a drink later?" Shelby asked in a soft voice.

"Am I your consolation prize?" Muriel walked back into the room, with more than a touch of humor in her voice.

"Truthfully, your cousin was more a passing fancy, so no, you're not."

A low chuckle stopped Shelby from continuing. "The forbidden fruit, eh?"

"Cain is more like the whole tree, but you're a different animal altogether, aren't you?" Shelby watched Muriel cross her arms and lean on Cain's desk. "I just thought that since you've lost so much today, you might want to unwind a bit. Once you're done, of course. I like you, Muriel, and now, more than ever, you could use a friend."

"Where would you like to go?"

"How about someplace neutral? The bar at the Piquant, perhaps?"

Muriel opened the door and waved, signaling that Shelby should go first. "I should be done by eight. If you like, I'll just meet you there. We wouldn't want your bosses to think any less of you if you're seen riding in a car with me."

"It's a date, Counselor."

The way Shelby looked at her as she spoke made Muriel feel as if the excitement in her life was about to begin, and bullets and explosions would have nothing to do with it.

CHAPTER SIX

Cain had silently gazed out the window for fifteen minutes after Merrick had finished bringing them up to date, and Emma knew she wasn't daydreaming. Like a master tactician, Cain was going through all her options before deciding on her next move.

"You aren't leaving the hospital, so forget it," Emma said just as calmly as Cain had begun ordering Merrick to call her doctor back to her room. "And before you give me any crap about it, you were shot two weeks ago. You're an amazing healer, but that bullet collapsed your lung and did a lot of damage."

"Merrick," Cain said.

The guard stood up and left the room.

"Emma, I need you to listen to me, all right?"

"Forget it. You can't charm your way out of here. I just got you back, and I'm not taking any chances on anything happening to you. You'll leave here just as soon as the doctor says you can."

"Deal."

Emma narrowed her eyes. Cain Casey never gave up so easily on anything. "What are you up to?"

"Nothing. I just want to talk to the man. Lass, I have to try my best to protect my family, so I'm not going to lie to you. I said I wouldn't, and I'm not going to, okay?"

"We're not going to be fine if you push yourself too hard and something happens to you. What about us if you aren't here to protect us?"

Cain pulled her down so Emma was lying next to her with her

head pillowed on her shoulder. "Did I ever tell you what my father Dalton said about the Casey clan and their place in the world?"

"I've heard a few aspects of this story, but I have a feeling there's another chapter."

"Ooh, I'd hate to think I've become predictable, but yes, there's another one. My father and I were sitting in my granny's living room looking at my granddad's coffin, with an Irish flag draped over it. The rest of his men sat in the kitchen drinking and telling stories. There's nothing like an Irish wake."

Emma ran her hand in a slow circle on Cain's stomach as she listened. It was how they'd spent many of their nights together after making love or just waking up together. Cain had also fallen back into their routine as she rested her hand on Emma's hip, and she would stop every so many words and kiss the forehead so close to her lips.

"How old were you?"

"Thirteen, and full of piss and vinegar. Thinking back now, I'm hoping me mum's curses don't come true, since our boy is getting close to that age." Emma laughed against her side, and her breath warmed Cain's neck.

"Getting back to my story, my father stared at that casket a long time, but when I put my hand on his knee, he snapped out of his trance. He smiled and covered my hand with one of his big paws. 'You know something, Derby?' he said. 'You're a lot like my father. Not in looks, mind you, because he was blond and freckled, but in every other way. He was a Casey through and through.'

"These were the times I treasured the most. Just the two of us, alone, with my father telling me a story. 'Why do you think I'm like him?' I asked him.

"'You don't go backing down from too many fights, but you're smart enough to know who's going to be winning in the end. The one thing I want you to copy him in more than anything is how he died.'

"Since the Caseys never talked about death, I laughed, probably because I was nervous. 'I don't want to be dying, Papa, so what are you talking about?'

"'He died in his bed next to the one he loved, in his sleep. My old man did a lot of living before that night came, and that's what I want for you as well, me pride.'

"Dalton used to tell me all the time that Caseys were like bad grass. 'You can weed us out for a little while,' he'd say, 'but once we're rooted, you can't really kill us off. You're an offshoot of that blade of bad grass, so don't be wasting your time thinking about death. She's the one woman you'll keep waiting for years to come.'"

"He compared you to bad grass?" Emma laughed.

"He wasn't wrong, now was he? Giovanni Bracato and his sons have much to answer for, but that day won't come until I'm ready to ask the important questions myself. For now, we're going to do what he expects a weak woman to do. Only he doesn't know what we know— bad grass doesn't kill easy."

Emma pushed herself up. "You've already decided what you're going to do, haven't you?"

"Just this second lying here with you, so stop giving me those sad eyes. We're going to run to someplace where I can see a rabbit coming at five miles."

Emma's eyes widened at the admission, and she didn't say anything for a moment. "You're running? I'm not going to hear about this for years to come, am I? How in your weakened condition I made you do something you'll regret until hell freezes over, since that's what I wanted to begin with."

"This isn't running because I'm afraid. It's running like a small rooster from a big bird with a very sharp beak on its tail. Did I ever tell you that story?"

"Will I like it?"

"Better than that, little girl, you'll learn something too." She patted Emma on the butt, and Emma moved closer. "Dalton once told me…" Cain began.

Outside, her plan was set in motion, and it would bring them one step closer to finishing a tale she'd one day use to teach her son when it was his time to lead their clan.

CHAPTER SEVEN

W ell?"
     "I want those bitches to suffer, so I'm going to blow their lives and everything they hold dear to shit. I've already taken care of the club and the lawyer's office—got a few more to go. My guy's getting the supplies together to finish the job." Gino Bracato sat across from his father Giovanni's desk and was so angry he spit as he spoke.

He'd made a serious mistake when he let his guard down after his father had kidnapped Hayden Casey. With Cain in the hospital, all of them had expected Emma to roll into a ball and wait for someone to save her. So when she had Gino's baby boy kidnapped to use as bait to get her own little bastard back, it'd been like a bat to the face he didn't see coming. Touching his son was one thing, but Emma had also humiliated him by leaving him to wait in his underwear while his father made the deal for his release.

At Emma's order, Cain's men had taken him out of his mistress's bed and held him, his brothers, and his son hostage in exchange for Hayden. On the way out, he'd seen his men knocked unconscious, which he'd rewarded with a trip to the bottom of the river.

"Careful how you carry this out," his father Giovanni screamed. "We don't need any more heat from the feds or otherwise." He was confident there were no bugs since they'd swept the room just before the family meeting. "And you..." He pointed to his second eldest, Michael, next. "What the fuck happened?"

"The shooters didn't expect that kind of firepower at the bitch's house, Papa. We thought with her in the hospital, the muscle would be there taking care of her."

Stephano Bracato sat back and listened to the rest of his family argue over their mistakes. He was slowly taking over the drug trafficking in the city and along the Gulf Coast. If he took advantage of this opportunity and his volume grew big enough, he could break away from his father and his brothers.

"My problems begin when the four of you start thinking," Giovanni screamed.

Michael and the youngest son Francis cringed a little when their father's voice kept escalating.

"We have to finish this before Casey wakes up from whatever the hell is wrong with her and mounts a counterattack. I'm too close to finally taking control and driving all the other families out. No more fuckups."

"Do we have your permission to pick them up and take care of them permanently?" Gino asked.

"You see a clean shot, you take it." Giovanni pointed his index finger in Gino's face. "Do you understand me? I don't want anything fancy. I know Emma took your boy and caught you with your pants down, but I want you to put that behind you. Emma got her kid back, and you have Little Gino. That's the end of it."

"But, Papa—" Gino tried to sound pathetic.

"You screw this up for me and I'll cut you off." Bracato stood up and left the room, expecting to be obeyed.

Stephano, lounging on the sofa, watched the whole encounter and knew his brother Gino wouldn't back away so easily. When Gino had married the girl their father had approved of and had a child not long after, his three bothers just slapped him on the back and smiled. Gino could have control of the family if it meant keeping the old man off their backs.

"What's your plan?" Stephano asked Gino. "I know you, and I know that blond whore embarrassed the hell out of you."

"She and our old man may think that she's gonna die from a bullet she'll never see coming, but I'm not in a generous mood. I want more than anything to fuck that little slut over and have Cain watch me make her scream."

"Gino, you just heard Papa," Francis warned.

The anger in Gino boiled over onto his youngest brother. Grabbing him by the neck, he slammed him into the wall. "You gonna go running and tell like you did when you were four, you little pussy? Reach down and make sure you got some balls, Francis, and if you do, start acting like it. Papa hears one word about this conversation, though, and you won't have to worry about them 'cause I'll cut them off myself."

"Let him go," ordered Michael, who always figured he would gain control of the family when Gino's mouth got him killed. "And it might do you some good to listen to him."

"Fuck off, all three of you. If you don't want to help me, then fine. I'll take my men and get it done myself. Come with me, though, and I'll think about giving you each a turn with her."

Outside, Giovanni walked the length of his dock and jumped onto a boat moored at the end. Four men jumped in with him, and a fifth waited on the dock and cast them off.

"Keep an eye on my four geniuses in there," Giovanni ordered the guard staying behind.

"You got it, boss." Before the man made it back inside, the four brothers were gone, so he picked up the nearest phone. This one, though, was bugged.

Across Tchoupitoulas Street three men sat watching from a window, two of them with binoculars in their hands and the third hunched over a computer keyboard. "There's something coming over one of the lines in the outer office," Agent Lionel Jones said.

"Could be something going on with everyone making a run for the nearest door," Joe Simmons added. "The brothers evil left via cars, and Daddy just hit the water. Dumb fucks, they have to know we have all the exits covered."

"Just like we covered the big shipment of illegal liquor a few nights ago, smart guy? It's time for us to go back to good old-fashioned detective work and start tying all this together, because I don't think Cain's just going to sit on her ass and not take a shot back at these guys." Agent Anthony Curtis put his glasses down and increased the volume to listen to the conversation.

His fellow agents frowned at him, which made him throw up his hands. "I like Cain too, damn it, but we looked like idiots the other night. She didn't do anything illegal, but we owe her for getting stuck with this crap assignment."

"You know, Tony, we could've just looked in the damn crates. We were played, but Cain wasn't doing the string-pulling. It was Kyle,"

Lionel said. "And from what Shelby tells me, Cain's going to be out of commission for a while yet."

"People, do I have to remind you who signs your paychecks? We aren't here to coddle some woman who would like nothing better than to fuck the whole lot of us over just to make her kid laugh." He put his hands in his hair and pulled in frustration. "And is it so hard to remember it's Anthony?"

"Lionel's right, Tony. Cain isn't doing anything but lying in the hospital with a bullet I feel somewhat responsible for. Besides, Agent Hicks said she isn't our concern anymore." Joe tacked on the moniker just to aggravate Anthony that much more.

"You mark my words, she's going to come out of there swinging, and when she's done there won't be a Bracato left standing." Anthony looked at the other two and wanted to scream at their bland looks.

Behind him the door opened and closed, only adding to the tension in the room.

"Is it a private moment," Shelby asked, "or can anyone join in?"

"It's nothing," Joe said.

"Nothing? You're about to throw away your career and you call it nothing?" Anthony couldn't believe his ears.

"Who's throwing away their careers?"

"Like I said, Shelby, it's nothing. Tony's all bent out of shape that Cain isn't going down with the rest of these guys," Lionel supplied. "Our buddy's still smarting from the spanking Cain administered the other night when our raid netted us a shitload of legal liquor. I know she fucked us, but she did it almost with our permission. Not one of us thought to question Kyle or to check when all of a sudden she started burning up the wiretaps we left with information about her business. We just barged in there and watched Kyle shoot her for Giovanni Bracato. And even after that all we could do was salivate over the fact we'd caught her with a line of trucks full of booze—our payback for all those miserable days being holed up in places like this."

"We need to take a step back and consider what we're doing. Am I the only one who thinks we're getting way too chummy with the enemy?" Anthony asked.

Shelby put her hands on her hips and let out a long, even breath. If they didn't pull together and act as a team, they wouldn't be taking anyone down for anything, not even a traffic violation. "Listen,

Anthony," she started, trying not to antagonize him any further. "Joe, Lionel, and I are on the same page, so if you're not comfortable with that you need to say so now. True, we got scammed, but Joe's right. Cain did it fair and square. We've gotten too far in to turn back now. Cain and her people are talking to me, which means they're doing the same to you, with the help of our little toys."

"They're talking to you, Shelby, because they all want to sleep with you." Tony dropped down to a chair as if he were tired of trying to explain himself.

"Are you questioning my integrity, Agent?"

"No more than you're questioning mine. I want you to listen to me. All of this is going to turn out bad if you take sides. Giovanni Bracato is not as suave and cute, but Cain is no different from him. Pull back before it's too late."

"This has to be a team decision, Tony," Joe said, "and I'm with Shelby."

"Me too," Lionel chimed in.

"Then I'm asking Annabel for a transfer. I like my job and want to keep it, not to mention I have no interest in going to jail. Keeping Kyle company for years to come isn't something I relish." Anthony picked up his coat and walked out, leaving total silence behind him.

"It isn't too late, guys, if you want to join him. I think this is the best way, but it doesn't mean it's the only way."

"He'll drive around for a while and come back, Shelby. Don't sweat it. Tony's strung a little tight because his old man was in the agency and the rumors of him being on the take never did die down. Especially not after a big drug kingpin got away because the old man didn't play it all by the book," Joe said. "I'm thinking, though, that we've come too far with this for him to want out now."

"I hope you're right. Would this be a bad time to tell you two that I have a date for drinks with Muriel Casey?"

"I wasn't too worried about Cain," Lionel said. "But Muriel— keep an eye on that one, Shelby."

"You think she's dangerous?"

"Only in a quirky kind of way. Cain knew better than to get too close to you, but Muriel's the chance-taking kind of gal," Lionel explained, with a shy tilt to his head. "I just don't want what Tony said to be a problem for you, and you getting pulled in front of an ethics committee for one stupid night will be problematic in the long run when it comes to your career."

"Thanks, Dad, for your concern, but I know what I'm doing." Checking her watch, Shelby waved to them and headed back out to her car. "Don't wait up."

"You think we should have her followed, Lionel?"

"So she can have me singing soprano tomorrow when she grabs me by the short hairs? No, thank you, Joe." Lionel watched the sedan disappear. "We either have to trust her or we don't."

From the other direction their replacements for the night pulled into the lot. "Just one drink, Lionel. Where's the harm in that?"

"Said the spider to the fly," Lionel answered with a laugh. "I hope you're right, buddy."

The problem was, though, that they hadn't been right when it came to the Caseys in a good long while.

CHAPTER EIGHT

D rinks, huh? Not that long ago you were warning me to stay away from our attractive FBI Agent Daniels, and now you're going to wine and dine her." Cain winked at Muriel and smiled. "Of course, maybe if you interact enough with these people they'll finally figure out we're just pouring beer and having fun and aren't some two-bit gangsters with an agenda for mayhem."

"I give advice, cousin. That doesn't mean I take it. Shelby just felt sorry for me because I lost some people today, so she offered to cheer me up, nothing more. She's even more married to her job than I am, so don't go spinning any romantic notions over her offer of a drink."

It was just enough to give whoever was listening the right impression of their fellow agent. Merrick had found the listening device on a routine sweep an hour earlier. Her first reaction was to give Cain a complete rundown on paper of Emma's whereabouts and phone calls. She couldn't prove Emma had anything to do with it, but was pleased that Cain had at least listened to her concerns when she pointed out the intrusion on her privacy.

Muriel pulled a piece of lint from her pants and smiled, wondering what her father would think of her date choice for later. In the Casey family, her uncle Dalton had been the one to take chances.

"You, on the other hand, look a lot better, Cain. And Merrick tells me there've been some personal changes over here while I'm out slaving on your behalf."

"Going to add your own bit of advice? So far Merrick has been full of it when it comes to the subject. I'd appreciate it if you were a bit more supportive."

Muriel looked up from the fabric of her slacks. Her cousin usually didn't need assurance about anything. "Maybe she's just worried because of what happened. We both saw what that did to not only you."

"Maybe, but I have to believe that some mistakes are made to be remedied. If not, what's the point?" Cain's answer was just as vague. Her life might have been a game of cat and mouse with the feds, but her personal life was not. As much as she could, she'd keep those parts of her life private.

"Then go for it." Muriel put her hand over Cain's and spoke from the heart. "I think you're doing the right thing. There was plenty of blame for what happened, and you both lost a lot."

"Yeah, well, that's enough mush for one day. We have business to discuss." Cain sounded gruff, but she added a hint of a smile for her cousin's kind words. This wasn't the place to share the innermost part of her heart. Not that she didn't trust Muriel; it just wasn't anyone else's business.

"What do you want to do about what's happened?" Muriel really didn't expect a verbal answer.

For a long stretch the small listening device next to the bed only picked up silence, making the man across the street think it had been found and disposed of. He expelled a relieved sigh when he heard Muriel's voice again.

"Are you all right? You just drifted off on me there." Muriel made sure she sounded both concerned and a little distracted as she read the note Cain had spent all that time writing. "I should leave you to your rest."

"Thanks. I *am* a little tired, so if you don't mind coming back, we'll discuss our future plans tomorrow. Just make sure you file the proper insurance papers for all the locations." To make it sound as if she'd just awakened from a short catnap, Cain added a yawn.

"Anything you want me to get you before I go?"

"Just between you and me, I'd love some good Cuban espresso."

The listener scrunched his forehead in confusion at the odd request.

"I'll see what I can do about that tomorrow." Muriel stretched before bending to pick up her coat.

"Good. Try for first thing in the morning before they show up with the swill they serve around here. That way you can tell me how your date went."

"I told you, boss, it isn't a date." The reprimand from Muriel only got her another wink from the bed. It was time to go and see about Cain's request for a cup of coffee, or in this case to visit the other family head in the city with whom, unlike the Bracatos, they had a good working relationship.

Ramon Jatibon was a native of Cuba and, like Vincent and Dalton, had worked hard to carve out his piece of the city. For years he had carefully built the gambling empire that had helped finance his other enterprises, which his children now ran. As proud as Ramon was of what he'd accomplished, it was his twins, Ramon Jr. and Remi, who made his chest puff out when he talked of them. But they were currently in different states expanding the family's holdings, and it was the old man Muriel had an appointment to meet.

After taking the freight elevator to the first floor of the hospital, Muriel exited in the delivery area. She ducked around a truck unloading carts of clean linens and headed for the steps that would leave her close to the one destination the watchers would never notice her.

The bus pulled up to the stop, and after a brief ride Muriel hopped off and headed to the upscale mall close to the aquarium.

Along the way she passed the new casino, laughing as a group of tourists headed for one of the entrances. No matter how hard the legitimate gaming places tried to compete with people like this who were probably headed to the nickel slots, the man she was going to see was still doing a profitable business. Ramon's regular clientele was used to the special perks that were a part of the service he provided.

In a private back section of a dark bar on the eleventh floor, she greeted Emile, who had been with Ramon from the time he was a teenager and would gladly sacrifice his life to keep the crime boss safe.

"Muriel." Emile nodded and held out his hand. "Good to see you again."

"Thanks, Emile." She took his hand and watched as hers disappeared in it. "Is it me, or do you get bigger every time I see you?"

He laughed and put his other hand on her shoulder. "Go on in. He's waiting on you."

Ramon sat at the back table sipping from a glass of dark rum and smoking a very good Cuban cigar. Now in his mid-sixties, Ramon was still very attractive. His black curly hair, slightly graying at the temples, was thick, and his clothes were stylish in a conservative way. He looked like a businessman or lawyer unwinding with a drink after a long day.

He stood as Muriel got closer and rested the smoke in the ashtray. "It's been a while, *amiga*." Holding her hands in his, he kissed both her cheeks before pulling her into a long hug. Despite his years in the States, Ramon still had an accent.

"You know how it is, Ramon. Sometimes life gets away from us and all we can do is try to keep up."

"And sometimes it's just a pain in the ass, no?" He chuckled and pulled a chair out for her, signaling the bartender for another round. "Sit and have a drink with me and tell me what it is you need."

The cigar lighter came out again, and Ramon relit his cigar while the server put down two new glasses and carried the empty one away. Muriel looked at the blue flame coming out of the small blowtorch and enjoyed the aroma of the expensive smoke. She picked up her glass and took a small sip of the amber liquid, liking the way it warmed her as it went down. "You heard what happened?"

"Two explosions that big are hard to miss. How many did you lose today?" He turned his face away from her and blew out a stream of smoke.

"Too many, but I'm not here to complain about that."

"You know I'll do whatever you ask, Muriel. I have much to thank Dalton for from when I first got to this country, and I'll be forever in his debt. Without his backing and that of Vincent, I'd be a poor man. When he died I swore to help his children any way I could. I'm sure Cain would do the same for either Ramon or Remi." The way the *R*s in the two names rolled off his tongue made Muriel smile.

"How are they? I'm sorry for not asking sooner."

"They are both wonderful. Remi's getting ready for a move to California, and Ramon is in Vegas running the Gemini. Their mother misses them, but they try and come home as much as possible. My wife spends most of her time trying to find a girl for Remi, especially after seeing how happy Cain has been after settling down. She won't be satisfied until she has a brood of grandchildren to spoil."

It was hard to miss the pride in his voice, and just as quickly his face became sober. "You have no children, but Cain understands what I do about family. What happened at her home today, that is unforgivable and not the work of a real man. It takes no *cojones* to shoot at women and children." He leaned back in his seat and clenched his fist. "I've spoken to Vincent, and we agree this action and everything else that happened today shouldn't go unpunished."

"Thank you for your concern, Ramon. Our family greatly appreciates the willingness of the other families to stand with us." She reached across the table and put her hand over his. "You're right, of course. For years we've all been happy to make a living from our respective businesses, but our common enemy has grown greedy. However, that's not why I'm here." She leaned farther in and spoke softly almost into his ear, conveying all that Cain had put in her note.

"That's all she wants?" He seemed surprised.

"For now. When it's time, we'll have to sit together again and decide how the city will be restructured so that everyone is happy, but for now she just needs time."

Blue smoke circled above his head for a minute after he exhaled, and Ramon finished his drink. From his inner jacket pocket he pulled out a card with only a number printed on it and handed it to her. "When she's ready, just call. There are ways to do this without anyone having to know. I'm thinking that's what she wants." He smiled, still biting the cigar in his mouth.

"There's a reason you're still at the top of your game, Mr. Jatibon." The card made its way into her inner jacket pocket. "You never have to have it spelled out for you."

He spread his hands out to his sides and shrugged. "I try," he said, making her laugh. "This is a favor I look forward to doing. Surprises are sometimes the best part of this job. I'm still laughing at what those policemen must have been thinking when they opened those crates."

For the longest time the Caseys had been supplying his clubs with liquor, and some of the more requested choices were illegal in the United States, even if the taxes on them were paid. Sort of like the cigar he was enjoying. Just because the government couldn't appreciate a good Cuban smoke and a glass of Havana Club twenty-five-year-old rum didn't mean his customers didn't.

"I was there when they finally figured it out, and I can safely say they didn't find it as humorous as we do." She finished her drink in one swallow, then squeezed his hand. "Thank you for coming out of your way on such short notice. I won't keep you away from your lovely wife any longer."

They exchanged kisses again before Ramon and his bodyguard walked her to the elevator. Outside the sun had set, and, from the look of the trees, the wind had picked up coming off the river. She still had plenty of time to stroll to the luxury hotel the Piquant to meet Shelby for a drink.

Muriel buttoned her coat as she veered away from the river and walked up Canal Street thinking of the FBI agent. Shelby Daniels was the first woman who'd ever invaded her thoughts in the course of her day, and it was starting to concern her. It was dangerous enough to lose your head over a woman, but it was disastrous to be interested in one set on trying to catch you in a mistake only to lock you up for it. As logical as that sounded to her, Muriel still picked up her pace, wanting to see Shelby again.

"Let's just go see if there's anything to this luck-of-the-Irish thing," she whispered. Perhaps for a little while she could forget what had happened that day by losing herself in a pair of pretty blue eyes, because, from the expression on Cain's face, the storm was coming.

And Muriel was sure that when it did, Shelby would be the last woman in the world who'd offer her a safe harbor.

CHAPTER NINE

L ose something?" Cain asked without opening her eyes. She smiled when she heard the orderly's breath hitch.

"I'm just getting you some fresh water. I'm Todd, by the way."

"Thanks, but you finished pouring quite a while ago. Do you need something else?" It was the same guy she'd seen planting the bug earlier that morning.

For a split second Todd wondered if the guy listening in from wherever would make it there in time if something happened to him. He thought hard before opening his mouth and saying anything that would put his life in danger. "I was just hiding out for a while. My boss is the bitch from hell. You know how it is."

The smile that followed the statement was insincere since it was more of a smirk than a smile, and Cain fought the urge to force-feed him the surveillance equipment. "Trust me, buddy, there are worse things in life than a boss who's a little hard on you."

Her smile widened, but instead of offering Todd comfort, it made him suddenly want to get out of there.

"Much worse."

He practically ran from the icy tone of her voice, and she laughed as the door slammed behind him. For Cain the hospital flunky was just a minor annoyance, but she did want to know who had put him up to bugging her room. She had no proof but wanted to believe that it wasn't Shelby. She wondered if the friendly feebie had any knowledge of Todd and his little caper.

"Scaring the help again?" Emma poked her head in and gave Cain a mock glare.

"It helps pass the time while I'm being bored to death in here. Of course, there are other ways to do that which are much more fun." Cain held out her hand in invitation. She'd sent Emma on a small errand and found herself missing her more than she wanted to admit. It had been much too easy to fall back to the sense of completeness Emma brought to her life.

"That would be wonderful, but you have to be good. Nothing but kissing for a while yet, honey. Doctor's orders."

"Then come over here and kiss me."

Emma stretched out next to her and stroked Cain's cheek. She couldn't get enough of the feeling that came from touching her partner after four years of missing her. Slowly she leaned forward and pressed her lips to Cain's for a fleeting moment. Then she pulled back just enough that she could trace the full lips with her tongue, liking the way Cain moaned.

When Cain cupped her breast, squeezing gently as if to convince herself she really did have Emma there with her, Emma inhaled sharply. "Be good, honey."

"I'm trying, but I can't prove it if you keep on holding my hands captive." Cain laughed as Emma covered her hand to keep it from roaming but didn't remove it from her chest. Emma groaned at both the answer and the touch, so Cain moved her hand to Emma's back. "I'm sorry, love, I'll behave. Did you get the kids squared away?"

"Your uncle took them in for the night and said he'd have them back here first thing in the morning for a visit. Getting Hannah to leave here was a nightmare, though. She's madly in love with you already and didn't want to go anywhere if you weren't coming with us." Emma couldn't stand to maintain eye contact as she said the words. The more she saw Cain and Hannah together, the guiltier she felt. "I'm so sorry." The apology was muffled by Cain's hospital gown when Emma buried her face in her chest.

"You know what's important here and now, lass?"

Emma shook her head, and Cain could tell she was crying.

"That you and she are here with Hayden and me now, and we want you to be. Some things will take time, and we might have some setbacks, but we'll get through those together."

"I'm so lucky."

"Yes, you are," Cain joked. "I'm good-looking, have money, and am a wonderful catch."

"And so modest." The light teasing pulled Emma out of her funk, and she thanked God again not only for Cain's willingness to try, but for her willingness to forgive. "I love you so much. I never stopped." She kissed Cain again and tried to express through her touch just how much.

"I've missed hearing you say those words."

"Not as much as I miss saying them." The words were as open and honest as the expression on Emma's face.

Some days in the four years they'd been apart she had yelled them into the wind when she walked her father's land. She'd found some comfort in imagining the wind carrying them south to find Cain.

Cain brushed her fingers over Emma's cheeks, wiping away the last of her tears. Now free to let her heart feel again, Cain found her own comfort in the smooth, familiar skin. "You want to help me up?" Cain wanted to tell Emma something but didn't want to share it with a stranger. In reality she'd let the conversation go on long enough.

"Are you all right?"

"Just fine, love. I have to go to the bathroom, and the group of Nazis they call nurses around here want me to get up as much as possible."

Cain had to laugh when Emma took the opportunity to explore a little as they walked. The gown Cain was wearing gave her plenty of real estate to work with.

"I thought you had to go," Emma said when the door closed and Cain pulled her close.

"The orderly left a little gift earlier, and I wanted to tell you about it before our talk got any more intimate."

Emma shivered as Cain whispered in her ear. Even in the earliest days of their relationship, Cain could merely have recited the alphabet and Emma would melt from the sound of that low burr.

"I need you to get my robe and find a closet somewhere so we can talk."

"Who's he working for?"

"Robe and privacy first, lass."

They flushed and started a conversation about the house and

repairs to give their eavesdropper the impression of domestic bliss. Throughout the exchange Cain started yawning, making it clear she was headed for another nap. Instead, they made their way to the empty patient room next door.

"Can the feds do that?" Emma was frustrated that Cain had to exhaust herself just so they could converse. It was one thing for their enemies to pursue her partner when she was healthy and able to make the chase interesting, but this was cheap and petty. "You're in the hospital because one of their people shot you, for God's sake."

"We don't know it's the feds."

"Who else would it be?"

"If it's them, then I'm sure some judge signed something along the way that makes it all right, but I don't want to talk about that now." She motioned Emma closer. "They can tape me all they want when I'm at work or out, that I'm used to, but when I have to talk with my wife, that's off-limits."

"Am I still that? Or should I say, am I still that in your eyes?"

Cain ran her hand through Emma's thick blond hair until it came to rest behind her neck. "When you left, or when it finally hit me that you were gone, I tried for the longest time to hate you. I figured if I could get to that place, it would be easy for my heart to cut you loose."

Emma understood the way Cain felt, even though it was painful to hear. "Why didn't you?"

"Two reasons." Cain reached for one of Emma's hands. "One, because of Hayden. At night I told him stories about you and about us. He would lie there and listen, enjoying my little forays down memory lane until the day came that he didn't want to hear them. That's when I found myself lying in bed thinking about our time together because it was the one thing that brought me peace." She brought their linked hands up and put them over her heart. "I started as a way to comfort our son, then found you were ingrained in here." Cain bumped their hands over her heart. "No amount of anger or any other emotion is going to erase you from my heart. I love you, Emma Casey, and no matter your choices you'll always be my wife in here."

"I'll never give you cause to doubt me again. I swear it."

"If that's true, then nothing will ever harm us."

"What do we do about all this mess we're in, honey? You need to get better before anything else happens."

The big smile and slight tug encouraged Emma to sit in her lap.

"We're going to take all the time you want. Then and only then will we live up to my reputation as a Casey."

Careful not to put pressure on Cain's injured side, Emma leaned against her and pressed her lips to Cain's neck. "I'm not sure what that means, but at the moment I don't care." She placed a small kiss on the pulse point, enjoying the way it beat steadily against her lips.

Dr. Donald Elton hesitated before entering, but kept walking when Cain waved him in. "I thought you'd run off on me. And I'd ask how you're doing, but I can see that you're doing better than I am."

"Sorry, Dr. Elton," Emma said, moving off Cain's lap.

"Don't be sorry. I've always felt love is the quickest healer. You keep up the good work and she'll be back to full steam in no time." He looked at Cain and held out his hand. "What can I do for you?"

Cain started by explaining what had happened at their home and her business, finishing with what she wanted from him. It was difficult for the doctor not to give her what she wanted, especially after seeing the size of Emma's smile when she heard what Cain had in mind.

"You'll still need care," he warned.

"I'm not in any way suicidal, so don't worry," she assured him. "When certain people start asking, and they will, the last time we saw each other was a couple of days ago, and I left without your consent."

"You don't have anything to fear from me, Cain. Just promise me you'll come by and let me see my handiwork. It's not often I get to work on someone with such great muscle tone and bone structure. I'd like to see it when it's all working." When Emma's smile faded, he put his hands up in her direction. "I really am only interested from a medical point of view, so don't worry."

Cain chuckled and pulled Emma back down on her lap. "You got a deal, Doc. As soon as this is over, I'll run laps for you if you want."

In spite of her good mood, it still bothered her that she was running, since the Bracatos would think she was weak, but Cain had no choice. She didn't know what the future held, and in Cain's world that was reason enough to sweat.

CHAPTER TEN

When Muriel entered the bar at the Piquant, the jazz ensemble was just stepping off the small stage for a break. She'd been there often, and she knew that the musicians were always as good as the drinks the bartenders poured. Shelby sat at a table in one of the alcoves, her back to most of the patrons in the room. She had let her hair down and was running her finger up and down the stem of her glass, seemingly deep in thought.

"Some might say there's something really sexual about that." Muriel pointed to Shelby caressing her Manhattan glass and laughed. "Is something wrong? I don't mind taking a rain check."

"Please sit. I was just going over my day and the little surprise it came with."

One of the servers approached and pulled out her pad.

"Double Jameson neat, with an Abita Amber draft on the side," Muriel said before the girl could ask. "And bring the lady another."

"Trying to get me drunk?" Shelby flipped her hair back and smiled in a coy fashion.

"Not at all." Muriel threw her coat in the empty chair across from her, sat, and placed her hands flat on the table as if to stretch them out before reaching for a nut from the bowl close to Shelby. "I'm trying to get you to a place where you forget three little letters that are so much a part of your identity. And make you forget my last name."

"If what you're talking about are FBI and Casey, that'll take a whole lot more of these." She pointed to her drink.

"As they say, Shelby, the night is young."

With the quick efficiency the Piquant was known for, the drinks were delivered to the table with a fresh bowl of snacks. Muriel picked up the whiskey first and drained the glass. The smooth-tasting liquor blended well with the glass of rum she'd already had during her meeting with Ramon.

"Tough day yourself?" Shelby's blue eyes widened a bit at the ease with which the whiskey had gone down.

"Just trying to catch up with you."

"Now why does that make me think you don't say those words often in any situation?"

"See, you bring out the best in me." At the bar the green bottle came out again and the bartender poured Muriel a refill.

The murmur of quiet conversations filled the room, accentuated every so often with a laugh from one of the patrons, but Muriel was content to just enjoy the comfortable silence between them. It gave her a chance to look around and check if there was anyone of interest that Shelby should know about.

Dalton, Cain's father, had taught her and Cain to study a room. "Never sit and not look around you, girls. One day it may make the difference between finding an enemy or their bullet finding you." Her uncle repeated the lesson every time they were out together.

With a silent thank-you to the man who had taught her so much, Muriel finished her drink and reached for her beer, watching the stage. Every so often after she spotted them, though, she glanced at the two men sitting close to the bar. They had glasses of pale beer in front of them and were trying their hardest to fit in with a crowd that was just a bit out of their league as far as fashion was concerned.

"So what's tonight really about?" Muriel asked Shelby, trying to sound casual.

"What do you mean? This is just drinks, Counselor," Shelby answered with a smile, thinking that Muriel was flirting with her.

"So, not working tonight? You know, trying to find ways to dig up dirt."

Still not understanding, Shelby put her hand on Muriel's forearm. "I just thought after today you might need a friendly ear or shoulder, whichever you want. I told you that today and I meant it." She squeezed the solid arm under her hand and smiled. "This is just about one friend helping another."

Muriel looked at the hand touching her and felt like a block of ice had formed in her chest. This wasn't about two friends finding comfort in each other's company; it was someone trying to play her at what she thought was a vulnerable time. "That sounds really good, but could you excuse me for a minute?"

"Sure, I'll be waiting. Would you like another drink?"

Muriel shook her head, stood up, and grabbed her coat. Shelby was about to ask why when the attorney started walking to the bar without another word. Shelby pivoted in her seat to see where she was going. The bartender leaned over the counter and offered Muriel her hand in a greeting that spoke of an old friendship, then nodded as Muriel whispered in her ear. Shelby followed Muriel's finger as it pointed first to the table they had been sharing and then to another table not far from where she was standing at the bar. From her pocket, a roll of bills emerged, and Muriel put quite a few in the woman's hand. After that she saluted first Shelby, then Lionel and Joe, before walking out.

Wood-paneled elevator doors slid closed before Shelby could catch up with Muriel and explain she didn't know her fellow workers were going to be there. Any hope of building trust between them was plummeting as quickly as the elevator heading for the first floor, and she was furious. She loved her job, but there had to be more to life than the part that belonged to the government.

"What in the hell are you guys doing here?" She stood next to them with her hands on her hips, a clear sign she wasn't happy. "I don't appreciate being spied on."

"Come on, Shelby. It's what you do for a living," Joe said, trying to sound funny so she'd come off the ledge. "We just wanted to make sure you were all right with all that's happening. I'd be sick if you got caught in the cross fire, and I wasn't here to do anything about it."

"Did it occur to you two idiots that this had nothing to do with work? She lost two young associates today because some psycho who's out to get her cousin decided to blow up her office. I just wanted to help her get over that."

"We're sorry, but there's another reason for our being here," Lionel said. Before he could say anything else, the bartender Muriel had talked to before leaving came up and set a tray on the table.

"How are y'all doing tonight?" The woman had a pleasant smile, and Shelby found herself returning it. "Muriel asked me to set you up with the next round before she took off. She picked them out, so if you want something else, let me know."

Shelby picked up the glass. "What is it?"

"We usually call it a buttery nipple."

"Usually?" Joe asked.

"Tonight, with the size of her tip, she renamed it. Enjoy your 'it's as close as you're ever going to get.' Or should I make that plural?"

"Oh, yeah, they're related," Shelby whispered when she thought of Cain. And as had happened with Cain, Shelby was afraid there would never be anything between her and Muriel either, no matter how much attraction they shared.

The gulf between them was too wide.

CHAPTER ELEVEN

The next morning the doctor looked at Cain's injuries longer than usual. Uncovered, the gunshot wounds looked rather gruesome, but Dr. Elton said Cain would be almost back to normal in another month, barring any major setbacks. Cain and Emma smiled as he carefully enunciated that she would be in the hospital at least two more weeks so he could keep a careful eye on her.

"Good morning," Todd, their orderly, said as he walked in with an arm loaded down with towels right after the doctor left.

Todd was working the day shift beginning that morning, and he was starting his rounds in Cain's room. For the last twenty-four hours his new boss had been confined to listening to only the conversations that had taken place in the main room, but the two new hundred dollar bills in Todd's pocket were about to fix that.

"Just do it the same way as before, only this time pick someplace that isn't going to get wet." Those were his orders, and as he scrutinized the room, he chose the toilet paper dispenser. The talks with the FBI agent he was working for were emboldening him, and Todd had offered to take some pictures if the man could get him a small enough camera. However, the guy seemed content to stick to the bugs for now.

A little bit of what looked to Todd like silly putty was all he needed to put the device in place. He put the towels away, leaned to the dispenser, and whispered, "Testing one, two, three," before heading back into the room. The guard who sat with Cain sometimes was in the corner, but so was Cain's blond companion, and Todd ogled her for a moment longer than he intended.

"Is there a problem?" Cain asked. She'd had enough of this guy, and it was time to put a little fear into him.

The man listening from across the street leaned forward in his chair to get closer to the speaker and felt the beads of sweat break out across his forehead.

"No, ma'am, I was just getting your bathroom supplies put away. Can I get you anything else?" Alert, Cain did look a little more imposing, and he didn't want to hang around any more than he had to. If all the stories about her were true, he could only imagine what she'd do to him if she figured out what he was up to.

"Not a thing, but thanks for asking. I want to compliment you on the great job you and the others are doing in taking care of me." Cain felt a slight pinch to her side from Emma as she let her know she was laying it on a little thick.

God, what a sucker this idiot is. Todd smiled as he thought of her ignorance. "It's my pleasure."

With a flick of her hand, Cain sent Merrick after the short wannabe detective as he went about his other duties. "I think our little friend has a crush on you, love," she told Emma.

The man listening to them let out a relieved stream of air from his lungs when he heard Cain's comment. "Ah, my boy's eyes lingered too long on that bit of fluff you keep around, did they, Casey?" He'd known her long enough to realize she didn't ask questions of anyone without reason. When the idiot he'd hired had whispered into the bug, for a second he'd thought they'd blown it.

"I don't seriously think you have a thing to worry about." Emma leaned over and kissed Cain long enough for her breathing to deepen. Free to express how she felt, Emma was having a hard time keeping her hands to herself. "At the moment you have other concerns."

"Do tell," Cain said, before she gently took Emma's bottom lip between her teeth.

Emma pulled back just a little. "I'll be happy when I get you in a room with a lock on the door. For now you'll have to be content with me just sitting here and making eyes at you." Emma pecked the enticing lips once more before helping Cain to her feet. They'd started for the door when the phone at the bedside rang.

"Hello." Emma entwined her fingers with Cain's as she listened to the explanation on the other end. "I told you later on today, so don't bug your uncle Jarvis to bring you over here."

Cain smiled, imagining the answer their son most probably had practiced before calling.

"I know you miss her, Hayden, but Mom needs her rest so we can bring her home. Once she does you'll get to see her all the time, so just sit tight, and I'll come by and get the two of you later. How's your sister?"

The conversation obviously wasn't going to end soon, so Cain stepped into the bathroom and scouted around. Afraid if she bent over she wouldn't be able to get back on her feet without Emma's help, Cain took Emma's small mirror from the bathroom counter and ran it along the bottom of the most conspicuous thing in the room. She found what she looking for in the center, almost too close to the edge to be seen. However, something about it didn't seem right, aside from the fact they had used Todd to plant both the devices. He was ballsy, she gave him that, but he wasn't highly intelligent.

"I'll be over around four when Mom takes her nap to pick you both up." Emma wrapped the cord around her finger and smiled. Hayden was too smart for his own good sometimes, and he must have sensed something was up and was ready to come to the hospital and ask them about it. "Stop laughing or I'll tell her you're making fun of the fact she has to take a nap." She smiled at whatever his response was and glanced at Cain. "I'll tell her, sweetheart, and I love you too."

"Getting cabin fever already?" Cain asked. She stepped farther into the room to hide the fact she'd been in the bathroom at all.

"He just misses you and wanted to come see you. Though he used his sister as an excuse to get me to come earlier." Emma pointed to the bathroom and cocked her head to the side.

Cain nodded and sat on the bed. She really did need to have a long talk with Emma, but her options were limited as long as they were in the hospital together.

"He said Hannah was crying for you all morning, and we shouldn't keep her waiting."

"I'm sure he's done his fair share of missing you as well, Mama." Cain chuckled for the benefit of her listeners and pointed to the IV in her arm. She wasn't anywhere near being up to her full strength, but it was time to go back to work.

With a sigh Emma took a Band-Aid off the table and went about the task of what she assumed Cain wanted, without any interruption in their innocent conversation. "I guess he thought he could talk me into letting him stay home from school another day." The small catheter slid out of Cain's arm, and Emma let it just drop to the ground as she covered the puncture with the strip.

Cain was now free of her IV pole. In her purse Emma had the necessary prescriptions they'd need to see Cain through the next few weeks. There was no reason she couldn't start taking her medications orally.

"And you didn't fall for that?" Cain said. "What kind of mother are you?" She stood and gratefully accepted Emma's help in getting on a pair of pajamas and robe, tossing the hated hospital gown on the bed. The fatigue from such a simple act amazed her, but she just plowed through it and stood once again. "How about I take a nap now, and I'll be ready for him by the time he gets out of school. Besides, I'm sure Hannah would love to see you."

"Then let's get you tucked in." The bed linens rustled as Emma pulled the blankets up and fluffed the pillow. "I love you, honey."

She whispered the sentiment to the standing Cain and almost cried when Cain pulled her into the strongest embrace she could manage. Hopefully all of this wouldn't take long and they could return to the business of rebuilding their family.

"Trust me, lass, everything's going to be fine."

For the first since Emma had come back, she totally believed that.

CHAPTER TWELVE

Giovanni Bracato would have worried about Cain, but his sons had done such a thorough job of blowing holes in her defenses and strongholds, he seriously doubted she would recover in time to give him any problems. By adding connections from Latin America he could expand his operation enough to muscle out Vincent and Ramon.

He sat across from his new suppliers and tried not to reveal his reactions, since he wasn't familiar with the three men. Things were going well, and he didn't want to screw them up by giving them any reason to doubt the sincerity of his word.

"So as you can see, Señor Luis, we have the market and the ability to move the product into the city. I just need your guarantee that the supply will flow steadily from your end." Giovanni had a hard time keeping a smug expression off his face as he adjusted his girth in the upholstered seat and reached for the cup of coffee one of his men had taken from the waiter and served. With his other hand he patted the briefcase lying on the table to his left and finally let the corners of his mouth curl upward slightly. "Let me worry about the street sales, and you just collect the cash."

Francis stepped up beside his father and snapped open the case containing stacks of hundred dollar bills and a brand-new 9 mm handgun. "What my father means is, you'll collect the cash and weapons as per our agreement."

"What about customs?" Juan Luis leaned forward and pushed aside the coffee with a look of disgust. A thick lock of dark hair fell into his eyes as he spoke, and he pushed it back impatiently. "With all the new security measures your government has put in place, how do we know you can get all you're committed to into the country? Because once it's ordered, *amigo*, you're responsible for it. I don't give a fuck if it makes it in or not."

"Because I just gave you my word." Giovanni had to stop himself before he tacked an insult to the end of his sentence. "That should be good enough."

An older gentleman sat to the side smoking a cigar and listening. Giovanni had dismissed him as an advisor and concentrated on negotiating with Juan, who up to now had asked all the questions and done all the talking.

"Your word means *mierda* to us." Juan's mouth went up in a sneer when he said the Spanish word for "shit." "With all the heat you have on you right now, you're lucky we're even here talking to you."

"You listen to me, you little pissant," Giovanni said, ignoring his son's hand on his shoulder as he aimed his finger at Juan, seated directly across from him.

"Please, Mr. Bracato, my nephew is a man used to speaking his mind. There's no reason for name-calling." The older man put his cigar down and patted the young man sitting next to him on the leg. "We are simply protecting our livelihood. Surely you can understand my family's concerns."

"Who are you?"

"I am Rodolfo Luis, and it's my coke you are buying." He picked up his cigar and pointed it at Giovanni. He looked like he wanted to snap Bracato's finger off. "Speak to me like you just did to my nephew, and I'll have you drawn and quartered like in days of old." He took a drag off the smoke to keep it lit and snickered. "Though we use chainsaws now to make it easier on ourselves."

"Come on, Tío Rodolfo. This asshole knows the score." With a snap of his fingers Juan leaned over and pulled the open briefcase over. "We'll hold on to this in good faith."

"Just remember that you fuck me and I have enough men to take you out," Giovanni threatened. He felt his ears get hot when the three men just laughed in his face before leaving. If the dealers decided to renege on their deal, five hundred large of his money was walking out with them for just meeting with him.

"Pop, you shouldn't have lost your cool like that. We need these guys." Francis dropped into the chair Juan had been sitting in.

"You think I don't know what I'm doing?" Before his youngest son could answer, Giovanni slammed his hands down on the table. "You don't know fuck. I was making deals and getting this family to where we are today from the time I was ten, so don't tell me how I should or shouldn't act."

Across the street Lionel and Joe sat in the service truck trying to drown out the rest of the restaurant noise to hear what was going on. They had followed the Bracatos to Costello's, an Italian restaurant toward the back of the Quarter, only to lose sight of them when they stepped into the private room in the back. Whoever they were there to see was already behind the oak-paneled doors when Joe and Lionel arrived. Since only the two of them were watching and trying to listen in, they never saw the car pull out from the block behind them or the Luis family depart through the kitchen.

"You want to go back to the house, Papa?"

"What I want to know is where your brothers are. I hate walking into a meeting looking like my family has better things to do than meet with the fucks who hold our future in their hands. Where are they?"

"I don't know. Maybe they were taking care of the business we discussed yesterday. If you want I can start calling around and see if I can find them."

With a little difficulty Giovanni pulled away from the table and lumbered to his feet. "Forget it, let's go. We'll catch up with them later on tonight. I want to make sure my guy at the Piquant keeps an eye on the greasers who just left with a shitload of my money."

The briefcase Giovanni was talking about sat between Juan and Rodolfo on the way back to their hotel as they laughed about the fact that the older Bracato obviously didn't know that his son Stephano was already selling their drugs in Mississippi. When they turned onto Royal Street in the French Quarter past the front of the restaurant they had just left, Rodolfo pointed at the van parked across the street. "See, *mi hijo*, these are the things you have to look out for when you come to America." He used the nickname "son" for his nephew because he thought of his sister's child as his own. Juan's father had left long before his birth, moving to the next town and the next woman waiting to be used.

The man hadn't gotten far before Rodolfo's men caught up with him and returned him to the Luis estate. The penalty for deflowering, then leaving Rodolfo's little sister had been a slow death straight from the imagination of the man who controlled most of the coca plants in Mexico.

At the back of the property that bordered the mountains, they stripped the handsome drifter who considered himself a ladies' man and tied him to a tree. Then one of Rodolfo's men coated his genitals in honey and stepped in the fire-ant pile at the base of the tree. The miles of beautiful countryside ate up his screams as the little insects chewed away at what had been a source of great pride. The men went back a couple of days later to scatter his bones.

"Every place you visit, you need a *padrino* to warn you of what dangers lie in wait," Rodolfo continued.

"A godfather? I don't understand." Juan looked at the van as it disappeared around another corner. "Who was that?"

"You just listen to your *tío*, and I'll teach you how to swim in waters other than those in your own backyard." He patted his nephew's leg and closed his eyes for the rest of the ride. What Rodolfo didn't realize was that in these waters, the sharks didn't work for the government.

CHAPTER THIRTEEN

The door to the hospital sunroom was closed, and three guards discouraged anyone from entering. Merrick and Lou lowered and closed all the blinds, cutting off the view of the gardens. A watcher would have to blow his cover to discover what was going on inside.

After stepping out and away from prying ears, Cain and Emma slowly strolled toward the sunroom arm in arm, resembling any other devoted couple. This would be Emma's first trial as they started to rebuild their relationship based on an equal partnership. The test would be tame, but like nothing Emma had ever seen before.

If the scene she walked in on alarmed Emma, no one could tell from her expression. She stayed at Cain's side and helped her into a comfortable chair. Merrick already sat nearby, and she merely nodded to them and smiled slightly. With at least ten other chairs to pick from, she chose the arm of the chair Cain was occupying and put her hand on the shoulder of the woman she loved.

Todd was the only person showing any emotion at all. He was trembling but didn't want to make any sudden movements lest the gun jammed in his mouth go off and leave his brains scattered across the expensive wooden blinds designed to make the room warmer.

"What do you want to do with him, boss? My finger's getting tired," Merrick said in a bored tone as she shoved the silencer attached to her gun farther into Todd's mouth.

"Why don't we let him have the use of his mouth back for a little while so we can have a chat." Cain lifted Emma's hand off her shoulder and gave the palm a kiss.

"I don't know why I'm here." Todd was on the verge of tears.

He'd been walking out of the employees' lounge when the big man behind him had grabbed him and brought him here. "Please, this is some sort of mistake."

"You know what I detest more than a liar, Todd?" Cain asked the question, but her eyes never left Emma's face.

He shook his head, but the words refused to come out of his mouth until Lou cocked the hammer on his pistol, pressed it to the back of his head, and said softly, "The lady asked you a question, and I suggest you come up with an answer."

"No, ma'am."

"She hates anyone who tries to hurt our family more than anything else in life," Emma finished for her. "Some of us are lucky and she forgives our indiscretions, but luck isn't running in your favor today."

"That's right, love." The palm close to Cain's lips received another kiss, and she smiled after delivering it. "What I want to know is why? How much was it worth to you to betray my family and me?"

"I don't know what you're talking about," Todd pleaded.

"I realize that your salary here must be pathetic, but that's no reason to keep lying," Cain said in a bored-sounding voice. "Let me explain to you how this works and why we're here. First, the human body has only two knees. Once I order Merrick here to put a bullet into both of yours, I'll be forced to move to things like your elbows, then your head. By my count, that leaves you four chances to answer correctly before you run out of options. Believe me, Todd, there's no turning back from that last shot."

With Emma's help, Cain climbed to her feet and moved closer to the man who just that morning had been feeling like the reincarnation of super spy. Todd manfully tried to meet her gaze, but he couldn't. There was nothing in the blue eyes that stared back at him. Nothing at all.

"Second, I never invite anyone into a meeting like this without finding out most of the answers first. That way, I know when you insist on lying to me. If that's how you want to play it, we'll go ahead and move to the head option now." Cain stood inches from him, and he had to lean back to see her face. "Shall we try again? How much did it take to get you to plant bugs in my room?"

As fast as he could, Todd pulled out the two hundred dollars and held them up to her. "I'm sorry. I didn't mean anything by it."

"Such a clichéd answer deserves the same response, don't you think?"

Cain stepped back as Lou punched the back of Todd's head so hard he fell face down on the floor. The groan Todd released at the sudden pain made Emma flinch, but she didn't say anything or make any move to leave.

"I don't care about your apologies or anything else. What I want is the name of whoever paid you." She motioned for Lou to pick him up so the idiot could see her before she continued. "And think very carefully before the words 'I don't know' come out of your mouth. Because you'll regret them more than you'll ever imagine."

"I don't know his name, I swear. He works for the FBI. He showed me his badge. I got a hundred for the one next to the bed and two for the one in the bathroom this morning."

Todd was talking so fast Emma thought he would pass out. Not once in her life had she seen such fear in another human being, but instead of condemning Cain for having to resort to violence and intimidation, she tried to concentrate on what had landed Todd on his knees.

"How did he contact you?"

"He just walked up to me in the parking lot one night before work. Somehow he knew I worked on your floor, but I wasn't assigned to your room so I switched with a buddy. This guy, the guy who paid me, he said he'd call me here if he needed anything else." All the excitement he felt when the agent first approached him had disappeared and felt pale in comparison to the fear he was experiencing now.

"What did he look like?" Cain sat again as she asked the question and tried to ignore the pain in her side.

"Dark hair, not as tall as you, and built kinda stocky."

"And that would describe half the men in the city," Merrick said.

"If I knew more, believe me, I'd tell you." Todd put his hands together and held them up to Cain.

"Todd, I want you to listen to me very carefully." Cain leaned forward and pinned the man with her eyes. "I'm thinking of letting you walk through that door in a few minutes—"

"Please, let me go and I won't tell a soul about this."

Lou drew back and hit the side of his head, knocking Todd down again and leaving him woozy.

"I'd appreciate if you let me finish. I said I'm *thinking* about it, but if I do, you're going to walk out of here and never, and I mean never, be seen in New Orleans again. Don't go to your apartment. Don't call your girlfriend if you have one. Just go."

Cain waited until Lou had peeled him off the floor again before she finished. "If I hear of you talking to anyone, Todd, you remember today as the warning. Next time, if there *is* one, I'm going to tell Lou here to just put a bullet in the middle of your forehead, and I'm going to leave you to rot where you fall."

Her words caused a wet spot in his pants that spread in the direction of the floor.

"Do we understand each other?"

"Perfectly." Todd stood with as much dignity as he had left and walked toward the door, hoping Cain didn't change her mind before he made it outside and to freedom. Fortunately, she'd let him keep his money, though he wasn't sure how far two hundred and thirty bucks would get him.

"What do you think the FBI is after now?" For years Emma had wondered what happened when Cain went off to meet someone who was causing her problems, but any questions she had were finally put to rest. After having witnessed this incident firsthand, she found a certain lure in doing business this way.

Most of society obeyed rules because they feared the consequences of breaking them. In circumstances like this, Cain made the rules and enforced them no matter what happened. Being completely honest with herself, Emma realized why this rogue who lived life on her own terms kept her enthralled.

The money and the life that Cain had afforded her weren't paramount; she loved this mix of devil and compassionate soul. Now, even if it cost her the lasting paradise her mother loved to preach about, Emma would never run from the truth of who she was, and she would accept whatever she had to in order to stay at Cain's side.

"I thought you said they would lay off after what happened at the warehouse that night."

"They did—well, as much as the feds are ever going to lay off our operations. This isn't the feds, though, baby," Cain said. As she watched Todd walk to the door, she thought of how lucky he was. She'd gone easy on him because of Emma, but in the future she couldn't afford to be so generous, and she hoped Emma would hold up. "We're dealing with someone else here, and they're not interested in what we're up to."

"Then what are they interested in, and how do you know that?"

"Why do you want to know?" Merrick asked Emma.

"For the love of God," Cain said, exasperated with Merrick and her suspicions. What they were talking about, even if Emma was wired, was no different that what the FBI was pondering as well.

"The equipment is too antiquated to be FBI, and I'm only guessing here, but I think they were just interested in finding out how healthy I am. Half-dead targets aren't as much fun, I'm assuming. If not, the final blow would have come by now." She'd given Emma the best answer she could think of.

"You're thinking Giovanni Bracato?" Merrick asked.

"Why not? Word on the street is that every one of the goons lying dead outside our house was on Stephano's payroll. The club and Muriel's office, though—that wasn't him. Something so splashy isn't his style."

"Gino Jr.," Merrick said.

"That's what I'm thinking too. What I need now is two good weeks to get back on my feet. Then we finish this."

"And we do it together," Emma added.

"You're left out from now on only if you want to be, lass. That I promise you on my mum's grave. But I want you to walk into this knowing what the outcome's going to be."

Emma put her hands on Cain's cheeks and bent down and kissed her. She obviously knew what she wanted and was staking her claim to it.

She pulled away, but not so far that Cain couldn't see the openness in her eyes. "No mercy, my love. If they go after our children and you, I want you to show no mercy."

"Then we want the same things."

"Forever," Emma said.

More than anything, Cain wanted to believe the sincerity in Emma's eyes and the fervor of her tone.

CHAPTER FOURTEEN

S helby?"

"Speaking," Shelby said into the phone balanced on her shoulder. She was in the office for the afternoon finishing up the report on the Barney Kyle incident. "Can I help you?"

"This is Agent Franks. Conner, remember?"

"I remember." Shelby had first been assigned to Conner's team before Kyle had poached her for his, thinking her looks would help further his investigation against Cain. Now she wished that she'd stayed with Conner, since he'd shown her the ropes so well.

She pictured the short redhead assigned to different areas around the city, currently assigned to Ramon Jatibon and his gambling ventures. "What can I do for you, Conner?"

"Are you all still tailing Casey and gang?"

"You need to come in more often. Didn't you hear?" she asked, wondering if one more person was going to rub it in. The day after they'd wrapped up the warehouse inventory, someone had left a bottle of whiskey on her desk with a sticky note attached describing what to look for when confiscating illegal liquor.

"I'm not calling to razz you. I just thought you might want to know that Ramon and a couple of his goons just drove up to Mercy Hospital with a big bunch of flowers. Any guess as to who he's here to visit?"

"What's Cain doing with him?"

"Look, I have to go. He's heading inside." The phone went dead, and Shelby was left listening to the dial tone.

The drone let her concentrate on what the next-best move should be, and Shelby didn't wait too long to decide. She punched in a number and waited for it to connect. "Joe, where are y'all?"

"Are we speaking again? I thought you were mad at us."

"Come on. Tell me where you are."

"Outside Giovanni Bracato's house watching his guard pick his nose. Where do they find these geniuses? He should know you have to wait till you're alone to fully enjoy the nose-picking experience."

"As fascinating as that sounds and as much as I want you to continue down this interesting subject path, I need to ask you and Lionel a favor."

"Ask away."

"Meet me at Mercy and see if you can zero in on a conversation happening on the fifth floor."

Joe banged his head on the small desk in the back of the van and groaned. "Do you remember a woman named Annabel Hicks? A very scary female when angered, who also happens to be our boss, in case that happened to slip your mind. Leaving the scene of a stakeout she assigned wouldn't be a wise career move."

"Have I led you wrong before?" Shelby gathered up her things.

"Would you like the list in chronological or alphabetical order?"

"Please, Joe?"

"All right, but if Lionel says no, you're on your own." The argument was weak, since Lionel was already in the driver's seat with the engine running. "We'll be there in five, and if Giovanni commits some heinous crime in his front yard, you're explaining it to Hicks."

"You're the best, Joe."

"Yeah, yeah, that and a hundred bucks will get me into a movie with a Coke and popcorn."

They were set up and searching for what Shelby wanted when she pulled up, but it was slow going because of all the equipment interference.

"As far as we can tell, they aren't in the room you told me Cain is occupying," explained Lionel. He'd pulled up the blueprints to the building to aid in the search, but Cain and Ramon had effectively shut them out.

"What do you think he's doing here?" Shelby asked.

"One of two things. He's here only as a friend paying a social visit, or we got the head of one family cahooting with the head of another," answered Joe.

"Cahooting? Is that even a word?" Lionel asked. "I say it has to do with everything that's happened. We've watched Casey long enough to know she isn't going to just lie down and take someone blowing up her property and shooting at her house while her children and her woman are inside."

Joe leaned over and punched his arm. "Her woman? Who are you, king of the jungle? I have to agree, though." He said to Shelby, "We followed Bracato to Costello's Restaurant today but couldn't see who he was meeting. There's too much activity in town for something big not to be happening. I think the deck's about to be reshuffled, and whoever's left will control much more than even we can imagine."

"Do any of the players have enough muscle to wage a turf war?" Lionel asked, still searching the floor for any sign of Cain's or Ramon's voices.

"If brains are the deciding factor, then Cain, Ramon, or Vincent could end up running the rackets for years to come," Shelby said. "My money's on Cain."

"Are you up for this?" Joe looked at her, wanting to see her face when she answered. "If she goes to the mat to destroy those who tried to hurt her family, we have to put her away. I don't care how much you like Cain and Muriel. No one's above the law."

"Don't worry. This isn't personal. I know what my job is, and I intend to do it."

❖

"Señor Jatibon, it's so nice to see you again," Emma said when he stepped into the sunroom and handed her a bouquet of flowers. "Thank you so much. I'm sure Cain is going to love them." She handed them to Lou at the door and followed Ramon to some chairs by the windows.

"Please, Emma, call me Ramon." He kissed both her cheeks, showing no surprise at her being there. "How is the patient?"

"Much more of this place, and she's probably going to plan an escape. You know Cain as well as I do. She can't sit still for long, so thank God she's back on her feet and able to move under her own steam. She just had to run back to the room for a minute. She shouldn't be long."

"She can take all day if she wants, my dear. This old man never misses the opportunity to spend time with a beautiful woman," Ramon said. "How are you and the children after what happened at the house?"

"Hayden says he's okay, and I hope there's no lasting effect."

"He's a good boy. I'm sure he'll be fine."

"Hannah is too young to really understand, so I'm hopeful it won't be a problem, but getting out safe is enough to be thankful for. Cain has good people working for her, and they handled things flawlessly. Though I never want to go through that again. Cain and the children are my life."

Ramon leaned forward and put his hand on her knee. "Never forget that, Emma. Cain and I are from two different cultures, but in here"—he tapped two fingers over his heart—"we are the same, and we feel the same when it comes to our children and our wives. You have my oath that I'll do whatever it takes to keep the peace and all of you safe until this is over."

"Thank you, Ramon. That means a lot."

"Yes, it does, and I owe you a debt for coming to our aid," Cain added, from the door. "Are we ready?"

"My plane's waiting for you, Cain." Ramon stood and offered his hand. "No one will be the wiser until it's too late. I've also made arrangements for Muriel and the other people you want to take. Vincent and I'll keep an eye on things until you get back."

"I'm thinking two weeks."

"It can be two months, *amiga*. Everything will be waiting for you when you return. Then we will sit and discuss what needs to be talked about." He was glad to see Cain up and walking around, but she looked tired. "Is there anything else you need?"

"Just time to heal." Cain looked at Emma before finishing. "But now that I've found my strength, I don't see that being a problem."

"Then we will be unbeatable."

"Count on it, Ramon." She held out her hand to Emma, who readily took it. "Count on it."

It was plain to Ramon as he looked on that the missing piece of Cain's fractured soul was back and appeared ready to take her place in Cain's life.

CHAPTER FIFTEEN

I'm not going anywhere without my parents," Hayden said. He was standing next to the car Mook had used to get them to the Lakefront Airport, holding Hannah's hand and refusing to board the plane about twenty feet away.

"Then get in here before we leave without you," Emma said from the door of the plane.

It had taken some coordination, but they had apparently managed to get everyone to the airport without picking up a tail along the way. Merrick and Mook would be traveling with them in Ramon's plane, and the rest of Cain's crew was already en route.

"Mama!" Hannah yelled, clapping her hands. "Where's Mom?"

"She's inside waiting on you, sweetie. Are you ready to take a trip?" Emma hurried down the short flight of steps so she could pick the little girl up and hug and kiss her before giving her son the same treatment.

The greatest gift, aside from getting Cain back in her life, was having Hayden not flinch when she touched him. He had actually initiated some of the contact in the last few days, and Emma had to fight the urge to sob every time he did.

"Do we get to find out where we're going, or is this a game of twenty questions?" Hayden put his arm around her waist and followed her back to the plane. He was joking, and at the moment they could have just been flying around the city and back. She knew he didn't care, that it was just nice to all be in the same place at the same time.

"What, you don't like surprises?" Emma said, trying to keep a straight face. "I'm sure the burden of being taken out of school will be worth your while when we get there."

"You don't know, do you?"

"You think you're so smart, don't you?"

He arched his brow, resembling Cain so much it took Emma's breath away. "Oh, all right. Cain knows how good I am at keeping secrets, so no, I have no idea." She laughed as she bumped hips with him and cocked her head in the direction of the plane. "Go on. She's been looking forward to you getting here."

"Thanks, Mama."

That was new too, and it made Emma sigh.

"You're very welcome." She kissed his forehead before sending him on his way. "Let's go get you strapped in, Miss Hannah."

The crew closed the door behind her and continued their preflight checklist.

In the back of the plane Cain sat in one of the leather chairs, trying to get as comfortable as possible for the two-hour flight. Dr. Elton wasn't thrilled that she was getting on a plane or leaving his care, but he understood her dilemma. He'd felt a little better when Emma told him Cain had arranged for medical care once they arrived at their destination.

"Hey, pal, how's it going?" Cain asked Hayden as he stepped closer. They took turns looking each other over, making sure the forced separation, which had been much longer than Cain would have liked, had done no harm.

For Hayden, the too-few trips to the hospital were as much about making himself feel better as they were about visiting Cain. His mother was such a huge part of his life that the thought of losing her made him ill. "I'm better now. How are you feeling?"

"I'm okay, Hayden. I want you to stop worrying. I'm going to be fine. There isn't any reason for you to think about this anymore. We're going away so I can finish healing. Then I'm coming back to take care of this just like I always do." She waved him closer and whispered the last part. "Only now I don't have to do it alone."

"You don't think she'll leave again, do you?" he asked.

"I wanted to talk to you before now, but haven't had the chance." With the hand of her uninjured side, Cain waved to her chest. Just behind their son she could see that Emma was having a hard time keeping Hannah in her seat, the little girl obviously wanting to be with her and Hayden. "Are you all right with everything that's happened? Your mother being back in my life also means she's back in yours, and I don't want you to feel like I'm pushing you aside."

"I'm just glad you're happy. I talked to her a lot when she came home from the hospital every night to have dinner with us. You were right that night we went out before you got shot. She's my safe haven, and I'm glad to have one again. I was so mad at her I didn't realize how much I missed her."

He needed some contact with Cain, but was afraid to hurt her so he put his hand in hers. "That doesn't mean I want our relationship to change, but I do want a chance to get to know her better. No matter what, Emma's my mom, and I'm glad she is."

"You're the best kid I could have hoped for, Hayden." Cain pulled him forward and put her arm around him.

"Just wait till you get to know Hannah. That kid is a riot." He kissed Cain's cheek and looked back at the little girl. "You should be glad I'm not the jealous type, or this could get ugly."

"Mama, please. I wanna see Mom and Haygen. Please." The little girl kept looking back at the two talking. "Please."

"Mom did a really good job when it came to telling her about us," Cain said. "Hannah's going to be fun to have around."

Hayden went to the little girl and picked her up, causing Emma to shake her head. Having Hannah exposed to the rest of the Casey clan was going to spoil the little girl rotten. In only a short time she'd come to love being with Hayden, who often carried her around the house, showing her family treasures and telling her the same stories about their family that Cain had told him through the years. The adventures of the Casey clan were much better than any book, and Hayden seemed to love retelling the tales as much as he liked hearing them.

"You want to tell Mom hi before we take off?" he asked Hannah.

She nodded and pressed her forehead to Hayden's, glad to have a brother who understood what she needed. "How's your owie, Mom?" Hannah asked when she took a seat on Cain's lap. "You stay with us now?"

The engines kicked on, and Emma urged them all into their seats before they took off. To keep the peace Cain moved so that they could all sit together for at least a little while. As the navigator came out to tell them they were getting ready to start their taxi to the end of the runway, someone started pounding on the door of the plane.

"Late as usual, and for that I apologize." Cain shook her head as she explained to the man in the cabin, who looked a little shocked. "I know you just closed it, but could you?"

With quick efficiency the crew opened and closed the door so they could admit their last passenger. Merrick was the first to wonder what the woman was doing on board, but now wasn't the time to start questioning Cain about anything.

The late arrival walked over to Cain and kissed her cheek. A well-tailored jacket hid the two Glock 9 mm pistols she always wore but did nothing to conceal her athletic body and long legs. Katlin Patrick had worked for Cain since her graduation from college with a business degree, an education her benefactor had insisted on and paid for. Having worked her way through Cain's business, she now was in charge of security for their shipments and also the day-to-day operations of Cain's legitimate entities.

They were seldom seen together, and Cain doubted anyone other than Muriel and Jarvis knew they were kin. Their family ties had been kept out of the police files for good reason. Cain had trusted Katlin on more than one occasion to represent her at various meetings and never feared betrayal at the hand of the woman, who, like Muriel, shared her blood.

"Sorry I'm running late, Cain, but there was a problem at the warehouse, then at the hospital, that I had to take care of."

Cain nodded and pointed to an empty seat. "And is it a problem still?"

"You know better than to ask."

"Emma, do you remember the black sheep of the family?" Cain pointed to Katlin.

"I think we've met, but I'm sorry…I can't recall the name."

"Not to worry, Mrs. Casey. Cain keeps me well hidden among the grunts. Helps to keep a low profile when I'm the designated watcher." The plane had started to move, so Katlin just smiled and waved. "I'm Katlin, Cain and Muriel's cousin a couple of times removed."

"You know everyone else, so let me introduce you to the newest member of our family." Cain took Hannah's hand in hers. "This is Hannah Casey, our daughter."

"Pleased to meet you, Hannah," Katlin said with a smile.

Emma looked on, amused. Katlin might have been a couple of relatives removed, but once again the Casey genes had won out. She had the characteristic dark hair and height, but one difference made Emma think she might be able to give Cain something she'd wanted from the time they'd met.

Instead of being the same incredible blue as Cain's, Katlin's eyes were a shade darker green than Emma's. When they'd started talking about having children, Cain had told Emma she wanted to hold a baby with her shade of blond hair and beautiful green eyes. Perhaps that would be possible since here was the proof.

The flight ceascd to fascinate the kids, and they drifted off to sleep before they were over Tennessee. Cain doubted the other passengers were sleeping, but all of them had their eyes closed and their breathing was relaxed. To her surprise Emma hadn't said anything after greeting Katlin and asking Hannah if she had to go to the bathroom. Unless they'd been apart for so long she'd forgotten Emma's moods, she was thinking about something pretty hard.

"What's making that frown line appear in the middle of your forehead, love? Is something wrong?"

With a sigh, Emma folded her legs under her and rested her head on Cain's shoulder. "You never forget anything about me, do you?"

"We've only been apart four years, but it could've been forty and I'd still remember all those little things that make you who you are. Or at least I'd like to think so."

The line Cain had spoken of disappeared with Emma's smile. "Nothing's wrong. I was just thinking about something."

She kissed Cain before the question of what could pop out. "Would it be all right if we talked about it later?"

"It's nothing I can help you with?"

"Oh, it's definitely something you can help me with." She laughed when Cain smirked and leered at her. "Trust me, I'm looking forward to that too, but what you're thinking about right now isn't it."

"Then you take your time and leave me to my lascivious

thoughts." With a slight bend of her neck Cain placed a kiss on the tip of Emma's nose. "But if you need to talk to me about anything, you know where to find me."

"Actually I have one question. Where can I find you for the next couple of weeks? We're in the air, so it's safe to tell me now."

"I didn't tell you because I wanted to surprise you, not because I didn't trust you with the information." She twirled a strand of blond hair around her finger, loving the way Emma smelled. It wasn't often that she ran across anyone with the same scent.

Hayden's head shifted away from the window at that moment, and he woke up without either of his mothers noticing. It was a good opportunity to study the reality of the love the two shared and compare it to the memories he relived late at night when he was alone in his room. Not since Emma had left had he seen Cain's face so relaxed or anyone sitting that close to her. He was glad to see he hadn't just made up something unrealistic to help him accept what had happened. Here before him was the love he remembered seeing for as long as he had memory of being alive.

"Will you promise me something if you can?" The injury was an inconvenience since Emma wanted to sit in Cain's lap and be as close to her as possible.

"Sure." The thoughts of the gunshot wound were going through Cain's mind as well. "I'll give you anything I can if it'll take that frown off your face."

"Tonight, when we get to wherever we're going, will you sleep with me?"

"I'd like that." A pain from moving her arm made Cain grimace, but she brought her hand up anyway and cupped Emma's cheek. "You haven't gotten used to sleeping alone, have you?"

"I could be sleeping in a single bed, and it'd still be too big without you lying next to me. Four years' worth of nights is a long time to do without you." She didn't mean for the tears to come, but they filled her eyes anyway. "I missed you so much, and I'm so tired of crying."

Cain rubbed her thumbs along Emma's face until she'd wiped away the few tears that had actually fallen. "There's no need for that, lass." She took a deep breath and released it. "I'm so sorry."

"For what?"

"I shouldn't have let four years go by. I'm just glad you had the courage to come back and show me what a jackass I've been because of pride."

"You want to make a deal with me, boss?" Emma rubbed the back of Cain's neck as she tried to get the sad look off her partner's face. "We both agree we were a little wrong, a lot sorry, and we'll move on. How does that sound?"

"Like a deal I can live with."

Their conversation died as they felt the plane start to descend and the landing gear come down. Unable to contain her curiosity, Emma leaned over and looked out the window. The familiar landscape made her laugh, then kiss Cain.

"Does he know we're coming?"

"Yes, your dad knows we're coming, and he's thrilled to hear we've set things straight between us."

Emma kissed her again and couldn't resist joking. "Not too straight, I hope."

When Cain laughed, the knot in Emma's stomach loosened and she almost forgot it was there. The more things relaxed between them, the more she was convinced that they would regain what they'd thrown away and build from there.

CHAPTER SIXTEEN

W e're staying with the Raths for a while, lass," Cain said when they landed. "Your mother's leaving in a couple of days to visit her brother and his family in Illinois. Once she's gone we'll move over there, so I hope you don't mind. Or we could just stay with the Raths and have Ross come over and visit."

Emma nodded as she stepped down to greet her oldest friend in Haywood, who seemed even more excited to see the children and their resemblance to Cain and each other than she was to see Emma. Maddie was a couple of years older than her, but their friendship had started years before in high school and had grown until they knew each other's secrets.

When Emma had come back four years earlier, it had been Maddie who had held her as she cried over the decisions she'd made in leaving Cain and Hayden and having Hannah alone. Maddie had also been a huge help after Hannah's birth and loved the little girl like she was a part of her family. She had done it without ever judging Emma for her decisions and for the fact that, given a choice, she would run back to Cain just as quickly as she had run home.

"You look a lot happier than the last time I saw you," Maddie said as soon as the door of the big SUV closed behind Emma. It had been only three weeks since Emma had left for New Orleans and just a few days since the Raths had escorted Hannah down south, but Emma and Maddie were used to speaking every day.

"You're looking at a woman who's been given her life back, Maddie. She still loves me. Even after all I did, she's forgiving me a little more every day."

"Of course she is, sweetie. You're a hard one to say no to. Then to top it off, you come with cute stuff in the backseat. Cain doesn't have a chance in hell. Is she doing all right with the injury? I still can't believe she got shot trying to save you."

"I can. You know how she is if family's involved."

The familiar bulk of Jerry's Ford Expedition was close behind them, and Emma stared in the side view mirror at Cain sitting in the front seat talking to Jerry. What Maddie had said brought that one moment back to her in vivid detail. When Cain had grabbed her and thrown her to the ground to keep her safe, Emma knew she had a chance. Cain was many things, but she had a hard time hiding her feelings from those people she really loved. Lying on the floor of the warehouse that night, Emma had seen enough in Cain's face to reignite her hope.

"When I got there that night she was so mad at me, but when the chips were down, as they say, her heart overruled her brain." With a deep breath and one last glance she faced her friend. "So, how long have you known we were coming?"

Maddie let out a long laugh as she looked both ways at the intersection that, with a left turn, would lead them home. "She called a couple of days ago and asked us to play intermediary with your father, since she didn't want to take the chance of calling over there and having your mother answer the phone. Cain sounds really nice, Emma. I'm happy for you."

"Thanks, pal. I'm looking forward to spending time with you and Jerry."

"Sure you are." Maddie laughed again as Emma's attention dragged back to the vehicle behind them. "I'm sure you'll be able to concentrate on what I'm saying or remember my name even if tall, dark, and devastatingly good-looking isn't anywhere in the area. On another subject, I thought Cain's cousin was coming with you."

Emma was about to say she *had* brought a cousin, but decided to keep that information to herself for now and tell Maddie about the cousin she knew about. "Muriel couldn't afford to be away from the twenty phone lines she constantly has going and the contacts Cain will need when we get back, so she's still working. Only she's doing it from Vegas under the watchful eye of an old friend of the family, Ramon Jatibon's son Mano. She took her father with her, and the people who work for her are busy trying to find a new office location."

"Isn't it dangerous to leave them back in New Orleans if all the people with guns are with you here and in Nevada with Muriel and her father?"

A familiar fence line came into view, and Emma looked out into the fields to see if she could spot her father. She felt bad for not calling him as often as she'd wanted to, but with Cain in the hospital, then taking care of the kids, it was always too late to phone him when it crossed her mind.

She was so happy she'd taken his advice and gone back to New Orleans in search of the love she'd lost. In his own quiet way, her father had always had her happiness in mind, and he'd demonstrated that by being willing to throw her mother out to make it happen. Carol Verde might have been disappointed in her only child, but Ross was proud of her and the family she'd built with Cain.

"I know it's a strange concept to wrap your brain around since Cain doesn't exactly walk on the right side of the law, but she has a strong sense of honor. It isn't her style to leave anyone, especially any innocent, in harm's way. True, we left with a lot of the muscle and the rest is with Muriel, but some of our friends are keeping the peace while we're gone."

Emma was irritated as well as a little disappointed in Maddie. She wouldn't stand for anyone, even an old friend, to malign Cain's character.

The yard in front of the house was still dormant because of the cold weather, and Emma could hear the wind blowing down from the north when Maddie pulled up and shut off the engine.

Maddie put her hand on Emma's wrist. "I will never, and I mean *never*, judge you for any choice you make, Emma. If this is what makes you happy, then I'll be happy for you. I didn't ask that to cast doubt on Cain, or you for wanting to be with her. But I know why you left her all those years ago, and I don't want the same thing happening if and when the heat starts to rise again. And my gut tells me her getting shot means someone has a huge toll to pay."

"I told her forever, and that's what I plan to deliver. As for the heat, the bastards who shot at my children and me deserve whatever Cain has planned for them. It may be wrong to wish ill on someone, but I hope she kills every last one of them."

"I'm sure she won't disappoint you, or us, for that matter. You know how I feel about Hannah, and what those bastards did makes my blood boil. Anyone who'd dare point a gun in her direction deserves everything the devil has planned for them."

"Amen, sister," Emma said, finally breaking a smile.

After a sudden cacophony of slamming car doors, about twenty of Cain's guards started setting up the security system that would be in place by nightfall.

"Maddie, it's nice seeing you again." Cain offered her hand, and Emma busied herself with getting a sleeping Hannah out of her car seat. "Did I pass?"

Maddie looked up to Cain's twinkling blue eyes and had to laugh. She loved Jerry with all her heart, but the first time Emma had shown her a picture of Cain, she could understand what being with another female was about. Add Cain's charm to her looks, and Maddie instantly liked her.

With one hand Maddie tried to smooth her brown hair as the wind blew it into her face. As it swirled around, Cain could see the blond highlights in it and guessed the combination came from Maddie's time in the sun and had nothing to do with an expensive salon.

"You have beautiful hair."

Maddie blushed. "I…thank you."

"Well, did I?" Cain asked again.

"Pass?" Maddie brought her other hand to her head and tried to control her locks. "I have no idea what you're talking about."

"Honey, stop giving Maddie a hard time and come inside. I don't want you catching anything in this cold weather."

"Yes, Mother." Cain winked in Maddie's direction before following Emma.

Maddie muttered to herself, "My God, Emma, a nun wouldn't have a snowball's chance in hell at telling her no."

And no was the last thing on Emma's mind, no matter the question, when it came to Cain.

CHAPTER SEVENTEEN

"Mama," Hannah said, still sounding like she was on the verge of unconsciousness.

"Go back to sleep, sweetheart. It's all right." Emma sat down and ran her fingers through her daughter's black hair.

Hannah opened and closed her little hand in an effort to get Cain to come closer when she saw her standing at the door. When Cain sat on the bed, Hannah put her head in her lap. Emma stood back, wanting to give Cain time with their daughter so that they could establish a relationship.

Not caring if she tore every stitch the surgeon had so skillfully put in, Cain lifted Hannah off the bed, then held her and rocked her until the blue eyes closed again in sleep. But before Hannah gave in to her exhaustion Cain whispered, "I love you, baby girl."

For once Cain wished there really was an afterlife where the dead went and were able to view the living. She smiled to think that her parents and siblings were looking down and seeing how beautiful the family she'd been gifted with really was. She placed her hand on her wound so she could bend and kiss Hannah's forehead before she stood and started out of the room.

Emma leaned against the doorjamb and watched the touching scene.

When Cain turned around her smile widened, and once the door was closed she pulled Emma to her. Never had she been on the receiving end of such adoration mixed with a little bit of lust.

"Come on, honey, let's get you settled in. You look a little tired." Emma pulled on Cain's hand to lead her to the bedroom next door.

"Mrs. Casey, is this some plot to get me alone?"

Emma's sultry laugh confirmed that fact. "I'm merely looking out for your well-being, love, nothing more."

"Hell, I must be losing my touch."

Emma led her to the room at the center of the hallway and pushed her gently inside. "Trust me, hot stuff, you haven't lost a thing."

From the window they could see the men and women they had brought with them still working to get the precautionary system in place. Emma was surprised to see Hayden with a piece of electronic equipment in his hand, walking to the utility pole across the street.

"What's he doing?"

"Learning the business from the ground up, like every Casey before him. Just 'cause you're born with the name, you don't automatically get to be the leader. Hayden knows that without anyone telling him, just like I did."

Emma leaned against Cain and wrapped her arms around Cain's waist. "Before that happens you'll teach him everything you know, right?"

"I know you don't agree because he's your son, but—"

Emma pressed her fingers to Cain's lips. "He's *our* son, and you'll teach him everything you know, right?"

"And then some, love."

"Then let's leave him to his work, and you and me get into that nice comfortable bed."

Emma helped Cain with her shoes and took off her own heavy sweater before pulling back the blankets and climbing in beside her. They had to reverse sides from their usual sleeping arrangements because of Cain's injury, but when Emma rolled over and snuggled up, it felt just as wonderful as she remembered.

"Tell me about the Raths," Cain said as she rested her hand on Emma's hip.

"What do you want to know?"

"Whatever you want to tell me. I'm just curious." She moved her hand from Emma's hip up her side close to her breast. "They sounded nice enough on the phone."

Emma felt like Cain was pouring liquid fire along her skin. While she'd missed Cain for a variety of reasons, when she was really honest with herself, she had to admit that the sex always came close to the top of the list.

"Maddie and I went to school together. Well, for a little while, anyway. I was just starting high school, and she was a senior. We hit it off from the beginning, and even though she didn't want to go to college, she was the one who really encouraged me to attend Tulane."

Emma moved so that she was almost on top of Cain, without putting any undue pressure on her chest. "When I came back here alone and knowing I was going to have Hannah, I cried on her shoulder the most. My father loves me, but he was at a loss as to what to do with me except try to convince me to go home to you and work it out, and my mother was just her usual self. Maddie understood me, but even she wondered why I'd run home and desert the two people I loved most in the world."

"It was a dark time, love." The long breath Emma let out warmed Cain's chest, and Cain ran her fingers through Emma's hair to offer comfort.

"To tell you the truth, I never understood it myself." Emma sighed. "I was so lonely, and I missed you so much. It's a miracle Hannah survived. I was so sick and didn't want to eat. It was the most miserable time of my life."

"Was Maddie there when Hannah was born?" Cain asked to keep their talk going. Having Emma get some of that hurt out would only help the two of them in the future.

"She, Jerry, and Daddy were the only ones who came with me to the hospital, but once Hannah was born and they knew I was all right, I sent them home. I remember sitting in the hospital holding my baby, staring at yet another Casey and crying because I was so happy and so miserable at the same time. Did I tell you that I brought some whiskey with me?"

Cain smiled and shook her head.

"I did, and I baptized her Casey-style just like I remember you doing with Hayden. Then I told her about the proud clan she was a member of. I swear if she could've talked right then, she would've told me to take her home to you."

"Considering you and she lived with your mother all that time, it's a wonder she's so spirited."

"It's that strain of Casey bad grass running through her veins. My mother had about as much chance of breaking her spirit as she did yours. I'm just glad I don't have to raise her alone anymore. Hannah's a beautiful child, but let me tell you, she's a handful. Sort of like someone I know and love."

Emma moved toward the lips she couldn't get enough of. Just as the kissing started, Cain's wandering hand finally came to rest on her right breast, and Emma's nipple came to life when Cain squeezed.

Their time on the plane, the cuddling they had done, and now this were making Emma want things she didn't think Cain was capable of delivering because of her wound, but she certainly didn't want to stop. She pulled back from Cain's mouth long enough to check for any discomfort.

"Come back down here, love," Cain said in a gentle voice. "I missed you something fierce, and I'm tired of waiting."

"I really want to, but you're hurt." She knew her protest was weak at best.

"Tell me you don't want me, and I'll leave you alone."

Emma didn't answer and was on the verge of giving in.

"Tell me you're not sopping wet, and I'll stop touching you."

That did it. Emma lowered herself for one more kiss before getting off the bed.

She knew Cain was about to groan in frustration, but she just locked the door, then stood in the sunlight so Cain could see her. It would've been nice to have more privacy so they could really be uninhibited, but she craved Cain, and she had some idea how they could be together without causing her any more pain.

Emma slowly undid the buttons on her shirt one by one, well out of Cain's reach. She wanted to peel away every stitch of clothing, laying herself bare for Cain's pleasure. If Cain touched her before she was finished with her little show, she'd give in to whatever Cain wanted before she was done. The shirt dropped to the floor from her fingertips after it had slid down her arms. A dark green silk bra covered her full breasts, and the sides of Cain's mouth lifted in a smile.

"We've been shopping, have we?"

"I remember someone once telling me green was her favorite color," Emma said, moving her hands to the top button of her jeans. She was a little nervous because her body wasn't the same as when

Cain first fell in love with her. Two pregnancies had left her with more than one stretch mark.

"Are there some matching panties under there?"

The second button came undone, and the question shored up some of Emma's confidence. "Maybe." The other two popped open and Emma wiggled her hips, making the jeans shimmy to the floor and pool at her ankles.

Now the bra and a thong in the same shade of green were the only things hiding any imperfections Emma thought she had, and when a full minute went by without Cain saying anything, she wanted to cry.

"I know after Hannah—" Emma started, fighting the urge to put her clothes back on and wait until it was darker and Cain didn't have the chance to study her this closely.

"I know that after Hannah you're as beautiful and sexy as the first time I saw you like this." Cain swung her legs over the side of the bed and sat up. "You have nothing to fear from me, sweetling. I want you so badly right now that I'm afraid of scaring you."

"You could never do that."

Emma watched as Cain unbuttoned her own shirt and stood, once she'd reached the top of her belt. She was mesmerized as Cain started to take off her pants. If this was a dream, Emma hoped nothing would wake her up. In a short time Cain was naked except for the stark white bandage around her chest that the surgeon had put there that morning.

The floor felt cool under Cain's feet as she moved closer to Emma, and it crossed her mind to punch Giovanni in the face when they finally met. Because of his orders to have her shot, she couldn't carry Emma to the bed like she wanted. Staring at the strings holding Emma's undergarments together, Cain reached for them. She stopped at the last minute, looking at Emma's face as if asking for permission.

"Touch me before I die from wanting you to."

The thin straps of the expensive underwear came apart in Cain's hands when she pulled them, running her hands down Emma's butt to get them completely off. Then she unhooked the matching bra.

When they met skin to skin Emma almost came from the exquisite feel of having Cain like this again. "Please, baby, I can't wait anymore, but I don't want you to hurt yourself."

"You don't mind doing most of the work for a little while until I can move without hurting?"

"Are you kidding me?" Emma took Cain's hand, led her back to the bed, and arranged the pillows so she would be comfortable, only to have Cain rearrange them.

"I need to lie down a little flatter for what I have in mind." Cain stretched out and extended her hand in invitation. Emma straddled her at the waist, giving Cain a wonderful view of pale, soft skin.

Cain started at Emma's knees and slowly caressed her way up the smooth thighs to her hips. Cain felt like she was rediscovering a landscape that she hadn't visited in a long time. To avoid pulling on her stitches, she continued from there with only one hand to the pink nipples that had puckered to the point of looking almost painful.

"Cain." The name came out of Emma's throat with difficulty as two fingers pinched and pulled on her nipple. "Baby, I really need you to touch me somewhere lower."

The bed was a beautiful old brass one with a headboard almost as high as the wall behind it. Cain studied the metalwork for a minute and figured it would make a wonderful handhold. "Like I said, I have something in mind."

"Please, baby."

"Come up here, Emma."

Emma stood up on the mattress and walked to the head of the bed. No way was she going to chance dragging herself across Cain's body and have to stop if anything went wrong.

"Are you sure?" she asked, with one foot on either side of Cain's head.

"I don't mean to be blunt, love, but sit."

Emma did as she was told, and Cain took a deep breath. This was definitely a scent unique to Emma, and having her in this intimate position was like coming home. With a flat tongue, Cain slid from one end of Emma's sex to the other, dipping in just a little, causing Emma's fingers to clutch the bed as tightly as the walls of her sex closed around Cain's tongue.

"That feels so good." Emma threw her head back when Cain wrapped her lips around her clitoris and sucked it in with as much pressure as she could.

Cain's hands on her butt encouraged Emma to move all she wanted, and she did, but not enough to lose contact with Cain's mouth. Four years of wanting came to an end much too quickly, and she felt the first spasm shoot from her groin throughout her body. Emma couldn't keep from screaming, no matter how many people were in the house. Just as quickly her need overwhelmed her and she started to cry. She needed Cain to reclaim what was hers, and she wanted it now.

"It's okay, love. Move on down here and let me take care of you." Emma heard the words and nodded as she moved back to her original position, and the tears of happiness intensified when she felt the two long fingers slide in and fill her to the core.

Knowing what Emma craved, Cain situated her hand so that her thumb would provide the right stimulation whenever Emma moved.

This time Emma tried to use a little control, slowing down and bringing her hands to her own breasts and squeezing them.

"That's it, let go for me. I want you to relax and feel how much I missed this with you."

She gazed down at Cain's beautiful face and was glad she didn't have to explain the emotions running through her heart. The ability to string words together had left her, and she could only concentrate on Cain's fingers sliding in and out of her with every thrust of her hips. Every position they'd tried in their time together always felt good, but this was one of her favorites.

It left her open to Cain, who could see how much Emma enjoyed her touch—the way the muscles in her thighs bunched with every jerk and her hips sped up in a way some would have called wanton, desiring to reach the peak Cain was leading her to. Cain knew that Emma would jump without fear because at the bottom was always a set of strong arms to catch her and keep her safe.

Emma pulled on her own nipples when she felt the walls of her sex start to spasm. No amount of control or slow going would prevent the orgasm she couldn't hold back any longer. Emma's hips sped up for only a short time before she slammed down on Cain's hand one last time and stilled with her breasts just barely grazing the muscles of Cain's abdomen.

Cain had always considered Emma's letting her see her at her most vulnerable point the greatest gift Emma could give her.

"Are you okay?" Emma asked as soon as she was able to get enough air in her lungs.

"Shouldn't I be the one asking you that question?" Emma was lying against Cain's uninjured side, and Cain ran her hand, soaked with the evidence of Emma's passion, up her chest. "God, I love the way you feel." Slick fingers encircled a nipple, getting it to come back to life. "I love the way you smell."

Cain buried her face in the blond, disheveled hair. "And I love the way you taste." The confessions ended when she brought her hand up and licked her fingers clean.

"You keep that up and I won't ever let you out of this room."

"Is that supposed to be a threat?"

Emma sat up enough to see Cain's face. "It's what you want it to be, just as long as I get to return the favor."

"You know you're free to do whatever you like without threats."

Cain's statement earned her a kiss before Emma got back on her hands and knees over the long stretch of skin below her.

"Let's see if I remember how to make you feel as good as you just made me feel."

"Well, if you don't, please take all the time you need to get it right."

"I seem to recall you liked this," Emma said, as she slid down, planting kisses along the way.

The muscled legs spread, and Emma stopped in the right position and cupped her breast, squeezing long enough to get the nipple to harden for what she had planned.

Feeling the feather-light touch of Emma's nipple on her clitoris drove Cain mad. It didn't take long for her right hand to land on top of Emma's head, encouraging her to keep moving down. "Don't be cruel now, lass."

"I have no such intention." The promise of bliss was just on the tip of Emma's tongue, or that was what Cain thought when Emma spread her open and lowered her mouth. And that was all she used for the longest time, just the tip of her tongue. The gentle touch coaxed her clitoris to harden to the point where Cain thought she would have to start begging for Emma to do something about it.

"Tell me what I want to hear," Emma said when she pulled back and gazed up at Cain. At times like this in the past Cain had let her defenses down and showed what was in her heart. Not because of the possibility of good sex, but because Emma had the ability to strip away everything Cain used to shield her soul from the world. "Tell me," she said a little more firmly.

"I love you." Cain cupped Emma's cheek in her palm.

Three such simple words, but they conveyed every ounce of what she felt for this woman. The only woman she'd let in, only to have Emma slice her heart in two with such ease it had amazed her for months after the door had slammed behind her. To say the words again now was to lay herself open and bare once more, and she knew Emma could see the fear in her eyes. Cain was holding nothing back, which scared her more than anything Giovanni Bracato or anyone like him could do to her.

Emma kissed Cain's center before moving back up to lie next to her. "Say it again," she said, with her hand flat over Cain's heart.

"I love you." The words didn't sound as haunted, and Cain closed her eyes for just a moment as if to gather her defenses. "And there'll be no other for me as long as I draw breath."

"Then we have something in common, my love. Because for me there's only been you, and there'll only be you for the rest of my life. Thank you…"

Emma didn't have to say the rest. She pressed her lips to Cain's as she slipped her hand between Cain's legs, this time applying the pressure Cain so desperately wanted. To try and keep her from moving too much and hurting herself, Emma draped herself over her lover's body as her fingers moved easily over the wet heat. "Now you let go for me, love. Show me that you still belong to me."

It was the same soft voice that Cain heard in her dreams, luring her to the pleasure always just out of reach, because every time she reached for Emma she would disappear into mist. This time, though, the pressure continued to build, and she could feel the compact body pressed up against her and heard the loving words being whispered in her ear. "Aaaah." The groan signaled that Cain had reached the point of no return. "Fuck."

Emma just smiled against her skin at the vulgarity. That was just Cain, she thought. A unique combination of polish and rough edges.

When Emma pressed harder, the orgasm overtook Cain, and she clamped her legs together to make Emma's hand stop moving. The intense sensation was almost painful, and, as her nostrils flared with one last explosive breath, the final spasm rushed through her body. When Cain opened her eyes again she was surprised to find tears spilling from them just as they had from Emma's before. Emma never lifted her head from her chest, but Cain could feel Emma's breath and the touch of her hand as it left its warm haven and rubbed her lower belly.

"I didn't hurt you, did I?"

"You did once, but I'm thinking it's getting better." Cain laughed in a carefree way Emma hadn't heard since they'd seen each other again. "And what of your hurts, my love?"

"With you by my side I'll never need anything else."

"May that always be true."

"Oh, it will." Emma kissed the shoulder she'd been resting her head on before moving to Cain's lips one more time. As much as she didn't want to, they had to get up. Hannah would be waking up from her nap, and Hayden would most probably be finished and coming back in. "Are you ready, or do you want to get a little nap in before you go face the masses?"

"I think I'd better get up. Three weeks is long enough to be lying about doing nothing."

"Cain, you were shot. Give yourself a break."

When Cain sat up and put her feet on the floor, Emma pressed up to her back. "It's true I was shot, but now it's time to build my strength back up. Want to sneak down the hall and take a shower with me?"

"I wonder how thick these walls are?"

The only answer Emma got was a knock on the door. Cain stood to see who it was and what they wanted, but Emma cleared her throat. "I'd hate to ruin this wonderful afternoon by having to get into a fistfight with whoever is going to ogle you from the other side of that door if you answer it dressed like that. I'm almost positive there's a robe in the closet."

The possessive comment made Cain's chest puff out a little and a huge smile break out across her face. When she looked at the bed, the sight of Emma sitting there with the sheet pulled up just under her arms was enough to make her want to go back and spend the afternoon exploring the skin that lay beneath the thin cover. "Have I told you recently just how beautiful you are?"

"You're killing me here, baby. Put something on before the whole house knows what we're doing." The favor asked almost in a whine prompted Cain to the closet as the person awaiting entry knocked again.

There was only one robe, but when she headed for the closet she watched as Emma picked up the shirt Cain had been wearing and put it on. It was an old habit of hers on most mornings when she felt chilled and found some shirt of Cain's lying about. The shirt covered as much of her as the robe did of Cain.

When Cain finally made it to the door, Maddie was standing in the hall with an amused expression. She glanced from the woman who was clearly naked under the robe to the bed that looked like it had been put to good use. "I thought you might want to know that your other surprise for the little woman has arrived and is having coffee downstairs. Or maybe he's down there having his horizons expanded? At this point it's a toss-up, and here I am not having time to take a cold shower."

The teasing had been done in a tone low enough for Emma not to hear her. Maddie remembered the young girl who'd always been embarrassed to talk about anything intimate. Hopefully from the scream she'd heard earlier, Emma had gotten over her self-consciousness, at least when it came to Cain Casey. Maddie was amazed as she watched Cain's blush run up from her neck like a fire through a dry field.

"Please tell me you're kidding?" Before they'd left New Orleans, through mediation from Maddie, Cain had called Ross from a secure phone and told him what their plans were. He'd said he'd get to the Rath place as soon as their plane landed to see them all back together. "This isn't exactly how I planned on him finding out just how together we are."

Maddie peeked in to see Emma picking up clothing and placing the folded items on the bed as she went along. "Honey, as much as he wiggled around in that chair downstairs, the man had a smile about a mile wide the whole time, and please don't take that the wrong way. He realized a long time ago how happy his little girl is when she's with you. I just think he's thrilled that she's found that happiness again."

With nothing else to pick up, Emma moved to the door to see what the hushed conversation was about. "Hey, Maddie, is something wrong?"

"No, I just thought you wouldn't want to sleep the afternoon away, and Hannah should be up soon."

"Thanks, we're just going to freshen up. Then we'll be right down." Emma noticed Cain's face, which still bore some signs of her blush, and gave her an easy way out. "Go on in, baby, and I'll get our stuff together." She pointed to the bathroom to the right of them. When the door closed and the water started in the shower, she opened one of the bags and pulled out a fresh set of clothes. "So how much did you hear?"

"Enough to be envious." Maddie laughed and sat on the bed. On the top of the dirty clothes was Emma's discarded thong. "Good Lord, does this happen often? Your underwear bill must be outrageous. Though how much can this dental floss cost?"

"You'd be surprised. Now leave me alone so I can enjoy the afterglow."

"Oh, honey, I'm not teasing you..."

Emma arched her brow much like Cain would have done in the same situation.

"Well, not as much as I could. You look like a woman in love, and it looks good on you. Are you sure about this?"

"I'm positive."

Cain stood in the doorway and wondered if Emma was now the one in need of saving. "Em, the water's running. Are you coming?"

"Not yet, but with a little luck, I may soon," she whispered to Maddie, then gave her a wink.

Maddie shook her head and laughed. Her friend had most certainly changed, but it was a change for the good. Emma had come into her own, as the saying went, and as accomplished and strong as Cain looked, Emma was her proverbial match.

The groan Cain let out as Maddie went down the stairs was testament to that.

CHAPTER EIGHTEEN

They're gone?" Shelby tried to massage away the headache that was building behind her left eye. She'd spent the morning trying to get in touch with Muriel, willing to apologize for something she had nothing to do with, if only she'd just pick up. "What exactly does that mean?" she asked the person calling, the guy Agent Hicks had assigned to unofficially keep an eye on Cain and company.

"It's not a difficult concept, really, or am I speaking too fast? They're gone, all of them. I took a walk up to the fifth floor this morning when I didn't see Emma Casey arrive at her usual time."

Shelby interrupted and hoped this guy didn't blow apart an already shaky situation. "Did it occur to you that she might just be running late?"

"Gee, I wonder why I didn't think of that," he answered tersely. "I waited almost two hours before going across the street sans the coat and tie, and I even picked up flowers in the lobby so I could pretend I had the wrong room. No one was on the door, and the bed was made up and ready for another patient. She's gone."

"Why don't you get back here? You can give us a report about what you have so far." She was still talking into the phone, but also getting her jacket back on. It was time to visit Annabel Hicks and convince her to put together another team for Cain, as well as Vincent's and Ramon's organizations.

An hour later Joe and Lionel were back, along with their old partner Tony. The agent Annabel had put on Cain reported that Emma had left the hospital the night before at her usual time, flanked by at least six guards, including Merrick and Lou. Shelby wasn't the only one who thought that was more than a little strange. The Cain they'd studied for so long that they knew how she took her coffee was never left alone and vulnerable; she never went anywhere without one of those two a few feet away.

After a fan around the city, they were all shocked to find not only Cain, but also her immediate circle and most of the people on her payroll, and Muriel, gone.

Tony looked at all of them, then lashed out at Shelby. "You wanted to befriend these people. I hope you see now she's played us like a bunch of assholes again."

"Was there some warrant for her arrest that I don't know about?" Shelby shot back. "We've already had one agent who made this all about personal shit, and he's currently cooling his ass down at central lockup. If you want to join him, tell us now before some other innocent person gets shot."

"Innocent? Do you want to fuck her so bad that you'd sit here and tell us Casey is innocent?" Tony stood up so fast his chair clattered to the floor.

"God, Tony, you should just turn in your badge and give Bracato a call. I hear he's got an opening after Kyle got caught. After all, if a person has been under the microscope before, they deserve everything they have coming to them, am I right?" Shelby slammed the door behind her.

"Anthony"—Joe said the name with a good amount of sarcasm—"that was way out of line. I suggest you tell Agent Hicks you'd rather serve on some other team. I can't speak for Lionel, but I have no use for you. Any man, or woman for that matter, I can't trust to watch my back isn't someone I want standing with me."

Lionel looked from one man to the other before standing. "That's right, Joe. You speak for me too. I'd rather not have you on our team, Anthony. And you owe Shelby an apology. We all do for ever doubting her loyalties."

"Joe, come on. You know as well as I do Shelby has some personal bias." Anthony's volume rose a little when Lionel left the room. "And she has the nerve to accuse me of not looking at this with a level head."

Joe glared at Anthony and wondered what had happened to make him so bitter. Everything had been fine until the day Muriel had waltzed into the warehouse where Kyle had shot Cain and handed their asses over to them on a platter. "I don't know what your problem is, but you'd better figure out how to make it right before I go to Agent Hicks myself and file a complaint. Lionel's right. You owe Shelby an apology, and it better be heartfelt."

Joe had started for the door to see where Lionel and Shelby had disappeared to when he thought of one more thing. "Maybe you ought to take some leave. You know how these petty personal vendettas get around to the other agents." It was a low blow, but Joe wasn't in a generous mood. "Isn't that what got your father in trouble in the first place during his stint with the bureau?"

"Fuck you, Joe."

"No, Tony, if anyone's getting fucked it sure as hell isn't going to be any of the three of us. Unless one of us gets lucky, then it'll all be voluntary, don't you worry."

"It's Anthony. Is that so fucking hard to remember?"

❖

Shelby gripped the steering wheel hard, trying to bleed out her anger through her fingers. What Anthony had just spouted off about had hurt, but it wasn't all wrong. When she'd become an agent, she'd thrown herself into the job.

The night on Vincent Carlotti's plane when Cain held her life in the palm of her hand, along with the bugs she'd planted, those lines between right and wrong had been blurred but not erased. This case had become a little personal for her as well, but not because she wanted to bed Cain Casey. She'd just come to see that the members of the Casey family weren't the monsters so many had made them out to be.

After glancing in the rearview mirror and noticing that the redness of frustration had faded from her face, she started the car and headed to the one place where she might find some clues as to what had happened to the amazing disappearing Caseys. She was certain that Muriel had set up temporary offices at the scene of the FBI's embarrassment to rub it in their faces.

The warehouse along the river where Cain had shipped her load of legal liquor, only to be shot for it by Barney Kyle, had a few men walking along the roof with high-powered rifles strapped to their backs and a collection of BMWs parked in front. The kind of car young, snotty attorneys working for Muriel would drive.

"I'd like to see Muriel Casey, please," Shelby told the receptionist.

"Do you have an appointment?"

The question made her wonder if Muriel was there and surveillance had just missed her. "She's here?" she asked, unable to hold back her curiosity.

"I didn't say that. I just wanted to make sure I hadn't missed rescheduling you." The receptionist ran her finger down the old appointment book page. "And you are?"

"Agent Shelby Daniels."

Finally escorted into the office of one of Muriel's associates that she had met earlier, Shelby bluntly said, "I need to talk to Muriel or Cain Casey."

"Of course you do, but they're both out of town, so I can't help you there." The young man pulled his wallet out and retrieved one of his cards. "As you can read there, I'm an attorney, not a travel agent, and I'm a peon in the firm, so they didn't run their itinerary by me. If Muriel calls I'll pass along the message you'd like to talk to her."

"You have no idea where they are?"

"Not a clue."

His smile made Shelby want to pull back and punch him. "And I'm sure you'd just give up the information if you did."

"Of course I would, so there's one possibility you might want to follow up on. Spring's almost here," he replied, to her confusion.

"What in the hell is that supposed to mean?"

"I believe that's when pit vipers shed their skin. Since I haven't officially received my fangs, I'm not real sure where one goes to do that. But a boy can dream, can't he?"

"I wouldn't be so sure." She threw her own card at him and stood up. "Just give her the message."

The one good thing about dealing with a lawyer like this one was that she'd completely forgotten how pissed she was at Anthony.

She slammed her car door, then punched the steering wheel. As she shook out her hand, she thought of a simple solution and sped back to the office.

With Joe and Lionel looking on, Shelby called the sheriff in Haywood, Wisconsin. Cain had probably taken her family there.

"Sheriff Dobbs, I need you to drive out to the Rath and Verde farms."

"Jerry or Ross in trouble?" Ignatius Dobbs leaned back in his chair and put his feet up on his desk.

"No, sir. We believe that Cain Casey's back in the area and need to confirm that fact." Shelby rubbed her forehead, trying to keep her headache to a minimum.

"I'll go out there myself and look around, but I haven't seen anything out of the ordinary in the last week or so."

"It would've been today, Sheriff."

"Let me get to work, then."

If that's where Cain had run to, surveillance was going to be the logistical nightmare it had been the first time around.

❖

Ignatius pulled off to the side of the road near the Rath house and watched the activity there. He laughed when Cain Casey stepped out onto the porch and waved, clearly inviting him to join her.

"Sheriff, it's good to see you again." She held the screen door open when he pulled up and rolled his window down. "Can I interest you in a cup of coffee?"

"You don't seem surprised to see me," Ignatius said.

"I just wonder who called you, but I think I can narrow it down." Holding her side, she grunted as she sat across from him. "Was it Shelby, Lionel, or Joseph?"

"Agent Daniels wanted me to come check if you're doing okay."

Cain laughed and nodded. "Wanted to know where to send flowers while I'm recuperating, did she?" When Emma stepped into the room and patted Cain on the shoulder before handing the sheriff a cup of coffee, she continued, "Did the concerned FBI agent tell you anything else?"

"Nope." He took a sip of the coffee and lifted the cup in Emma's direction in salute. "Just wanted a report of your whereabouts before they made the trip for no reason, I guess. Before you came along we didn't have too many FBI stakeouts. After I got a taste of Agent Barney Kyle, I can see why some peace officers have trouble working with the feds."

"I have no right to ask you this, Sheriff," Emma said. She squeezed Cain's shoulder before she went on, "but I want you to tell Shelby that we're not here."

"Why would I do that?" He took another sip and studied the couple. "You're not doing anything but visiting friends, right?"

"Agent Kyle shot Cain on the order of a mob boss in New Orleans. So far the FBI has refused to give us any more information on what happened and who else might be involved. We came here so she can heal, but also so we could get out of the line of fire." Emma delivered the information with a quaver in her voice. "We have children, Ignatius. If you don't do it for Cain and me, then think about them."

Ignatius focused on Cain. "I have your word that recuperating is all you're doing out here."

"Just recuperating and spending time with Emma, I swear," Cain said with a wink. "But if this is going to cause you problems, then do what you think is right."

"Mabel down at the diner hasn't stopped talking about you since you left, and if Mabel likes you it's a safe guess that you're okay. Just behave, and I'll take care of Agent Daniels. Turns out I came out here and didn't find anything but cows."

"Moo moo," Cain said before she laughed.

❖

The chatter around the city for the next week was almost deafening. Not only were the authorities searching for and asking what had happened to the Casey crew, so was anyone working for Gino Bracato. Cain had done such a good job of vanishing that no one had a clue where to start looking, no matter how much money or muscle was dangled in front of them.

News did come on the eighth day of their disappearance, but it wasn't what Bracato had planned. Cain might have taken her gang with her for the protection of her family, but she still had an army of snitches working the streets, and his family's name was coming up more often in connection to the attacks on the Caseys.

As for Cain, her daily walks with the children were making her feel better and stronger, and it had been a boost for everyone when the local doctor said it was time for the stitches to come out. The wounds were still healing, and Cain was slowly regaining full health.

Emma watched as Cain threw her coat on, intent on sneaking out to the back fence with the satellite phone in her hand like she had all the other times it had rung. Whoever was on the line obviously didn't mind interrupting Hannah's playtime with her favorite new block-building partner.

"What's going on?" she asked before Cain made it outside.

"I'll tell you as soon as I'm done with this call. For now could you go keep an eye on Hannah? Hayden's out for his morning run with Mook and some of the others."

Seeing that her daughter was fine, Emma returned to the back door and watched Cain's face as she spoke sporadically, as if either asking questions or verifying information. When she hung up she immediately dialed another number and did most of the talking. Emma didn't worry until she saw Cain run her hand through her hair. It was a move she knew well, and it bespoke either worry or frustration. Neither emotion was good for Cain's convalescence.

"Problem?" Emma pulled Cain's sweater tighter around herself as she joined Cain in the yard. She'd put it on when she felt the wind pick up. The business of Cain's world had left them in peace for eight glorious days, which was more than she could have hoped for.

"Giovanni's number-one son was responsible for the bombs at Emerald's and at Muriel's office." Cain opened her coat and wrapped Emma in her arms to keep her warm.

"How do you know?"

"The little shit just planted one at Vincent's place, or at least he tried. The guy he hired ran into a couple of Vinny's more unreasonable guys and, if I had to guess, got one hell of an explosive enema."

As gruesome as the thought was, Emma snorted into Cain's chest, picturing what her partner had painted. "Who tipped him off?"

"One of our guys on the street. Gino Jr. never did learn the cardinal rule of keeping your mouth shut. Bragging only leads the police to your door or, worse, someone like Vincent Carlotti. The little crazy bastard might have done us a favor, though." Cain kissed the top of Emma's head.

Emma ran her hands up Cain's back until she locked them behind Cain's neck. "Why do you say that?"

"Because now Vinny really does owe us a favor, and Ramon will be told of our immediate and lifesaving actions. When the time comes or, I should say, *if* the time comes that I need their help, it'll be a guarantee."

She massaged the tense neck and tried to read what was going on in Cain's mind. "Honey, you have to know that both those guys would come running if you just called. I saw what they did for you and our family when you got hurt."

"Emma, my father taught me that some help comes back to haunt you, some is freely given, and some is given because it's owed. Sometimes you have to pay for the help that haunts you with something you don't want to part with. That's the worst. Freely given help is good for everyone: we help because we love the other person. But help that's given because it's owed is a blessing, just like the second. Vinny is my friend, like Ramon, but I want to live my life and run our business as debt-free as I can." She stopped her lecture and kissed Emma's cheek. "Do you understand?"

"By you helping him, he helps us in return because he owes you a debt?"

"You're a fast learner, lass. Maybe I can retire after all this is over and hand the business over to you."

"No, thanks, you can keep your job." Emma took a deep breath and held it as she looked up at Cain.

The last eight days and how they'd spent them returned to the forefront of her mind. They had walked with their children and visited with her father every day, strengthening the ties necessary to rebuild their family. Every night she and Cain had relearned each other in the most intimate and sensual ways possible, waking naked and smiling every morning.

"Go get your coat on, lass." Cain swatted her gently on the backside and nodded toward the house.

"You need to make another phone call?"

"No, I want you to take a walk with me and tell me what's on your mind. If this is going to work, then you have to share with me what's making this worry line get deeper. After all, it's what you keep telling me to do." She ran her thumb down the middle of Emma's forehead.

The little part of her brain that had kept her alive screamed what Merrick had been telling her from the moment Emma walked back into her life. Maybe the worry line had to do with the fact that Emma wasn't being totally up-front with her about how she felt.

"Whatever it is, I'll listen. Then we'll fix it, if that's what you're worried about. Unless you're wearing a wire under that bulky sweater of mine." She ran her hand up Emma's side more in a tickling fashion than in a distrusting one. "Then we'll plug you full of holes and feed you to the cows."

They walked back to the house together and picked up not only Emma's coat but a blanket as well. Emma wanted to share one of her favorite places with Cain. Maddie waved them off from the family room where she had Hannah engrossed in dressing up her dolls, shooting a wink their way when Emma held up the blanket and pointed to the back of the yard.

Soon they crested a hill and came upon a fairly good-sized lake.

"What a beautiful place." Cain looked around the area before sitting down next to Emma. "I don't know how I missed this the last time I was here."

"The hills around it form almost a perfect bowl, so unless you wanted to do some leg work by climbing, there's no good reason to come up here. See over there?" She pointed to their left. "It's the only way to get in without having to make the climb, and that's how the cows get in here. When I was little and someone else owned Jerry's place, I'd sneak over here and sit along these banks for hours, just looking at the water or the clouds floating by." Emma felt melancholy.

"We'll have to ask your father for some of your baby pictures while we're here. I don't think I've ever seen any of them." Cain pressed her back against the tree where they had laid the blanket and pulled Emma into her arms. "You have an unfair advantage since you've seen all of mine."

Emma couldn't have asked for a better segue into the conversation she wanted to have, so she looked up at Cain's face and reached for one of the big hands to hold. "My mother didn't believe in wasting money on what she called frivolous things."

"Children are never frivolous things, love."

"I know that, and I knew it back then. That's what I thought about when I sat here. I daydreamed about the family I'd someday have.

About the person who would help me and love me the way I wanted to be loved."

Cain let go of her hand and ran her fingers along Emma's jaw down to her neck. She forgot sometimes what a fragile soul her lover was and how many hurts had laid the foundation for the woman she'd become. When they had first started living together, Cain wondered at times what made Emma so skittish. She always seemed to be waiting for the blow to knock her down because of some unforgivable mistake.

"I'd be willing to bet that in all those daydreams your brilliant mind never came close to me. Am I right?" The kiss she gave her after the question was as long and as loving as Cain could make it.

"After I met you I thought of this place again, and you're right. That's when I knew I didn't have enough imagination. I dreamed of someone strong to keep me safe, someone to love me. Little girls normally want those things, but I wanted something even more."

"What's that, sweetling?"

"I dreamed of someone who saw *me*, who really saw me and wasn't disappointed with the sight."

The confession broke Cain's heart like nothing else could have. Her eyes filled with tears for the little girl who for so long had only had a father who loved her, but who wasn't willing to fully stand up and fight for her. She liked Ross, but a part of her believed he had somewhat failed his daughter.

"Oh, lass, I saw you all those years ago in my pub, and I've seen little else since. After today we're going to leave the hurts and disappointments of that little girl here, 'cause she's found what she sought. I love you and, more importantly, you belong to me. I'll let no more pain touch what's mine."

"I know, and I love you for it. When I found you and we had Hayden and filled that house up with love, toys, and pictures, I always felt like it was a dream. You showed me it was all right to want those things Mother told me for so long I didn't deserve. I wanted them enough to start believing they were something I deserved because I loved you."

Cain kissed her again and smiled at the confidence building in Emma's voice. "You deserve so much more, and if I can, I'll give you everything and anything you want."

"Do you mean it?" Emma pressed her palms to the sides of Cain's face and gazed into her eyes. Cain nodded, and the silent answer gave Emma the strength to do what her father had told her when he left her at the airport. *Go and get what's yours, and don't ever settle.* "I want to have another baby."

If Emma had asked for anything else, a laugh would have come bubbling out when she watched Cain open her mouth, then click it shut a couple of times. The color drained from Cain's face so quickly that Emma was afraid she was going to pass out. "Did you hear me, honey?"

"Yep." Cain uttered the affirmation in such a small voice Emma barely registered it.

"I know we have a lot of rebuilding to do before we get to the point where you're comfortable with the idea, but I just wanted to tell you that's what I want." Her speech sped up as nerves took over. "And if you don't ever want it, then I guess that's okay too. This isn't something someone can foist upon—"

Any other words were stopped by the lips that covered Emma's in a kiss filled with passion. Without too much effort Cain rolled them over so that she covered the more compact body with her own, never releasing Emma's mouth.

Slowly Cain pulled away, leaving Emma breathing hard. "I want that as much as I want you right now."

The desire in Cain's voice made Emma moan and lift herself so she could reach the tempting lips again. This time when she pulled away she lowered her hands to the button of her jeans and undid them enough so Cain could fit her hand inside. "It's too cold to take them off completely, but if you don't touch me right now you're going to have to carry me back." Her last thought before the long fingers sliding over her robbed her of the ability to think was how thrilled she was her hopes hadn't been shot down.

"I love you, lass, and I'll love as many children as you wish to bring into this world with me."

It was done. No matter the consequences, Cain set her sights on trying again, regardless of her self-doubts. With so much to fight for, she was ready to enter the fray, no matter what waited for her at home.

It was time.

CHAPTER NINETEEN

A s Ross stared out at his barn from his living room and sipped his coffee, he thought of the spring they'd brought baby Emma home from the hospital. The ordeal of childbirth had wreaked havoc on Carol's body, and the doctor had told them it would be risky to have other children. For a man who'd come from a family of ten, it was the hardest news he'd ever had to take.

It had made no difference. He looked out at the yard and in his mind's eye could see the small blond tagalong hanging from the fence waving to him when he'd ride back from the fields. Emma had filled his heart so completely, Ross hadn't regretted not having any others. Yet he'd let Carol subject her to the kind of treatment she didn't deserve. At night when he had trouble sleeping, he'd pray God would forgive him for his weakness. He should have done something about his wife a long time ago. He certainly didn't miss her right now.

Jerry's truck pulled up to the house, and as Ross watched Cain get out of the cab and survey the area, he wondered how she'd gotten away from Lou and Merrick. She seemed to be back to normal, and Emma had told him that Cain had a little pain only if she moved too quickly. Grabbing another cup from the kitchen, he carried the pot of coffee out to the porch and sat in one of the rockers.

"It's a beautiful morning," Cain said, not taking her eyes off his fields. "Not heading out today?"

"Just spending a lazy morning in for a change. There's enough feed in those bins to keep until this afternoon. Why, you looking for a job?"

Cain slowly shortened the distance between them and picked up the cup he'd filled. "I actually miss our little rides out to see your lost flock of bovines. And I miss the talks we had when I was here."

"Cain, am I anything like your father?"

If it seemed a strange question, Cain's face remained passive and relaxed. "You're like him in some ways, but overall I'd have to say no. I mean, you love your child, and I think you have a connection to the past and your family's traditions that would most probably have made you friends, but Dalton Casey was one of a kind. Why do you ask?"

"I wonder sometimes if my child will speak so highly of me as you do of him. I see it in Hayden as well when he talks about you. Lately I've felt like Emma got the short end by being born into this family." He took an interest in the bottom of his cup, not having the courage to face her judgment of him.

"Did Emma ever tell you the story of how we met?"

The question made Ross stare off into the distance, as if the answer would somehow be broadcast on the front of his barn. "She just mentioned you one day. I can't recall if there was a story of how she met you attached to that."

Cain launched into the story, not leaving out anything about the night that had changed her life forever.

Ross laughed, trying to picture Cain covered in beer and not getting angry about it.

"Do you know what happened for the next year and then some?"

He shook his head and set his chair in motion. This was a nice way to spend an early morning.

"She got me to court her in a way I'd never dreamed of. It was always dinner, a movie, maybe, or something that we could spend time together getting to know one another. When all those dates ended, I got a kiss and a nice pat on the head before she sent me on my way. At first I thought it was cute, then it got frustrating as hell, but I never pushed her any further than she was willing to go."

Ross glanced at Cain, feeling better knowing that his little girl hadn't gone to the big city and run wild.

"You have nothing to be ashamed of, Ross, and you didn't fail. What you did was raise a young woman with self-respect, who demanded the respect of others. The woman I married was raised by a man who loved her and was enough of a parent to make up for anything lacking in her life."

"She made you wait?" Ross asked in an amused tone.

"And then some, old man, so wipe that silly grin off your face. You raised a good girl, and it just about killed me."

Ross finished his coffee, relieved that he hadn't failed Emma as much as he feared.

Cain set her cup down and stood up. "Take me for a tractor ride, Ross."

He cranked up the new piece of equipment Cain had bought him during her last visit. For the longest time he really did think it was just about the ride, but at their second bin Cain started talking and asking his opinion on a few subjects. Ross kept quiet until she was done, stunned by the way her mind worked. In the time Cain had spent in the small community of Haywood, she'd considered every consequence to every problem that faced her and the action she'd have to take to fix each one.

"What do you think they'd say?"

"I honestly don't know, Cain. That's something the Raths have always wanted, and it was denied them. If it came to pass, then I really don't see them turning down the opportunity. No one would get in any trouble, right?" Ross took his hat off and scratched the top of his head. This was certainly more intrigue than he was used to.

"Life isn't always a hundred percent guaranteed, Ross, but I don't plan mine that way. When I do something like this, I cover every possible angle. Don't worry. If the heat comes down, I'll be the only one sitting in the pan."

Ross put his hat back on and his hand on her shoulder. "You won't be alone. Emma made you wait, but she did some waiting of her own. If you go down for any reason, she'll never be happy with anyone else."

"Thanks for the advice, and I'll do my best to keep my nose clean. And thanks for hearing me out. I had some doubts, but you helped me through them."

"Anytime. If you learn to like talking to me, maybe I'll see my grandchildren more often."

"I wouldn't worry about that either. All this fresh air has my mind humming, so I think I have a solution for that little problem too."

Cain took her time getting off the tractor. She'd seen the doctor in Haywood a couple of times, and he'd said her injuries were healing nicely, but not to push herself. The wound was a little past the itchy stage, and she could get by with a smaller bandage.

Back in the yard, she shook Ross's hand. If she hurried, she could make it back to Maddie's in time to have breakfast with Emma and the kids.

Ross waved, feeling melancholy for the opportunities with Emma he'd squandered, but the emotion eased with the knowledge that his daughter had found someone to share her life with who wouldn't repeat his mistakes.

CHAPTER TWENTY

"Did you have fun playing dairy farmer, love?" Emma was still in her robe and pajamas when Cain walked into Maddie's kitchen. She held a platter of pancakes and was serving the kids.

"I had a good time, thanks for asking. Why, don't you think I'd make a good cattle baron?"

"For about a week, then I figure you'd be running cow races on the side to pass the time."

When Hannah saw her new favorite person, she climbed down from her chair and went to sit on Cain's lap.

Cain kissed Hannah's head and smirked at Emma. "You want to stop sassing me and get Hannah and me some pancakes, eh?" Cain tried to take on a Northern accent. "Or better yet, why don't you sit, and I'll get Hannah and you some pancakes."

"You aren't going to spill anything, are you?" Emma tried her hardest to keep a straight face.

"Oh, yes, because that worked out so badly for you," Cain shot back. "You didn't drench me in beer on purpose, did you?" She stood, took the platter from Emma, and put it and Emma on the counter, causing both Hannah and Hayden to laugh. "I told your father that story this morning."

"You told my father I worked in a bar?"

"Why, did you tell him you met me at Sunday mass?" The familiar arched brow appeared, and Emma broke out in a long laugh. Cain hugged her, and the merriment died down to a long sigh.

"Mama, Grandpa Ross said he was coming by to pick me up for a ride down to the feed store," Hayden said.

"Can I come too?" Hannah squealed. The excitement in her voice was hard to miss.

Emma was waiting for Hayden to say no and explain why Hannah couldn't go, but was surprised when he said sure, as long as it was all right with Emma and Cain. Emma gave him a hug and kiss for his generosity.

"Finish up, Hannah, so I can get you dressed if you're going with your brother," Emma instructed as she gave Cain a plate of pancakes and a cup of coffee, as well as a wink. "You finish up too." Emma wished every morning with her family could be as uneventful as this one.

Forty minutes later Ross stood smiling as Emma strapped a thrilled Hannah into her car seat in the back of Ross's extended cab. Merrick, Lou, and Mook loaded into a rented Suburban behind them. Ross and Hayden would have a chance to visit, but the guards weren't going to let either of the Casey children out of their sight.

"Want to take a ride?" Emma asked Cain. "I want to talk to you about something else in private, so Dad said we could use his place."

"Would this talk entail the wearing of clothes?"

"Well, for a little while anyway," Emma answered, feeling aroused.

When Katlin started for the vehicle Cain and Emma were taking, Cain waved her off. "Take a break. I doubt there'll be a hit team waiting for me at Ross's place."

"You're the boss." Katlin wandered back inside.

The ride was quiet as Emma leaned against Cain, looking out the window at the landscape that had changed little since she was young. She was starting to miss New Orleans. When she got out of the truck, she took a deep breath before following Cain onto the porch of her childhood home.

"Will you rock me?" She looked at the old rockers on the porch as she asked and thought of all the times she'd spent sitting in them holding Hannah. "If your side hurts we can just go inside and talk."

"I'd love to rock you."

To get more comfortable Cain took off her jacket and used it as a blanket over both of them. Shedding the extra layer allowed her to feel Emma pressed up against her.

"We need to get one of these for the house," Emma said.

"Can you go back to that house after what happened?" Cain didn't want to pressure Emma. She simply wanted to give them all what was best, and since she hadn't been there when the shooting happened, she'd have to rely on Emma for guidance.

"We'll get to that, honey, but I want to ask you something else." The boards under their chair creaked every time Cain rocked back and forth, a comforting sound in the otherwise quiet morning. "I can understand that Katlin is your cousin and she works for you, but can you tell me why Merrick can't stand her?"

"What?" Cain pulled her head back to look at Emma's face to see if she was serious. "They hardly know each other." She paused and started again. "I take that back. They hardly see each other, so I don't think they'd know enough about one another to not like each other."

"I'm telling you, Merrick bristles whenever Katlin walks within two feet of her." Emma unbuttoned one button over Cain's stomach and slipped her cold hand inside. "At first I thought it was something sexual, but then I remembered Merrick already has a love in her life, so there might not be enough room for Katlin."

"What did you do, bug my house?" Cain stopped to kiss her just because Emma's lips were so close. "How do you know all this stuff?"

"Because the love of her life hasn't changed in all the time I've been gone." The hair around Cain's ears ruffled a little in the wind, and Emma combed it back with her fingers. "Not that I can blame her, really."

"If I'm supposed to know who you're talking about, I'm still at a loss."

"It's you, honey." She pressed her fingers to the soft lips and smiled. "I didn't say you returned Merrick's feelings, and if you slept with her when I wasn't with you, I don't blame you." Emma pressed harder on Cain's mouth when she tried again to say something. "I know you didn't, but if you had, I wouldn't have had the right to say anything."

"You have every right to say whatever you like. Just like I have the right to be honest with you. But when it comes to Merrick you have nothing to be worried about. She works for me and that's where it ends." Cain had pulled the small hand away and held it to her heart.

"Let me tell you something, darlin'. If you'd found some cowpoke out here to spend time with, he'd be planted under a pile of manure by now."

"Have I told you lately how romantic I think you are?" Emma kissed her, but Cain laughed. "What's so funny?"

"You left me because you thought I planted some guy who put the moves on you, and now you think it's romantic."

"Well, time has shown me that I'll never find a better champion than you, and you'll never do something to harm someone if they didn't throw the first punch. Sitting here alone all that time made me realize that I love you, all of you, and I don't want to change who you are."

"I love you too, and it's good to know that you feel that way. As for Merrick and Katlin, I'm at a loss there. I haven't noticed any strange behavior."

"That's because you have me to look out for you and notice the things that you'd most probably find trivial anyway."

Cain stopped rocking as she thought about that and resumed the motion when she started talking again. "It could be something important, though. I can't afford for two of my most important people be more interested in getting laid than in watching for what's coming at us."

Emma pinched a bit of skin on Cain's abdomen between her fingers and laughed. "I don't think you can control who your employees date, honey. Unless, like I said, Merrick is still interested in you. Then you can be as controlling and cold as you want." The last bit was delivered with a bit of heat.

"This really is bothering you, isn't it?"

"Considering she thinks I'm wearing a wire in my bra and has a tendency to undress you with her eyes at every given opportunity"— she pulled her hand free and held up her thumb and index finger an inch apart—"it bothers me a little." Emma released a sigh and put her head down on Cain's shoulder. "When I first got home I'd sit out here and think of how I'd finally given her the chance to get close to you."

"Put those feelings to rest, lass. Nothing went on at the house that wasn't going on before you left. I trust Merrick with my life, but not with my heart. I've only done that once, and she's sitting in my lap now."

"Thanks for saying that."

"Anything else you're worried about?"

Emma shook her head.

"Then you keep an eye on what's going on between Merrick and Katlin and let me know if there's something I should be worried about. I don't want to change the subject, but now's a good time since it's just the two of us." Cain pulled her closer and tried to make her hands behave and not veer somewhere that would cut their talk short.

"Before any other shit happens to make Giovanni think he's closer to taking over, I have to go back and deal with all this. We had a life before all this, with a certain number of businesses and a feeling of safety in our home, and I fully intend to return to that security. If you want, we can start fresh somewhere else. You taught me that a house is just that, a place where you keep all your stuff; but having you and the kids there makes it my home."

"When do you want to leave?"

"That's the other thing I want to talk to you about—"

Emma pulled back far enough so she could point her index finger at Cain. "You said no more leaving me behind."

Cain took hold of the menacing pointer and bit down gently on it. "Calm down, wild thing. No one's leaving you if you don't want to be left. What I was going to tell you is I want the kids to stay here with Jerry and Maddie, along with a few of the men. That house has enough bedrooms to put up Mook and some others until we're done. It's okay, though, if you want to stay behind. I'll come back as soon as I can."

"You can't be that delusional, can you?" Emma put her hand back in Cain's shirt after another button came undone. "If you're going, I'm going with you. While we're there you can take care of whatever you need to do, and I can tend to what we're going to do about the house. Just think of it this way. If we're there together we'll have each other to rely on."

"Are you sure you don't want to stay here?"

"I'm as positive as I am about wanting to show you my room right about now," Emma said as she pinched an alert nipple. "That way if my mother ever gives me another problem, I'll tell her what I let you do to me in that little bed."

Cain let her up and took her hand. She figured another month of recovery and she'd be carrying Emma wherever she wanted to. But for now, the sway of those enticing hips wasn't a real hardship to study all the way up the stairs.

Emma smiled at Cain when they reached the top step, because while she was positive their relationship was built on more than sex, it was good to see the want back in Cain's eyes.

CHAPTER TWENTY-ONE

K atlin sat on the porch and stared at Merrick, who stood by the car looking like she wanted to figure out a way inside the house without having to use the door Katlin was sitting beside. They eyed each other, neither of them making a move.

"How about me and you go for a little ride and leave the guys to watch the house?" Katlin asked Merrick. She'd closed the book she was reading and was trying to gauge Merrick's mood.

"What do you want?"

Saying something like "world peace" occurred to her, but she thought for once she'd hold her tongue to keep things civil between them and see what Merrick's problem was. "I'd like to have a little talk. Think you can stand me long enough to do that?"

"I'll take the ride, but as for the rest I don't know what you're talking about." Merrick moved to the driver's seat, and Katlin just reversed course and headed for the other side of the car. Before the tires of the truck hit the black highway, Merrick was talking. "Why are you here?"

"The same reason you're here. Cain invited me and I came. Why? Why do you think I'm here? Or better yet, why do you have such a problem with it?" Just as an aggravation, Katlin kept her face toward the window, not giving Merrick the opportunity to view her profile.

"You don't belong here. For once you shouldn't have taken Cain up on her invitation." Merrick headed for the Verde farm, and Katlin did nothing to stop her. They rode in silence until the entrance to Ross's place came up on their left, and Merrick turned in. The sun was starting to go down, the house was dark, and the truck Cain had driven Emma over in was still parked in front of the house.

"Your problem isn't me, Merrick. Your problem is that the blonde won out. You work for Cain just like I do, only I don't want to fuck her."

Katlin finally did face her when their truck stopped well short of the house. It was as if Merrick had just grasped what she was saying.

"Are you insane?"

"I'm not crazy, just observant. You're nice to Emma because you have to be, but you can't hide the anger inside when she reaches out for my cousin and Cain welcomes her. It's time to face the truth. Cain's truth. And *her* truth is most probably upstairs with her right now. You should just go ahead and accept that and move on."

Merrick flattened her hand out on the middle of the steering wheel as if she wanted to slap Katlin for saying it out loud. "When all this is done, Emma won't have the courage to stick it out. There's no way she's going to be able to accept what Cain needs to do to win against Giovanni Bracato. And when that reality sets in, Cain's going to be left hurt and bleeding again at the hands of the blonde you're so accepting of."

"I have another prediction for the future, and that ain't it." Katlin put her hand up to stop Merrick's verbal assault. "Don't bother to say anything, and rest assured I won't mention this talk to Cain." Katlin grasped Merrick's arm and squeezed just short of being painful. "But you do anything to Emma or Cain to sabotage their getting back together, and I swear that whoever bothers to look for you will never find you. Do your job, and the rest is none of your business."

"And this is your business?"

"Cain is my cousin, and her happiness means the world to me. It's the least I owe her for giving me the world."

"You don't have anything to fear from me. Don't worry."

❖

Emma rolled over and found an empty bed next to her. Their cuddling and talk on the porch had led to a lazy afternoon in her childhood room doing things her mother would have burned the house down for if she'd known. "What are you doing way over there? I'm cold."

"Sorry, love. I heard a car coming and wanted to see if we had company."

Emma was glad to see Cain move with more of her usual smooth style and glad that her chest bandage was smaller.

"Please tell me it's not my father." She put her hands up to her face and tried not to think about some of her and her father's conversations lately. "I swear after that first afternoon when we got here, he doesn't do anything but blush when I talk to him."

"It's not your father. It's our two tense birds you were telling me about earlier. Whatever they're doing, they're doing it well away from the house."

"Then come back here, and remind me to get a gun when we get home. That way I can fire off a few warning shots if I want to spend time alone with you and someone threatens to interrupt us."

Emma molded herself to Cain's side and rested her head on the broad shoulder. After they'd made love the first time, they'd finished their talk, so Emma knew just what Cain had in mind and why Katlin was here. Feeling like there was nothing she could add, Emma had initiated another round of lovemaking that had left them tired enough to sleep.

"How do you think Merrick's going to take the news?"

"Lass, Merrick works for me. I want her to be satisfied with her job, but it isn't my duty to coddle her."

"I'd certainly hope not. That position in your life is filled, thank you." She kissed the skin close to her lips before pushing herself up. "And as much as I enjoy your coddling, I think it's time we tell your little lost souls out there what you have in mind."

They dressed and stepped outside where, from the porch, Cain waved the two nearer.

Slowly Merrick moved closer, took one last look at Katlin, and made her promise again.

"What we talked about stays strictly between us. You have my word," Katlin said.

Cain took a seat in one of the rockers, and Emma sat on the arm of the chair with her hand on her partner's shoulder. They appeared to be a couple no one, not even someone like Kyle, could ever break apart.

"We leave in two days," Cain said as Emma caressed the back of her neck to keep her relaxed. "I want most of the men to head back tomorrow and be in place when we return. That also gives Muriel time to do her part."

"What's Muriel doing?" Katlin asked.

Merrick glared at her and shook her head. "Whatever it is, I'm sure she doesn't need your help, and you should learn not to ask about things that don't concern you."

"Merrick's right, Katlin, but you'll have plenty of time to learn. When we get back I want you with Lou and me."

The smug smile faded from Merrick's face, and she stared at Cain as if her boss had lost her mind. "Where am I going?"

"Merrick, I want you with Emma."

"No way!"

Cain kept Emma by her side by putting her hand on her leg. "I'm only going to explain this once, and if you can't accept it I'll have to live with that." Cain pointed to the chair Merrick had jumped out of when she registered her objection, clearly expectng her to sit back down. "I think you're the best at what you do in my organization, and I need that reassurance guarding my wife when we go home."

"Cain, I think Lou can handle taking care of Emma," Merrick said again.

"I've made my decision, Merrick, and I want your answer now." Despite their friendship, Cain didn't like to be second-guessed by anyone who worked for her.

"My answer is yes, you know that."

"Good. Like I said, I want Emma taken care of by the best."

Merrick didn't say anything else, realizing this might be a blessing after all. If she spent that much time with Emma, she could expose her for the fraud she was.

CHAPTER TWENTY-TWO

Hayden was tying the laces of his running shoes when Cain stepped out on the porch early Friday morning. "Can I talk to you before you head out?"

"Sure." He didn't look up, still sulking from the night before when he'd learned that he'd be staying behind again. He didn't seem very mature at this point, though he was always trying to convince Cain otherwise.

"We're leaving later on today, and I wanted to talk to you before that." Cain took a deep breath, and the cold air was almost painful. "I know you're mad, and there's nothing I can do about that, but I need you to look out for your sister while I'm gone. Even though you can't do all the things you think you're ready for, you're still our next generation. If something happens to me, you'll be responsible for keeping your mother and sister safe, and I just wanted you to know I have every faith that you'll do a good job."

Cain interpreted his silence as anger, and she left him to it, not wanting to push him any further than he was willing to go. She'd never forced him to do anything he didn't feel comfortable with.

Hayden kept tying his laces, head down, though he jerked it up when the door closed.

"Mom, wait." He caught up with her on the steps leading back to her room. "I know you think I'm too young, but I could help if you take me back. I also know you're not going to. I'm not happy about it, but I understand. And what you asked me for outside"—he pointed over his shoulder with his thumb—"thanks for trusting me like that. And you have my word I'll take care of Mama and Hannah. Just be careful this time, huh? No more getting shot."

Cain stepped down and opened her arms. "Thanks, son, and I'll try to keep my head low. You remember one more thing, okay?"

"Anything for you."

"It seems like a long way off, but when you turn seventeen, no more leaving you behind. That's when I started, and my father before me. Think you can hold out that long?"

"Mama isn't going to talk you out of this, is she?"

"She made me swear if by then you're still interested in the family business, I'd teach you everything I know."

Just as she expected, he stepped back and offered her his hand. To shake it meant the oath she'd made would be as binding as if she'd signed it in blood. With a serious face to match his, Cain took his hand and returned the firm grip. "You have a deal."

His smile was back. Cain knew that four years and a couple of months seemed like a lifetime, but it was a target to shoot for.

"Thanks, Mom, for giving me the chance."

"You should know me better than that. I'm not giving you anything you haven't worked for and deserve. Remember that when you show up on your first day." She laughed along with him and pointed up the stairs. "Go tell your mother good-bye so she can get over her crying jag before it's time to go."

"She's dressed, right?"

"Everybody's a comedian," Cain said.

After a cup of coffee, Cain went back upstairs and stripped off the borrowed robe. "Everything settled with the boy?"

Emma lay on her side watching Cain with a smile on her blotchy face. Hayden had just left. "Whatever you told him sure made him look happy."

"I just gave him the timeline we talked about. He always wants to go so bad and is disappointed when I leave him, so I gave him a realistic goal. Why? He wasn't trying to talk you into taking him, was he?"

"No, he wants me to spend every minute when we get to New Orleans keeping you safe." As sweet as that sentiment sounded, Cain was a little disappointed that he'd thought only of her and wrinkled her forehead.

Emma ran her fingers over the frown lines. "He wanted me to

watch out for you since he knew you'd spend the same amount of time and effort taking care of me. I must be moving up in the world if I'm in your league."

"Of course you're in my league. You're his mother. I tried, but I never could fill that part of his life you were responsible for." Cain handed Emma the cup of coffee she'd fixed for her and lay down. "Though I did a pretty good job if he wants me to spend all my time watching you."

"He's twelve, honey. Tell me you haven't already filled his head with tips on how to deal with girls?" She wrapped her hands around the warm cup and leaned against the strong body behind her.

"I'm going to tell you the same thing I tell the feds." Emma pinched her on the leg.

"What?"

"I refuse to answer that on the grounds that it'll incriminate me."

As Cain's hand landed on Emma's middle and was deciding which direction to head, the door to their bedroom opened and a little head peeked in. Their first morning in the Rath house, Cain had learned a quick lesson on how to pull a punch when she woke up to a face about an inch from hers. Hannah might have been born looking like Cain, but she'd inherited Emma's love of cuddling.

"Good morning, princess," Cain said in a soft voice. She could tell by the slump of the shoulders and Hannah's eyes that she wasn't quite awake yet. Sharing this time with her in the morning was making Cain regret having to leave, but the sooner they got things under control, the sooner they'd be able to enjoy any special moments fully. "Did you have a good sleep?"

Hannah burrowed into Emma's chest and put her hand in Cain's. With the lethargy of early morning, she nodded and closed her eyes.

"Don't want you to go, Mama."

"I don't want to go, but when we come back Mom is taking us all to live in New Orleans."

"Promise?"

"I do, sweetheart. And even though Mama and I are leaving, we'll be calling you all the time."

Hannah seemed satisfied for the moment and closed her eyes again when Emma started singing to her.

Cain lay there content for the moment until she heard the front door open and close and Hayden's footsteps on the stairs. Like his sister, he poked his head in and then walked to the bed when Cain waved him over.

"Watch out for her while we're gone, and call me if you see anything out of the ordinary, okay?" Cain pulled her hand out of Hannah's grasp and put it on the little girl's back. "I know this isn't what you had planned, but I'm counting on you."

"Don't worry, Mom. I'll take good care of her. Could you just hurry it up and come get us? Baseball season is starting soon and I wanted to try out for the team."

"You got it, kiddo."

The four of them enjoyed one more breakfast together before Merrick and Katlin pulled the cars around to pack for the trip to the airstrip. Emma kissed both of the kids again and stepped off the porch to the car door Cain was holding open for her.

From the way her bottom lip was trembling, Cain could tell she was about to start crying again. "It's not too late to change your mind, you know."

"I want to go with you, honey. It doesn't mean, though, that I won't miss them."

"I know, baby, and it's what makes you a good mom." Cain hugged her before helping her into the truck. They pulled away slowly so Hannah could wave to them, and she kept at it until they could no longer see her. Cain sat in the backseat with Emma and held her close. "I'll make this as quick as I can."

"I'm not worried about that, love. I know you're going to try your hardest to make this as painless for everyone as possible. Just don't ask me not to worry about you and the kids."

"I'll be fine, and the only thing that could happen to the kids is getting calluses on their hands from milking too many cows." Cain pulled her closer and figured Emma had something on her mind she hadn't found a way to express yet. "Why, are you worried?"

"It's just that Bracato came after us in the house. Do you think he'd send someone out here to hurt them? And my mother's coming home soon. I don't want her to discover that Hannah's at Maddie's."

A little of Cain's anger escaped her control, and she tensed, but it had nothing to do with what Emma had said. She had pushed her recovery to the limits because she intended to pay Giovanni back for that insane afternoon at her house. And she was sure her men could deal with Carol Verde on the off chance that she came snooping around.

"That's why I chose to bring them here, lass. This is a great place because it's in plain sight. That's why it was so easy to spot Kyle and his men. Anyone who doesn't belong here will be dead before they step foot out of the car."

Emma's laugh sounded much better than her tears. "You're incredibly sexy when you're threatening bodily harm. You do realize that, don't you?"

"I'm glad you think so. If that's the case, the next couple of weeks should be rather interesting for you." Cain cupped the smooth cheek and stole a kiss. "By the time I'm done, you'll think I'm the sexiest person alive."

"Too late on that one, studly. I already think that."

The plane was sitting on the end of the short strip, and Muriel was there.

"Ah, good, the gang's all here," said Cain as she returned the wave.

"You didn't tell me Muriel was coming with us." Emma covered the hand on her middle and ran her fingers over Cain's skin.

"She didn't tell me definitely, so I thought we'd surprise you if she was able to make it. Look, she's got a tan."

Muriel opened the door of the truck for them and offered Emma a hand. "How's the crabby patient?"

"She's doing just great, so I wouldn't be pushing my luck and calling her names. Give her a couple more days and she's liable to take a swing at you." Emma stood on her toes and gave Muriel a kiss.

"After I tell her all the stuff I got done, she wouldn't dare."

Muriel and Cain eyed each other with mock glares before wrapping their arms around each other. From childhood, they had acted more like siblings than cousins.

"Did you get to speak to Ramon again?" Cain asked once they were airborne, running her fingers gently over her chest, trying to stop the itching of the healing wound.

"A couple of times, and then he met with the people you asked him to. They were interested in a deal if you agree to meet with them too, once this is all over."

"For what? They can't seriously think I'd be interested."

"Not interested, cousin. More like your willingness to let them deal with the other families."

Cain nodded, but didn't comment for a long time. "They can hope, but I'll have to think about that."

"They realize that, I think, so they told Ramon to convey their willingness to be patient until you're ready. On another subject, my staff has moved into new office space."

"Muriel, that's great," Emma said.

"Not when your dear spouse gets the bill. They figured you wouldn't mind if we upgraded a bit."

"Of course not, the mobster's made of money," Cain said.

"You'll be giving them all raises when you see what else they got you." Muriel dug through her briefcase for the right paperwork. "Your new deed, barkeep."

The address at the top made Cain smile. When she was a kid, both her father and uncle had talked about this old warehouse by the river where their grandfather had worked as a young man fresh from Ireland. The property had been part of a furniture store chain for years, and they hadn't been interested in selling off their holdings in pieces. Years and urban renewal in that part of the city had eventually changed their minds, but the warehouse Cain had been interested in for sentimental reasons had been the one thing the company had hung on to.

"What made them agree to sell?" Cain looked up from the document to her cousin, delighted.

"Not to sound like a canned movie, but you gave them an offer they found hard to refuse. The space downstairs is big enough for what you have in mind for the new club, and with a little insulation and work, the other five floors will do nicely for the new digs of the Casey Law Firm. Hell, they even threw in some furniture they didn't feel like moving out."

With Cain's trust, Muriel had already negotiated, signed the act of sale, and cut the company a check. "If the crew working on renovations keeps up their pace, we should be in there in three or four months. That means you'll have to stick to the pub for your drinking pleasure until they're done."

"What about our friend Blue?" Cain asked. "Has my lucky manager been behaving himself?"

"I've had a couple of our men sitting on him." Another folder came out of the bag, and Muriel flipped through the paperwork and pulled out some photos. "The dumb bastard's been busy." The first picture she handed over showed Blue standing next to a new Porsche.

"Man, baby, I'm not sure how much you pay your people, but if you're looking for a new club manager, I'm interested," Emma said, peering at the car.

"I pay a good salary, and with some careful planning, he could afford this ride. Problem is, though, our boy Blue likes to spend his days at the track, and he's got the luck of a two-legged dog in heavy traffic." Cain examined the next picture taken at the horse track. The wad of bills in Blue's hand didn't compute. "Who's he been talking to? Or should I ask, who's he working for?"

Muriel handed over the last one taken at the same track, only now Blue was sitting in a box watching the race through some binoculars. It was the man standing next to him that made Cain crumple the picture and throw it to the floor. Stephano Bracato didn't look too interested in the afternoon horse racing.

"He spent the afternoon with Stephano, losing steadily and drinking. Before they parted in the parking lot, Bracato handed him another thick envelope and they shook hands. You'll have to talk to him, but I'm guessing his going out to his car had a lot more to do with knowing what was going to happen than sheer luck. The little son of a bitch even called to ask if you were still going to pay him even though the club was gone."

"Where is he now?" Cain's voice dropped to a dangerous tone, and not even Emma's calming presence was enough to relax her.

"Little place off Airline Highway watching the ponies run at Belmont. I got Karl sitting in there having Cokes and placing a few bets to make sure he doesn't disappear."

They'd started to descend, causing Cain to look at her watch. It was still early afternoon, but the skies over New Orleans were gray and heavy with rain.

"Merrick."

Merrick materialized at Cain's side.

"I want you to take Emma to Uncle Jarvis's. Don't take any detours," she warned, looking at Emma.

Before Emma could start to protest, Cain put her hand up. "Not this time, lass. For an envelope full of money, Blue traded the lives of people who were guilty of nothing more than trying to make a living. Our talk might be long and ugly, and I don't want you exposed to that."

"You'll call and tell me if you're all right when you're done?"

"I sure will."

"And you'll have Katlin and Lou with you all the time, right?"

"I'll have a couple more than that, as will you." Cain stopped to place a kiss on the tip of Emma's nose. "I plan to put a wall around you, with Merrick as the cornerstone."

"Just don't be gone long." Emma rested her head on Cain's shoulder and sighed. "I understand why you have to do all this, but after having you all to myself for these past weeks, and knowing this is dangerous, it's going to be hard letting you go."

"I'm thinking this bloke is going to start talking the minute I see him, so you're not going to be by yourself very long."

"I'd like to go by the house instead of Uncle Jarvis's when we land to look at the damage and see what we can do about that situation. What do you think?"

Cain looked over Emma's head at Merrick before answering.

When she nodded, Cain agreed with the plan. "Just remember to stick close to Merrick until all this is done. That house won't mean shit to us if something happens to you."

"I'll keep my head down if you remember to do the same, Casey."

The time had come for Emma to stand up for what she wanted and to keep her word.

CHAPTER TWENTY-THREE

Blue sat at a table in the back corner staring at the closest screen and screaming for a pony named Eagle's Talon to get his ass moving. From the pile of ripped-up tickets on the floor around him, Cain could see his luck, or lack of it, was holding as steady as his losing.

The off-track betting bar Blue was sitting in reminded Cain of a cave. With the total lack of windows the patrons were bathed in the glare of television sets and neon. They all looked zombielike.

Without having to be told, Lou headed to the chair behind Blue, and Katlin stood behind Cain, who sat in the table's other chair. The look of panic in Blue's eyes was clear even in the dim lighting. He pulled his drink closer as if trying to find protection behind the glass of rum.

"Cain, what are you doing here?"

"It should be obvious. I'm here to see you." Cain crossed her long legs and leaned back. "I hear we have a lot to talk about."

Blue laughed and stood up, getting ready to deny whatever she was accusing him of. "I'm just placing a few bets, boss. What's to talk about?"

"I suggest you take your seat, Blue," Lou said from behind him. "You make me ask again and I'll break your kneecaps so you don't forget your manners. The lady wants to talk to you, so sit and talk."

"Come on, Cain, there's no reason for the muscle. And where's Merrick? I'm sure she'd vouch for me. I didn't do nothing wrong."

A waitress came over with an empty tray and picked up Blue's glass. "Can I get you anything?"

"A shot of Jameson, neat," Cain answered.

"The good stuff's extra."

Katlin waved a twenty in front of the waitress. "This ought to cover it."

"Now, Blue, what makes you think I'm here because you did anything wrong?"

The question sounded innocent enough, but Blue hadn't worked for Cain for a couple of years without learning a few things. There was something behind it.

"That's what I'm saying. I'm just sitting around waiting to go back to work." The fresh round of drinks was placed on the table, and Blue smiled up at the girl he'd been trying to flirt with for the better part of the afternoon.

"Of course you're out of work. That's as good a reason as any to set up my family and get some of my people killed. You were just looking out for your own interest. Who could blame you for that?"

Blue spit the rum he choked on back onto the table. Swallowing wrong set off a furious round of coughing, and he knew the color of his face lived up to his name. "Wha…what?" he finally got out through the wheezing.

"Let's go for a little ride, Blue," Cain said. She stood, pulled out a money clip, and peeled off a couple of bills. The waitress reappeared as if by magic. "What's your name, darlin'?"

"Mitzi." She looked greedily at the crisp one hundred dollar bills in Cain's fingers. "You need another drink or something?"

"No, Mitzi, I need to know where the back door is. Then I need to hear you give a complete description of me. If you can do that"—the money clip came out again and Cain peeled off another two hundred—"you can go shopping for something pretty."

"The door's by the restrooms, through there." She pointed to Cain's left. "And you, it's going to be hard to say anything about somebody I've never seen before."

Before the money exchanged hands Cain laughed, never taking her eyes off the woman. "See, Blue, we just met, and already this girl's got something up on you. She's smart, and she knows when to keep her mouth shut." Cain handed the money over and walked out the front.

Behind her Blue was about to scream when Lou put a small knife up to his throat.

"You gonna be needing change on that twenty?" Mitzi asked Katlin.

"Keep it, sugar. I'm not as generous as my friend, but not many of us are." The third race Blue had bought tickets for concluded, finally breaking his losing streak.

"Hey, I won." He held up the stubs now worth five grand.

"On second thought, sugar, I think this might just be your lucky day." Katlin ripped the stubs out of Blue's hand and gave them to the waitress. "Go buy yourself that something pretty my friend mentioned."

"That's mine," Blue whined, temporarily forgetting the trouble he was in.

"It's just not your lucky day…again…you fucker," Lou whispered before pushing him toward the door. "Let's go so I can explain to you what the trifecta of screwups means."

CHAPTER TWENTY-FOUR

Y ou ever get the feeling all hell's about to break loose and there's nothing you can do about it?" Joe asked. It was starting to frustrate him that everyone they'd targeted was being so circumspect. "Maybe if we recap what we have so far."

"This started with us following Kyle's lead by raiding Cain's warehouse and finding a legal shipment of liquor," Shelby said.

"Right, only the real crime was Kyle shooting Cain on Giovanni Bracato's behalf. As retaliation for losing his inside man, Bracato orders the hit on the house, Muriel's office, and Emerald's." Joe was pacing now as Lionel wrote the timeline on the board in the conference room they were using. "We have no real proof he ordered the hits, but who else would have held such a grudge against her?"

"Did we check with the police that day about any identification on the people Cain's crew was able to bring down?" The blue marker in Lionel's hand was starting to dry up from all the writing he'd done. "I don't remember reading that in their report."

"You're right," Joe agreed.

"If we had the names we could run down any leads on who they were working for. It could make it easier for us to find a way to bring someone in for questioning. At this point I don't care who it is, just as long as we get a little something out of it."

Shelby ran her hand through her hair and felt tired. They'd spent so many hours at the office trying to prevent the mayhem they were all waiting for that she was starting to feel like she'd never have any personal life. "I did ask about that, and the detective on the scene said there was no ID on any of the perps. If I was a betting woman, I'd say

Muriel or Merrick has those right now and knows who they worked for."

"You wouldn't want to call her and ask her nicely to let us have a look at them, would you?" Joe drooped his lips into a pathetic frown and cocked his head to the side like a begging puppy.

"I'm sure she'd not only do that, but tell us exactly how her cousin has evaded detection from doing God knows what for so long." She gave the answer in the same teasing tone as she addressed Joe's question. "Come on, guys, we've been at this for days, and it isn't getting us anywhere. How about we knock off early today and start fresh tomorrow?"

"Yeah, I can't really see anything shaking out today."

❖

The inside of the Casey house seemed dark and ominous because the back windows had been boarded. When they reached Cain's office, Emma had to put her hand on the doorjamb to steady her balance. Behind her, Merrick still looked irritated at having to be stuck with her as long as Cain ordered. "You know, Merrick, if you stop sulking long enough, you might find that my company really isn't all bad."

"I'm not sulking." The long sigh that followed didn't make Merrick sound all that convincing. "Are we almost finished here? Cain and the others might need me."

"If you find this assignment so unacceptable, I'll be happy to talk to her tonight and see if she'll change her mind. I'm sure Cain can find someone else to work with me."

Emma ran her fingers along the holes in the leather chair and closed her eyes. It chilled her blood to think of her lover sitting here. "There's no sense in you being miserable and making me miserable watching you frown all day long."

"No, I appreciate your concern, but she's right," Merrick conceded. "You need someone competent to watch you, and I'll do it as long as necessary. Do you want to start calling repairmen? I could get the household staff to give me a list of who we've used in the past."

"Maybe tomorrow, but for now I want to talk to Cain about all this. Fresh paint and new windows might fix what's broken, but I don't know how the kids would react to coming back here."

"How do you feel about the prospect?"

"I'd be happy living in the pool house out back, Merrick. Just as long as I get to share it with her. I was scared before because I didn't fully understand."

"And now?" Merrick didn't look entirely convinced.

"We've talked a lot in the last few weeks, and now I understand far better what makes her tick. Before, I just knew about what she needed from me here." She waved to indicate the house. "But what she needed to get done out there was a foreign concept."

"She'll still need to do all the things you left her for. It might be even worse."

Emma's grip on the leather chair strengthened. "The upstairs looks just like this. Those men and the people who sent them came solely to harm my family. I'm sure it was only business to them. They didn't think or feel anything, so I can only return the favor. Whatever she has planned for them won't be enough."

"That's a good start, Mrs. Casey. Shall we go?"

The small phone in Emma's purse rang as they headed to the car, and she answered it as Merrick opened the back door for her. "Hey, baby, everything going okay?"

"Just like I said, piece of coconut custard pie," Cain said. "Listen, I was thinking—"

"Always a dangerous proposition," Emma interrupted. "I'm sorry, honey. I couldn't resist. What were you thinking?"

"How about you go buy yourself something devastatingly sexy for tonight, and I'll take you out to dinner?" Cain relaxed into the leather of the vehicle and watched suburbia melt away as they entered the city. Somewhere behind her, Lou and Katlin were following with the little package they'd picked up at the bar. "It could be our coming-out dinner."

"You outed me years ago, lover."

"My, we *are* in a playful mood, aren't we? I was thinking perhaps some veal at Eleven 79."

"Let's see. Who, pray tell, has a standing reservation every Friday night? They're known for their northern Italian, right?"

"I really may just retire now and let you handle things from here on out. It's nice to see you didn't lose that observant streak of yours living the quiet life in Wisconsin." The back of the vehicle was filled with Cain's laughter. "It's Friday night and Mr. Bracato, the senior scumbag, has a standing reservation. And yes, they are known for their renditions of certain Italian dishes. What do you say, Mrs. Casey? Care to join me?"

"I'd love to. Hold on, baby. Just let me tell Merrick about our new destination." They headed back toward Jarvis's house, so Emma leaned up and tapped Merrick's shoulder. "Merrick, could you please take me downtown." Then she asked Cain, "Can I pick up anything for you while I'm out?"

"Do you remember how to spend real money?" Cain asked.

"I can muddle through. It's easy when you're so encouraging."

"Sorry to cut this short, but I've got to go. Have fun, and I'll see you at Uncle Jarvis's soon." There before her was the warehouse Muriel had bought while they were gone. The workers were packing up for the afternoon and starting to pull out of the parking lot. "I love you, and tell Merrick not to lose sight of you. I have plans for you later."

"I love you too, and be careful."

Emma knew this was her first true test, but unlike Blue, she planned to prove just how loyal she was to Cain.

CHAPTER TWENTY-FIVE

Cain's footsteps echoed hollowly as she walked to the center of the room. There was no furniture in the new Emerald's yet, considering the sawdust and hanging wires, but she could envision the final product. The unfinished carved oak bar fit in well since the builders had left alone the brick walls as well as the old wood floor along the perimeter of the new dance floor.

From the back a large door opened, and Lou pulled the SUV in far enough for the door to close behind him.

Blue started for Cain, and Katlin caught him just before he touched her, dropping him to his knees with a kick to his legs.

"Please, Cain, don't do this. I didn't do anything," Blue pleaded.

"How do you like the new place?" Cain asked, as if Blue had never spoken. "We stock the bar, get some tables and bar stools, and we're back in business."

"It's great. I can't wait." The tears were starting to fall down his face. He never figured he'd be in this position. Assurances had been made that he would never have to face Cain's anger. "Is that why we're here? To talk about the new club?" He tried to play the innocent again.

Lou and Katlin both took off their jackets, folded them, and placed them on the shell of the bar. Then Katlin found a chair one of the contractors had been using and brought it over for Cain.

Sitting, Cain balanced a folder on her lap and crossed her legs, the picture of relaxation. "No, Blue, that's not why we're here. I'm going to explain a few things to you before we get started, and if you're a good boy, we'll be out of here in no time."

"Great! Like I said, I didn't do nothing wrong, so I have no idea what this is about."

"See," Cain said, as she glanced up at Lou, who'd almost finished rolling up his sleeves and was shaking his head, "already you're lying to me, and I haven't even asked you anything. Lou, you want to show Blue what happens when I know he's lying."

When Lou's fist connected with Blue's side, it was strong enough to knock him face-first to the floor. Katlin helped him back to a kneeling position by yanking him up by the hair while he cried openly.

"See how we play the game now?" Cain asked.

Blue nodded vigorously.

"Good, very good. First, how much did it take to give up the men who worked for you? Two guys who were just looking to make a few extra bucks while they were in school. How much?"

"I don't know—"

Blue never finished the statement as Cain waved her hand at Lou again.

The second blow caught him on the jaw, and he dropped as if he'd been axed. Again Katlin picked him up off the floor.

"You know, Lou, maybe you should hit me too. I deserve it for giving this dumb fuck a job in management."

The two guards laughed as Cain said to Blue, "Since 'how much' was too difficult for you, how about who offered you the money?"

Blue just shook his head. "Please, Cain, you know me."

She opened the folder and looked at a picture before holding it up for him to see. "I thought I knew you. I thought you were smart enough to know something like this wouldn't stay a secret very long." The picture was of Blue shaking hands with Stephano Bracato after Bracato had just handed him an envelope full of money. "Was the money so good that you forgot what I'd do when I found out?" Her booming voice echoed through the place. "Did you?"

"I didn't mean nothing by it."

Nothing else came out of his mouth when Lou hit him again.

"How much did it take to endanger the lives of my wife and children? Because let me tell you something, Blue. The only reason this isn't going to take very long is that nothing happened to them. After Danny Baxter tried to rape Emma, he found relief in hell when I was through with him. It took hours for me to finally kill him, and he thanked me when I did."

His tone tough and threatening, Blue took one last chance. "Did you have the balls to pull the trigger, or did you have your flunky do it? It was just money, Cain. I didn't think Stephano or his family would be stupid enough to go after you."

"You thought wrong, then, didn't you? How typical of you. You gambled and, big shocker, you lost." She leaned forward in the chair and looked into his eyes. "How much did it take, Blue?"

"Ten thousand." He straightened his shoulders, starting to feel confident. "Ten grand, just to open up early and let some guy in the storeroom. Stephano told me he was acting as an intermediary for his brother Gino. Part of the payment was telling me what time the thing was supposed to go off."

"You know what the problem is with people like Stephano, Gino, and the other two idiots Bracato brought into this world?" She held out her hand, and Katlin passed her the gun she'd just attached the silencer to. "As they go around playing gangster, they mess with people's lives. They're the ones who have flunkies do their dirty work because, as they say in the movies, they haven't made their bones. It's easy to kill someone when you aren't there to see it, to see the bullet go in and splatter someone's brains on the floor."

"Cain, what are you talking about?" Blue couldn't believe his eyes when he saw the gun.

"That their price was ten thousand. Mine's a lot cheaper."

"I'll take whatever you're offering for the information," Blue said eagerly. "Better yet, just consider it a favor, to repay any ill will between us."

"You're right, boss," Lou said. "I should slap you for hiring this idiot."

"I'm not offering money. I want to give you a bullet. If you can take it and walk out of here, then we're even." Cain stood up and pressed the pistol to his forehead. "You can tell Gino and his brothers when you see them in hell that he shouldn't have fucked with me. And to answer your question, I never get someone to do the dirty work for me when it's personal. Unlike the wannabe you dealt with, I made my bones a long time ago."

Blue's response died in his throat when she pulled the trigger.

"What do you want us to do with him, boss?" Katlin asked. She took her gun back and put it in the holster strapped to her chest.

"Find a way to have him delivered to Bracato. I say we give him a little preview of what's coming."

❖

The glass elevators stopped on the second floor in the Canal Place shopping center, and Emma and her two shadows stepped off. A large portion of the floor was taken up by Saks Fifth Avenue and the little designer shops within the store. It had been an old haunt of hers when she lived with Cain, a place to either pick up some things for herself or items like her lover's custom-made shirts. During her time in New Orleans, Emma had been one of their best customers.

"Mrs. Casey, it's so good to see you again. We've missed you."

The middle-aged man was wearing the best tailored suit Emma had ever seen, other than those Cain owned, and he seemed very familiar, but for the life of her she couldn't remember his name. The disadvantage to frequenting Saks was that their employees didn't wear name tags; they just wore small pins with the establishment's initials.

"It's good to be back," she tried, searching her mind for a name.

"Kevin, ma'am, at your service." There was no judgment in his voice and no hint he minded her lapse in memory. "Is there something special you're looking for today?"

"Of course, Kevin. How's Ralph doing? That's your partner's name, isn't it?" She looped her arm through his when he offered it, a little angry at herself for not remembering him. Kevin had been the best guide she could have hoped for to help her fit into Cain's life—well, as far as clothes had been concerned. When they'd first met, she'd joked that you could still smell the hay in her hair.

He led her to a comfortable space at the center of three boutiques within the store. A quick call to his assistant meant hot Earl Grey tea and peanut butter cookies were on their way out.

"Ralph's doing fabulous, thank you for asking. Just between us, the business you gave me helped me finish putting him through culinary school. After he graduated and paid his dues at one of the downtown hotel kitchens, he got a position at Eleven 79. Not to brag, but it's one of the hardest places to get a reservation these days." Kevin took a seat next to her and put his hand over hers.

"Well, I hope Cain still has some influence around town, then. That's where she's taking me to dinner tonight and why I need something to wear. Living on a farm for years hasn't exactly chicced up my wardrobe."

"No problem. Enjoy the cookies and tea, and we'll put some selections together for you. I'm sure Ms. Casey will want to take you to some other places as well, and it'll save you some return trips. May I be the first to say it's good to have you back, Mrs. Casey."

"Thank you, it's good to be home." Emma leaned back and waved to the two chairs across from her. "You two might as well sit. We're going to be here for a while."

Merrick unbuttoned her jacket and grabbed a cookie before taking a seat. "Sit, eat, Walt. You heard the lady. We might be here awhile."

❖

Standing at the sale rack, Shelby couldn't believe her eyes. They'd used all the means at their disposal to find the Caseys, and here, sitting like a leading lady of New Orleans having afternoon tea, was half of the equation. Since two of Cain's people were positioned so close and looked so relaxed, Emma had obviously gotten through the door Cain had locked four years ago. It never hurt to see, though, and perhaps exploit the brief encounter they'd shared at the hospital. Surely Emma wouldn't forget that she'd cried on Shelby's shoulder after Cain had been shot.

"If you like, you may step into the dressing room, Mrs. Casey," Kevin suggested.

His appearance made Shelby hang back.

"If any of the sizes or colors don't work for you, just ring. I'll run downstairs a minute and pick up some shoes to go with these selections. My assistant will be right outside the door. If you like, we could also pull your card at the cosmetic counter and put together a kit for you."

"Thank you, Kevin. That would be great. Could you add a bottle of Dolce and Gabbana? It's Cain's favorite."

"Of course, ma'am. I'll have all that delivered wherever you like within the hour so you don't have to worry about toting it out of here."

"Thanks again." Emma stood up and laughed as Merrick snagged another cookie before following her toward the large dressing room. "Do you think Bracato's got a hit man in there ready to plug me full of holes?" she asked, pointing to the large room she was headed toward.

Merrick pulled out her phone and held it up. "You want to call her and tell her you want me to sit about a mile away from you?"

"I'm beginning to see the downside to this arrangement," Emma said, and pointed her finger at Merrick before taking another step. "No critiquing my choices."

"The one thing I can admit to without hesitation, Emma, is that you always looked like a million bucks no matter what you were wearing. Money or no money, you, lady, have style to spare. Though, if you ever tell anyone I said so, I'll deny it."

Emma merely nodded and closed the door between them. Kevin had done a good job. The little black dress on the hook by the mirror caught her eye first. If she wanted to take Cain's mind off business for even a minute tonight, this was the way to go.

She held it to her. It took everything in her not to flinch or make a sound when she looked past her reflection in the mirror and found someone else in the dressing room. She was standing at the back out of sight with her arms folded, looking like she was sizing Emma up.

The blue jeans, sweater, and loose flowing hair made Shelby appear years younger. "Agent, are you here to help me shop?" With a surprisingly steady hand, Emma put the dress back and leaned against the mirror with her arms folded, copying the trespasser's pose.

"I'm here because I'm worried about you." Shelby moved closer. "I lost contact with you and have been wondering if you're all right."

"I've never been better. If you don't mind, though, I'm in the middle of something."

"Do you want to be dragged down the same road as before?" Shelby unwittingly started on the path Kyle had tried to walk long before. "You have to know this is going to end badly, right?"

Emma let her arms drop and put some space between her and the agent. Something about how Shelby had gone about trying to get close to her made her angry. She and Cain were under enough pressure without having to deal with someone who only months earlier had been interested in her wife.

Knowing that Shelby would react as a professional and what side of the law it would put her on, Emma opened the door and waved Merrick in. Doing so would put her squarely on Cain's side. "Could you call Cain and ask about those reservations? We wouldn't want to be late because of any unforeseen nuisances."

Merrick glanced from one woman to the other and walked out to do Emma's bidding, leaving the door open. Emma knew she'd inform Cain just who Emma was stuck in the dressing room with. When Kevin returned to see how Emma was doing, Merrick waved him off.

"We'll talk about how she got in there and past you later," Cain said once Merrick was through explaining. "Did she try to talk her away from the dark side?" Cain asked. She was on her way back to the house, and the fact that a Bracato had so easily turned someone in her employ for so little money was starting to make her madder than when Blue had repeatedly tried to lie to her.

From the time Cain had taken over after her father had been killed, she'd tried to stay out of the way of the other families. She didn't agree with some of the things they were involved with, but she'd looked the other way because it wasn't any of her business. What irritated her was the fact Bracato that had come to her doorstep offering money to her employees to help him harm her family. He had crossed the line that all the family heads had honored until now.

"I guess that's what's happening while I'm out here talking to you," Merrick said. "But I have to admit Emma looks cool and collected."

"Not that I don't trust her, but let me talk to her and see if she needs any backup."

Cain gazed out at the passing houses as she waited. "Hey, lass, I hear you've acquired a new shadow. You're moving up in the world."

Shelby didn't back away from her, as if anxious to hear Emma's side of the conversation. "How does a black dress sound to you?"

"Still not alone, are we?"

"What do you think?" Emma looked at Shelby and shook her head.

"Buy it. You want to look good, considering how many eyes will be on us." The car came to a stop in front of her uncle's house. "Do you need me to come over, baby?"

"I'm just interested in what two blue eyes think about what I'm wearing and how I look in it. But the most important thing now, I guess, is what time I have to be ready. I think I can handle the rest." Emma left the statement hanging, wanting to see if Cain really did trust her.

"I'm sure you can. Give my best to the friendly agent, but make sure she leaves the room before you take off any clothes. I prefer to be the only one besides Victoria to have a look at all your secrets."

"Will do, love. See you at home." Emma folded the phone and handed it back to Merrick at the door. "If there isn't anything else, Agent, I'm sure you heard we have reservations for tonight, and I don't want to be late."

Shelby graciously conceded and started for the door.

"Oh, and don't ever try that game with me again. Kyle tried and even succeeded, for a while at least. Having you play the same old tired game makes me think the supposed bad guys have a new flunky."

"There's no way in hell I'd work for someone like Bracato."

"Accosting someone in a dressing room doesn't do much to make me believe you. I suggest you get going since I'm sure there's some van you have to outfit with surveillance equipment, but trust me, that's as close to Cain as you're going to get."

"Is that a threat, Mrs. Casey?"

"No, I believe that's what's called a promise. It can't have slipped your mind that one of your own tried to kill Cain less than two months ago."

"He wasn't one of ours," Shelby said.

"Then we really are in trouble when the FBI starts bringing criminals to a bust to do their work for them."

Emma slammed the door in Shelby's face before she could respond.

CHAPTER TWENTY-SIX

I'm going to take a shower, Uncle Jarvis. Just send someone up if Emma calls."

"Cain, I'm sure she's fine. She has Merrick and Walt both with her."

"Did I say I was worried?" Cain asked as she left the room feeling like she was about to jump out of her skin.

The hot water felt good against her skin, and she stood there with her head down and her hands pressed on the side of the tiled wall, letting it hit her shoulders and the back of her neck. Thinking about the coming night, she didn't hear the glass door open. As she felt two arms slide around her waist, she smiled.

"Miss me?" Emma asked. She had almost started stripping on the stairs when Jarvis had told her to hurry before Cain rattled apart.

Cain pressed Emma to the opposite wall. "Just a little. Did everything go all right?"

"I got a dress and some other things the salesman talked me into, but Merrick gave me the thumbs-up, so I'm sure you won't mind. As for our friendly agent, I'm sure she's off somewhere thinking of ways to take you away from me."

Moaning when Cain's lips started up the side of her neck, Emma let her head fall back farther.

"No one's going to take me away from you." Cain pulled back as she got to the curve of Emma's shoulder. "God, you taste good."

"I'm the best appetizer going, honey. I don't care what everyone says about the restaurant we're headed to tonight. Let's go lie down for a little while." Emma's knees felt weak, and the lower Cain's hands slid along her body, the harder it was to calm her breathing.

When Cain accepted the invitation and led them out of the shower and to the bed, Emma's nipples instantly became stone hard in the cool air. But the feel of Cain's body covering hers as soon as her wet body hit the bed added the mix of excitement she'd been craving all day. The exhilaration of all that skin coming into contact with hers made her wrap her legs around Cain's hips and pull all of her weight on top of her.

"I want to feel you," Emma said when Cain tried to roll off. It was hard to find words with the muscles of Cain's abdomen pressing against her sex. Adding to that, the muscles in Cain's shoulders were flexed and looked even sexier with the droplets of water from the shower beading on her skin.

"I want to feel you too, and I can't if I don't have room." The wound in her side ached a little, but Cain ignored it and concentrated instead on the puckered nipple so close to her hand.

For Cain, touching Emma had always been about love. It had been beautiful to watch the shy farm girl evolve into a woman who knew what she wanted and wasn't afraid to ask for it. Both facets of Emma's personality were equally beautiful to Cain because, as adventurous as her wife became, a bit of that young woman she'd first met was still locked inside her.

"I used to think about you like this," Cain said. Her palm covered Emma's breast, and she could feel the small nub pressing against her palm.

"Like what, baby?"

"When we first met, I'd take you out and talk to you and maybe dance, but on the way home I used to imagine what it would be like to have you stretched out like this with my skin touching yours. What it would be like to touch you because that's what you asked me to do." Cain moved her hand and wrapped it around Emma's breast so she could lower her lips and suck gently on the neglected nipple.

Cain had been forced to exercise tremendous self-control the day Emma had called her back to that small apartment. When she walked in and saw Emma naked from the waist up, with only her arm covering her chest, Cain had wanted to devour her whole. The memory of the first time Emma pulled away from her and exposed herself to her hungry eyes would forever be one of Cain's favorites.

Women were something Cain knew and enjoyed, but Emma had been worlds apart. From her first look Cain had just sat and stared so hard that Emma had grown nervous and asked if something was wrong. "You're just so beautiful," Cain had told her.

"Please, I want you to touch me now," Emma said.

Cain let go of the nipple in her mouth and dragged her hand farther down Emma's body. Long fingers parted Emma and found her wet and ready, but Cain didn't go inside.

Instead, she stroked from one end of the heated flesh to the other, until Emma pushed her leg between Cain's.

"Look at me, Emma."

When she opened her dark green eyes she looked like a woman lost in the passion Cain was creating.

"I want to see you while I'm loving you." Cain's fingers slid up and separated as they came to Emma's clitoris.

"Please, baby." When the fingers stopped and squeezed, Emma's hips surged off the bed. "Go inside, Cain. I need you."

Emma tried to keep her eyes locked to Cain's as Cain slid her fingers where Emma most wanted them, but it took all of her concentration to not just lie back and enjoy the fire consuming her body. No words could describe how Cain made her feel as her fingers stroked away Emma's worries and the walls of her sex did their best to keep Cain inside.

The battle was lost when Cain lowered her head and sucked on her pulse point. Emma closed her eyes and moved her hips in time with Cain's hand, trying to make the moment last as long as she could. With an impressive show of strength, Emma pulled Cain's head up and pressed their lips together. The tongue in her mouth drove her blossoming orgasm to the point of no return.

"Don't stop," Emma demanded as her head fell back to the bed and she arched into Cain. Emma dragged her nails up Cain's back, trying to keep their bodies together. The rush of pleasure peaked, and Emma grew taut as a scream ripped from her throat. "Whoa."

"Whoa?" Cain said after Emma's tremors subsided. "My lass has been on the farm a little too long."

The comment made Emma start laughing, and she had a hard time stopping. "No, don't go," she said, still chuckling when Cain began to move off her. "I like being pinned down by you almost as much as I like being teased by you." With gentle fingers Emma traced Cain's face before she cupped her cheek.

"Yes, but just think of where all the pinning and teasing lead." Cain kissed her one last time before sliding off. "However did I live all this time without you?"

Emma's eyes filled with tears. She was the only one who got to see this side of Cain, the woman so many respected and more than a few feared, who could with just a few words express all that was in her heart. "I've been asking the same question about you for a long time."

"Don't cry, love. I look at you sometimes and feel like there isn't enough air in the room to fill my lungs. I never imagined a woman could so completely own me. Then I met you." She placed her hand along Emma's jawline and wiped the few tears away with her thumb. "Will you let me know if I ever do something to disappoint you? I don't want to be without you ever again. Four years was a long time not to know true happiness."

"Honey, you never disappointed me." Emma leaned into the strong hand, then draped herself over Cain's body. "I disappointed myself. I'm your wife, and I shouldn't have believed anyone but you."

She put her lips to Cain's forehead. "I love you. That means for better or for worse." Her lips moved to Cain's eyelids. "In sickness, health, and gunshot wounds." Emma whispered the last part into Cain's ear before she placed a kiss just below it. The laugh that it caused in Cain shook her body a little.

"For richer or for poorer"—the other ear was given equal attention—"till death do us part." Emma finished the vows with a kiss that left no room for doubt about how she felt or how strong her love was for Cain. "I belong to you and will have no other in my life except you."

"That's the sweetest thing you've ever told me, but I don't want to own you, love."

Emma quit smiling and started to roll off, thinking Cain still wasn't ready to fully commit.

"Don't go. I like being pinned down by you," echoed Cain from what Emma had said earlier. "Do you trust me, Emma?"

"With my life." She answered without hesitation and didn't try to hide anything from Cain.

"Then don't worry when I say things like that. I didn't mean that I don't want you. Nothing could be less true."

Emma relaxed, and she tried another smile.

"I don't want to own you. I want to know you're my equal in every way."

"Can I tell you something and not have you think I'm crazy?" Emma put her head down on Cain's shoulder, and her hair fanned out across her lover's chest.

"It's just us here, and I'll never think you're crazy."

"I like that you're stronger than me, Cain, and not just physically. You give an order, and people obey because they want to, not because they fear you. I love that about you, and I'm happy you're the one who protects our children and me. I feel safe. What I meant was, I don't want to be treated like a prized cow. I want people to look at me and know that I belong to you, that I'm your responsibility as well as your partner."

She went willingly when Cain flipped them over and hovered over her. "I want them to know that I've chosen to belong to you. I want all that…but is that what you want?"

Cain took a deep breath and released it slowly, as if trying to organize her thoughts. "I'm not sure why this talk has become so serious, but perhaps it's a good thing." She slid off Emma again and, this time, off the bed.

After taking something out of the small desk, and before Emma could panic, Cain returned and knelt next to the bed. "When all this is over I want to give you something I was remiss about before." She held a small green velvet bag tied closed with a tiny cord.

"Soon we'll stand before God and our friends, and I'll claim what's mine. And I want you to do the same. We belong to each other. I love my children and my family, but all that's incomplete without your love and belief in me."

"I do love you," Emma said.

"I know you do." Cain had a little trouble getting the bag open, but when the contents slid out into her hand, Emma put her hands up to her mouth in awe. "You lived with me all that time, and I never gave you a proper ring."

Cain held up the first ring, and the diamond sparkled in the waning light from the window. "The jeweler told me the stone is flawless. To me it represents my love for you. Perhaps my life isn't perfect, but I try very hard to make you feel cherished and loved as flawlessly as I know how. When you look at it I want you to remember that."

She held it up close to the ring finger on Emma's left hand. "Emma, will you have me?"

The question was barely out of Cain's mouth when Emma said simply, "Yes."

Cain held another ring, a simple gold band with two sapphires embedded in the metal. "This ring is a partner to the one I just gave you. Two more stones in honor of the most precious things you could have given me, our children." The second one slid home, and Emma gave in to tears.

"Can the guy who sold you this add more to this one?" Emma pointed to the second ring.

Cain didn't answer the question verbally; she just handed Emma the bag, then kissed the tip of her nose. The bag weighed just enough for her to know it wasn't empty. When she tipped it over, another two sapphires rolled out into her palm, to be added to the ring if they had more children. "You *do* want us to work, don't you?"

"That I do, lass, but before you go planning something, you might want to hear what I have to say."

Emma pressed her hand to Cain's lips and stopped whatever was getting ready to come out. "Later." She looped her other hand around Cain's neck and pulled. "Much, much later."

Again Cain just grunted when Emma pressed her thigh between her legs. In retrospect Cain had chosen a rather strange way to propose, naked and just after making love, but Emma wouldn't have wanted it any other way. Whatever confessions Cain had would have to wait.

This was an occasion Emma didn't want marred by anything.

CHAPTER TWENTY-SEVEN

Emma turned Cain in the shower so she could rinse out the shampoo she'd worked in. "Blue was responsible for bombing the clubs and Muriel's office?"

"He didn't set the bombs, but he let in the guys who did. Not that he admitted it, but he was also giving Stephano Bracato information about all of us." She wiped the residual suds from her face before lowering her head again so Emma could repeat the process. "You have to understand that Bracato and his sons have no honor. They aren't going to be satisfied with just my heart on a platter; they want to hurt me first by taking away everything dear to me. It got Marie killed and will make them keep coming until their sick needs for vengeance are sated. But I'm not just going to sit back and let that happen, no way in hell. I'm sorry if you think I'm a monster."

"Don't apologize. You're protecting your family, end of discussion. I meant what I said, Cain. I'm here for you no matter what. Though when you see the tab for this afternoon, you may tell me to head back north."

"The designer shops around town are going to start sending me thank-you cards again, aren't they?"

"I believe Kevin said something about the wine being on him tonight." Emma guided Cain's dark head under the spray of water so she could rinse all the lather she'd worked up again while they'd been talking. "The FBI may not like you, my love, but Kevin simply adores you."

"Who's Kevin, and why haven't we met?" They stepped out of the large shower together, and Cain accepted a towel from Emma.

"He's my personal shopper, and while you've never met him, he's memorized your account number. With your line of credit you might even make him forget Ralph."

Cain laughed as she helped Emma into her robe. "I know I'm going to be sorry, but who's Ralph?"

"The chef at the restaurant you're taking me to, and also Kevin's partner." With her robe tied, Emma walked back into the bedroom and gasped at the number of packages stacked around the room.

"Is the little black dress you promised me in one of these boxes?"

"Along with a few other things, apparently." She lifted the lid of one box that looked too small for anything she'd tried on in the store and closed it quickly when Cain stepped up behind her. Cain appeared amused as Emma's face suddenly got hot. "Why don't you get dressed and go downstairs and wait for me? I'm sure Uncle Jarvis would love to have a drink with you."

"Tell me what's in the box and I'll be happy to."

Emma put her body between Cain and the box in question. "What's the matter, honey, don't you like surprises? I believe that's what you're always telling me."

"Ah, don't I even get a hint?"

"Knowing Kevin the way I do, it's made of silk. Satisfied?"

The smile that had attracted Emma in the first place grew even broader. "Not as much as I'll be later when I help you out of the dress. It's got to be something, to make you blush like this." Cain ran her long finger up Emma's cheek till it brushed through her wet hair.

"If you want to make it to dinner some time tonight, might I suggest you stop doing that, and most certainly stop looking at me that way." Emma admired all the naked skin on display and for once felt like just staying in.

All those months on the farm she'd dreamed of the nights like this when Cain had made sure she enjoyed herself, no matter if she did a little business also. She'd seen the envy on a lot of women's faces when she walked into a place on Cain's arm. Emma knew most of them would have been all too happy to trade places with her—to see Cain standing before them naked and hungry.

"I thought you liked it when I looked at you this way?"

"I do, but you said it was important that we go out tonight, so stop it." Emma felt chilled a minute later when Cain stepped into the closet to pick out a suit, and her white shirt almost crackled from the starch.

Emma slapped Cain's hands away and fastened the buttons herself, along with the belt, as soon as she tucked the shirt into her lover's pants. When Emma finished she handed Cain the jacket and stood on her toes for a kiss. "Wait for me?"

"I'll leave you alone to get ready. Just call if you need me."

With a hard tug on the black belt around Cain's waist, Emma stopped her before she made it to the door. "I need you."

"Lass, I love you with all that I am," Cain whispered before she kissed her again. "But I'm only human, so behave."

"You can stay if you want to."

"I'm looking forward to being surprised." Cain waved at her before closing the door behind her.

When Emma was sure Cain wasn't coming back, she opened the box Kevin had included with all her purchases and smiled when she read the card.

> *Welcome home, Mrs. Casey. I hope you don't mind, but I wanted to add a little something for Ms. Casey from me for bringing you home. You were sorely missed.*
> *Kevin*

She lifted the black silk undergarments out of the box and smiled. She didn't realize that Kevin kept her preferences and sizes for absolutely everything in his files. The panties with matching strapless bra she would need for the dress she was wearing that night were a brand she'd been partial to after Kevin had pointed them out. The real deciding factor was the reaction she'd gotten out of Cain the first time she'd worn them, and she was hoping for a repeat performance later that night. "When you say a little something, Kevin, you aren't kidding."

The night promised more than one possibility now, Emma thought as she smiled.

❖

The tension in the study was almost palpable when Cain walked in to find Katlin and Merrick both holding what appeared to be Cokes, staring at each other like they were ready for the next round. "Did someone ring the bell and we've all retreated to our neutral corners?" Cain asked. They all sat in silence for almost ten minutes, neither of them willing to break the calm.

"Do you want something to drink, boss?" Katlin finally asked.

Merrick blocked her on her way to the bar. "I think I'm capable of pouring a drink."

"If you'd bother to learn what Cain likes, then you wouldn't have to ask," Merrick shot back.

The two were so busy sniping at each other they missed Cain's smile.

"Short blond women with green eyes. You should know since you got to spend the day at the mall with her," Katlin retaliated. "Did she buy you something pretty too?"

"Katlin, enough," Cain ordered. She accepted the glass of whiskey from Merrick and sat down on the sofa. "Did we finish all our chores today, Katlin?"

"Just like you asked, no problems. What's tonight's game plan?"

"Dinner, and perhaps a little something after, like we talked about earlier. We'll just play it as it comes. This place we're going tonight is small, so only the two of you, and maybe Lou. Make sure you have your licenses on your person. This is our coming-out party, but someone invited the men in gray." Cain took a sip and shook her head. "Leave it to Emma to go shopping and find a fed in the designer section."

"The fed was shopping the sale rack," Merrick said, with a laugh of her own. "If she hadn't snuck into the dressing room, Emma would've never seen her."

"Why do you think so?" Katlin asked.

"Because you can always count on certain things." Merrick pointed at Cain. "The boss likes aged whiskey, and her lady never shops the sale racks."

Cain laughed at Merrick's gentle teasing.

"Though you're the one to blame." She pointed to Cain again.

"Guilty as charged, but"—Cain looked toward the door—"you don't find visions like that one on the sale rack."

Emma stood in the doorway and waited. She'd slicked her hair back and pulled it up in a sophisticated swirl. Her new shoes were comfortable but still made her calf muscles stand out a little. However, the dress stilled anything else from coming out of Cain's mouth for such a long time that Emma thought something was wrong.

"Do I look okay?" She rested her hands on her stomach as she tried to calm her nerves.

She hadn't even thought of wearing a dress like this for a long time and hoped she still looked decent enough to pull it off. The strapless top of the silk sheath wrapped around her body showed just a hint of cleavage, and the bottom stopped at midthigh, barely hiding her thigh-high stockings.

"I would have to answer that question with a big no," Cain said as she rose from her seat.

"I could change."

"Let me finish, lass. You don't look okay. You look absolutely stunning."

Emma smoothed down the short dress before looking up at Cain. "Really?"

"I wouldn't lie to you, love. You look so good it's going to be hard to concentrate on business, but that might not be so bad. Let Bracato sweat out what we're up to while I spend the evening staring at you. Just promise me one thing."

Emma took the hand that Cain was offering and smiled as she soaked up the praise. "Whatever you want."

"You take me shopping sometime and introduce me to Kevin. This guy deserves his own store if this is one of his selections, though you'd look good in a gunnysack."

"Have I told you lately how much I missed you?"

"Just a little while ago, actually. But as good as it is to be missed, it's even better to be found." She pulled Emma forward and kissed her like no one else was in the room. In a sense there wasn't, since both Merrick and Katlin considerately stepped out.

"Let's call the kids before we head out," Emma said when they pulled apart. "Maddie should be putting Hannah down in a little while, and I don't want to miss talking to both of them."

"That's why our reservations aren't for another hour." Cain sat back down on the sofa and picked up the phone. After getting a report from Maddie, she talked to Hayden. "Make sure you're making yourself useful while you're up there. I don't want the Raths thinking we raised you to be afraid of work."

"Don't worry, I'm earning my keep."

She had to pull the phone away from her ear when Hayden put Hannah on the phone because the excited girl was so loud. Both Caseys took turns catching up on the first day the kids had been without them. Emma finished by checking in with Maddie.

"Are you ready?" Cain asked before she initiated another kiss.

"Kiss me like that again and my answer will be yes, but not if the question is out to dinner." Emma handed Cain the dress's matching jacket and shivered when Cain helped her with it, then slid knowing hands down her sides and pulled her close. "I love you, Cain."

"And I you, sweetling. Let's go set the city on fire."

For once since meeting Cain, Emma was grateful for their entourage of guards. The memory of Cain's chest darkening with blood was still fresh, and if they had to travel with this much company to prevent a repeat performance, so be it. Whatever kept Cain whole and alive.

CHAPTER TWENTY-EIGHT

Giovanni Bracato sat with his eldest son Gino and daughter-in-law Eris in the corner of Eleven 79, named for its address in the warehouse district. As the hostess seated the Caseys almost in the center of the room, both men stared at them, seething, but Eris appeared almost dazed.

"The wine list, Ms. Casey." The waiter handed Cain a thick leather-bound menu. "If you like I can make a few recommendations."

"What are you in the mood for, love—red or white?"

"Red, I think."

After Cain ordered wine, she returned the menu and glimpsed Giovanni and Gino whispering furiously. "Well, part of our party's here," Cain remarked as she picked up Emma's hand and kissed her palm. "Where do you suppose the rest of the players are?"

Emma leaned forward, giving Cain an excellent view of the tops of her breasts, and brushed a strand of hair behind Cain's ear. As Emma kissed the exposed ear a moment later she whispered, "Table near the entrance to the kitchen, three guys. Seems you rate over the FBI, honey, if that's the best table they could get."

"And they say crime doesn't pay," Cain joked. "Good job, Emma."

She pulled slightly back from Emma when a man dressed all in white approached their table and waited to be addressed. "Yes?" Cain asked.

"I'm sorry to disturb you, Ms. Casey. Mrs. Casey." He bowed his head to them. "I'm Ralph, and my partner Kevin told me you'd be joining us tonight. I wanted to welcome you and treat you to dinner."

"Thank you, Ralph, but that really isn't necessary."

"Then may I serve the menu I devised just for the two of you? I really do owe you a great deal. Mrs. Casey helped Kevin move into management at the store, which helped me get through school without owing a small fortune."

Emma dropped her hand to Cain's thigh, treating it to a slow massage. "Please, Ralph, call me Emma, and this is Cain. We love to be fed, so begin whenever you like."

Sitting by the kitchen, agents Joe, Lionel, and Anthony were enjoying their appetizers and talking into their sleeves every so often to Shelby and another agent in the van next door. Agent Claire Lansing, a computer-surveillance expert, had been assigned to the team per Shelby and Joe's request. They planned to phase Tony out soon, afraid that his hatred of Cain would cloud his judgment.

At the other end of the room, Giovanni and Gino could barely fit in their booth. Giovanni hadn't touched his food yet, unlike his son Gino, who was holding his fork like a shovel and stuffing his mouth with veal. Next to him his wife Eris limited her movements to taking healthy sips from her drink. Her husband grabbed the plate of pasta sitting before her and replaced it with his empty dish.

"Fucking Christ, how much of that shit did you snort before we left the house?" Gino asked Eris. The circles under her eyes were as black as her shoes, and she looked anemic from the lack of food after the drugs and alcohol had stolen her appetite.

"Leave me alone, asshole." Eris slurred her words. "I didn't want to be here tonight, so who gives a goddamn how much blow I had before we got here."

Her father-in-law looked at her with disgust.

"What's the matter, old man? Don't care for what you see?"

"Gino, you better deal with this problem, and soon. We have enough to keep us busy for the rest of the fucking decade." He downed his glass of wine in one gulp. "I can't believe that Casey bitch lived. Look at her with that little blond slut, acting like she doesn't have a care in the world."

"Don't worry about it, Papa. It's under control." Gino's fork was loaded with pasta, and some of the sauce dribbled on the napkin under his chin.

Chewing with his mouth full, he waved over one of his men from the bar. "Take her home, and no stops along the way." He pointed to Eris. "Get something to eat and go to bed, and when I get home, we'll discuss your behavior." He dropped his fork and squeezed her arm until she whimpered. "Get out of my sight."

"I see that Gino needs some lessons in manners when it comes to treating his wife with respect. I wonder if she stayed off that shit long enough so baby Gino won't have any lasting problems." Cain made the observation as she fed Emma a bite of her appetizer.

"I might be hooked on drugs myself if I had to live with that animal," Emma answered. "I held that little baby not that long ago, during that infamous kidnapping episode that started this whole mess, and he seemed responsive. Maybe she had a shred of maternal instinct left when she found out she was pregnant."

"Maybe," Cain said, distracted. She shifted her attention from the two buffoons to the three sitting at the other end of the room.

"Anything?" Anthony asked into the mike in his sleeve as he lifted his glass of ginger ale.

"Are you sure you gave us the right table?" Claire responded. "Because all we're getting is a big jumble of background noise."

"Middle table, the one we marked as number four when we came in and canvassed earlier. You should be getting something."

Shelby sounded impatient. "One of these days you're going to figure out all these people we chase aren't complete idiots. They're keeping their voices low enough so they become part of the background, even with the most sophisticated equipment. We're concentrating on Bracato and son since they've been nice enough to speak clearly."

"Keep trying Casey and the woman with her," Anthony said. "I just know she's up to something."

"Is there ever a clever way to hide that you're talking to your wrist?" Emma asked, as she leaned in and kissed Cain's ear again.

Before she said anything, Cain took hold of Emma's hand and kissed her on the wrist while looking at the three men. "Unless you do it like this, there isn't really a way."

No one but Cain noticed a deliveryman walk in carrying a box and his clipboard. After a brief conversation with the hostess, he was directed toward Bracato's table.

"Mr. Giovanni Bracato?"

"What do you want?"

"Delivery for you, sir. If you'd just sign here." The deliveryman handed over the box.

"What the fuck is that?" Gino asked.

"How in the hell should I know? I'm eating dinner, for God's sake. Who has something delivered to someone in a restaurant?" He ripped the tape off the top, noticing that the label didn't have a return address.

When he removed the top, most of the people sitting close to them put their napkins up to their faces. From the stench, Giovanni had to guess the fish resting on the bottom was more than a few days old. He shoved it at the first waiter who appeared, but made sure to pick up the enclosed note.

Blue sends his regards.

It was short, but conveyed the point quite admirably, and he flipped the card over and over in his fingers before looking at his son. "Who's Blue?"

"The manager of Cain's club, Emerald's. He's working for Stephano now since the tragedy that put him out of a job." He laughed at his own joke, oblivious to Giovanni's rage. "He's given us quite the insight into Casey's business."

"Shut up before we end up in jail."

"What was in the box, Papa?"

Giovanni leaned over and whispered in his son's ear. "A message for you and your idiot brother. Blue, or whatever his name was, is fish food. For a fucking Irish Mick, Cain's up on Italian customs. Make sure you find your brother tonight and tell him someone sold him out."

A wave of panic swept over Giovanni so fast, he was afraid his dinner was going to reappear. Before the waiter could get back to the kitchen with the box, a man at the back table stopped him and peeked inside it. Giovanni kicked himself for being so busy trying to burn a hole in Cain's head with nasty looks that he'd failed to see the more-than-obvious feds.

"Man, that smells like a dead fish," Joe said, holding his nose.

"Good detective skills, Simmons," Anthony said sarcastically. "It's a message from someone to Giovanni. Someone he knows and more than likely worked for him is dead."

"Who do you think sent it?" Lionel asked.

"I'm sure it was the Girl Scout feeding tiramisu to the blonde as we speak. Tonight was nothing but them showing who has the bigger dick." Anthony angrily handed the box back to the restaurant worker.

From the van Shelby laughed and shook her head. "If Tony's comparing Cain to Bracato, my money's still on her."

"You sound like you really admire her," Claire said.

"It's more like a healthy respect for her as an opponent. Most of the agents who've tried to nail her in the past have tried to categorize her, but that doesn't work because Cain's hard to define. She believes every problem has a solution, then proves that it does."

Claire removed her glasses and chewed on an earpiece. "Like I said, it sounds as if you find that admirable."

"Let me put it this way. Some people study cobras and may even think they're beautiful or admirable because they can survive. But I doubt they ever forget they're deadly snakes. That's how I feel about Cain Casey."

"That she's a deadly snake."

"She's not remotely snaky, but she *is* dangerous and deadly. Kyle didn't see it, and I don't think Bracato and his crew will either. She's circling but isn't the least bit ready to strike."

"Would you like to tour the kitchen before you go?" Ralph asked the Caseys.

Hearing his voice prompted Claire to put her glasses back on and fool with the powerful mike to try and listen in on their conversation.

"We'd love to." Emma answered for both of them. "That was excellent. In fact, I've already told Cain we have to come back soon."

"I'm glad you enjoyed it." Ralph pulled Emma's chair out for her and helped her up. "I come to work every day and feel like I'm living a dream. Thank you both for trying the place."

"You're quite welcome. And thank Kevin for his little gift. I'll put it to good use."

Cain helped Emma with her jacket, peeling off some money to pay the bill. She enjoyed watching Emma fall back into the wife-of-Cain-Casey role she'd long ago perfected. Anyone who met her seldom forgot her soon. Emma made others feel loved and at peace.

Most of the kitchen workers glanced up from their tasks and smiled as Ralph took Cain and Emma through. The space looked chaotic, but in actuality it was like a coordinated ballet. Each person had a role, and the whole of their skills produced the food the restaurant was quickly becoming known for.

"I hope to see you both again soon," Ralph said as he showed them to the back door. "Here you go." He handed the keys to his car over to Cain. "Keep it as long as you like, and if you need anything else, just call me again."

"When you finish tonight, Ralph, our car and driver will take you home, and I'll have your car delivered to you no later than noon tomorrow."

Cain and Ralph shook hands again, and Ralph returned to work.

Forty-five minutes later, Joe went to the bathroom, taking the long way around to peek into the kitchen to see what Cain and Emma found so interesting. Merrick and Katlin hadn't moved from their table. Only the larger guard Shelby had reported earlier had stepped out for a smoke behind the building. The Bracatos were also watching the entrance to the kitchen, waiting for the women to reemerge and hoping to follow them to their next destination.

The chef the Caseys had been talking to was busy flipping something on the multiburner stove with no audience but the people who worked for him.

"Fuck, fuck, fuck," Joe muttered as he continued into the kitchen, sure that Emma and Cain were gone.

"Sir, I'm sorry, but you can't come in here," a waiter emerging with a loaded tray said. The sudden stop he'd made trying not to crash into the agent made the plates slide precariously to the edge. "Can I get you something?"

"I was just looking for some friends." He glanced around, trying to spot a nook the women might have slipped into. "I saw them come in here and was waiting to tell them hello."

"Unless your friends work for the restaurant, there's no one back here, sir." Another man dressed in kitchen attire took Joe by the arm and led him back toward the tables. "If you need anything else, please ask your waiter."

"But I saw them come in here," Joe insisted.

"You were just in the kitchen. They're not here. It's just employees, I tell you."

"The bird we've been watching has flown," Joe said into the mike in his sleeve.

"Not through the front door," Claire answered.

Joe looked out the window to confirm that the driver and five other guards Cain had arrived with were still there. Most of them were leaning against the car talking and smoking cigarettes.

"I realize that." Joe stepped through the front door and headed to the back of the place. "There's a back door through the kitchen. What we don't know is what they left in." He looked at the door Cain had obviously used, then the parking lot. Cain had outfoxed them again since the getaway had to have been planned ahead. "She knew we'd be watching."

"Not a stretch, Sherlock, since we're always watching," Anthony said as he joined his colleague.

"If you're not out here to help me, can I suggest you just fuck off?" For the first time since they'd met, Joe used his height and weight to try and intimidate the shorter agent, making him take a step back. "I've had it with the attitude, just like I've had it with this case. We're no closer than Kyle to catching this woman doing something wrong."

"Perhaps it's time we took a page from our old boss's tricks," Anthony said, looking at the smug guards.

"That's it. Get the fuck away from me." Joe called for Lionel inside and headed to the truck across the street.

Anthony walked toward the city, alone.

CHAPTER TWENTY-NINE

Y ou can come out now."
Emma laughed at Cain's words, watching as Lou emerged from the backseat where he'd crouched down.

"You'd think they'd learn to count heads by now," Cain continued. "It's not like they haven't taken a million pictures of everyone on my crew."

"The feds slip up every so often, and you're complaining?" Emma asked.

"Me complain?" Cain laughed at her as they stopped for a traffic light. "Never."

"Now where are you taking me?"

"For a little after-dinner drink and some light conversation with some very heavy hitters in the drug trade."

Cain sucked in a breath when Emma pinched her, scowled, and asked, "You're getting into the drug business?"

"Get real, pumpkin. Of course not. Giovanni Bracato and the merry band of evil spawn he calls children are, though. He doesn't realize we're onto his new source of income and its ramifications."

The French Quarter was directly across from them as they waited on the other side of Canal Street for the light to change.

"What's that?"

"The bigger he gets, the more money he'll have coming in and the more powerful he'll become. Once he hits the street with all that muscle we won't be safe for very long, and none of the other families will either."

Cain pulled over and stopped before they arrived at their final destination. "I'm not going to let that happen, and I'm not having my children or my wife walk around surrounded by protection all the time."

"Whatever you think's appropriate, honey," Emma said, patting Cain's cheek. "I'll just follow your lead."

They stopped in front of the Gemini Club, which was owned by Ramon Jatibon. He had named it, as he'd done most of his businesses, for his twins. Looking at the place, Cain wondered who Ramon had on his payroll from the police department, since they ran without much legal interference.

People usually lined up to get in the club on the first floor, and the gambling operation on the second floor, while small by comparison, rivaled any in Las Vegas. Some federal agencies and the police were interested in the upper part of the building but hadn't found anyone willing to talk on the record about Ramon's activities.

"Oh, I remember this place." Emma moved closer to Cain and placed a kiss on her cheek as she maneuvered the small sedan to the front entrance. "Which of our dates was it that you brought me here?"

"You don't remember?"

"Of course I do. I just want to know if you do." Emma took Cain's hand and stepped into her arms. "I have total recall when it comes to our dating days. When Hannah gets older, if she runs into someone like you, hot stuff, I want her to see a little waiting won't kill her."

"Are you kidding? I lost more brain cells walking around in a constant state of horniness than I would've if I drank heavily. But you're right. If anyone comes near our little girl, there'll be problems." Cain bent and kissed her before pressing her lips to Emma's ear. "So, lass, which date was it?"

"Fourth, and the one that got you this close"—she held her thumb and index finger a smidgen apart—"from getting lucky."

"Now she tells me," Cain said.

"There's something about watching you gamble that makes me hot."

"Good to know, but tonight you're going to have to settle for drinking and dancing."

Emma rolled her eyes and muttered back to Lou, "I guess we'll have to muddle through somehow." The big wall of a man laughed.

They were inside quickly after Cain dropped the car keys into the valet's hand and the bouncer at the door pulled aside the velvet ropes holding back the crowd. A few people pointed toward them and whispered.

The multilevel room was crowded with people either enjoying conversations and drinks or dancing to the small band playing slow jazz numbers. Cain pulled out Emma's chair for her as she looked around the room for the players who were always scattered amid the regular patrons Ramon pulled in nightly.

"Is he here?" Emma asked.

"Table toward the back close to the stage. Two men with their heads together. The older one. Dark suit. Looks like a kindly grandfather."

Emma glanced at the table. "Want to get his attention?"

"How do we go about that?" Cain smiled down at Emma.

"Well, you could send him a drink." She put her hands over those on her shoulders. "But that'd be the unexciting way." Before Cain could answer, Emma stood and stepped into her arms. "Now, if you asked me to dance, I bet he'd notice you."

"The way you look in this dress, he's not going to be the only one noticing me. And he and everyone else in here are going to be jealous as hell they aren't me."

"Thanks, love, no need to flatter. You know how much I love your arms around me."

Cain led her to the dance floor and put her hands on Emma's hips, feeling Emma's hands in her hair as soon as they started to sway to the music. His alert brown eyes following their every move, the man called over a waiter as soon as he'd finished lighting his cigar. Knowing their fish had taken the bait, Cain relaxed and enjoyed the feel of Emma in her arms. At times like this, even though the night was the beginning of business, Cain felt the world slide back to a comfortable and healing place. Spending time with Emma helped her let go of the pain she'd forgotten she carried, since it'd become such a part of her. The real pleasure came from the knowledge that she wasn't alone, not even for things like this.

"When all this is over I want you to promise me something," Emma requested.

"Whatever you like, since I'm going to like whatever it is."

"I want about a week with just you and me on a beach somewhere, and I mean just you and me. No kids, no guards, and no one taking pictures."

"I know just the place, love, and I'm going to enjoy taking you there." The song came to an end, and Cain watched as Ramon walked toward them carrying two glasses.

"Perhaps I'll put you on my payroll if you come and liven the place up with such beauty every night." Ramon handed Cain a whiskey and Emma a glass of wine.

"Does your wife know you just come here to flirt, my friend?" Cain asked.

"I wasn't talking to you, Cain, so leave an old man to his fun." Ramon leaned over Emma's hand and pressed his lips to it briefly. He liked to joke around, but not enough to insult. "May I escort you back to your table?"

Emma smiled at Cain and winked, accepting Ramon's arm.

"How are your friends from warmer climates?" Cain asked as soon as they were all seated.

With his hands spread out in a gesture of innocence, Ramon laughed and shook his head. "Rodolfo and I aren't friends. Not like you and I are. He and I are acquaintances with a mutual respect. He comes here to drink my liquor and enjoy the music with the understanding I don't want any part of that shit he peddles."

Cain nodded slowly, distracted by her thoughts. "The word on the street is he cut a deal with Bracato to expand his operations here."

"They had one meeting, but I hear they don't feel comfortable with each other yet. But"—Ramon put his finger up for emphasis and leaned farther in—"I did learn that Giovanni put down a nice chunk of cash as a show of good faith. And he still doesn't know his number-one son is already doing business with Juan and Rodolfo in Mississippi."

"Did you speak to Rodolfo on my behalf?" Cain asked.

"I did all that Muriel asked of me, my friend. Actually I, as well as my children, would like to see how this plays out. We're having a similar situation in Vegas, and I hope to learn from your outcome."

Cain laughed at his tact. "Or my mistakes, right?"

Ramon laughed along with her and stood. "Please, I know you don't often make mistakes." He patted her shoulder with affection before adding, "It's a trait that reminds me so much of my daughter Remi."

"Thank you, Ramon. You and your kids are always welcome to call on me for help."

They watched him return to his true passion, the gaming tables upstairs. Another round of drinks arrived without prompting, and Cain arched a brow in the waiter's direction.

"The gentlemen by the stage sent them, Ms. Casey. The older man would also like a moment of your time."

In answer, Cain picked up her glass and saluted Rodolfo Luis with it before taking a sip. Immediately Rodolfo and his companion stood and headed in their direction. Under the table Emma rested her hand in the curve of Cain's thigh.

"Señora Casey, it's nice to see you again and looking so well." Rodolfo extended his hand to Cain.

"Please sit, Señor Luis, and please, it's Cain." After the handshake she introduced Emma. "This is my wife, Emma."

"A pleasure, ma'am, and this is my nephew Juan." The younger man sat and had a hard time keeping his eyes off Emma as well as a smirk off his face. "How are you feeling after your accident?"

Emma's hand tightened at the word "accident," and Cain could see her jaw clenched in an effort not to say anything.

"I'm feeling fine. Emma's taking really good care of me." With the admission Cain felt Emma relax.

"Good." Rodolfo smiled as he leaned back farther into the leather chair. "I hate to intrude on your evening, but would you give me a few minutes of your time?"

"I'd be glad to," Cain answered, since it was the main reason they were there.

"Alone," Rodolfo added.

"Whatever you have to say, you can say in front of Emma."

The hand on Cain's leg tightened again. "It's all right, love. I have to go to the ladies' room anyway."

Everyone stood when Emma did. "Save my seat," she told Cain before placing a gentle kiss on her lips.

Without another word, Emma stepped away with Lou following close behind. Juan also stood and headed in the same general direction, leaving his uncle to the business that needed to be discussed.

"What can I do for you?" Cain asked.

"We'll get to that, I'm sure, but first I wanted to ask you about Bracato. I hear from Ramon that he's the one who ordered the hit on you."

Cain ran her finger along the rim of the glass before her as she pinned the head of the Mexican drug cartel with a cold stare. "Big Gino and my family have a history, but I'm sure you don't want to waste time on our differences. Bracato has made it clear he wants a war between our families, and I don't intend to ignore that. If you want to do business with him, do business with him. That's none of my concern. Only warn your people not to mistake my disinterest for leniency. If they get in my way, there will be consequences."

Rodolfo's smile faltered for a second, then grew larger. "There's no need to threaten me. I have no dog in this fight. My family is only interested in making money, and I trust you'll not interfere. I plan to do business with Bracato, but that's all."

"Let's just say I have different plans for Big Gino and no interest in your business. You have my word."

Rodolfo extended his hand again to seal their bargain. "Perhaps I should've offered you the deal first. You'd be a much better partner and more lucrative to my bottom line."

"Thanks, but I'm not interested."

"My nephew and I'll be in town awhile longer if you change your mind."

"Thank you again, but don't lose sleep waiting up for my call." Cain stood and offered her hand again.

Seeing that Cain was almost done, Emma started back, only to be stopped by Juan Luis when he stood in her way. He was dressed in black, which made his palms look stark white when he held them up.

"A moment of your time, Emma."

With Lou so close to her, Emma felt safe enough to not call for Cain. "What can I do for you?"

He laughed and edged closer, and Lou stepped closer too. "I was watching you earlier, and maybe it's me who should be asking you that."

Emma cocked her head to the side and locked eyes with Cain for a second before directing her attention back to Juan. "What's that supposed to mean?"

"You look like a woman who enjoys certain appetites." Juan stayed put when Lou looked mad enough to kill. "What I can't believe is all that hunger can be satisfied by another woman."

"Not that anything about my life is any of your business, but no part of it lacks anything. Even if it did, I'm sure you're the last person I'd call." She ran her eyes from his feet to the top of his head, thinking that what she saw could define the word "lacking."

"And just for your well-being, might I suggest you never offer me anything at all or speak to me in this manner. Sometimes Cain can be dangerous to your health when she breaks that short leash she keeps her temper on. This might be one time I release it myself."

She rolled her hips as she walked away, and he laughed again. "This isn't over, Emma, and nothing about another woman scares me."

Emma barely heard the comment over the music, and before she got too far away, said, "One more thing. My name, it's Mrs. Casey. Try and remember that as well."

This time Lou laughed.

CHAPTER THIRTY

You're becoming a fucking disgrace. You know that, right?" Gino slammed the front door, dragging Eris in from the car after he'd collected her from the bar she'd insisted the driver take her to after she left the restaurant. Gino was furious and had screamed at her all the way home. She'd twisted an ankle on the way in but was in no pain since she was so high.

Eris kept walking to their bedroom, not wanting to listen to his ranting any longer. She'd heard more than enough of it in the car, and her neck was starting to tense up from the headache she felt coming on. That wasn't going to stop him, though, since she could hear the click of his heels on the tile floor right behind her.

"Don't walk away from me. I'm not finished talking to you." She lost her balance when he grabbed her shoulder and spun her around. "I'm sick of you embarrassing me in front of my father."

"Then stop insisting I go with you whenever you have to meet with him. I hate sitting there watching that fat pig stuff food in his mouth like—" A hard slap stopped the rest of the insult from pouring out of her mouth. Blood readily replaced the words, and Eris reeled. Their relationship had started to crumble, but Gino had never resorted to violence before.

She peered up at him with a mixture of disbelief and pure hatred. "Do you feel like a man now, you fat son of a bitch?" Her hand came away from her face extremely bloody, but the cocaine in her system masked the pain. "Get the fuck away from me!" she screamed when Gino tried to help her up.

The baby started crying after Eris's voice rose, and she heard the nanny go in to check on him. Eris had been hooked on Gino's product when they had met—nothing extreme, just enough to make her days more enjoyable. After they'd gotten serious about one another and decided to marry, she'd cleaned up and given up her little friend, as she called the white powder.

Because she was going to have children, she had made her decision easily. Kids had enough to deal with without being born sick because of her. Now, though, she couldn't have cared less about herself or her husband, and instead of maternal feelings for her son she had only guilt.

Everything had changed after she'd had Little Gino and gotten pregnant again right away. She'd done everything right and fought off her demons without giving in to the craving for drugs, but she'd lost the second baby anyway. Only the small vials of white powder gave her solace after that nightmare.

"Clean yourself up before that woman you hired to take care of my son thinks you're a bigger loser than I do. There isn't any reason for you not to be taking care of him." He batted her hands away and pulled her to her feet. "Little Gino doesn't even know you. He fucking thinks that idiot you hired is his mother, but maybe that's a good thing."

"You're right, but what'd be even better is if he didn't know either one of us. Then he might have a fighting chance."

This time he walked out and left her on the floor after he'd hit her again, only this time he'd used a closed fist.

Gino started the car and waved off the men standing outside ready to follow him. He didn't need an entourage outside his mistress's condo all night. He was firming up thoughts of how to rid himself of Eris when his car phone rang.

"Yeah?"

"Did Papa call you?" Stephano asked.

"I had dinner with him and haven't heard from him since." The streets were quiet and free of traffic, so Gino picked up speed. "Why?"

"I got a call from someone in Luis's organization about problems in Biloxi. Something about thinking we don't have enough cash flow for both operations."

"That's your problem, brother."

"No, Gino, this is *our* problem, since I cut you in. If Papa finds out about our extracurricular activities, my ass won't be the only one in shit, so don't try to walk away from your responsibilities. I'm going to meet with these guys, but I want you ready in case I need backup."

"Do you think you can handle this alone? We don't need you fucking up our new deal." Gino pulled over and looked at the dashboard clock. The green numbers read 1:48, and something wasn't right. Rodolfo's men weren't the middle-of-the-night, clandestine type.

"I'm not the fuckup in the family, so shut up. Just forget I called and forget our deal in Biloxi. I'll handle this myself."

"Stephano!" Screaming his brother's name did no good. The connection was dead. Gino immediately dialed Stephano's number to find out where he was, but didn't get an answer. "You stupid bastard." Gino called his two other brothers. If he was right, they didn't have much time before Stephano was lost to them forever.

Francis was in for the night and couldn't leave without raising their father's suspicions, so Gino tried Michael next.

"Just get out and look for him, Michael," he said as he drove to Stephano's favorite club.

"I told you two I don't want any part of this business until you come clean to Papa."

"Fine, but if something happens I'll be sure and let the old man know how helpful you were."

Gino slammed on his brakes in front of the club and asked the bouncer if he'd seen Stephano, getting a head shake no.

"Where are you, little brother?" Out of ideas about where to look, Gino drove to his mistress's house, intending to leave his phone next to the nightstand in case Stephano needed him.

His instincts told him Stephano needed him more than ever, but he was out of his reach now.

❖

The silence closed in on Stephano as soon as he shut off his engine in front of the abandoned-looking place. As he checked the address he'd scribbled on his bar napkin, all he could hear were the ringing phone and some slight clicking noises coming from the engine as it started to cool.

Stephano stood outside his car ignoring the phone and dismissed any fear at meeting at such a peculiar location and time, not wanting to jeopardize the connections driving his lucrative business dealing on the Mississippi coast. Family loyalty was one thing, but this was business, and that, his father had always taught him, came before anything else.

The closest structures were abandoned tenement buildings Stephano figured were used as crack houses. Adjusting the semiautomatic in the small of his back, he summoned up the swagger in his gait and strode to the door, which had opened when his car alarm chirped.

"Let's get this over with. It's damn late," he told the guy at the door. In the faint light coming from the street, he could see his earlier guess was right. Homemade pipes littered the floor, evidence that the local dopeheads visited frequently after making a score. "Where's Manuel?" Stephano asked without giving the first guy he passed another look. Manuel Cusso was the guy Rodolfo had entrusted the Louisiana, Mississippi, Alabama, and Florida territory to. He was always straightforward during their dealings, and they'd formed a friendship along the way. That was why this meeting seemed so strange.

"In his condo in Miami, if I had to guess, but then again I don't give a fuck about the people you keep company with, little man."

The familiar voice chilled Stephano more than the hands pressing him roughly to the wall in front of him. After a few pats along his body, he was relieved of his only weapon, then pushed roughly into a chair almost in the center of the room. Another, much cleaner-looking one, sat a few feet in front of his, and its occupant looked like someone waiting for a cup of coffee. He'd always envied the cool demeanor.

"Comfortable? This won't take long, but I don't want you to be miserable during our talk." Cain uncrossed one of her long legs and kicked a crack pipe in Stephano's direction with the tip of an expensive shoe. "Do you ever stop to wonder what drives someone to get hooked on something that'll ruin their life? What prompts them to sit in rat holes like this and spend their days sucking on crap like that?" She pointed to the pipe at Stephano's feet.

"You dragged me here to ask me that?"

He winced involuntarily when someone jerked his arms back and tied his hands together. He tried not to show either pain or fear, because he was in the deep end of the pool and a shark was swimming lazily toward him. Stephano's dreams about dying at home in his bed after a long life were rapidly dimming.

"It's a rhetorical question, so no, that's not why you're here."

"Cain, you have to know if you hurt me, my father's going to bury you. I never figured you for stupid." Stephano shifted to find a more comfortable spot, and a few creaks escaped from his chair.

The laugh that bubbled up from Cain's chest chilled him. "Thank you for the compliment. At least I think it was a compliment. Stupid is something I try to avoid at all costs. Stupid gets you dead. Stupid gets you caged in some penitentiary. Stupid gets you tied to a chair someplace where no one of consequence will ever find you." She crossed her legs again and cocked her head slightly to the side as if studying him. "The question is, do you know why you're here? Is it because of greed or stupidity? Or perhaps a little of both?"

"Come on, Cain. I know you. What do you have against me? You wouldn't kill someone because of their last name, would you?"

"Please." Cain cocked her head to the other side, only this time she frowned. "You're not going to sit there and act innocent, are you?"

"You're the head of your family. You know what that's like. My father's no different from you. The grudges between you two have nothing to do with me. Just like all these goons standing around here, I was following orders."

"So you were following orders, or did you feel some overwhelming compulsion to hang out with Blue? I didn't realize your charity of choice was to give large cash donations to gamblers with shitty luck." The laugh came again, and again it gave him no comfort. "But enough about that. Blue's a *dead* subject. Why we're here seems like a more interesting topic of conversation."

"Why are we here?"

Katlin took a case out of her pocket and placed it on the windowsill behind her. She then took the time to study the area outside. Stephano knew Cain and her guards would've taken extra precautions to lose any shadows interested in them. He'd even heard rumors of escape routes dug from private homes for just such occasions, so he was afraid that any help from the feds would never materialize.

"I'm here to share with you what you've shared with so many." The needle came out of the little black case, looking surreal in Katlin's black gloved hands.

A bead of sweat rolled down Stephano's neck.

"You're here to sit back and enjoy the ride," Cain said. Someone standing next to Katlin lit a small cooking torch and poured a bag of white powder into a small metal container. "I've never indulged, but from what I've read on the subject, I understand that's exactly what it feels like. A nice long ride no one wants to end."

"That's too much," Stephano protested weakly. A slight chemical smell in the air mixed with the mildew and rot, and he could almost feel death walk through the door.

"Are you kidding? I spared no expense on your behalf, Stephano. If a little makes you fly, then I want you to soar. And if you're worried about the quality, don't. I had one of my associates buy it from one of your dealers." The plunger squeaked when Katlin dipped into the hot liquid and filled the syringe. "I would think you deal only in quality."

Stephano was mesmerized as Cain pulled a switchblade from her pocket and opened it with practiced flair. He closed his eyes as it sliced through his sleeve and barely opened them when Katlin tied the rubber tubing into place, making his veins plump up like they were anxious for what came next.

"Don't do this." He knew the plea made him sound small and weak, but Cain's expression didn't change. "You've always been so sanctimonious, but we aren't so different. Except for where we come from, we've got the same blood running through our veins." Someone out of his eyesight tapped on the vein in the bend of his arm.

"You ask for salvation by insulting the memory of my father, saying our blood is the same?" Cain pressed her hands together to keep from hitting him. "You and I are nothing alike. I indulge in what I peddle, so to speak, so why is it you look at that needle with such fear?"

Katlin stepped closer, inserted the tip of the needle into the bulging vein, and barely pushed the plunger. Cain judged from the way Stephano's carotid was pumping, the coke would course through his body rapidly. And from the way his eyes were glassing up, the high would kick in sooner rather than later.

"See, that's not so bad, is it? See what you've been missing just pushing this crap to other people?" Cain nodded, and another shot hit Stephano's system.

"I feel so great I could run a marathon," the condemned man said. He sounded as if he were vibrating with energy, and the ropes around his hands pulled tighter as he pushed against them. He apparently thought it wouldn't be too difficult to break free and seemed oblivious to the ties biting into his skin.

Cain watched Stephano slide further and further into a world the cocaine was creating in his head. From what she could see of his hands, they were swelling and turning blue as he pulled on his bindings. She couldn't tell if they bothered him.

"You can't hurt me, you know." His head fell forward, and he laughed so hard his eyes filled with tears. "Even after all we did to you, there's nothing you can do to hurt me."

Cain held up her hand, making Katlin hold back on the huge syringe that still held three-quarters of the original amount. "What things?"

Stephano jerked his head up, as if remembering Cain was still there. "What do you care?" The laughter had died down to some high-pitched giggles, and he appeared to be enjoying himself.

"I don't. I just thought you would get off on the telling. If what you did hurt me, just think what telling me about it will do."

The smile on his face made Cain think he agreed with her logic.

"You still crying over that retard you were related to?"

Cain used every bit of her self-control to refrain from getting up and slitting his throat when he spoke of her sister in such a flip tone. "If you're referring to my sister Marie, then yes. Her death is something I'll never get over."

Stephano's head fell back, and he started laughing again. He laughed so hard he choked on his saliva, but for the longest time, he didn't stop. "She cried for you in the end, you know. Really, she cried for you the whole time, but after the show Danny put on, we just ignored the whimpering. The way that little simple brain thought you would save her from the bad men was heartwarming."

So caught up was Stephano in the telling of the story, he never noticed that Cain was almost breaking the arms of her chair. "I wanted to call you so you could hear her screaming, but Gino wouldn't let me."

"Gino was there?"

Cain barely recognized her own voice.

"Was he?"

Everyone jumped as Cain shouted.

"Yeah, we both were. Danny called us after he nabbed her. You should've heard him. He couldn't believe he caught her so easily. He really wanted your woman, but you ruined that for him. Kept going on about how he got a hard-on every time he looked at the blonde you were fucking every night, but that the retard would really get to you." He stopped talking and smacked his lips together like he was thirsty. Even though they were still sitting in the dark, dank room, Cain knew that his senses were heightened, giving him a feeling of euphoria.

"Finish your story, Stephano, and I'll let you go."

"He had her tied down when we got there, had her spread out and naked like some sort of freak show. The retard shut her eyes and just kept calling your name over and over. I'm not into that shit, but for a fucking deadhead, she was kinda hot."

Cain's hand shot up, and when Lou pulled his gun out and pointed it at the man's head, she warned him with her eyes. As painful as it was, she wanted to hear the end of this story. "Why were you there?"

"I just went to watch, but Gino, he wanted in on the action." He shook his head and laughed again. "He's my brother, but that bastard will fuck anything. The burns on the tips of her nipples, those were mine. I couldn't just sit there with my dick in my hand the whole time doing nothing. Gino got a real kick out of the way that got her hips to buck."

"Give me that fucking torch." Cain held her hand out as she stood.

Without being asked, Lou ripped Stephano's shirt open.

No matter how much shit Stephano had in his system, he must have noticed the smell of burning hair and flesh. He screamed like a volcano erupting as his nipple disappeared, eaten off by the blue flame in Cain's hand. "You bitch, you said you'd let me go if I told you." He was crying when she moved to the other one.

"You're right, asshole. I'm going to let you go, all right." She pushed the plunger all the way down and stood back as Stephano started to convulse. Before long he started to shake from the seizure that had taken over, and he was choking on the foam spilling out of his mouth.

"Bon voyage, asshole, but don't worry. You won't be traveling alone. I'm sending your whole family on the same trip."

Stephano's chair started to shake from his jerking, but no one tried to stop him. At one final moment his body went completely taut, the ropes finally snapping under the pressure. Then he slumped, overwhelmed by the lethal dose of drugs.

"However we finish this, I want them all dead. None of the Bracatos will escape, but I want Gino and his father saved for last. Just like Danny, they'll pray for death when I'm through with them."

Katlin and a couple of the men stayed behind to remove any evidence. She put the syringe and needle back into her case, as well as the rubber tubing, then cut the ropes off without too much worry for his hands. He wouldn't feel anything now.

Finally, she used with a disposable wipe doused in bleach to wipe down Cain's chair. If anyone happened to discover Stephano, they wouldn't be able to extract any DNA.

"Problem is, like Cain said, no one who matters will find you. The crackheads will come strip you of anything valuable, then leave the rest for the rats." After making sure nothing could tie them to the scene, Katlin rifled the body for one more thing.

On Stephano's right ring finger rested a signet ring bearing the Bracato family crest, a gift from their father, a duplicate of the one he wore proudly. Engraved inside each one was the name and birth date of the son to whom it belonged. It was one of a set of five Cain planned to collect before all this business was over. To see it again, off his son's finger, would send Giovanni the same message as the dead fish announcing Blue's demise. Still wearing her gloves, she jerked the ring off, walked to the car, and handed it to Cain.

"We're good to go, boss."

"Rest up, Katlin. We're just beginning."

Katlin knew Cain's comment was fueled by rage about Marie and that if the Bracatos wanted quick and painless, the devil wasn't in the mood to hear their pleas.

Chapter Thirty-one

For one brief moment Cain could hear the echo of laughter when Marie and Hayden had played together, enjoying each other's company. Not a day went by that she didn't miss her sister, but she realized that while Hayden hid his feelings on the subject well by not talking about it much, Marie's vicious murder had left a hole in his heart. Compared to what Marie had endured, the syringe full of liquefied cocaine she had just given Stephano was a gift.

In a lot of ways, this night resembled the night four years earlier when Danny had tried to rape Emma, causing her to leave Cain because she believed Cain had killed Danny in revenge for an act that never took place. Only this time Cain really *had* taken a life, a life that had ended in a sputtering mess of twitching muscles and tense limbs. Stephano's death had eased some of Cain's guilt over her failure to protect the most innocent of her responsibilities, but now came another test.

A light under the door flashed every so often, and Cain guessed Emma was watching television, trying her best to wait up. She paused, her hand on the knob, wondering how Emma would react this time around. "The proof is as easy as opening the door," Cain whispered before doing just that.

The television was on, but Emma sat in the middle of the bed staring at the door, willing it to open. When it did, she could see from Cain's clenched jaw that she was upset. The sitting and waiting had been murder, but now she needed to help.

Without a word, she pulled Cain into the room and locked the door. When she finished, a pile of clothes lay on the floor and she was lying skin to skin with Cain as she held her.

"Tell me what happened." Emma's tone showed no trace of indecisiveness.

"Stephano came to the address. Alone, like Lou had asked him to on the phone." Cain relaxed into Emma's chest, enjoying the methodically moving fingers combing through her hair. "We treated him to some of the shit he sells, and it made him really talkative…"

As her voice died away, she expelled a big sigh. "Maybe some part of him knew I'd never let him walk, so he wanted to inflict the maximum amount of hurt before his time was up."

"What could he possibly say to hurt you?"

Cain closed her eyes as if reliving the little speech Stephano had given about that night. When she opened them again they stung from unshed tears. "He was there the day Marie was killed. He tortured her too, and laughed about it." The sheets wrinkled in her fists as she gripped them, trying to fight the urge to go out and find the rest of the Bracatos and inflict some pain immediately. "Thing is, Danny put on a little show for not just Stephano, but for his big brother Gino. That bastard took a turn with her."

Emma held Cain as her tears fell, something that rarely happened. Cain had always had time to spend with her younger sister. She had taken such good care of Marie that Emma had been sure Cain would make a wonderful parent and therefore had loved her even more deeply.

❖

Fourteen Years Earlier

"Why do you look so nervous, Emma?"

"Are you kidding? You haven't done anything but talk about your sister and your family for weeks. What if they don't like me?" Emma was enjoying their rare time alone as Cain drove them to the Casey home for a casual Sunday lunch.

"Lass, quit your worrying. Marie's going to love you, and so will Billy and my mother." She squeezed Emma's thigh and smiled. "Just remember she gets confused at times, but just be patient with her." Two of the guards opened the front gate, and Emma waved, recognizing them from the pub when they accompanied Cain.

"I remember." She smoothed down her dress for the hundredth time since Cain had picked her up. "Do I look all right? I don't want your mother thinking I'm not right for you."

Cain's blue eyes softened. "You look fabulous. At least I certainly think so."

"I just want them to like me."

Cain got out of the car and walked to Emma's door. When she opened it she crouched down and pressed her palm to Emma's cheek. "Do you think you're right for me?"

"With all my heart."

"That's all that matters."

Before Cain could say anything else, the front door opened and Marie pressed herself to her sister's back. "Hi," she shyly said to Emma. "We're going to be great friends."

The words proved that Cain was right. Life might have given Marie a mind that wouldn't mature like most, but her heart had fared just fine. Emma smiled and gazed into eyes so like Cain's that she felt an instant affection for the girl who was so important to the woman she was falling in love with, although Marie's eyes were missing the mischief always shining in Cain's.

❖

"Do you remember the day you introduced me to Marie?" Emma brushed back a thick lock of Cain's hair and held it in place when it kept falling forward.

"I remember how well you and she got along."

"Do you know why we got along?" Cain shook her head, and Emma kissed Cain's forehead before answering. "Because Marie told me something that I'll always treasure."

"What?"

"She said you'd found someone who would love you more than she did. Then she told me how lucky I was."

"Why?" Cain moved to get a better look at Emma's face, never having heard this story.

"Because I'd never have to be afraid. If you could keep me safe, you would."

Emma could see the wounded look her words caused. She had to tell the first part of this memory, though, so she could get to the wisdom that had been Marie.

"You didn't fail her, love, and no matter her handicap, Marie understood more than you think. She finally said that you couldn't be everywhere, and sometimes bad stuff happened. When it did, you still loved me and didn't want it to occur. It just did sometimes."

"But she didn't deserve what happened to her."

"No, she didn't, but it wasn't your fault, and it wouldn't have taken place if you'd known about it. That's the important thing here, love. *If* you'd known. You didn't, and it's time to stop beating yourself up about it. What happened to Marie happened because Danny was a sick bastard."

Emma rested her head on Cain's and sighed. "I almost wish he'd taken out his need to hurt us on me. Maybe that would've saved her."

In an instant their positions reversed, and now Cain was doing the holding. "Don't ever say that. Even though I lost Marie, I thank all that's holy you don't have to live with the pain of what he could have done that night."

"Thank you for feeling that way, but I want you to forgive yourself for Marie." Emma straddled Cain's lap so they could look each other in the eye. "Will you at least try?"

"I'll try."

"And will you promise me something else?"

"Name it."

"Heap on Gino Bracato the same pain he gave Marie. She was your sister, but she was my family too. I don't know what happened to Danny, and I don't care to know exactly what happened to Stephano, but Gino deserves to suffer."

Cain put her hands around Emma's hips and pulled her forward in a hug. "Thank you for that, but I don't want you to say or know things you'll have a hard time living with later. I treasure your compassion and the fact that you haven't had to make any pacts with the devil yet. Because, believe me, he exacts a heavy toll at times."

"Don't patronize me, Cain."

Cain smiled. "I'm not patronizing you, love. I'm just looking out for you."

"But I can live with this wish." Emma pushed herself up so Cain could see her eyes and the sincerity in them. "No one lives a complete life if they don't learn from their mistakes. I adopted my mother's perspective and considered everything either black or white, right or wrong, in its place or out of it. When I met you, I fell in love with you, but part of me thought what you did to earn a living was wrong."

"But I am. Wrong, I mean, in the eyes of the law."

"So what? Special Agent Kyle was supposed to be the law, and look what happened. I know now that you don't go out of your way to hurt people, and what you do and how you do it isn't hurting anyone but the IRS." Emma pressed her fingers to Cain's lips to keep her quiet for a while longer. "There's something else. You know when to avenge a wrong done to someone you love, and just because you do, you're not a horrible person."

"That's a change of heart," Cain mumbled, the fingers still pressed to her mouth.

"It's just the truth, sweetheart. Marie's life meant more than Gino's, so it'd be wrong to let him get away with what he did."

"And he won't. I'll swear to that on a stack of Bibles."

Before Cain could continue, the phone on the nightstand rang. It was one of the only secure lines in the house. "Casey," she said. "No, it's not too late, don't worry about it." She pulled Emma closer and listened to whatever the caller was saying. "I'll try and make it in the morning."

"Anything wrong?"

"Just a strange invitation. Nothing to worry about."

"Good. Now we can go to sleep." Emma snuggled up to Cain's side. They would have many of these talks, she was sure, especially once Hayden came of age, but they'd get through them if they just said what was in their hearts. That and love would keep them whole.

CHAPTER THIRTY-TWO

W hat happened tonight?" Merrick looked as if she couldn't wait to hear the answer to her question.

Katlin stared at her over the rim of the glass of whiskey she'd just poured. After dropping two cubes of ice into the crystal tumbler, she poured another two fingers. "Do you usually talk to other people about the jobs you do for Cain?" She gulped the whiskey, and though she wanted another one, she shed her jacket and sat down. "If you do, you've got a problem."

"Why do you insist on being so impossible?" Merrick asked.

"Look, lady, as much as I enjoy pushing your buttons, I don't have the energy to fight with you. If you have an issue, take it up with Cain. I'm going to bed." Katlin got up and headed toward Jarvis's small guesthouse near the pool.

"Fuck me, man," Katlin mumbled when she heard the echo of Merrick's footsteps right behind her. "What?"

"I'm worried about Cain, so I'd like an answer to my question." Merrick followed Katlin inside and stood with her hands on her hips.

Not caring what Merrick did, Katlin hung up her jacket and put her shoes in the closet. If the next day was going to be anything like this one, she needed some sleep. With a sigh she lay down and closed her eyes.

"Are you just not going to answer because it's me, or is it just an annoying habit of yours to ignore people?" Merrick asked.

"Look, I don't know why Cain chose me for this position instead of you. I don't question my employer. If you have any complaints, problems, or concerns, Cain's upstairs just waiting for you to bother

her. But you and I aren't friends, and I'm not into heart-to-heart discussions."

Merrick watched Katlin rub her neck as if trying to work out a knot. "This isn't getting us anywhere, so how about we start over?"

"Look, like I said, I'm sorry if I usurped your position with Cain, but I didn't ask to be here, so starting over sounds good. Unless it means using knives and guns instead of words, or something equally drastic," Katlin quipped. "I have a water bazooka, and I'm not afraid to use it."

"Duly noted." Merrick tried to sound bored, but she couldn't stop her smile. "I know why our positions changed so quickly. I'm just not happy about it."

The rubbing stopped, and Katlin opened her deep green eyes and hiked her brows in Merrick's direction.

"Like she said, she wants the best person taking care of Emma."

"Yeah. I can't be everywhere at once, so I'm glad you were available to pick up my slack," Katlin said, and had to laugh when Merrick blew on the tip of her index finger, her hand in the shape of a gun.

The firm mattress barely budged when Merrick sat on it, and because she did, Katlin kept her eyes open.

When Merrick asked, "Will you tell me what happened tonight?" Katlin was tempted to knock out another smart-ass comment, but instead, with an almost technical detachment, she recapped everything Stephano had done and said before the end. She was almost shocked to see tears welling up in Merrick's eyes.

"When I first came to work for Cain, I'd never dealt with somebody like Marie and I tried to avoid her. Thing was, though, Marie had a way of breaking through and making you like her. When Cain found her all broken like she was, I begged her to let me be the one to take care of Danny. I wanted to skin him slowly, but I never would have guessed he'd invite the Bracato boys to be there." She tilted her dark head back and blinked furiously to clear her eyes. "Did killing him bother you?"

"Why would you ask me that?"

Merrick's hands went up in a gesture of ignorance, then just as quickly dropped back down. "You just seem like something's wrong."

"I had a hard time standing there listening to him go on like that about her. When he bragged about burning her nipples with his cigar, I got so mad I wanted to vomit. Killing him didn't bother me at all. What *did* bother me was that he only got to die once."

"Thanks for telling me." When Katlin started rubbing her neck again, Merrick hesitated. "You want help with that?"

"Thanks, but you don't have to."

"Is it the guns I wear that intimidate you big Casey/Patrick types?"

Katlin laid her hand flat on her chest. "You know the answer to the Casey side of that equation, but the Patrick part doesn't scare easy either."

"Then get up and take your shirt off."

The command sent a shiver through Katlin's long frame, making her laugh. If she was honest, Merrick *did* scare her a little.

"Need help with the buttons?"

"I think I can manage." Taking her time, Katlin presented her back, not really caring to see Merrick's reaction since she couldn't lie to herself. It never got her anywhere, and she knew Merrick was obviously infatuated with Cain. This was just a massage, because when it came to her heart, Katlin wasn't willing to be a substitute for anyone who couldn't give her everything.

When Katlin first removed her shirt a little past her shoulders, Merrick thought Cain was disrobing before her. The cousins had the same strong neck and musculature along their upper back, but on Katlin's back, dipping down her shoulders and wrapping around her biceps, was a dark blue intricate design of a warrior whorl. The tattoo, composed of small lines, looked like an old armor design.

As Merrick started at the middle of the design and worked outward, Katlin shivered and said, "In ancient Ireland, the warriors painted on their clan's design before they went into battle so they could carry their fighter spirit with them. Every man willing and brave enough to pick up arms against his country's enemies had the right to apply the paint." Merrick ran her fingers along Katlin's upper arms, but she still wouldn't budge. "I've never found that exact story in any book, but my Granny Casey told it to us as kids all the time."

"Your grandmother's very wise, and you've carried on your traditions well." With very little pressure Merrick turned her around but didn't try to look at Katlin's naked chest. "I'm sorry for being such a bitch before. I can see you're taking good care of Cain."

"An apology from the mighty Merrick?"

The question was light, and Merrick didn't try to break the hold Katlin now had on her neck, surprised at herself for being so docile.

"Tell me, what do you see when you look at me?"

"What do you mean?"

"What do I mean?" Katlin pulled Merrick closer and grasped her sweater. "Do you see a copy of what you can't have?"

"No, I just see you," Merrick said.

"Go telling lies like that, darling girl, and you might find yourself someplace you don't want to be."

"Like where?"

"In my bed," Katlin said. "Then where the devil will that get you?"

When Merrick touched Katlin's waist, she felt a scar there. Katlin was tall like Cain and built as solidly, but Merrick noticed subtle differences. Her hair was dark, but not jet-black like Cain's and her children's, and she was a few inches shorter. The deep voice was similar, though, and made Merrick breathe faster.

"Someplace safe, I suppose—someplace I've been seeking." Katlin reeled her in a little more, and Merrick could feel the heat emanating off Katlin's body.

"What have you been looking for, Merrick?"

Merrick stroked higher along Katlin's back and responded when soft lips came up to meet hers. "An ally and an equal." Merrick pulled away, but only enough to form words. "Just how tired are you?"

"I'm fresh enough for whatever you have in mind," Katlin answered readily and stumbled only a little when Merrick pulled her forward by her belt.

"Then let's go." Merrick handed her the shirt she'd just taken off.

"I see you're a tease," Katlin said as she slipped the garment back on.

"Tease?" Merrick walked up to her slowly this time, jerked her belt open, and unzipped her pants. Without losing eye contact with Katlin, she pushed past the Jockeys and down to Katlin's sex, chuckling at the moan and the involuntary hip thrust that came when she pinched her hard clitoris. "I never tease when I want something. Try and remember that." She squeezed harder and Katlin closed her eyes.

"What do you want?" Katlin asked.

"I want to take care of this for you slowly until you beg me to fuck you." With that she pulled her hand free. "But first I want you to help me give Cain a present."

"Now?"

"The quicker we finish our business, the quicker we get back here for more pleasurable pursuits." When she slid the fingers she'd just had in Katlin's pants into her mouth, Katlin finished dressing in record time.

"Let's get going." Katlin strapped on her guns and opened the door for her. "In this condition, I'll kill anyone who slows us down."

"Good to know, darling, because it just might come to that if we're lucky." Merrick grinned, ready to lead Katlin to hell and then back to her warm bed. Tonight would be the beginning of new alliances.

CHAPTER THIRTY-THREE

Cain sat at breakfast drumming her fingers on the table, her plate full but untouched. From the set of her jaw and the even, strong beats of her fingers, Emma knew this was the calm before the storm.

"Did I ask you for this?" She raised her hand from her lap and opened her clenched fist so the others could see what she was holding.

"No," Katlin answered, putting her hand on Merrick's arm and keeping her in place when Cain leaned forward a little and cut loose.

"Then why the fuck did you do it?" All the dishes on the table clattered when she shouted and pounded her fist. Emma righted Cain's coffee cup, stood behind her, and put her hands on Cain's shoulders, trying to calm her.

"We just thought—" Katlin started before Cain lit into her again.

"No one, *especially* me, is paying you to think. I expect you to do what I tell you to, when I tell you to. That's it. If that's not working out for you, then get out of my sight."

"Cain, we meant no harm, we just thought—"

Merrick stopped when Cain's hand went up.

"Whose idea was this?"

Again, she held up her hand as if the two guards hadn't seen what was in it, even though they'd presented it to her when they arrived.

"Mine," Katlin and Merrick answered together.

Emma noticed something that hadn't been there before, something sweet, if not ludicrous. Katlin stood slightly in front of

Merrick as if protecting her from any threat, even if it was Cain. But if anyone in Cain's organization could take care of herself, it was Merrick Runyon. Emma didn't have time for any more speculation, though, because Cain slammed her hand down again. Only this time two matching rings lay in front of her.

"Emma, would you please take Merrick and excuse us." As Cain spoke, her eyes never left Katlin's. Cain smiled faintly when Emma bent and kissed her before she left. She didn't say anything else until the door closed.

"What's this about?" Cain pointed to the rings on the table.

"Michael and Francis Bracato were a liability to you. Now they're not, and no one's the wiser." Katlin kept standing since Cain hadn't invited her to sit down. "They weren't part of the main business we're after, so Merrick and I took care of them for you."

"Without consulting me first. If you don't see this as a problem, then I want you gone today."

Experience kept Katlin's mouth shut because she knew Cain was deadly serious. A wrong comment now would land her on the curb so fast it would take it a minute for her shadow to catch up.

"This isn't exactly what I had in mind when I brought you in. Having more responsibility was something you asked for, remember?"

Katlin took a deep breath, but still didn't say a word.

"Remember?" Cain repeated, with a little more heat.

"I remember, but anything I say here's going to piss you off more than you already are." Trying to appear calmer than she felt, Katlin ran her hand through her hair and kept eye contact with Cain. "If this is too big for you to ignore then I'll clear out, if that's what you want."

Cain glared at the door when someone knocked. "What is this, no one wants to listen to me anymore?"

Cain clearly didn't expect an answer, and Katlin prudently stayed quiet.

"What?"

"I know you didn't want to be disturbed, honey," Emma said, having heard Cain's comments about being disobeyed. "There's an Agent Curtis here to see you. I put him in the solarium to wait. Since it has glass walls, I figured the men outside could keep an eye on him."

"I keeping telling you, you get any smarter and I'll give you my job," Cain whispered into Emma's ear.

"No, thank you. Taking care of you is my job and my first priority. Should I tell him you'll be a little longer?"

"Don't worry about it. I'll see what he wants." Cain left her food forgotten and strode out of the room with only a small nod for Katlin. As Emma passed her, she patted Katlin on the arm and smiled reassuringly.

❖

Anthony sat in a wicker chair and stared out on a yard that resembled a well-maintained park. It pissed him off that criminals like Jarvis and Cain lived so well while people like him worked hard for peanuts. Just the furniture in the room probably cost more than he made in a year.

"Anthony, to what do we owe the pleasure?"

Cain's voice from the doorway broke through his anger-induced haze, and he cut his eyes her way.

"I'd appreciate if you addressed me as Agent Curtis."

Releasing a deep breath slowly while trying to get over her anger, Cain centered herself. The quickest way to end up where she didn't want to be—in trouble with the law—was to enter a meeting angry and out of control. In this case, having Katlin and Merrick hand her Michael's and Francis's rings that morning after having killed the two Bracato brothers the night before had left her in a foul mood. She expected her staff to be obedient.

"And I'd appreciate being left alone, but you're here bothering me, so we don't always get what we want, do we? I have some business this morning, so why don't you tell me why you're here."

"I need you to answer some questions, and I'm not leaving until you do."

Muriel watched from the study, trying to figure out Curtis's game. She'd been in her suite of rooms upstairs when Emma called her and told her to get down to the solarium as soon as possible. From the set of Cain's jaw, she was afraid that the agent might get a response he wouldn't like, so Muriel quickened her pace.

"Do you habitually invade people's homes and threaten them,

Agent Curtis?" Muriel asked as she strode to the chair across from his, acting as if she owned the place. "Perhaps you haven't had the opportunity to speak with Agent Hicks—your superior, I believe," she added, just to put him off a bit more. "After the warehouse fiasco, we've agreed to play nice until everyone's had a chance to recover. Should I get her on the phone?"

"Agent Hicks will give me a raise when I show her what I gathered on your client last night. You didn't think you'd get away with that shit, did you?" he asked, pointing at Cain. He almost laughed out loud when he saw the perpetually cocky Cain Casey visibly pale. "I love it when people screw up, and I have 8x10 glossies of the whole thing."

When, for the first time, Cain noticed the folder lying on the table next to the agent, she almost jumped from her chair and ripped it open to see just how much he'd caught on film.

Muriel squeezed the arms of her wicker chair enough to make the material creak. Across from her she was seeing the same thing Curtis was looking at, a visibly rattled Cain, which was a first. "Cain, why don't you head on up and keep Emma company. I'll handle this."

"No, I want to hear what he has to say." Her voice came out in a raspy whisper, and Cain stopped herself from continuing, not wanting to sound any weaker. "You want to do this here or somewhere where you can gloat for your friends, Anthony?"

"I'm tempted to show Shelby and the others exactly what you're made of, Casey, but here's good for now. If you don't tell me what I want to know, then we'll have to make this a little more official."

Muriel knew that Cain's face, devoid of emotion, hid the fact that a million thoughts were running through her head. Curtis was being cryptic on purpose, and the strategy was working.

"You want me to become your informant?" Cain sounded incredulous.

"You're going to do it and be happy about it."

"I tell you what, Anthony. You show me what's in the folder and we'll see. If not, no deal."

Muriel wanted more than anything to tell Cain to shut the hell up. Daring FBI agents into gambling with your future was not a smart idea. "Cain—"

Cain raised her hand as if she'd just released the dice in this dangerous game of craps.

"What's it going to be, Anthony?" Cain asked him, sounding more and more confident.

"I tried helping you, but now I have to go to Agent Hicks and give her my report." He stood and picked up the folder they were all staring at. Stopping at the door, Anthony glanced back. "You know something, Casey? When I started this job I vowed never to make it personal, and I've done a really good job. This time, though, it's going to be a pleasure watching you go down. You think you're so fucking smart, but you're just like the rest of the scum we deal with—stupid as a sack of dried shit."

Muriel waited until she heard the front door close and they were alone. "How big a problem is this?"

"Cousin, you should know by now that to everything there's a time and place. Now isn't the time or the place for this conversation."

"I can't plan if I don't know what I'm up against."

"I need some time to think, Muriel, so drop it."

Cain's voice rose higher than she would have liked, but she wasn't familiar with the feeling of panic. She'd been careful, or so she thought, but if Anthony had gotten film of what she'd done to Stephano, a jury would probably lock her away for life. He hadn't taken her up on her offer, so now Cain just had to wait and see what Anthony did with his information.

She abruptly stalked out of the room and, outside, jumped into the first car she found with the keys in it. Before anyone had a chance to respond, Cain was out the front gate headed downtown. It almost felt like fear was chasing her down the street.

CHAPTER THIRTY-FOUR

Gino Bracato sat in the chair next to the bed and alternately looked out the window and stared at the still form on the bed, oblivious to the ringing phone and doorbell. His wrinkled clothes smelled of his mistress's favorite perfume, but he didn't care about his appearance. Instead, the unmoving chest of his wife Eris mesmerized him.

He'd intended to ship her off to the first rehab center that would take her, but when he'd gotten home he'd found her already gone. No matter how hard he shook or slapped her, Eris hadn't responded. The large pile of white powder on the nightstand close to where her head had landed explained everything. She had finally found a way to escape him and his family, and he couldn't follow her.

"Mr. Bracato?" the nanny asked. "Please, sir, I need to see you, if I could."

"What is it?" He opened the door just a sliver.

"Your father has called so many times and would like to speak to you. He sounded upset. Would Mrs. Bracato like for me to bring the baby in? She likes spending time with him in the mornings."

"No! My wife's sick and doesn't want to be disturbed. Keep my son away from her, and tell the rest of the staff to stay out."

"Yes, sir. I'm sorry I had to bother you."

As soon as the nanny left, Giovanni yanked the master suite door open and shoved his way in.

"When I fucking call you, I expect you to pick up the phone and talk to me," he screamed. Stopping, he stared at the lump on the bed and sneered. "You know what your problem is? You've lost control of your house, boy. Your wife should know better than to lounge around after nine o'clock. It's time for you to start teaching your wife who's in charge here just like I have at home."

"She's dead," Gino whispered. He buried his face in his hands and tried his best not to cry in front of his father. Despite all their problems, he had loved Eris once and never dreamed their relationship would end like this.

"Fucking shit," Giovanni said. "What happened?"

"Looks like she snorted enough blow to fry her brain. I was out last night and came in to find her like this. What am I going to do, Papa?"

The slap to the side of Gino's head almost knocked him off the chair.

"First, you start sounding like the man I raised and not some weak pussy. All we have to do is get rid of her, then report her missing. They can't find her here, Gino, or you'll go down for this no matter how it happened.

"Go get cleaned up, because there's nothing we can do about this now in broad daylight. We have bigger problems, and I need your help."

"What's wrong?" Gino stood up and walked away from his father, trying to put some distance between them.

"Your brothers are all missing. I've been to all their houses and checked all the places they could be, but no one's seen them. Stephano and Michael pull shit like this all the time, but Francis knows better than to keep me waiting. We're meeting with the Luis family this morning, and he was coming with me." He shook Gino by the shoulders. "When was the last time you saw them?"

Stephano's late-night call for backup rushed back to Gino with such a vengeance, he slumped down on the end of the bed. If something had happened to his brother, his father would never forgive him for putting a woman before his family. "Yesterday afternoon when we were all together," he lied. "I didn't hear from them after that."

"Take a shower and get dressed," Giovanni ordered. "And don't forget to lock the door on the way out. We don't need anyone wandering in here while we're gone. Tonight after we find your brothers and get business squared away, we'll deal with your little problem. At least most of the people who knew your wife knew what a junkie she was. Nobody'll even miss her."

Except me, Gino thought, as he looked back at the woman he'd once loved.

CHAPTER THIRTY-FIVE

Think this is some trick to pull us away from something bigger?" Claire asked.

"I've been wrong so much lately that I'm not even going to guess." Shelby studied the people around Cain and didn't spot a viable threat. Cain sat totally alone near the rail in Café du Monde, resembling any other tourist. "I've only seen Cain like this one other time—the first time she saw Emma after she got back to town."

"After seeing them last night, I'd say that they've solved their problems. You're dying to go over there and talk to her, aren't you?"

"I may want to, but I've broken more than my share of procedures when it comes to Cain Casey. Eventually all that could catch up with me."

Claire shut off the camera they had trained on Cain drinking coffee. "Why don't you take a break?" She pointed to the camera. "We seem to be having technical difficulties."

"Thanks, Claire."

The noise of the French Quarter increased when Shelby opened the door and climbed out of the van that sported a local plumbing company's logo. Noticing Emma approach the café from the direction of downtown, headed for Cain's table, Shelby stopped abruptly after stepping off the curb. Plans forgotten, she calmly returned to their air-conditioned haven, took the headphones from Claire, and waited for the conversation across the street to begin.

"Want to talk about it?"

Cain shook her head and ran her finger around the rim of the generic white mug. A plate full of the powdered beignets the place was famous for sat untouched next to the mug.

"Just felt like a cup of coffee, huh?"

"Something like that." Cain finally picked up the cup again and took a sip. "This place is a tradition for me, and God knows more than one tradition has shaped my life." She cut her eyes briefly to the van across the street and wondered who, in addition to Shelby, was listening in.

"This place is mine alone, not like the club and the bar. I used to come here early some mornings after leaving the pub or after dropping you off to people-watch. Your apartment wasn't far from here." She pointed down the alley across the street. "Trying to figure out what was going on with them helped me sort out what was going on in here." Cain tapped the side of her head.

"I can go," Emma said.

Cain grasped Emma's wrist. "Not yet. Are you here alone?"

"Same as you, so no lectures, okay?"

"Sometimes, lass, no matter how much you think we're alike, we're not. My being out here alone isn't the same."

Emma jerked her arm away, and her upper body slammed into the back of the chair. "I thought we'd come to an understanding."

"What, that I'd give everyone in the world who's pissed at me a free shot at you?"

"No, that you would let me in." Emma put her hands flat on the table. "That you'd treat me like I'm something more than an ornament for your arm for nights like last night."

Cain widened her eyes slightly, and Emma stopped talking.

"I can't talk about something I don't know anything about. I can't lead you into something I don't know a way out of myself. Do you understand me?"

"No."

"Then this is what we call putting your chips down. If you don't understand, then you have to trust me to guide you until you do. Do you trust me that much?"

"Yes," Emma said without hesitation. "I don't want to destroy the trust we've built up since I've been back, but I don't want to be shut out of part of your life like I was before."

Before Cain made any more declarations, she pulled her phone out of her jacket pocket and dialed her uncle's number, getting Lou. "Café Du Monde, and make it fast. Merrick's package seems to have walked out the door without her. After the dressing-room incident I'd have thought she'd have been a little more vigilant."

"You promised," Emma said in a dejected tone. "And I believed you."

Not wanting to draw any attention to them, Cain grasped the seat of Emma's chair and pulled her closer. "I said a lot of things, but so did you." The pain in Emma's eyes was almost enough to shatter her resolve, but Cain kept going. "Now listen to me and believe me when I tell you this isn't the time or the place to talk about this."

"But, Cain—"

Cain took advantage of this opening line. "I'm tired of talking about this, Emma." With another quick tug Cain yanked Emma's chair across the sticky cement, bringing her wife even nearer. The rest of the talk was so low the microphone trained on them couldn't pick up what they said.

Shelby and Claire watched as Emma pushed away and stood up, then almost ran out of the café, dodging a few cars as she crossed the street and started down the alley next to Jackson Square. She made it almost to the end close to St. Louis Cathedral before Cain grasped her bicep firmly and whispered in Emma's ear again, not letting her go when she tried to break free.

"Our job is to observe, that's all," Claire warned when Shelby put her hand on the door.

"Cain's a lot bigger than she is, and it looks like Emma doesn't want to be part of this talk anymore." The sound of a slap echoed in the van, and a stunned Cain stood on the flagstone looking like her next victim would be Emma.

They didn't exchange any more words until a black sedan pulled to the intersection and Lou climbed out from the backseat. With one last glare for Cain, Emma started toward Lou and the car. She never looked back once she started walking, but neither did Cain when she set off in the opposite direction.

"Joe, you got her in sight?" Claire asked as she started the van.

"Our target's entering the cathedral. Maybe she's going to confess her sins and decide to lead a life on the straight and narrow?" Joe and Lionel watched from a park bench in Jackson Square, confident that the black iron fence and shrubbery would keep Cain from seeing them. "Stay put for now, and I'll let you know where we're headed next. Lionel and I are going inside."

"Just remember that she knows you." Shelby's voice popped into the conversation.

"Don't worry. We look like tourists today. She'll never spot us." He walked across the grassy area around St. Louis Cathedral that was usually full of artists, street performers, and tourists.

To their surprise, Cain walked toward for one of the confessionals at the rear of the church. They knew she was Catholic; they just assumed she wasn't a practicing Catholic. The light on the side Cain had entered lit up, signaling that she was now on her knees waiting for the priest.

"Wouldn't you love to be able to listen in on that conversation?" Lionel asked.

"It wouldn't be admissible in court, but for pure entertainment value, yeah, I would. Thing is, though, I'm not sure what to make of this." Joe waved his hand around the vestibule. "We've been following her for so long, I thought I knew everything there is to know about her. But today something's off, and I can't pin it down. Being out alone, rare but not strange." Joe held up a finger as if counting off a list. "The fight and this, though, way off the radar as far as previous behavior goes."

A nun close to them put her finger to her lips and smiled, softening the reprimand.

Inside the confessional a wooden door slid back, and a million memories flooded Cain's mind as she looked at the man on the other side of the grate. Father Andrew Goodman had graduated from high school with Cain's father, and despite the different paths the men had chosen, Andrew had remained a good friend.

For years he'd joked that Dalton needed a friend with such high connections to keep him out of trouble. After burying Dalton, his wife, and two of their children, Andrew had stopped joking and started praying for Cain and her family.

"Are there blessings left for the wicked, Father?"

A small laugh escaped Andrew's lips as he leaned farther in. "God doesn't see us as wicked, my child. He loves you no matter how bad you think you've been." He put his hand up to the barrier between them. "It's good to see I still have some influence over you. Thanks for taking me up on my invitation."

"I thought I'd come in from the storm for a little while, and you're always a good harbor." Cain pressed her hand to his and felt the heat through the decorative wooden grate.

"It's raining outside?"

"More like invaders at my gates ready to storm the manor."

"You're early and I still have confessions to hear, so will you do me a favor? One that'll make your mother happy."

"Sure." Cain was amused.

"Go out there and say five Hail Marys and five Our Fathers while you wait for me. If you can spare the time, I'd like to have morning tea with you."

"I'll try anything to make my mother smile down on me from heaven," Cain joked. "Of course if you hear a sudden boom in the next few minutes, you know I got struck by lightning."

The prayers came with no effort since Cain's mother had repeated them from the time her children were learning to talk so they would have the starting point to talk to God that every good Catholic had. Cain didn't think of them very often now, but she wasn't completely faithless. A part of her wanted to believe in a heaven and a hell, even if that's where she would one day find herself—as long as those who'd hurt her loved ones suffered along with her.

Joe and Lionel were shocked when they saw Cain genuflecting before the altar. She scooted into a pew, pulled the kneeler down, and folded her hands together in prayer once she was on her knees. From their position on the other side of the church, they could see that her lips were moving in obvious prayer. Her behavior was certainly new and interesting.

CHAPTER THIRTY-SIX

Watching a man pull a cart full of art and finding the entire situation absurd, Emma didn't bother to notice her surroundings. *Why should I, since I have someone to do that for me?* She glanced behind her at the loyal Lou. The surveillance van Cain had pointed out earlier was still there, so she kept her comments to a minimum.

Juan Luis and three of his men rushed from the coffee shop on the corner and surrounded Lou before he could pull his weapon.

"Good morning, Emma," Juan said.

Judging by his dark suit with a white shirt and red tie, she would've pegged him as a bank president or something just as mundane if she hadn't known he sold drugs.

"Perhaps you'd like to join me for a cup of coffee or breakfast?"

"I thought I made it clear last night I don't want anything to do with you, and my name is Mrs. Casey. Is it really that hard to remember, or do we have a language problem?"

"Let me explain something that I imagine your servant here understands. I asked merely to be nice, but answering no isn't an option. As for 'Mrs. Casey,' we both know that title doesn't exist, so I'll call you whatever I like."

From the expression on Lou's face, Emma was sure he wanted to kill her for antagonizing Juan, but she kept up the sarcasm. "Do women in your country find this attitude appealing, Mr. Luis?"

"Any woman in my country would die to be in your position now. You're the first woman who touches a place in me that makes me want to conquer something or someone to prove myself to you." With the calm movements of a man used to being in control, Juan folded his hands in front of him and gave her his best smile. "How could you possibly say no to that?"

With the movements of a woman who'd reached her breaking point, Emma started laughing, aware from one of her college courses that a proud Hispanic man wouldn't take too kindly to a woman deriding him when he was trying to prove just how powerful and charming he was.

"How could I possibly say no to that?" She repeated the question between gasps of air. "Easy. I'm not one of the many women from your country who wants to be in that position. Just in case I wasn't crystal clear last night, I'm with Cain. I'm with her not only because I love her and we have children together, but also because I'm gay. If I hadn't picked Cain years ago, I'd have some other woman in my bed, so thank you for the invitation and the dramatic way you chose to deliver it, but no thanks."

"You'll find that what you've been missing is the right—"

"Please don't finish that sentence with 'the right man.'" Emma quit laughing as her anger returned, and she lowered the tone of her voice. "Lou, let's go. Even though Mr. Luis isn't from the United States, I'm sure he knows the consequences of shooting someone on a busy intersection. New Orleans's finest would love such an open-and-shut case with so many witnesses around."

"Not so fast," Juan ordered. He held his hand up as if trying to regain control of the situation, but the gesture didn't stop Lou from moving. "I said stop."

With a small wave, Lou greeted the newest person to join in on the fun.

Emma, expecting Cain, was surprised when she saw Shelby waving back.

"Mrs. Casey, could I have a word with you?" The three men with Juan hid their guns behind their backs when Shelby arrived. "You too, Lou."

"Emma is busy at the moment, so get lost," Juan said, returning his attention to Emma.

"Too busy to talk to an FBI agent?" Shelby pulled out her

identification and thrust it in Juan's face. "We really frown on uncooperative individuals."

"What can I do for you, Agent Phillips?" Emma asked, thinking that the morning had truly spun off into the bizarre.

"Just a few minutes of your time. Unless you have unfinished business you'd like to wrap up."

Emma snorted and motioned back to the Café du Monde across the street. "Why the hell not."

"We aren't finished, Emma," Juan warned as she started to leave.

"Listen to me. There's nothing to finish since nothing ever started. I tried to caution you last night, but I'll have to tell Cain about your idiotic behavior. Perhaps if she speaks to you, you'll believe I'm not interested."

"I'm not afraid of the infamous Cain, so don't make idle threats."

"You should be, butthead," Lou added. "When she has something to say to a woman, she doesn't need three guys to back her up. I'll admit, you caught me unawares today. But that won't happen again, so I suggest you bring more guys to back up your big *cojones* act."

Luis made a fist and spoke to Lou in a controlled tone. "This isn't over. Tell your boss that."

"I'm sure Mrs. Casey will tell her everything she needs to know. Now why don't you take your thugs and slither back to whatever jungle you come from, spunky." Lou offered his arm to Emma and walked her back across the street.

Shelby followed but crossed walking backward, not taking her eyes off the men standing ramrod straight in the alley.

"As you Americans say, this isn't over by a long shot," Juan whispered.

❖

"Claire." Joe spoke softly into the mike hidden in the mouthpiece of his cell phone.

"Yes?" Claire sat in the van alone, watching Shelby take a seat across from the most fashionable woman she'd seen in ages. Studying Emma Casey, she understood what kept Cain so interested. Emma didn't just have looks; the confrontation with Luis confirmed that.

"Anything interesting happening outside?"

"That would be putting it mildly. I'd explain, but I'm busy right now. What can I do for you?" She adjusted the focus on the small telescope bolted to the floor at one of the widows, bringing the players at the table into better view.

"Just checking in. Cain's praying, of all things, so we're stuck in limbo here until she's done." He laughed before adding, "Considering how short her confession was, we may be wasting our time chasing around after her."

"Or maybe she had a hotline set up at home to save time?" Claire ventured, waiting for the waiter to finish so Shelby could begin her talk. "Sorry, Joe, gotta go."

"Problems?" Shelby asked, and pointed to the spot where Juan and his men had encountered Emma and Lou. Lou was sitting at the next table with his arms crossed over his chest.

"Nothing we can't handle," Emma answered, meaning herself and Lou. "Since I've become Miss Popularity, maybe I just should stay home more. Can't go anywhere these days without attracting an unwelcome crowd."

"Does that include me?"

Emma drummed her fingers on the Formica-topped table much like Cain had done that morning and expelled a long breath. "Look, I appreciate you sitting with me that night Cain got shot. Perhaps I never took the time to say that, but we're not friends. We're not friends now, and I don't plan to include you in my appointment book for shopping and lunch dates so, yes, that includes you."

"I just worry about you."

"Ha!" The short laugh came out so loud that several people stopped what they were doing and stared. "Is that sort of like the IRS showing up at your house just to see if you're financially secure and help if you're not?" Emma moved her hand so the nice young woman who was waiting on them could put the mugs down. "We've already entertained one of your coworkers today, so forgive me if I come off a little short. I was an idiot to think you'd ever really leave us alone."

"What do you mean you entertained one of us this morning?"

"That's it." Emma pushed the mug to the middle of the table and stood up. "Lou, could you call for the car. We're leaving. I've had enough bullshit for one day."

"Wait," Shelby tried. She stood up, but she instinctively refrained from touching Emma. "I really don't know what you're talking about."

"Then call the office and get an update. I'd think, as FBI, you'd be better informed than this." She strode out and started up the street from where she'd come earlier that morning, leaving Shelby confused.

"Claire," she whispered.

"I'm on it. None of our team members should have contacted the Caseys this morning. I personally checked with Agent Hicks before we headed out. You'd think she would know, since she *is* in charge." She spoke to Shelby as she held up her phone to the other ear, waiting to be put through to operations.

Shelby returned to the van. "There's one thing I know for sure," she said as she closed the door behind her.

Claire held up a finger and finished her call. "What's that?"

"The farm girl's here to stay, and she's grown a long set of claws and fangs since she left the city four years ago. I thought she was the sweet and innocent one."

"Silly rabbit," Claire joked. She switched off all the equipment, since they were in a wait pattern. "No one's scheduled to visit the Casey house today, but the small team assigned to the location saw Curtis go in and come out about fifteen minutes later. Since he's a fellow agent, they didn't call it in."

"I wonder—"

"What he was doing there?" Claire finished. "Whatever it was set off this shitstorm we're riding out now."

"What could he have told them to make both Cain and Emma venture out with so little protection?"

Shelby voiced the question out loud, but Claire didn't think it was directed at her. She hadn't been with the team long enough to know the dynamic among the agents. So far she surmised that Shelby, Joe, and Lionel worked as a cohesive team, but Anthony had his own agenda and played it out with no thought of keeping the others informed. He was following the path of the infamous Barney Kyle.

"Do we break up and follow Emma?"

Shelby closed her eyes for a long moment and shook her head. "No, we follow the plan and wait for the guys to report in."

"Joe did report in while you were across the street. They're hanging out by the gift shop until Cain finishes her prayers."

"She's praying?" Shelby's eyes popped open. "God help us all."

Claire laughed, then stopped when she saw that Shelby was serious. For once in her life she wanted to slap herself for giving up a nice comfortable desk job.

Chapter Thirty-seven

R eady?" Andrew asked when Cain finished her prayers.
Both agents saw the problem facing them when Cain and the priest stood up and walked toward the altar and the door to the left of the ornate area. No way could they follow without blowing their cover.

Andy bowed his head and said the appropriate prayers before removing his vestments, kissing some of the items before storing them in their proper place. When he was done, he wore the black shirt with the stiff white collar and the dark pants Cain remembered from her childhood.

"It must be nice to have such an orderly and predictable job."

Andy laughed. "God manages to throw in a few wrenches for even us of the cloth to deal with, child, so don't be thinking I have it too easy." They headed to the rectory for the tea he'd offered. "Though I don't have the luxury of sex to take the edge off when things get too out of control, like you do."

Cain felt a weight lift from her shoulders. She was glad she'd accepted Andy's invitation to visit, which he'd offered by phone late the night before. He might be a priest, but every so often he reminded you that under the collar still beat the heart of a man.

"True, Father Andy. Sometimes I like to compare people who don't like women to vegetarians."

"Interesting analogy, and I do like the way your mind works, so lay it on me." He opened the door and waved her in.

"If God had meant for people to be vegetarians, a good steak wouldn't taste so divine. Following that line of thinking, neither would a woman."

"You owe me another set of prayers for that one." He shook a finger at her before speaking into the intercom. "Megan, please bring in some tea for two when you have a chance."

The leather chair next to Cain's, set in the alcove of a large bay window, let out a woof of air as Andy fell into it. Outside, the gardens were being tilled for their spring plantings.

"You know, the day they made me bishop of this area, I sat in this room with your father and enjoyed quite a few drinks from a rather good bottle of whiskey he'd brought. In spite of all that pomp and circumstance, I remember our conversation more vividly than anything else." He sighed as if lost in thought. "Strange where we both ended up—those skinny little boys who used to throw rocks at passing trains way back when."

"Trying to corrupt you even back then, huh?"

"Heavens, no. More like reminding me about life and taking time to live it."

"Why did you like my father so much, Father Andy? You had to know some of what he stood for, all of it going against the church's teaching."

Megan's entrance with their tea gave Andrew time to think of an appropriate response. He knew how important Dalton had been in Cain's life and how much she still missed the man who'd molded her. He looked Cain in the eye and waited to hear the click of the door before he answered.

"If you ever tell this to anyone, I'll have to deny it," he began. "The church sometimes misses the old proverbial boat on a lot of things. I loved your father, and he was one of my best friends until his death because he was an honorable man who loved his family and those loyal to him. How can that be wrong, no matter what he did for a living?"

"You won't get me to disagree, and I've tried my best to follow in his path, but I don't think I'm walking it as well as he did."

Andrew realized that from Cain's slumped shoulders that the admission had cost her dearly. Cain's father had brought her up to ignore and defeat weakness, no matter what her action cost in terms of her soul.

"The wolves are baying at my door, and I don't know how to keep them out."

Andrew recalled Dalton's final visit. He'd taken time to visit Andrew the day before Bracato's henchmen had gunned him down. As if a premonition had sent him to seek out his old friend, he'd come to ask a favor.

❖

Sixteen Years Earlier

"Andy, is it true that confession is good for the soul?"

"And for the spirit, but only if you mean it." Andrew often had theological discussions with Dalton's wife Therese, but seldom with Dalton. "What troubles you, my son?"

"Wiseass," Dalton shot back. "I want you to hear my confession and say a prayer for my family."

"Could you clear the rest of my afternoon?" Andrew asked the secretary on the other end of the intercom. "I'm not making fun of you, Dalton, but if you're here asking me that, you must think it's important."

He had spent a couple of hours after that trying to keep a neutral expression on his face as Dalton spoke. Several times, Andrew longed for the barriers of the confessional so his look of surprise wouldn't halt the words streaming from his friend's mouth.

When Dalton finished, Andrew stood, placed his hand on his friend's head, and prayed for his soul with all the fervor in his heart. "Now that we're done with that, what's the favor you need?"

"In case something happens to me, I want you to promise you'll offer the same absolution to Derby Cain and Billy if they ever come to you. My life is so unpredictable at times, I'd feel comfortable moving on if I know they can rely on you. Your friendship has been a gift for me all these years, and I wanted to thank you."

"It would be my honor, Dalton. You didn't even have to ask."

In a voice tainted with weariness, Dalton said, "I just feel better knowing for sure. If I leave Derby all alone, I want her to have somewhere to go."

❖

Dalton had died the next day, and if the church teachings were true, he'd gone with a clean slate. Therese and Billy had followed not long after, then Marie. Andrew pondered how much self-reliance Derby Cain must possess to bear that pain every day.

"If my life of watching other people live their lives and giving advice on how to do it better has taught me anything, it's this," Andy said, wanting more than anything not to let Dalton down. "Those who want to beat you down can't succeed unless you give them a lot of help. God grants us free will to live life as we choose, Derby. You've taken a wife, you're raising a fine son, and you've done everything possible to protect them both from harm."

"But look at how I failed Marie and my mother."

He took her hand. "No, you had nothing to do with that. What happened was God's will, and nothing, no matter how hard you tried, could have prevented it from coming to pass."

"God's will? That's the best you got?"

"Just like your father, I swear," Andrew said, shaking his head. "You simply can't control everything in your life. Things happen, and you have to accept them and try to find a way to keep going forward." He held up his hand to keep her from interrupting. "I know it's easy to say, but sometimes simple is exactly what's needed. Would it be fair to Emma and Hayden if you just accepted defeat?"

"What kind of question is that?" A little of Cain's fire seeped into her answer.

"One that begs an answer."

"I'd never give up and abandon my family. You know that. If you don't, you didn't know my father and what he taught me at all."

"I knew your father better than most, and how he raised you and all he taught you." He squeezed her hand before letting it go and leaning back. "Why are you here, besides the fact that I asked you?"

"To be honest, I don't really know. It's a little about respect, a little about being summoned, and a little about finding answers to the million questions in my head. I certainly enjoy having someone safe to talk to and not have what I say come back to bite me on the witness stand."

"Then you've found the one reason your father came often. The church is for everyone, Derby, even those not in the pews every Sunday. I can give you absolution for your sins."

"Even if I have every intention of sinning again?"

Andrew laughed again, feeling like he was spending time with his childhood friend. "Even then. The other thing I can offer," he continued on a more serious note, "is a little wisdom. No one can be strong all of the time, no matter how broad their shoulders. When your load gets too heavy, let the woman you've chosen help you."

"I thought the church frowned on the fact that I love a woman."

Andrew exhaled a long sigh. "Someday all believers will see love for the beauty that it is, no matter where it's found. That day hasn't come yet, but some of us are a little ahead of the times, no matter how many years we carry around with us."

"And the wolves at my door?"

"Neither the church nor I has an answer for them." The whirl of a leaf blower came through the window, and Andrew waved to the young man operating it. "However, I do know who does have an answer to that question."

"Father Andy, if you tell me to pray on it and it'll come to me, I may have to smack you one."

The laugh lines around her eyes were a sign that her smile was genuine and that she was teasing.

"I see some smiting in your future, if you don't behave," Andrew shot back. "I was going to say that the one person who could answer that was your father. After all, he was a man of honor, but also a man with more than his share of enemies. So he had a philosophy about what the two of you liked to call wolves."

Cain leaned forward and put her hands on her knees. "How much easier would my life be if he'd lived?"

The question didn't seem directed at him, so Andrew stayed quiet.

"There was still so much he didn't tell me before he left."

"Knowing Dalton the way I did, I can tell you he didn't choose to leave. He got his money's worth out of each day God gave him, and if he could have, he would've bargained with the devil himself to stay for a while longer and watch you shine."

The easy silence came once more, broken when Andrew said, "Hell, I miss him so much I would've made the bargain myself."

"I'm sorry, Father. I didn't mean to come here and upset you with old memories."

"Don't worry about that. I'm an old man who gets more sentimental every day." He slapped his hands together. "So on to the answer to your question. Dalton Casey believed that man had dominion over the animals."

"Is this a riddle?"

Andrew shook his head. "If man has dominion over all the animals, then you can either tame the wolves causing you trouble or give them a new scent to follow. What's most important here is not to show fear for any reason. Accept the things you can't control, Derby, and plan around them. But you *can* control some things, so start thinking about how to keep yourself and those around you safe. It wouldn't hurt to keep them out of jail too."

As Cain smiled and sat quietly, she brushed back some mussed hair, an old habit that made Andrew see her incredible resemblance to Dalton. "I can see why my father loved you, but why did my mother?"

"Not everyone can be shown the way by taking the same road, child. I listened to your father and didn't judge, because that's not my job. To Therese, I was Bishop Goodman first, a man of faith who helped her find peace by praying for her family. It took me an age, it did, but she finally also accepted me as Andy, the guy who shared a few whiskeys with her husband on Saturday afternoons.

"But your father liked coming here for another reason, especially toward the end of his life."

"Another riddle?"

"Just an observation, but perhaps useful, and the real reason I asked you here today." With his fingers steepled on his chest, Andrew stopped talking. "I don't often call my parishioners so late in the evening, bothering them while they're with their families."

"Well?"

"He was right about you—a bit impatient." The reprimand was a bit sterner this time, and it made Cain's jaw click shut. "Tell me, have you ever heard the expression 'blessed are the meek, for they shall inherit the earth'?"

"It's part of scripture, if I remember my religion classes in school."

"Good. Do you think that God would bless those who help unfortunate children?"

That Andy took the long road to get to every point didn't escape Cain, so she put her empty cup down and relaxed into the comfortable chair. If anything, their visit was helping her forget Anthony's intrusion and its ramifications. "If life was fair, my answer would be yes, but it seldom is, so my answer is maybe."

"Excellent. I see your brain is still capable of firing on all cylinders. In this case, the answer you're looking for lies with you."

He held his finger up and she stayed silent.

"Your father took an interest in our youth-development programs, sponsoring certain things so the church's outreach programs would touch many people's lives. He would sit in here with Anya and talk about them for hours."

Cain laughed, but played along. "And Anya is?"

"The director of the youth sports programs. Would you like to meet her?"

She threw her hands up and laughed again. "Sure, I've got all day."

After a short phone call, an athletic-looking woman with auburn hair and dark skin stepped in, introduced herself, and offered Cain her hand. The three talked about Anya's job and how successful her programs were in the city's most poverty- and crime-ridden neighborhoods.

Wasting time carrying on such a conversation seemed surreal to Cain, but Anya sounded so enthusiastic about her causes that Cain listened with genuine interest.

"It was nice meeting you, Ms. Casey," Anya said as she stood up, holding an envelope Cain hadn't noticed before. "Thank you for listening to me, and just remember, every little bit helps. I also wanted to tell you how fond I was of your father. Mr. Casey did a lot of good, and we still miss him." She dropped the envelope into Cain's lap and started to leave. "Would you mind throwing that away for me? I found it outside and don't need it."

The innocuous white envelope felt heavy, and out of curiosity Cain opened the flap. She couldn't control her brief look of shock but quickly slid the cool veneer back into place. "Ms. Sterling?"

The woman stopped, her hand already on the doorknob. "Yes?"

"The new volleyball program you wanted to start, how much do you need?"

"We could do the whole thing for twenty-five thousand."

"You'll have a check today." Cain tucked the envelope into the inside breast pocket of her jacket. "And if you ever need anything else thrown away, give me a call."

"You don't have any questions?" Anya asked.

Cain turned to Andy as she answered. "I have faith enough to know when to consider something as good fortune for helping those less fortunate."

"God bless you, then," and with that, she was gone.

"Does the church realize aiding known criminals is part of your daily job?" Cain waited until the door was closed before posing the question to Andy.

The bishop put his hand on his chest, his eyes wide. "You're a criminal?"

"Now who's the wiseass?"

"Guilty as charged," Andy joked. "Anya's a wonderful woman who's done a lot of good. Her partner works in the FBI forensics lab here in town and in that position sees some rather interesting things."

"I'll just bet."

"Last night when an agent came to her partner and asked for something without following protocol, it piqued her interest, and she said she felt like she was seeing a ghost from the past. She remembered Anya speaking of Dalton often, and someone in the pictures looked an awful lot like him. Anya called me last night, concerned, and I don't need to tell you what a horrible position you'd put her partner in if you let anyone know about this conversation."

"You have my word, Father Andy."

"I don't know what Anya wants thrown away. I just know she needed a donation to start something that'll bring happiness to kids no one wants to think about. If you decide to make that dream of hers a reality, it's certainly up to you. That's why I called you to come today. One thing about her, though, bears mentioning. A fledgling program to do outreach in the housing developments, funded by your father, saved Anya's mother, who was walking the streets selling her body and using the profits to feed a habit that spiraled out of control."

Cain nodded. "I guess to her it didn't matter that it was bootlegger money."

"It didn't matter to anyone who benefited from Dalton's generosity, but he learned an important lesson from the act. Her fortune came back to bless him more than once, but don't think she'll always be there to help. When Anya sees an injustice she can do something about, she acts. Lucky for all of us that she's found someone to share her life who feels the same way. To her it's just that simple. Do you understand? What happened today may never happen again, so don't help her if that's what you think you'll be getting in the bargain."

"Perfectly, and your call couldn't have come on a better day."

"Just remember her donation and take care of yourself. I told your father I'd look out for you, and you don't want to make an old priest a liar. It's sacrilegious."

"Thanks again, Father Andy." Cain stood and prepared to leave, hatching a plan.

"Want to go out the back?" Andy pointed to a door near the bay window. "I can have my car take you home."

She shook her head and stepped closer to him. "My father always said you have to be seen to play the game. To do that I have to go out the front door. 'Cause you know what?"

"What?"

"I'm ready to play." She wanted to see just how good her opponents really were.

CHAPTER THIRTY-EIGHT

Cain strode confidently up the main aisle, with only a quick glance to her right where the gift shop was located, before stepping out into the cool early afternoon. A car was parked across the street in front of the community theater, just as Cain had requested in a short call from Andy's office. Since Shelby and Claire were on the opposite side of the square, Cain didn't expect a tail, at least not from them.

Joe and Lionel made it out in time to see her jump into the back and close the door. Now that no one would see him, Joe pulled out his phone and called for backup. He described the car and its general direction, then called the surveillance van on the radio to join in on the conversation Lionel was already having with them. Joe knew that if they'd had the advantage, Cain had swiftly taken it back.

The car stopped at Vincent Carlotti's offices so Cain could take care of some business before heading to her home, since she was ready to finish what she'd started with Giovanni and his sons. When they got to the house, Cain sat back and studied it.

It looked exactly like it did the last time she'd walked out the front door to head for the warehouse where Kyle had been waiting to kill her. Not a single paint chip was out of place, but Gino's men hadn't come from the front. Like his father, he'd taken the coward's way and approached from the back, and that was where the real savagery lay.

Cain had to take a few breaths before she could open the car door, though she knew Emma had tried to prepare her when she'd explained the damage. Now it was time to see for herself what had happened while she was in the hospital, and why Giovanni Bracato's family would never come out of this intact.

Voices were filtering from different parts of the house, but Cain zeroed in on the one that belonged to the person she wanted to see. Emma was in Cain's office sitting in the big leather chair full of gunshot holes, signing a contract with the moving company that was transporting the furniture to storage while the house was repaired.

"Just make sure everything that's not already broken gets wrapped and packed really well, especially the things in my son's room upstairs."

The foreman was examining every square inch of the room while he listened. "We'll be careful, ma'am. Can I ask what happened in here?"

"My wife hired a group of killers to shoot the place up so she'd have an excuse to remodel," Cain answered from the doorway.

Emma slid the papers across the desk. "Funny guy."

"But you love me anyway. Imagine that."

"Yes, imagine that."

The look between them was smoldering, and the man with the contract in his hand stood there staring.

"Do you have something else for me to sign?" Emma's eyes never left Cain's, but her question did snap the worker out of his trance.

"No, ma'am, I'm sorry." He crumpled the papers in his hands a bit as he stumbled toward the door.

"Mrs. Casey, I was wondering if I could have a few minutes of your time?" Cain bent a little at the waist and held her hand out. "That is, if you're free and could perhaps show me a room in the house that isn't full of holes."

They were on the first few steps heading upstairs when both Lou and Merrick started to follow them.

"Don't even think about it," Emma warned. "As a matter of fact, I want you both to stand here and shoot anyone who tries to climb these after us."

Cain laughed softly as she followed Emma to what had been their bedroom. The space looked no different than the last time she had stepped out for the ill-fated meeting with Kyle. A shirt lay thrown over a chair near the closet and a half-full glass of water sat on the nightstand, but what caught Cain's attention was the way Emma was staring at the picture still sitting near the phone.

❖

Fourteen Years Earlier—Vincent Carlotti's Restaurant

"Tell me something," Emma leaned over and whispered in Cain's ear.

Emma was afraid the butter knife in Cain's hand was going to bend from the pressure she was putting on it. The black dress and heels Emma was wearing had obviously put Cain on high alert from the time she'd picked her up.

"What?"

Emma laughed at the way Cain's voice cracked on the simple word.

"You're playing with fire, lass, and you're about to get burned."

Emma always dismissed the idle threats, knowing Cain was, above all things, noble. "I've been playing with fire for months now, so I'm pretty good at it," she said. "But enough about that. I believe I asked you to tell me something."

They were seated in a booth at the back of one of Vinny's places having dinner, so no one even glanced at the table full of tough-looking characters sitting close to them. The tablecloth gave Emma enough privacy to put her hand on Cain's thigh and scrape the expensive material of the slacks with her nails.

"First tell me, Ms. Verde, do the residents of Haywood, Wisconsin, know what an incredible tease you are?" Cain captured her hand and kissed her palm.

"I'm not teasing, honey." Pulling her hand free, Emma placed it on Cain's chest and ran it up until it was resting behind her neck.

With only a very slight tug, Cain's head came forward and her lips pressed to Emma's. The sound and feel of a flashbulb going off separated them, and Emma almost felt sorry for the poor guy with the camera surrounded by Cain's pit bulls. She would have felt more sympathy for the man if he hadn't just interrupted the best kiss of her life.

"Guys, I don't think he's going to sell the thing to the feds. Let him go," Cain ordered. She handed over a hundred dollar bill and asked for a copy of the picture.

❖

That photograph had sat in Emma's apartment until the day they'd moved in together. Emma could still feel Cain gently holding the side of her face as she returned the kiss. Cain's tenderness had made her feel incredibly adored, and she'd missed seeing this reminder of it during the years she'd been away.

"You never did get around to asking me a question that night." The hands she'd been thinking about rested on her shoulders, and she could feel the solidness of Cain's body as Cain pulled her closer.

While she'd been studying the photo, Cain had removed her jacket and thrown it on the bed. "Do you remember what you wanted to know?"

Her breathing hitched when the hand at her neck slid down and Cain cupped her left breast. "I was going to ask if you liked my dress, since you never said anything when you got there."

"I see." Cain trailed her hand down to Emma's stomach, then back up to her other breast. "How thoughtless of me not to tell you how beautiful you looked." A very slight pinch to a very alert nipple made Emma lean farther back into her embrace. "In reality, though, love, you always look beautiful, but I never want to be thoughtless and not tell you so."

"You make me feel beautiful." The picture came into Emma's focus again, and she smiled as the roving hand made its presence known again. "You always have."

"You'll always be beautiful to me." Cain stopped teasing and just held her. "Can I tell you anything now?"

"Just a few things, but they'll be painless."

The cheek Emma had slapped was still slightly red, and she laid her palm on it in a comforting gesture. "I'm sorry. I didn't mean to hit you so hard."

"Don't worry about it."

They gazed at each other a moment longer before Cain walked them to the bed, knelt between Emma's legs, and started whispering in her ear. With the radio Cain had switched on before that, even the most sophisticated listening devices couldn't have deciphered what she was saying. "Never apologize for doing something I asked you to do. Our little ruse this morning flushed out the watchers quite nicely, but I really need you to be more careful about leaving the house alone. Agent Daniels and whoever she was with were easy to spot, but where there's one fed, there's always more. They're like cockroaches that way, and the other ones were in the square."

"Still, I shouldn't have hit you so hard."

"Put that aside for now, because I have more important things to talk to you about."

They stayed in that position for twenty minutes, Emma never breaking the silence, only nodding every so often when Cain asked if she understood something.

When Cain finished, Emma examined the contents of the envelope Anya had given Cain, then stood and dropped all of it into the fireplace. She burned its secrets until nothing was left but ashes.

"How would you like to take a ride downtown?" Cain asked her as she stood at the floor- to-ceiling window and pulled the heavy drapes aside. The van parked across the street looked empty, but it was hard to tell with the tinted windows.

"Are you sure you want to do that? Agent Curtis seemed so sure of himself."

Someone took a series of photos as Cain laughed at what Emma had said. The moving company Emma had hired had acquired a slew of new employees that morning who'd left more than they'd carted out. The fruits of their labors while taking inventory were helping the guys stuck in the van outside looking in. When the music had come on and the two women had lapsed into silence, the men assigned to the surveillance chuckled, figuring Cain and Emma were busy making up for the earlier fight.

"And just how do you know that?" The curtain fell back into place as Cain stepped closer to Emma. "Not working the other side already, are you?"

"Get real." Emma picked up the frame on the nightstand and

handed it to Cain, then looked on as Cain removed their photo and pointed to the inside corner. The thought of someone listening in on their most intimate moments infuriated her.

"By the way, after you left this morning Muriel and I had a talk. She really wants you to call her once you decide on anything."

"Why take Muriel when I can take you?" Cain put her arm around Emma.

"True. I'll do my best to protect you, honey, but I really want you to call her. On the way to pick her up I can tell you about the visitor I had this morning."

"And here you've just gotten back to town, lass. You're such a popular girl."

"You have no idea." Emma straightened her clothes and started for the door. "You should keep a close eye, Cain. The competition is getting fierce."

Emma looked over her shoulder and winked, knowing that nothing in the world could compete with what she found in Cain's eyes.

CHAPTER THIRTY-NINE

D id anyone find them yet?" Shelby asked the dispatcher on the way back to the office.

"The group you lost this morning outside the cathedral just walked in and asked to speak to Agent Hicks," the man answered with a laugh.

"Cain Casey is in the building?"

"Along with Emma and Muriel Casey. That's what I'm telling you."

More than one agent gathered around the monitor with Annabel Hicks and stared in amazement at the feed from the waiting room. Cain sat in one of the beige plastic chairs with her legs casually crossed, like she had just checked in for a massage appointment. Next to her, Emma ran her index finger along Cain's hand, which lay open in her lap. Muriel was reading a file and ignoring the camera in the corner of the room. All of the watchers noticed one thing—the Caseys acted like they visited the enemy camp every day.

A young agent wearing a conservative gray suit walked into the area and verified, "Ms. Casey?"

"Yes?" Cain and Muriel answered together, looking at each other as if they were going to enjoy the upcoming meeting.

"My apologies. I meant Cain Casey."

"What can I do for you?" Cain didn't stand up, and she didn't pull her hand away from Emma's.

"If you'd come with me." The agent pointed to the hallway behind her. "Agent Hicks will be with you as soon as possible. Your friends can wait for you here."

"Cain—" Emma began, stopping when Cain squeezed her fingers.

Cain stared at the camera, ignoring the young agent who obviously still expected her to stand and do as she was asked. "Agent Hicks? I came here today voluntarily. If you don't want to talk to me, fine, but I don't have time to play games. The thirty minutes I've been sitting here is the extent of psychological bullshit I'm willing to put up with."

After the tough talk, Cain got to her feet and offered Emma a hand up, and to the consternation of the observers, all three Caseys headed toward the exit. Before Cain touched the doorknob, Annabel Hicks took the agent's place.

"Ms. Casey, I'd like it if we talked before you left."

Cain knew it was as much of an apology as she was going to get.

"Mrs. Casey and Ms. Casey are more than welcome to join us."

They followed her into one of the interrogation rooms, and Cain smiled when she glanced at the wall of mirrors. She wondered if just the sight of them intimidated people into confessing before they knew what they were doing.

"What can I do for you?" Agent Hicks asked.

"I thought I'd save you the trouble of having to find me."

Annabel didn't know what Cain was talking about, but she had no intention of revealing that. "Considering our situation and what we both do for a living, Ms. Casey, let's not pretend the Bureau would have any trouble finding you if we needed to. The city has eyes and ears in the most unlikely places, wouldn't you agree?"

"If you're referring to the multitude of listening devices your people planted in my house this morning, then I'd have to agree. You really should inform your men that most moving guys don't spit and polish their shoes, and I sincerely hope you had a warrant for all of those, especially the ones in the bedroom."

Cain looked from Hicks to the mirror beyond her and the collection of people undoubtedly standing behind it watching like an audience at a high-stakes chess game. "While what my partner and I do behind closed doors isn't to everyone's taste, I'm positive it's legal. What are you hoping to gather from anything you hear in there? Your agents hoping to learn some new moves to spice up their pathetic little lives?"

"I'm sure the agents have followed the letter of the law. You and

I both know I can't stop the surveillance unless you decide to take up another kind of business."

"Then go ahead and arrest me, since according to Agent Curtis you have enough evidence in your possession to lock me away."

"Agent Curtis?" It was too late. Annabel's surprise not only showed, but it seeped into her voice. "What's he got to do with this?"

Muriel took over the meeting and explained the visit earlier that morning and why Anthony had been there. The observers all wanted to bang their heads into the glass when they heard what the idiot had done and what it would mean to their team. Agent Hicks would never believe he was acting on his own.

"Ms. Casey runs a reputable business and is an active and contributing member of this city, Agent Hicks. If she wasn't, I'm sure your digging would have uncovered something by now, so it's rather insulting to her and to our family to have a member of the FBI come to our home and threaten her into becoming an informant.

"I'm sure my client would love to serve the government as an informant if you decide to open a pub. She could regale you with tons of information on how to pour beer, but otherwise, I want this constant harassment to stop."

Muriel pulled out a file from her bag and slid it over. "This is our complaint citing that you've lost control of some of your agents, resulting in my client being shot. With Mr. Curtis's actions this morning, we now see the kettle has been put on the fire to again build up steam. I don't want to take a second chance with my client's life, so don't view this as something against you, Agent Hicks."

Annabel never took her eyes off Muriel's face, and she carefully formulated her answer before opening her mouth. The last thing she needed was another fiasco like Kyle, but Anthony Curtis had been up to that point an exemplary field agent. Even if he had gone to see Cain with no one's knowledge, she was going to trust his reasoning since he hadn't given her a reason not to.

"I know it's your job to represent your client in the best possible way, Ms. Casey, but I'm going to fight any complaints brought against Agent Curtis."

"Because you've seen his evidence and find it incriminating enough to allow him to constantly meddle in my family's affairs?" Cain asked. She signaled Muriel not to interrupt. Cain was confident that

Muriel would keep her from saying too much, but she needed to buy some time and space, and Curtis was her ticket. It would be much harder to finish her business with the Bracatos if the stepped-up surveillance continued.

"I'll do it because Agent Curtis is an important part of our team, a man above reproach when it comes to his job."

"What Agent Hicks is trying to tell you, sweetheart, is she hasn't seen Anthony's little envelope either," Emma added. "Makes you wonder. If you had become an informant, would he have shared that information with Agent Hicks?" Emma looked first at Hicks, then at the wall of mirrors. "Ambitious people awe some people and terrify others. I think Cain awes those who associate with her. Can you say the same about Kyle and Curtis?"

The same agent who'd originally come for the Caseys sidled in and whispered something in Hicks's ear, and overhearing a snatch of the conversation, Cain figured they'd now found Agent Curtis.

"This conversation isn't about Barney Kyle, so let's stay on point." The calm exterior was still in place, but Hicks's façade was starting to show fractures around the edges. "I know I've taken more than enough of your time, but I'd like your indulgence a bit longer."

"Take all the time you need, Agent Hicks, but I'd like it if you'd resolve this today."

Unlike Annabel's, Cain's hands as well as the skin around her eyes were relaxed, even though for her the stakes were much higher.

"Did you two really need me to be here for this?" Muriel asked after Annabel left the room.

"Hot date you aren't telling us about?" Cain countered.

"Maybe. Women do find me somewhat attractive, you know."

"Because you lie on all those Internet dating questionnaires."

Shelby snorted on the other side of the glass at Cain's teasing. Muriel didn't need to use a dating service any more than her cousin did. She felt a small pang. After Joe and Lionel had showed up at the Piquant the night she and Muriel had met for drinks, Shelby had never heard from Muriel again.

"If you want my advice," Cain continued, "you should go for the girl behind curtain number two." Both Casey cousins had noticed the number of the interrogation room on the way in. "Just make sure you don't talk in your sleep."

Before Shelby could give another thought to what Cain had just said, the door to the room opened and Annabel asked, "Where is he?"

"He's just going through security now, ma'am," one of the agents responded. "I left word that he was to report here before attending to anything else."

As Anthony went through the security measures set up in the building, he never took his eyes off the envelope he'd shown Cain that morning. It was going to be the center point of his defense if the direct order he'd gotten to report to Agent Hicks meant trouble.

Anthony walked through the door, aware that the conversations had stopped, and he could feel everyone's eyes on him. He glanced at the collection of agents first before he noticed who they were monitoring. He couldn't believe his eyes when he saw Cain Casey sitting in the room joking around with her cousin and her partner and obviously calling his bluff.

"Hand it over," Annabel demanded. "And before you think of asking 'what,' let me inform you of the surveillance report sitting on my desk. The report I read before meeting with the charming Cain Casey and her entourage."

"I was on my way in to show it to you." The envelope came out of his pocket. "After they left the restaurant last night, and the rest of the team lost them, an informant called and told me they were at Jatibon's place." Pictures of Cain and Emma sitting with Ramon were passed along to the rest of the group.

"Did you lose your phone on the way to Jatibon's Club?" Shelby asked.

"There was no time to waste, and I was afraid if too many agents showed up, Cain would notice us."

"Well, these prove Casey and Jatibon are friends," Joe said, holding up the best in the series of shots. "Wait a minute...didn't we know that already?"

"It's the next shots that show what your friend is up to." He tapped the pictures Annabel was looking at. "From the customs report, we knew Rodolfo Luis and his nephew Juan were in town looking to expand their business in Louisiana and Mississippi. But we didn't know who they were going into business with. From the amount of product these guys move, it had to be someone well connected, with an established distribution system already in place."

"And from these shots taken this morning," Shelby opened the folder in her hand, "it's more likely that Cain is telling the old man to call off his nephew." The images of Juan and his goons surrounding Emma were clear, and the man's intent was just as crystal. "If Juan Luis saw Emma Casey last night and behaved the way he did this morning, then her partner's conversation with Rodolfo probably had nothing to do with smack."

"Is that true?" Annabel posed the question to Anthony. "How long did the meeting last?"

"Long enough." Anthony collected all his pictures and shoved them back into the folder. "If none of you want to do your job, fine, but don't expect me to just sit back and let that tall bitch get away with one more thing."

"Your job is to follow my orders, Agent Curtis." Annabel walked up and took the evidence away from him. "At this moment I'm inclined to agree with Ms. Casey's attorney that these photos show little more than a personal vendetta on your part. Wait for me in my office. I'll be there as soon as I finish with our guests."

Annabel muted the sound on the monitor before she walked out, unwilling to share her apology with more people than those who had to hear it. Perhaps if it was sufficiently heartfelt, Cain would let her guard down enough so the agents assigned to her case would find something that would actually stick.

CHAPTER FORTY

For the first time that she could remember, Cain looked behind them as they pulled away and saw no tail. The freedom wouldn't last long, but their visit had accomplished what she needed. Doubt—in some cases it was almost like a virus in someone's brain. Cain had managed to plant the seed of doubt in Annabel Hicks's mind about her office's motives.

"Now what?" Muriel asked.

"We drop you off at your office, then wait." The leather of the seat creaked a bit as Cain relaxed into a more comfortable position. The clouds forming to the west were increasing the humidity as well as the ache from her still-healing gunshot wound.

"Wait for what?" Muriel persisted.

"For the thing I spend my life waiting for, cousin. The right time."

Their talk on the subject was over. Cain had always gone out of her way, as had her father and her uncle Jarvis, to keep Muriel above the fray that was their lives. She was the one Casey who worked exclusively for the family but was beyond reproach as far as the law was concerned, and nothing would make Cain do anything to change that.

"Are the other papers I asked for ready?"

"They're in the office whenever you and Emma want to pass by and sign."

The buildings of the warehouse district distracted Cain for a minute as she gazed out the window. Her head was starting to hurt from all the thoughts running through it.

Just like a master strategist, she had planned how to win the dangerous game they were playing, but unlike any game, this situation was starting to gain unexpected players and scenarios. She would have to be careful to maneuver without mistake.

"What papers?" Emma asked.

"I asked Muriel to draw up a new will, as well as the paperwork that would make us officially a family. They're no different than what we have for Hayden." Cain turned from the window to Emma. "If something happens to me, I want you and our children taken care of."

"Fine, but just make sure nothing happens to you."

Ahead of them Lou jumped out and opened the large door that would allow them to drive into the new club. The offices upstairs were starting to take shape as well, and Muriel's staff had been moving in and re-creating all the files lost in the explosion.

A team of carpenters was busy putting the finishing pieces on the bar. Eventually the top floors would be separated from the club area and also have their own side entrance. Unlike the last time Cain had been in the building talking with Blue, a cadre of craftsmen was working to meet Cain's opening-day deadline. They had two weeks left to finish, and the foreman was pushing everyone to the limit.

"Make sure they sweep every day, starting today."

"Cain, even the feds wouldn't bug your attorney's office," Muriel said.

"And one of their agents would never let a known mob boss in the city hire him to kill me, but what do I know."

"We'll begin today."

By the time they finished their business with Muriel, the sun was starting to set, and Katlin came in and asked to speak to Cain. Emma and Muriel were talking as Katlin and Cain sat with their heads together. Emma was listening to Muriel but also keeping an eye on Cain. From the time Katlin arrived Cain hadn't opened her mouth to interrupt. Whatever the guard was reporting, it had Cain's undivided attention.

"Are you sure?"

"The men I posted said Giovanni drove a van into the garage and left about forty minutes later, with Gino. And earlier in the day the two live-in workers left, with what looked like all their possessions. A cab took both women to the airport, where Gino's people put them on a flight to Mexico City. We know one lady was the full-time housekeeper and the other was Little Gino's nanny, but we don't know why they were let go."

"Why indeed?" The memory of Gino's wife from the night before popped into Cain's head. The amazing food in front of Eris had sat untouched, but she'd consumed glass after glass of wine.

"Our men followed the two Bracato idiots to their final destination, then took a short swim to find what was in the bag they dumped. It was definitely Eris. No visible wounds except some nasty bruises to the face, most probably courtesy of Gino."

"What do we know about Gino's wife?"

"She's dead, boss. What does it matter?"

"What do we know about the woman?" Cain asked again.

Almost as if she'd known Cain was going to ask that question, Katlin handed over a file complete with pictures. "Her name was Eris Dubois, and she was twenty-eight years old. She hooked up with Gino about three years ago. Dumb move. She was a little into the blow, and that's how the connection between them came about. Last year she checked herself into rehab, and a few months after that she was pregnant."

Cain flipped to the next item in the folder and chuckled, amazed that her cousin had gotten this information. "Is this an original?" She pointed to a sheet pulled from Eris Bracato's obstetrical file.

"Me, involved in such illegal activities?" Katlin joked. "Stop asking questions and pay attention."

Cain returned her attention to the page Katlin handed her.

"A few months after she gave birth to the next Bracato generation, Eris got pregnant again. Only thing is, the second time around they weren't so lucky, and she lost the baby about two months into the pregnancy. After that, she spiraled back into drugs and handed off the responsibility for the baby to the woman who boarded a plane yesterday."

As soon as Katlin stopped talking, Cain started tapping her fingers. She drummed in staggered intervals, stopped for a while, then resumed her disjointed cadence.

When Cain refocused, Katlin asked, "Do you want me to do any more?"

"Eventually, but for now keep your people on Gino's house and see what happens next." Gino was probably in an emotional tailspin.

No matter what a cold bastard he was, the woman was his wife, and he had to feel some remorse. "Remember, when I tell you to move, Katlin, I want you to be fast and invisible. Do you understand?"

"I know I disappointed you last night, but if you need me, I won't do anything else wrong."

"Don't go making promises you don't expect to keep." Cain laughed and put her hand behind Katlin's head, then looked beyond her at Merrick. "Are you sure you haven't found other alliances that invalidate ours?"

Katlin also looked at Merrick, who was standing next to Emma. "If you think that, you missed the point of last night. My alliances—I should say *our* alliances—are to you. When this started we had five problems, and now we have two, at least as far as the Bracatos are concerned. If that's not good enough, then I'll apologize again."

Cain squeezed the column of Katlin's neck and smiled. "I know why you did it, but if you do something like that again without my say-so, I'm going to kick your ass." Her voice was low, but the smile never disappeared. "Just this once, though, thanks. Because of you and Merrick we *do* have only two left, but it's those two that concern me."

"I'd be worried if Dalton Casey had raised Giovanni and Gino, but he didn't. We'll be fine, I'm sure of that."

On the other side of the room Emma continued to listen to Muriel talk, but her eyes never left Cain. She still needed to tell her about Juan Luis.

Almost as if he'd read her thoughts, Lou took Muriel's place and put his hand on Emma's knee. "How you doing, Mrs. Casey?"

"I'm working on my poker face, Lou, but aside from that I'm doing great."

"Have you had a chance to tell her what happened this morning?"

"Not yet."

He nodded again and sighed. "I guess you haven't gotten around to telling her about last night either?"

"Lou, I know you're unhappy with me, but when she got home last night, Juan the idiot was the last thing on my mind." Emma placed her hand over his. "I swear tonight over dinner, I'll tell her everything that happened. Just start praying now that she doesn't shoot me for waiting this long to bring the subject up."

"Aren't you glad you have Merrick and the others to keep you safe?"

Whatever else Emma was going to say died on her lips as Cain stood and buttoned her jacket. "How about an early dinner?"

"Sounds good." Before she got to her feet, Emma looked at Lou one last time and smiled.

The door of the car closed behind Cain a few minutes later, and she embraced Emma as they started to move.

Emma said, "Something happened last night and this morning you need to know about."

"Are you all right?"

Emma kissed a small scar on Cain's first knuckle. "I'm fine, and I want you to keep that in mind when you hear what I have to say." Before she lost her nerve she described the two brief encounters with Juan Luis, swearing she felt Cain growl when she told her what had happened that morning in the French Quarter.

"Did he touch you?"

Emma could have taken the question a number of different ways, but she took it for what it was—concern. Though Cain often told Emma she belonged to her, their relationship wasn't built on possession. Emma knew Cain belonged to her just as much.

"Lou was there both times, love, so no, he didn't. I also told him on both occasions who I'm with, but he didn't seem to want to get the message."

Surprisingly Cain laughed at the comment, making Emma squirm. "I'm not laughing at you, sweetling, or the situation."

"What's so funny, then?"

"After the last couple of weeks and what we've been through, I would've enjoyed seeing you put that asshole in his place." She kissed the top of Emma's head and pulled her closer. "And of course he didn't want to get the message. Men like Juan were raised to think the world and all the women in it are for their pleasure. In this case he's going to succeed."

Emma shot up at the comment, ready to face off with Cain. "I did not give this guy any encouragement."

"I know. I meant, if the attention of a Casey woman is what he wants, then he's getting it. Only once I'm done, he might not find it all that pleasurable."

Emma laughed, but worried that the last thing Cain needed was another battle to fight.

❖

As the waiter brought out the desserts Cain and Emma had ordered, the phone on Merrick's hip buzzed once, signaling she had a message. She flipped it open under the table, not wanting to draw attention to herself, but just as soon as she read the message, she smiled.

Have u eaten yet?

With one more glance around the room to make sure everything was still all right, she tapped Lou on the shoulder and pointed toward the ladies' room. Once there, she inhaled deeply before hitting the Reply button and sending a return message. She felt like scolding the sender for bothering her at work, but left the door open for whatever possibilities the night held.

"Problem?" Cain asked Merrick as she helped Emma out of the restaurant.

"Katlin just had a question, nothing serious." Merrick moved ahead of them to open the car door and avoid any more questions.

"Let it go, baby, we're on our way home," Emma said as Cain opened her mouth to say something else. "If it's something Katlin thinks needs your attention, I'm sure she'll be waiting for you when we get there."

"And if it has to do with our talk in Haywood on your father's porch?"

"Then I say we take a bottle of champagne up to our room and toast my good fortune."

Creases formed on Cain's brow when she tried to figure out what Emma was talking about.

"Your good fortune?"

"If Merrick has found someone who can take her mind off you, then yes." She kissed Cain on the nose. "My good fortune."

Merrick stayed long enough to see the couple retire upstairs, then set the house alarm before walking out the back door. At dinner she'd been thinking of her bed in the condo she owned not far from where the new club was going to open. One little question, though, had realigned her focus.

She opened the door to the pool house without knocking, then crossed her arms over her chest, the perfect picture of annoyance. "Do you usually bother people when they're working? Considering what we do, that could be a dangerous habit."

"You're not working now," Katlin said from the small kitchen.

"Your point is?" The phone on her hip buzzed once again with a new message.

Behave or there might be consequences.

"Is that a threat?" She took her suit jacket off and threw it on the sofa.

"The way I want the night to end"—Katlin finally stepped into the room and put a bowl of strawberries on the nightstand—"it wouldn't be prudent for me to make threats."

"Then what's this about?"

Katlin spread her arms out and shrugged her shoulders. "Call it settling a bet with myself."

"This ought to be good." Merrick picked up a piece of fruit. She bit into it, her eyes on Katlin as the juice ran down her chin.

"Before I tell you my bet, I've got a question for you."

Merrick nodded her head once as if to give permission for her to ask, but Katlin wasn't in a hurry. She sat in the chair across from where Merrick stood and looked her over from head to foot. "Do you plan on running out to find any more gifts for Cain tonight?"

"I think the last two we got her should suffice for now, so tell me your bet."

"Part of me thinks you're a tease." Katlin stopped and laughed at the scowl her statement produced.

"What's the other part of you think?" Merrick dropped her arms and spread her feet apart almost as if she were expecting an attack.

The dark shirt Merrick was wearing pulled tight across her

breasts, but Katlin decided the shoulder holster she was wearing rather than the cut of the shirt caused the pleasant sight. When she took a deep breath the material pulled even tauter, and Katlin noticed her nipples harden.

"That you'll make good on your promises." Katlin crossed her legs and pointed in the direction of Merrick's chest. "By starting with the gun and the shirt. You're just dying to show me something that'll make me wet."

"Am I now?" Despite the flip question, Merrick removed the holster and the Glock, dropping them on her jacket. "What are you going to do for me?" She opened the buttons on her shirt with the patience of a woman who had all night to reach her goals.

The navy bra looked exotic next to Merrick's skin, and the sight of so much skin made Katlin stand up and say, "I'm going to show you something I don't think anyone has bothered to in a very long time."

Stepping behind Merrick, Katlin lifted her fingers and with a quick twist unfastened the bra. She moved in close to reach for the button on her pants, and just as quickly they dropped to Merrick's ankles.

"Aren't you overdressed?" Merrick asked Katlin.

"I see now that you aren't a tease, darling girl, so we'll worry about me soon enough." When Katlin pulled her backward into her body, Merrick's abdomen muscles tightened under her hand, but that was her only reaction. Katlin guessed it was Merrick's way of trying to maintain control. "Kick your shoes off for me."

Free to move Merrick without tripping her, Katlin walked her to the chair she'd been occupying, stopping when Merrick's hands were on the back of it. Katlin mapped out Merrick's body with her soft yet strong hands, staring at her stomach, then moving around to her back, never stopping and going nowhere near where she knew Merrick really wanted her.

"Who's teasing now?" Merrick asked, having to look behind her to get a glimpse of her torturer.

"Teasing is arousal without the promise of release," Katlin said as her hands slid down until she was at the last barrier between her and Merrick's skin. But instead of removing the navy striped bikinis,

Katlin slid her fingers just under the elastic. "I can promise you won't go wanting."

"That sure of yourself, baby?" Merrick laughed softly and turned her head even more, so she could see Katlin's face.

"You're telling me you're not turned on?" Katlin squeezed Merrick's nipple until it felt like a small stone between her fingers. At the same time her other hand went down between Merrick's legs, finding her wet and hot. "Something tells me you believe my promise."

Merrick parted her lips to accept a kiss, groaning into Katlin's mouth as her fingers started to move. Every sweep downward coated her fingers so that they slid easily over Merrick's diamond-hard clitoris. Katlin never broke their kiss as she stroked faster, enjoying the way Merrick's ass pumped into her groin. As her excitement built, Merrick brought one hand up to cover the one Katlin had on her chest, making Katlin squeeze harder.

"Uh...don't stop," Merrick panted as she tightened when her orgasm started. "Don't stop." With one final push back into Katlin, Merrick came on her hand, glad for the strong arms holding her up.

When the spasms finally stopped, she went willingly when Katlin turned around and sat down with Merrick on her lap. She reached for Katlin's still-wet hand and linked their fingers together.

"What is it you think no one's bothered to show me in a long time?" Merrick asked, remembering something Katlin had said earlier.

"You're very good at your job, which takes strength and a certain attitude to pull off." Katlin stopped to kiss her again. "People respect your strength, but they sometimes forget to look past it and see how beautiful you are." Another kiss made Merrick move closer. "My job is going to be to remind you of just how stunning you are when it's just the two of us."

"Such sweet words"—Merrick stood with the grace of a cat—"make me want to make good on my promise." She unfastened Katlin's pants and with help threw them over her shoulder.

"What promise was that?"

Merrick dropped to her knees and spread Katlin's sex open for her pleasure. "I believe I promised to go slow enough to make you beg." She sucked Katlin's clitoris into her mouth, making the meaning of "slow" rather dubious, but then just as quickly she stopped. "And only when you beg am I going to give you what you want."

When she sucked on Katlin again, she had to laugh at the pained "please" that leaked from Katlin's mouth. It was then that she stopped teasing and gave them both what they wanted.

CHAPTER FORTY-ONE

The next two weeks were quiet. No one had spotted the Casey children yet, but the watchers saw their parents almost every night sharing quiet dinners at some of their favorite spots. Lou and Merrick were never too far away, and Katlin was barely a blip on the FBI's radar.

Muriel's offices and Emerald's were almost complete, and the club would open soon. Shelby and her team figured Cain would make whatever move she'd been planning then.

The one team of agents assigned to the Bracato family was working overtime to piece together what was happening and why they were missing so many players. After hours on the street and monitoring their wiretaps, they had concluded that Giovanni had sent three of his sons out of town to finalize whatever business they had with Rodolfo Luis.

"There's nothing new with Casey?" Annabel asked. After one too many embarrassing moments, she'd taken a more active role in all their ongoing investigations.

"No, ma'am," Joe answered. He opened the file in front of him in case Agent Hicks wanted a more detailed account. "Since they're set to open in a couple of days, we've added a few more guys at the warehouses and other places she might not think we're watching."

"You're delusional if you think she's not aware," Anthony interjected.

"Agent Curtis, do you have anything constructive to add to what your fellow agent is saying?"

"No, ma'am."

"Then why are you talking? I suggest you stay quiet and listen from now on, or I'll reassign you to desk duty. Are we clear?"

He lowered his eyelids a little, but merely answered, "Crystal, ma'am." He was convinced that he hadn't been transferred or bounced out of the agency because no one had found out about his illegal wiretap operation when Cain was in the hospital.

"You were saying, Joseph."

"We'll be ready if something happens. The shooting at her home, along with the two bombings, won't go unanswered. We predict a turf war between the Casey and Bracato families.

"But we don't know how the other families will react or if they'll get involved. If they want to gain more territory, they'd be smart to let the two families battle it out, then divide the city once they're done. That leaves us with one good scenario. Once the dust settles, we can put two of the four families out of business."

The agent assigned to Giovanni's family opened his file next. "Gino was bragging about both jobs, so we concur. If Casey moves, it's going to be against him first."

Agent Hicks nodded and placed her hands flat on the table. "Then let's keep our eyes open, people. I don't need to remind you how ill-advised another fiasco like the warehouse incident would be."

❖

Cain led Emma to the new bar and helped her onto a stool. Emerald's was set to open the following night, so they wanted to enjoy the quiet before the state-of-the-art sound system cranked up. Cain pulled a new bottle of their best whiskey off the shelf, picked up two glasses, and poured a finger of liquor in each.

"Here's to our success, darling girl." The clink of their glasses echoed in the empty space.

"That's a given, honey. This place is beautiful."

"Not as beautiful as the woman who shares my life, but if the lady doesn't mind, it'll be more beautiful because it'll share her name." With a quick tug Cain removed the paper taped up to the mirror behind the bar and revealed the name "Emma's" etched across the middle. "It isn't much, but I have a lot of birthdays and such to make up for, so it's a start."

Emma held her hands over her mouth and gasped as she studied Cain's offering. "Thank you, love, but it wasn't necessary."

"I wanted to do it. Do you know why?"

Emma shook her head and reached for Cain's hand.

"Because I want to come in here for years and dance with you pressed against me. Because I want everyone who enters this place to know who my heart belongs to."

"I belong to you as well, and I will for the rest of my life."

"Thank you." Cain lifted the delicate hand off the bar and kissed the back of it. "Tonight we finish what we started. The Bracato family will pay for every sin they've ever committed against us."

"Do you need anything from me?"

"An alibi later on tonight," Cain joked.

"Honey, I'll be happy to. You never have to ask."

"Merrick and some of the others will take you home. Go in through the garage like we've been doing, and no matter what, don't leave the house. I'll be there by ten at the latest, and I won't be calling. We can't afford any lucky intercepts now if I'm supposed to be in the house with you."

Cain joined Emma on the other side of the bar and walked her to the waiting vehicle with heavily tinted windows.

"You do what's right, Cain, but whatever you do, come back to me."

"You have my word, love."

They kissed, and Cain walked to the other side of the bar again.

There, she pulled back one of the industrial rugs to reveal a trapdoor. She'd wanted to purchase the building for so long primarily because of the door and where it led. Now more than ever, she thanked God her grandfather had told so many stories.

After Cain lowered the door behind her, Merrick replaced the rug before she joined Emma. In the rare chance someone investigated the club, the only thing they would find would be the two used glasses on the bar.

Below the building, Cain flipped on her flashlight and stooped to make it through the narrow tunnel, walking along the edge to avoid the inch of water on the center of the floor. A string of old lights was bolted to the wall on the other side, but they hadn't worked in a long time and she didn't intend to fix them. She didn't want to tip off anyone who didn't need to know of the tunnel's location.

After thirty minutes, she reached a rusty white iron door and pulled a set of keys from her pocket. Despite the door's age, the new security lock turned easily, and when she opened the door the dampness of the river hit her immediately, since she was now close to the port. An old beat-up Buick was parked where Katlin had said it would be, and Cain found the key. Her watchers would never notice the car with all the head-banger stickers on the back window.

At that moment the surveillance teams had another problem. Two of their major targets had totally vanished. Gino had left his house an hour earlier and disappeared into the crowd at a local mall. Whoever had helped him escape knew how to spot the feds' vans, and now the agents were at a loss.

"Houston, we have a problem," the one in charge of Gino said as he watched two of his men on the sidewalk in front of Gino's house search for signs of life.

"You locate your targets yet?" the dispatcher asked. He held his phone, poised to dial Agent Hicks's number.

"Negative. We're going to circle one more time, then come back here and wait for him." The two men outside shook their heads slightly. "Does Shelby have her target in sight?"

"They're in for the night after an early dinner and a stop at the new place before heading back to Jarvis's," Shelby reported. She and Claire were sitting in one van, while Lionel and Joe hung back farther down the street. "Do you need me to cut our backup loose?"

"Hold for now, and let me get Agent Hicks on the phone," the agent at Gino's said. "Something about this feels hinky to me, and I want to cover everyone's ass."

"I'm telling you, all's quiet here," Shelby said, "so let us know if you need more backup to canvass where they were last seen. Looks like we're going to have a slow night."

CHAPTER FORTY-TWO

The old recreational building smelled heavily of mildew and rot. Gino deserved nothing better for what Cain had in mind because of how dishonorably he'd lived his life. Plus, the site was set for demolition in six months to make room for a new federal building. Then they would find the man the FBI was out hunting for. Cain loved irony.

The stench came from the water left in the old pool, now green and slimy from neglect. It had been years since the sound of children playing had echoed off these walls, and the putrid remains of the once-chlorinated water now magnified the sound of Cain's footsteps.

Katlin stood at the edge of the deep end and nodded in Cain's direction. Outside, the night quiet was broken every so often by the sound of distant traffic. The area had once been home to some of the city's most ruthless gangs. Now the old tenement buildings, as well as all the buildings that had once made up the community, were a ghost town awaiting the wrecking ball.

"Beautiful night, isn't it?" Cain walked to the front of the building as though she were walking beside a pool at an expensive spa.

"Cain, you fucking asshole." Gino tried to break free of his bindings and the weight tied to his ankles. He stood in the middle of the pool, the water lapping the middle of his chest. Under the water his hands were tied behind his back, and his feet were also bound by the most common rope Katlin could find. When she and Lou had put him in, they'd looped another long piece that she held in her hand. "Once my father hears about this…Hell, I don't need him. I'll take you out myself."

The relaxed Cain peered out over the shallow end of the pool and cocked her head to one side, as if enjoying the positions they found themselves in. "Gino, I want you to listen to me, because I'm only going to say this once."

"Fuck you!" He tugged on the bindings on his hands again and stopped when the knots tightened to the point of pain. "Get me the fuck out of—"

His scream died in his throat when he saw Cain nod slightly in Katlin's direction. Katlin pulled on the rope, dragging him farther into the deep end. The outburst had cost him precious inches he could ill afford to lose if he didn't want a mouth full of the foul greenish soup.

"Ready to listen?"

"What do you want?" When something flitted against Gino's leg he shuddered and concentrated on Cain to avoid thinking about what could possibly live in this stuff. Trying to stay upright, Gino willed his body to relax and stared up at her.

"I want so many things we'll be here for a while yet, so hang tight."

"You fucking suckered me, Casey. Does it feel good to catch someone with their pants down?"

An urgent call from a business associate of the Bracato family had gotten Gino out of the house. After he and his father had dumped Eris's body, Gino hadn't wanted to socialize at all. He sat in the den most nights, watching television and holding his son as he ignored the ringing telephone.

"Sort of how you caught my father unawares the night you gunned him down in the street in front of our offices?" The back door where Cain had entered squeaked as it opened again for their last visitor. "Or is it like murdering my mother? What sort of man kills an innocent?"

"I had nothing to do with any of that, so why am I here?" The shallowest part of the pool contained no water, and Gino pressed his hands closer to his back when he saw a large rat standing on its hind legs sniffing the air. Whatever was in the water with him bumped into his thigh again, and he couldn't help but wonder if rats could hold their breath.

"You're here because after talking to your brother Stephano…" Cain stooped, took her hand out of her pocket, and laid the signet ring that belonged to the second oldest of the Bracato boys on the cracked cement at her feet.

The fact that it was in Cain's possession could only mean one thing.

"What are you doing with that?" Gino, starting to panic, rubbed his bound hands together as if trying to make his own ring reappear.

Cain laid an identical one next to the first ring. "Your brother Michael was next, and he folded like a stack of cards in a tornado." The last ring came out, and she finally looked up. "Unlike you with my sister, I didn't have the heart to be cruel to Francis, even though he was more than eager to help your father expand his drug empire. He was trying his best to prove he could keep up with his big brothers."

Gino screamed in outrage and almost fell forward into the slime. "You fucking bitch. He wasn't even twenty-five years old." His anger won out for the moment, and he forgot his fear.

"You're the last of them, Gino, which is good, since I have only one more question."

"You're fucked in the head if you think I'm telling you anything."

Cain put up her hand, her index finger and thumb a hair's breadth apart.

"Wait!" The word reverberated throughout the area, echoing Gino's alarm until silence fell again. He tilted his head up and looked at the ceiling, not wanting to know how many more inches he'd lost to pride.

"This is your last chance, so listen carefully."

"I keep telling you, my father...or should I say *if* my father had anything to do with the death of your father, he didn't tell me anything about it." If Gino had been able, he would've held his hands up in surrender to help his case.

"I believe you, Gino."

His head snapped up, and he smiled. "You do? I mean, of course you do, since I didn't know."

"And since you don't know anything, you're just wasting my time." Another nod of Cain's head and Katlin yanked on the rope again.

"Wait!" Gino yelled again, even more frantic this time. The water was making him itch, and when it reached his neck, Katlin stopped.

"You don't have many inches left, Gino, and you just said you didn't know. Why the wait?"

"He ordered the hit after your father slapped him back out of the neighborhoods he controlled. The merchants Dalton did business with started to complain when my father's pushers started hanging on some of the street corners. Once Dalton was finished, my father lost a handful of good men, and no amount of money on the streets helped my father find the bodies.

"One of the guys we lost was my cousin, but that's not what motivated my father to kill your family. That was your father's fault. Dalton wanted to send a message, and we heard it loud and clear. Problem with that was, Big Gino wasn't about to put up with some Mick telling him his business, so he returned the favor. He hired Danny. Your cousin jumped at the chance to get back at you for giving him every shit job in your organization."

As Gino gave the ropes one more jerk in an effort to break free, they cut deeper into his hands. "Danny still worked for Dalton back then and knew his schedule. When my father asked, he set up the time and place for the hit."

"And my mother and brother?"

"Your brother was a hothead, which sealed his fate, and your mother was a bonus. Danny told my father with both of them gone, you'd be easier to break."

The silence stretched as Cain balled, then relaxed, her fists. Finally, she asked, "Anything else?"

"That's all I know, I swear it."

"There's something else, Gino, and the price will be steep."

She summoned the newcomer over with a wave of her hand and waited for him to walk the length of the pool before continuing. "The information about the rest of my family was useful, but you haven't answered for one more person."

Cain accepted the bundle and kept it hidden from Gino's view.

Mook's brother, Patrick, who worked for Vincent Carlotti, stayed close.

"Marie, my sister, is who's left, Gino, and after my talk with Stephano I don't need to ask anything else, do I?"

"That was all Danny."

Dragging him back a few inches shut him up.

When Katlin stopped, Gino was forced to tilt his head back to keep his face out of the slime. "If Stephano told you different, then he's a lying bastard."

"The lying bastard was high as a kite when I talked to him, so lying was out of the question."

Her voice settled around him, making Gino force his head back farther in an effort to see her again.

"That's the one redeeming factor of the shit you put on the streets. It lowers your inhibitions enough that your answers aren't important because you don't fear any repercussions. The high must really be euphoric enough to make you feel invincible, but all it did in the end was snap his brain and his body like a twig."

Gino stared to the left, and Cain finally came back into limited view, since the only illumination in the dank place was moonlight. The whimper coming from the bundle in her arms made his blood run cold. "Please, God, no."

"Funny you should say that. I remember uttering that same phrase only three times in my life." Cain pushed the child's blanket back. He resembled his mother, the waiflike woman in the restaurant. "I remember all three vividly since I was standing in front of a coffin each and every time."

"Cain, he's just a baby." Gino glimpsed his son's hand as a little fist came up, almost as if he were trying to entice Cain to play with him.

"Don't worry. I'll be much more merciful with him than you were with Marie. She was as innocent as this infant no matter how much longer she had on this earth before you stole her life in the most degrading way your twisted little brain could come up with. Her innocence didn't stop you, did it?"

"I'm telling you, I wasn't there."

Cain's intense glare made him fight harder to free his hands.

"And even if I was, what does that have to do with my son?"

With one last kiss to the baby's forehead, Cain handed him off to Patrick. "We were raised by two very different men, but my father always tried to impress one thing upon me."

"What, to go around and fucking kill little babies?"

"To always live my life so that my sins wouldn't be visited on my children. Even people like us can live with honor. To have a code means we all promise to consider people like your son and my sister. When someone breaks that code of honor, though, the innocent pays the price of those actions."

Cain nodded, and from behind Gino came a splash, then an eerie silence.

"No!" It was the last word he uttered as Katlin pulled the final couple of inches needed to get the job done.

Resigned to his fate, Gino locked eyes with his judge for one last moment before the urge to fight took over and he struggled to break free as his lungs started to feel like they would explode from trying to hold his breath. Katlin had positioned him so that just his eyes and forehead were above the water line.

As the reality of his fate dawned on Gino, Cain could see the horror in his eyes and kept looking until all movement ceased.

Then Katlin pulled him farther into the deep end and retrieved the rope she'd used. When the property was razed, Gino would either be part of the foundation, or the mystery of his disappearance would be revealed. Either way, nothing at the scene could tie Cain to his demise.

Cain slid the fourth and final ring Giovanni had made for his sons into her pocket as she strode back to the car. "You live like a slimeball all your life, Gino, and sometimes it'll drown you."

The jingle of the ring in her pocket assured her that she'd almost won the game. She was missing only one piece.

CHAPTER FORTY-THREE

I know what you said, boss, but I can't find him."

Giovanni slammed his hands down on the desktop and glared up at his guard.

"We looked everywhere in town. We even shook down the woman he had on the side, but no one's seen him."

"No one just disappears into thin air. Did you go by his house?" Giovanni took his gun out of the top drawer and checked the clip.

"The only thing moving around Gino's place is the feds parked outside. I sent Chops inside, but the place was empty. Wherever Gino went, he took the baby and packed light."

When Giovanni stood up, he shoved the nine-millimeter into his waistband at the back. He'd wasted enough time worrying about what had happened to his sons; it was time to start doing something about it.

"The baby's probably with those women Eris hired, since she's too lazy to take care of my grandson herself. Come on. We'll check out some of Gino's contacts, then go meet with Rodolfo."

"You got it, boss."

"And tell the guys when they find Francis, not to let him out of their sight. That little idiot hasn't come home for the last couple of nights, and his mother's giving me shit about it. It's a fine time for him to grow a pair and start venturing out on his own."

Giovanni flipped the watchers off as he got into the back of his car, where agents observed his growing frustration with the situation through the camera lens pointed at him.

As soon as the small convoy left, the agent in charge called in for backup for the tail, needing to stay behind and wait for the rest of the Bracatos to show up. With all of the sons falling off their radar, the surveillance teams had adopted different modes of operation. Some were watching, and a larger group was out investigating.

Giovanni thumbed the bottom of his signet ring as they drove through the gates of his office building. He could somewhat understand that his eldest son needed some time after what had happened with Eris, but the other boys' absence had built a ball of fire in his gut that was growing by the hour.

Just that morning he'd taken some calls from some of Stephano's men who'd all but admitted that his two sons had an ongoing operation in Biloxi. They were starting to feel the heat from some of the other dealers in town and wanted permission before doing anything to rectify the situation.

His sons liked to indulge in women and a good time, but Giovanni had always taught them business came first. If their business was under fire and they were nowhere to be found, there was a problem. And if that problem turned out to be Cain Casey, the streets would run with her blood.

❖

Emma glanced around the room and tried to suppress a chuckle. The other people in the waiting room were scrutinizing them as if trying to figure out exactly how the odd conglomeration of people fit together. Next to her Cain sat patiently reading a golf magazine, not saying anything. She and Cain hadn't talked much when Cain had returned the night before, but after seeing the fourth ring, Emma didn't need to know anything else.

"How are you doing, lass?" Cain dropped the magazine and took both of Emma's hands in hers, as if she didn't want Emma to feel she was being ignored.

"Trying to conjure up good thoughts."

Thinking about the exam rooms beyond the door was making her nervous. After Cain's recent injury, Emma didn't want to see any more doctors.

"You don't have to do this."

Emma knew that only the curious people in the room kept Cain from pulling her onto her lap.

"I'm just nervous, honey, but I really want this."

Emma knew that Cain and their guards must have really glared, because suddenly the onlookers found their magazines fascinating. When she looked up from Cain's shoulder, she found the same charming smile she'd fallen for.

"Mrs. Casey," a nurse said quietly from the doorway at the end of the room.

Five people stood up.

"Guys, I appreciate your concern, but I think Cain and I can take it from here."

The actions of Katlin, Merrick, and Lou touched Emma because she knew they'd once again come to accept her place with Cain.

"How are the fertile Caseys today?" Dr. Ellie Eschete said. She and her partner had a great following with couples just like Emma and Cain. "And I see from your chart that your birthday surprise for Ms. Casey worked out, Emma."

"The surprise's name is Hannah and she's four, so thank you. Now, we're hoping to make it three for three, so give me some good news." Emma held up her crossed fingers. She was no expert, so she couldn't begin to guess how the gift that Cain's brother Billy had given her had fared after being in the deep freeze for more than four years.

Billy's gift had lived on past him, giving Cain the legacy she'd come to want. Emma just hoped it was still as potent as the man who had proved his love for his sister in such a thoughtful way.

The door opened again, admitting Sam Casey, Ellie's partner not only in business but also in life. When the greetings were done she sat on the edge of the desk, folded her hands, and rested them on her lap.

"You live with this bad weed and think there would be bad news?" From the first time they'd met, the luck of sharing Cain's last name gave Sam more leeway to joke around, even if they weren't related.

"What the comedian means," Ellie interjected, "is how ready are you to try again?"

"We're in the middle of some things right now, so we just want to check on the viability of another Casey baby. I did, though, start testing so that I can track my ovulation. Then when the time's right, we'll be ready. Right, love?"

"You know me. I'm ready every eleven months."

"Aside from the fact you're ready to try again," Sam said, "your donor's swimmers are doing great after their long nap. We tested just a small sample to be sure, but if you want another Casey baby, you'll get it."

She laughed when Cain pumped her fist at the news.

After Cain slapped Ellie on the back, she reminded Emma again of the things she should do to improve their chances of conception and gave her a chart to track her ovulation.

"It was great seeing you two again. Just remember that whenever you're ready, we'll be waiting."

As soon as they were completely alone in Ellie's office, Emma released the tears she'd been holding back, surprised when she found Cain crying along with her. "I never thought I'd be blessed like this again."

"Today's our new beginning…right here and now."

"Yes, it is."

"Then it's time to put the past behind us, Cain. What you started to protect us—it's time to finish it. I want more than anything to come back here and try for this baby. When we do, I want it to be born with nothing hanging over its head and no one looking over its shoulder."

Emma kissed Cain with the same passion she saved for their most intimate moments. She knew she was asking Cain to unleash the devil inside that Cain feared would drive them apart, but by doing so Emma declared herself as true a Casey wife as Therese Casey had been.

"Swear to me that'll you'll finish it."

"On my mother's grave, I'll finish it or die trying."

"Oh, no, my darling, dying is a long way off for you." Emma brushed back a lock of dark hair and smiled. "And when she comes calling, I'll be just a step behind you."

Emma finally trusted Cain to use any means necessary to finish what needed to be done, and when she did, Emma would be there with the love that would heal what haunted her.

CHAPTER FORTY-FOUR

W hat's going on now?" Joe telephoned to ask Shelby. He and Lionel were helping to canvass the Bracato brothers and babysit Anthony. Because Cain had become a virtual saint overnight, Agent Hicks had cut them loose from tailing her.

Shelby laughed along with Claire at the sheer boredom that faced them if their day continued on the same slow scale. "We're sitting outside the clinic and guessing Cain's just finished one more follow-up visit, since Merrick and Lou are back down here. I doubt they'll be deserting their charges in broad daylight." Running off a couple of eager security guards and an overzealous meter maid had provided their only excitement so far. "How's it going on your end?"

"Lionel's thinking of shooting Agent Surly if he makes one more snide comment, and we both agree the grim brothers four can give lessons on how to drop off the face of the planet." Joe stepped out of a café some of the agents assigned to the Bracatos said Gino liked to frequent and looked for the car the three of them were in. "Why do I feel we're always two steps behind these guys with no hope of catching up?"

"Because we're always two steps behind these people with no hope of catching up," Shelby said, making him laugh. A knock on the back door of the van cut short her razzing. "Joe, let me call you right back. If it's that woman again, I may shoot her this time instead of showing her my ID."

"Shelby, heads up. Our targets are mobile again," Claire said.

Shelby was so busy watching Cain and Emma that it took her a while to realize Merrick had walked up to the van.

"I see our company isn't the meter maid," Shelby said. She was seriously considering ignoring the knock, but Merrick and Lou weren't moving.

Merrick merely smiled as the back door cracked open. "I hope I'm not disturbing anything, but I come bearing gifts." She held up two cups of coffee but didn't try to come closer and peek in. "My boss thought a nice warm drink might make all these boring hours pass faster."

"Make sure and thank Cain on our behalf."

"Actually, Cain would let you rot out here, but I'll tell Mrs. Casey you appreciate her thoughtfulness." Merrick had begun to head back across the street when she snapped her fingers as if she'd forgotten something. "She also wanted me to inform you she was going shopping again and there was a great sale on suits, if you were interested. In case you lose us, we'll be in the designer section."

"Thanks." Shelby made sure the sarcasm was hard to miss. "Tell her no one likes a smart-ass," she added in a whisper.

It wasn't soft enough, she realized, when Merrick laughed and shook her head.

"Then perhaps you should ask to be reassigned. Smart-ass seems to be her specialty." With that, she walked back to her waiting car.

As pissed as Merrick had been when she was first assigned to Emma, she was starting to enjoy her company. Cain, she'd found through the years, had a wicked sense of humor, but after only a few weeks she was finding that Emma rivaled her.

"What, they aren't coffee drinkers?" Emma laughed at Merrick's still-shaking head.

"More like they're still in shock that they've run across someone who actually likes to mess with them more than Cain does." They all looked at the van, which had an electric company name on the side. "After all, you're not supposed to notice them because of the convincing camouflage."

"Kind of hard to miss a big-ass electric truck following you around all day. They'd be less conspicuous if they rode around on a huge pink elephant playing a couple of banjos." Emma waved one last time before accepting Cain's help into the car.

Even if the FBI was monitoring her every movement, Emma felt too good to be upset about it. A majority of the prayers she'd uttered in the quiet of the Wisconsin nights while she'd been apart from Cain had been answered in the last hour, and nothing was going to ruin that for her.

"Keep this up and your file may be thicker than mine," Cain said, once the door closed.

"I'm bad, but I'm not that bad, lover."

The car headed back downtown since Cain hadn't planned on separating from her partner that day. Even though Emma was going to the mall for a final fitting of her new outfit for the club opening, Cain had vowed to tag along.

"You're sure you want to watch me try on clothes?"

"I'm more looking forward to you stripping down for me, but I'll live. Everything for tonight is done, so I freed up my day. Just call me the official bag carrier."

"You do a good enough job, and I might hire you on a permanent basis." Emma leaned in closer and ran her index finger down Cain's chest. "But if you come with me, I won't be able to surprise you later on tonight."

"Then how about if I sit outside with the help and admire you from afar?"

Emma trailed her finger back up and was delighted with the shiver it caused. "Just as long as you're not too far away."

They both had to laugh at the gagging noises coming from Merrick in the front seat.

"Enough from the peanut gallery, thank you."

"I'm just thinking." Emma looked at Cain. "Any more of this, and you'll have to retire and become a florist or something equally romantic. At least those guys might leave you alone if they hear you spitting out all this mush."

"That's what I've been telling them all these years, but no one ever pays attention to me. I'm just a big mushball." Cain kissed the tip of Emma's nose.

At the mall Emma headed into the dressing room with Kevin leading the way after she introduced him to Cain.

Shelby and Claire stood outside close to the elevators, sipping the last of their cappuccinos and trying to blend in with the other shoppers as best they could, envious when they saw Cain hand Kevin an invitation to the opening of the club that night.

"I'm looking forward to seeing you and Ralph there tonight, Kevin," Cain said, putting her hand on his shoulder after handing him the envelope. "Any man who's that talented in choosing lingerie should be rewarded."

"Judging from Emma's comments about you all these years, I didn't think you'd disapprove."

"You definitely thought right."

The day had been so boring up till now, especially listening in on this drivel, that Shelby was almost tempted to leave, but she figured Cain would use the opportunity to pull off a major hit while they were out helping Joe and the others.

"Still watching the world pass you by, eh, Agent Phillips?"

The voice caught Shelby so off guard, she almost dropped her cup over the railing. "I'm thinking about retiring if one more person sneaks up on me today." Trusting Claire to keep things under control, Shelby focused on the subject of more than one thought over the weeks. "How've you been, Muriel?"

"Busy, actually." Muriel looked at where Claire was staring and laughed at Cain, who was making a face at her and crossing her eyes. "I'd ask what you've been up to, but I can see things haven't changed much."

"It's a job."

"I'm sure it is." Muriel opened her mouth as if to add something, but just as quickly she clicked it shut. "I'll let you get back to it, since it looks rather riveting. With any luck Cain'll start some sort of illegal cock fighting in designer shoes just for kicks. If not, I don't want to think what a waste of my tax dollars this is."

"Muriel, please wait."

Shelby's request stopped Muriel before she got too far away.

"It's my job. You may not like it, and you can play stupid and not try to understand it, but it's my job."

"Why do you care how I feel about it one way or another?"

"Because I thought we were becoming friends." Shelby eased closer, glad that Claire acted as if nothing was happening.

"I thought so too. Then something reminded me of the enormous gulf between us. As much as I'd like to, I think that gulf is too wide to breach."

She pointed to Cain. "In the end it's like you said—it's a job to you, but to me, it's my family. My loyalty is to her and my name."

"Even if that loyalty sinks you, Counselor?"

"Shelby, a word of advice."

Muriel's demeanor changed as her voice lowered, making Shelby understand she'd overstepped her bounds.

"Never speak of things you can't fathom. One of my greatest possessions is a book of family history that goes back generations. It teaches that the Casey clan, for as much as you have watched us, is exactly that to you—unfathomable. We have survived for hundreds of years because we know no other way than to be loyal to our own. So to answer your question, yes, my loyalty is hers even if it sinks me."

The rebuke was quiet but scathing, yet for some reason it impressed Shelby and clarified something about Cain and Emma's relationship. No matter how many Barney Kyles came into Emma's life, she would never again betray her loyalty to Cain, because that loyalty undergirded their relationship.

"I wonder what belonging to something like that feels like."

"Did you say something?" Claire asked.

"Nothing important." Shelby took her post at the center railing and watched not Cain, but the cousin who'd joined her. "Think we can finagle one of those invitations for tonight?"

"It's worth a shot, because something tells me tonight will be exciting only if we're in the middle of the action."

Chapter Forty-five

Make sure you keep an eye on your sister. Hannah's an angel with a streak of mischief." Emma put her hand over Cain's where it was resting on her abdomen. "She inherited that from your mother. She's always been a little hard to control too."

The soft laugh from behind her tickled her ear as Hayden replied to her from his end.

"When are you coming to get us? It's fun up here, but I miss you."

"I'm not sure what Cain's timetable is, but it should be soon. We miss you just as much."

That was true, but during the three weeks she'd spent with just Cain, the last of the doubts between them had faded and they'd reconnected so strongly Emma was still amazed.

"Nothing's wrong, is it, Hayden?"

"We're fine, Mama. Stop worrying. I just didn't want you to forget about us."

Months before, the statement would've sent Emma into tears, but now she heard the teasing in his voice.

"The Caseys are mischievous, son, but forgetful they're not," she said right back. "Stay warm, and I'll see you soon. I love you, baby."

"I love you too, Mama."

That she had come so far in that relationship too choked Emma up, and she had to pass the handset to Cain, though she kept the speaker on.

"How's it going, buddy?"

"Bet I can milk a cow better than you."

The greeting made Cain laugh. "I bet you can too, so I think I'll pass on losing any money to you."

"Tonight's the big night, huh?"

"Don't worry. When you get back I'll take you for a walk-through, and I'll make sure one of the men takes some pictures tonight so you can see how beautiful your mama looks."

"I wish I was old enough already." He laughed, cutting off any advice from Cain. "I know, I know—don't rush it."

"Damn right. How about we make you a deal? When you turn twenty-one, we'll open a new place and you can go with a pretty girl on your arm." Emma laughed, and Cain kissed her forehead.

"I forgot to ask. How did Mama like her surprise?"

"He knew you'd named the club after me?" Emma asked, coming up from Cain's side so she could look at her.

"I may have let it slip when you were in the shower last week, but he agreed that it was a good idea. What, you think you're the only one sneaking in extra phone calls during the day?"

Trying to appear innocent, Cain ignored the laughter coming from their son. "Kiss your sister for me, and tell Mook to keep his eyes open."

"How about you do the same?"

"Will do, buddy. I love you and we'll see you soon."

He said good-bye to both of them again before he put Hannah on for a minute, then let Maddie talk.

"That one's going to be a heartbreaker, Emma."

"You mean you think they both won't be?" Emma sat up after taking the handset back and turning off the speaker so Cain could answer a call on her cell phone. She watched as Cain grabbed a pen to write something down. "Are you doing okay with a house full of people, Maddie?"

"The kids are great, and I have to remind myself every so often that the men Cain left behind aren't field hands. Mook may carry a gun, but he's wonderful with Hannah and Hayden, and he helps Jerry when he can. Just a minute, I hear something."

"Is anything wrong?"

Cain stopped talking and glanced at her quizzically.

"It's just a visitor, but I can't make out who it is yet. Oh." Maddie exhaled loudly. "It's just your father."

"What's going on, Maddie? You don't usually hold your breath when you hear someone up the road."

"I didn't want to worry you, but your mother's started coming by and asking a lot of questions about you. Since I'd never tell her the kids are here, it makes for some scrambles at times."

Emma shook her head at Cain and smiled. "They're fine, love. My father just got there."

"What kind of questions is she asking, Maddie?"

"Just stuff like how often I talk to you and when you're coming home. Nothing real specific that raises any red flags, and you know I won't put up with her talking bad about you or Cain."

"Why the sudden interest, do you think?"

"I have no idea. Just finish what you're doing and leave the rest to Jerry and me. The kids will be waiting just like you left them."

"And I'm looking forward to seeing them and you, Maddie. Call if you need anything."

"You and Cain will be my first call, you know that."

"Problems?"

Emma stared at the nightstand a few moments longer before answering. "Problems?" she repeated. "I'm not really sure." She told Cain what Maddie had said about her mother.

"Does she know what the sudden interest is?" Cain pulled her shirt off and draped it over the arm of the chair near the closet. When Emma finally shook off her daze, Cain was dressed in just her underwear.

"I don't know what her sudden interest is, but can I tell you about mine?" For someone who'd been shot, Cain looked incredibly good.

The deep laugh chased a delicious shiver through Emma.

"What are you interested in, lass?"

"For one thing, I'm interested in expanding my wanton ways," she said as she stood up and presented her back to Cain, who seemed to take a torturously long time opening her zipper. She just let the dress fall to the floor, waiting to see if Cain liked what she saw. "Then I'm interested in hearing you moan."

"How, pray tell, do you plan to do that?"

Emma needed no further words as she guided Cain to sit, but not before her plain white boxers came off. Once Cain was sitting, Emma stood before her and released her bra. Cain's eyes were riveted as

Emma slowly peeled the straps down, exposing her chest a little at a time. The awkwardness of her inexperience had long vanished, and she now enjoyed seeing the raw hunger in Cain.

"How about these? This was my latest little gift from Kevin." Emma put her fingers in the sides of her underwear and smiled.

"Nice, but take them off," Cain replied, her voice husky. "I want to see all of you."

The black panties came down her legs, and Emma stood naked, wanting the need in her partner to rise a bit more. The throbbing between her legs increased when Cain's nipples grew hard just from looking at her. How easy it would be to rush and reach the pinnacle only Cain could bring her to, but tonight wasn't about fast. Tonight was about giving Cain the pleasure she deserved and making it last as long as Emma could drag it out.

With that goal in mind she grasped Cain's hands before she could derail her plans. She dropped to her knees and guided Cain's hands to the arms of the chair. "Just remember one word before we begin." Emma sat back on her feet and gazed up at Cain with desire.

"What's that?"

"Patience, love." Emma let Cain's hands go, knowing they would stay where she'd put them. "I want you, and I want it to last." She leaned over and bit down gently on an alert nipple. "Can you give me that?"

Cain put her feet flat on the floor. "I'll give you anything you want."

"Good." Emma sat back again so she could watch her hands wander from Cain's shoulders down her body. She smiled when she saw how tightly Cain was gripping the chair as Emma's unrelenting fingers traced every muscle in Cain's chest and abdomen. "Lean back and relax for me, baby."

"Relax, she says. Good one." Cain obeyed anyway, falling back farther into the chair.

Emma stopped roaming and rested her hands at the apex of Cain's legs. Their eyes stayed locked as Emma slowly opened Cain's sex and lowered her mouth. With a feather-light touch of her tongue she started at the base of the hard clitoris and worked her way up slowly.

"You're killing me with all this teasing, darlin'." Though Cain complained a bit, she never moved her hands, and Emma never stopped or changed her tactics.

The one thing she did do was moan as Cain grew wetter and disobeyed her by lacing her fingers through her hair. Wanting to take her to the next level, she stopped licking and started sucking before Cain could protest.

Emma inched her closer to the sheer definition of pleasure, but before that happened, she lifted her head.

"Lass, this is no time to be stopping." Cain's voice sounded almost strangled.

Emma pinched Cain's clitoris between two fingers, feeling how hard it was. "Tell me what you want." She pinched harder, liking the way Cain's hips bucked in response. "Tell me or I'll stop."

"I want you to love me forever." Her hips bucked again as Emma increased the pressure. "And I want only you in my bed till I die."

This time Emma had no intention of stopping. She sucked until the hands in her hair tightened their hold and she heard Cain scream her name, awed that she could affect Cain so powerfully.

Cain recovered quickly, though, and before Emma could say anything, she found herself on her back on the bed, soaked and ready. Cain's fingers slid in slowly as her thumb started its delicious stimulation. The kiss Cain had initiated swallowed each one of her moans.

Cain was so tender that a warmth went through Emma that formed tears in her eyes, and she held on to Cain until the walls of her sex clamped down around the loving fingers. As her orgasm washed over her like a Caribbean wave, Emma broke their kiss and arched her back, wanting to get closer, and as in all aspects of their life together, Cain held her and made her feel safe.

"I love you so much." Emma put her hands on Cain's cheeks and gave her a blissful smile.

"I love you too, lass, and I'm more than willing to do it again if I didn't get it right."

"Honey, if you want me to leave the room tonight, then you got it plenty right."

"Don't tempt me." Cain placed her hand gently on Emma's cheek.

"You couldn't be more wanted," she whispered, and Emma's tears finally fell.

The door that led to Cain's heart was locked once again, but now Emma was sitting on the inside where no one could touch her.

❖

They took their time showering and getting ready for their evening out. Cain stayed with Emma the entire time, watching as she put on makeup and fixed her hair, wearing a new set of underwear. Seeing so much skin on display, Cain was flooded with memories of Emma's pregnancy with Hayden, and she couldn't wait to see Emma like that again. At the moment she felt like a spoiled child who wanted the shiny new bike she'd admired forever, but needed to clean her plate before she was allowed to have it. Big Gino was now her only barrier to the future she wanted.

"Are you all right, honey?"

Cain looked up as Emma stood before her with a bow tie in her hand. "Sorry, you caught me daydreaming. Did you say something?"

"I asked if you needed some help." She held up the tie and received a nod. "You can daydream all you want as long as I fit in somewhere."

"You dominate my dreams, lass." Finished putting everything on but her jacket, Cain stood to help Emma get ready. They had to attend a dinner before heading over to the club, but they weren't in a hurry.

"Thank you for saying so, but now I need you to focus on tonight." Emma stepped into the dress she'd picked up earlier and let Cain zip her up. "Are our friends still out there?"

Cain walked to the window before answering. Stepping out to the balcony, Cain could see two surveillance teams. She lit a cigar as she observed the observers, pulling out her cell phone with a wink for Emma, who was slipping into her shoes. Cain knew that the watchers almost always wanted to ignore these types of calls, since she never used something so easy to listen in on.

"Lou, give us about twenty minutes. Then pull the car around."

"We're on it, Cain. You want to go out the back?"

Before she could answer, Emma joined her. "When you're married to someone like Emma Casey, you always escort the lady out the front door."

"Truer words, boss."

The camera captured the embrace followed by a kiss, and the powerful mikes recorded the words. "Think they're going to dinner at Carlotti's?" Claire asked.

"There's no way they won't be there," Shelby answered.

❖

After weeks of silence and inactivity, the opening of Emma's signaled more than a new place to dance in the city. As trucks made deliveries to Carlotti's Italian Restaurant, a wiretap on the office phone caught a conversation between the restaurant manager and his boss, Vincent Carlotti.

Vincent had told him to bump a major anniversary party scheduled in the private dining room. At first the agents assigned to him hadn't given it much thought, until the agents assigned to Ramon Jatibon reported two new arrivals at the Lakefront Airport. Ramon's twins Remington and Mano had flown in on their private plane, traveling very light.

"The families are circling the wagons, and they're probably going to discuss whatever's bought them all together in that private dining room tonight." More agents than Shelby thought worked in New Orleans now surrounded the restaurant owned by Vincent, waiting to catch snippets of the conversation. "The only ones missing are Giovanni and his boys, but that's another story they'll probably cover tonight."

Claire nodded and readjusted some of the gear for better reception. "Vincent's kid, Vinny, I know from my prior assignment, but what's the story on the Jatibons?"

"Street name Snake Eyes, the twins are the next generation of that family's empire. The daughter Remi will be the next head of the family, while her brother Mano runs their Las Vegas holdings. In a lot of ways Remi reminds me of Cain, at least when it comes to the revolving door on her bedroom. Just like our friend up there, Remi has had her fair share of beautiful women. The old man, Ramon, much like Vincent in his organization, still calls the shots, but the young guns wield a tremendous amount of power and influence within their respective families." Shelby tapped her finger to her chin, trying to remember what else was in the file she'd read earlier when they were informed of the twins' arrival.

"From what I know," said Claire, "part of the holdings of all three families is legitimate."

"True, but we're interested in the part that's not," Shelby said. She clicked the camera again, catching the Caseys across the street with their heads together. "And they're all smart. Dalton, Vincent, and Ramon raised pit vipers, but they're anything but stupid. All of the children are college graduates—Remi even went to law school—and all of them are master tacticians."

"Then how do we bring them down?"

"My father loves to build models of famous naval ships," Shelby said.

Claire laughed. "What does that have to do with anything?"

"He taught me that no matter how good the design of any ship, it always has flaws. Most are minor, but they're flaws nonetheless."

She concentrated on Claire, knowing Cain wouldn't give up anything but soft whispers to Emma. "Find those flaws, and enough of them, and you can sink anything. These guys are smart, but no one's perfect. Our job is to find the flaws."

CHAPTER FORTY-SIX

Welcome back to Carlotti's, Mrs. Casey." The head waiter escorted them through the din of the main dining room to where the rest of the families were waiting.

"Thank you." Emma was perfectly content to walk at a leisurely pace while hanging on Cain's arm. "It's good to be back."

For once the notoriously prompt Cain was fashionably late, but Emma could tell by their gait that Cain wasn't worried about it.

"Is everyone here, Dominic?"

"Yes, ma'am. We were waiting for you and Mrs. Casey before we started preparing the salad. Mr. Vincent ordered the crabmeat for everyone tonight, and we want it to be perfect." He bowed slightly, his hand on the doorknob.

Had it been anyone else, the forty-five minutes they'd kept Vincent waiting would have had them barred from the building for life. But Vincent was far from upset.

"You might want to hold off on that salad a little longer," Vincent said to the waiter, when he opened the door and escorted the two women in, then just as quickly closed it, not bothering with the lock. "Welcome, Cain." He took Emma's hand and kissed it. "Emma."

"Thank you for having us."

"Tonight is for you and Cain, so please don't thank me."

Emma looked up at Cain, not understanding but confident she would fill in the blanks later. With a wink Cain walked them to the empty chairs at the table and pulled one out for Emma, who casually glanced around the room, recognizing all but a few people. Everyone was dressed to attend the opening of the club after the meal.

"Emma, I believe you know everyone except Remi and Mano Jatibon, and Mano's wife, Sylvia," Vincent said, playing the good host. "Raul shipped them off to make even more money for him."

The twins, seated at their mother's side, nodded in Emma's direction. Vincent's son Vinny and Ramon rounded out the party, and they too nodded in greeting. At the center of the antique table stood a bottle of Irish whiskey and glasses for everyone. Standing, Vincent broke the seal so he could start pouring.

"For months we have been facing a problem." He spoke to no one in particular, and no one looked as if they were going to interrupt him for an explanation. "A problem that was growing stronger and more dangerous the longer we ignored it."

Ramon continued, "And while it was a threat to all of our families, from the beginning our snake had its sights on one more than the rest." He accepted a glass from Vincent, as did his wife and children.

Vincent picked up the tribute again, handing his son a glass. "We have all done our part to solve this problem, but one went beyond what was called for. For that we owe our gratitude." The next two crystal glasses went to Emma and Cain before he hefted the last one for himself. "Cain, Ramon and I have worked in this city for a long time, building a legacy for our children."

Ramon stood with his glass in hand again to tell part of the story. He had been the last to arrive in this country and this city, but he understood too well the importance of alliances. "Your father was no different, my friend. It still saddens me that you have had to go on without his counsel because of a pack of butchers."

"Tonight belongs to you for another reason, Cain." Vincent finally raised his glass and smiled. "And too long in coming, for which Ramon and I apologize."

Emma felt Cain's hand on her arm to keep her in her seat as she stood up and raised her glass as well. "No apologies are necessary among friends."

"Perhaps not, but we'll extend them anyway."

When Cain shook her head, Vincent laughed and said, "Your father and I shared a very long friendship, and I was so happy for him the day you were born. The pride in his face only grew in the days that followed. Dalton understood the importance of family and of loyalty."

His eyes then shifted to Emma. "You've given Cain the same gift Therese bestowed, and I see the same pride now blossom on Cain's face. So in a way, I'm happy we waited to have this meeting."

"Why?" It might not have been proper to speak, but Emma couldn't help herself.

"Because, beautiful one, our lives and our businesses exist for our families," Ramon answered. "We have to always remember that fact. It's why Vinny, Remi, and Mano are here, as well as my wife."

Vincent drew himself up, lifted his glass even higher, and formally addressed Cain. "Dalton had our respect and our loyalty because he earned it, and from your actions, Ramon and I can see he taught you well. I offer you the same, Cain. If you accept, I, Vincent Carlotti, offer you my friendship and my oath of protection to you and your family, should it be necessary."

Ramon lifted his glass as well. "My offer is the same, and I look forward to working with you."

"I accept," was all Cain said, with no hesitation.

"To the head of the Casey family, then," Vincent said.

Emma, Sylvia, and Marianna, Ramon's wife, kept their seats, but the others stood and raised their glasses before drinking. Something important had just happened, and Emma knew that while Cain had always had power, the night's events had just increased it tenfold. The old alliance had been formally re-formed, and Cain had replaced Dalton in the eyes of the other families. The muscle at both Vincent and Ramon's disposal came with that acknowledgement.

Like the men standing with her, Cain had just pledged her help in return, if it should be needed. That meant she'd made a commitment Hayden would be expected to honor, just like Vinny, Remi, and Mano were willing to do for their families.

"What we have agreed to tonight has made us all stronger," Cain said after she'd drained her glass. "To thank you for the honor, I come bearing gifts."

"Before you say anything, Vincent and I have something for you." Ramon accepted another drink from Vincent. "What you asked for, or should I say what you hoped for, I'd guess, is waiting for you. The place is a little open for our taste, though, so be careful."

"What did he say?" Shelby closed her eyes and concentrated on the voice speaking. They were sure Vincent was using some sort of jamming equipment, but they'd come prepared. The audio was low but decipherable.

"Something about a gift," Claire answered, as she too pressed the headphones closer to her ears. "We'll clean it up later in the lab."

"Joe?"

"Go ahead, Shelby." He was keeping his eye on the cars the players had arrived in. Most of the drivers were leaning against one of the SUVs, smoking and laughing at something one of them was saying. The muscle was stationed at all the entrances. A well-planned hit would take out most of the bad guys in town.

"Call me the minute that door opens and you see them all leaving, Joe."

"You got it."

Back in the restaurant, Cain said, "This time around it's worth the risk, Ramon. What's the old saying, 'a life without risks isn't worth living'?"

"I believe it should be a 'life without love' instead of 'risks,'" Marianna said. She smiled at Emma, who sat quietly next to Cain. "If that's true, your life is very worth living, so take Ramon's advice to heart."

"Thank you, Marianna." Emma also smiled, at the words and at the fingers squeezing hers gently. "And please don't worry about Cain. She has too many responsibilities to be going around doing foolish things."

"Is it official yet?"

"What?" The bottle Vincent had opened was almost empty, and Emma hoped the toasts for the night were done and someone would bring her a large glass of water.

"The reason you haven't touched that?" Marianna pointed to the drink.

"You'll be one of the first to know. I'm just following the doctor's orders in getting ready."

She laughed as she accepted a large juice Marianna got up and poured from the bar. "Once it happens I'll be happy to shout it from the rooftops."

"You might have to hurry for that, sweetheart." When Emma

looked up from her drink, Marianna pointed to the room where the others had disappeared. "The only other person I've known who is as crazy about such news is Ramon, so I'm sure Cain will beat you to shouting out the good news." Marianna stood and embraced Emma. "I'm happy you have found yourself back home."

"What in the hell are they talking about?" Claire asked. All of a sudden the interference had gotten so bad all the conversations disappeared, and then just as quickly it came back incredibly clear.

"If it's anything important then they're talking in code." Shelby hitched her shoulders a bit as she continued to listen to the women discuss what sounded like nothing. "It's hard to believe they met tonight so Marianna Jatibon and Emma Casey could catch up on old times."

"Shelby?"

Joe's voice startled her as she ran through the possibilities of what was really going on.

"Go ahead."

"Does this sound vaguely familiar?" With powerful binoculars he swept the area again, but no one in his sights had moved.

The question stopped her thought process cold, and something became clear to her, making her stare at Claire and panic.

"What's he talking about?" Claire asked.

"We need to get in there," Anthony said. "Get our boss on the horn and get us a warrant."

"I say we wait," Lionel said.

"Explain, please," Claire repeated. "If we blow our cover we'd better have more than a benign talk between two women."

"The last time Cain played us," Shelby paused, trying to get her thoughts in order, "for one brief moment we thought she'd screwed up and let us see into how her mind works. All of a sudden every conversation, every plan she was making was out in the open, and it was as if she didn't care who was listening."

"She had her own agenda." Claire sounded as if it all became clear to her as well. "And tonight is no different."

Not far from them Anthony was on the phone with Annabel Hicks. He was pleading his case, using the same rational argument Shelby was laying out for Claire.

Because he was, Hicks was hard-pressed to find any personal bias against Cain or the others. As soon as she finished talking to him she picked up the phone again and called one of their more reliable judges for the proper paperwork.

"What do you think she has in mind?" Claire asked.

Shelby kept listening as Emma, Marianna, and Sylvia talked about trivial matters. "Think about who's in there, and all we hear are the three least important ones. The major players must be gone, making whatever move they had planned all along."

The phone next to Claire rang, and both women just stared at it for three rings before Claire picked it up.

After listening to the person on the other end, Claire responded. "Yes, ma'am." She exhaled heavily after she switched the phone off and told Shelby, "With any luck we have about ten minutes before we raid the restaurant."

"Raid it? What in the hell for?"

Joe cut in on the radio. "The best Agent Hicks could come up with is liquor violations, whatever that means. It's an excuse, Shel, to get us into that room and prove your theory right."

"My theory? Oh, no, I'm not going on record as this being my idea. Because if we do this and we're wrong, kiss the investigation up to now good-bye. You know as well as I do, Joe, once Muriel and Cain finish fighting this legally, the law is going to bite us in the butt. And we're the law, God damn it."

❖

In a secluded basement room of the restaurant, the new alliance sat at a table where a lot of their previous meetings had taken place. Here, no matter how good the surveillance equipment was, the group was in a perfectly safe haven. Cain fished the four Bracato rings out of her pocket and placed them on the table, not needing to explain their significance.

"The city needs new territorial boundaries," she began as she lined up the rings. "I ask only that if you decide on a piece of the drug trade, you do it with someone other than the Luis family."

"They're the best connected, so why?" Vinny asked. "They could help us make a lot of money."

"His nephew has a problem with respect, especially when it

comes to my wife and her needs. Do business with him if you like, but understand I won't respect that boundary." She stared at Vinny. "If he goes near Emma again, I'll serve that bastard's dick to his uncle on a plate and force him to choke on it."

"Understood, Cain," Vincent cut in with a glare for his son. "After the gift of new enterprises you've opened up for us, we can abide by that. Ramon?"

"Our interests are elsewhere at the moment, so we have no problem."

His children nodded in agreement.

"Be careful with these people, though," Ramon said. "They may look gentle, but Juan Luis is nothing but a butcher." He cut his eyes to both Vinny and Cain. "He learned all his cruelty at his uncle's knee. Rodolfo drinks in my club, but I'll never have anything to do with him."

"Well," Vinny said, "someone has to control the drug trade in the city, or it won't matter how aligned we are. The money involved can build an organization strong enough to topple us all. That's what Giovanni and his sons were after." Even though he spoke out of turn again, his words rang true.

"It sounds like something you might be interested in." Cain threw the comment out as a test.

"Not if all of you are against it, but I'm warning you about letting some unknown get too well established. The city already runs red from those who want in and are willing to take a chance."

Like their fathers, Cain and Vinny had grown up together and more than understood each other. Ramon might have not had a history, but his children had a long one with the next generation. Remi and Mano had known Cain and Vinny since they were six, so the four of them would back each other up even if the majority of them didn't agree with a venture.

"What if we offered our protection as far as moving the stuff?" Remi said. "I think like Cain. If the drug trade doesn't touch our businesses, we might negotiate with someone like Vinny, if he's willing to take the chance."

Remi had enough of her father's trust to speak for him.

"What cut?" Vinny asked.

Vincent and Ramon looked at each other and smiled as their

children set their courses for the future. Judging from Vinny's question, the deal was done if the terms were agreeable.

"Twenty-five for us, twenty-five for Cain," Remi offered, and Cain nodded.

"Done." Vinny laughed and stood to shake hands with his allies.

Just then a team of agents led by Annabel Hicks entered the restaurant and headed for the private dining room.

CHAPTER FORTY-SEVEN

Lou was the first to intercept them before they reached the door. "Good evening, Agent Hicks."

"It's nice to be so well known." Annabel spoke almost as if she were joking with him and had no choice but to stop, since the man was so large. "Step aside or we'll move you. I don't care how intimidating you think you are."

"Is there a problem?" Lou asked.

"Open the door," commanded Annabel, Anthony Curtis at her elbow.

"Can I see a warrant?" Lou didn't seem fazed and didn't budge. "Since you can't answer a simple question, maybe your reason for being here is written on that."

"The lady said move." Anthony put two hands in the center of Lou's chest and shoved. Considering Lou's size, Annabel was shocked when he went flying into a table where a waiter had just served four heaping bowls of pasta.

The bigger shock came when Vincent came to the door and opened it himself. "What the hell is going on out here?"

"Where's Casey?" Anthony demanded, his words dying on his lips when he saw that smug smile from behind Vincent. "You can't be here."

"Agent Hicks, I want an explanation," the elder Carlotti continued.

They all watched as the diners who'd cushioned Lou's fall were helped off the floor by a team of waiters. The hot oil and garlic on one of the pasta dishes had splashed on Lou's face, forming angry red splotches.

"We have reason to believe," Annabel started, grimacing when the rest of the group they thought was missing came out as well, "that you have some illegal liquor on the premises. We have a warrant to check your licenses."

"Be careful, Vincent. The last time this happened to me I caught a bullet with my chest," Cain said.

Annabel was one of the only people in the place who didn't laugh. "That was uncalled for, Ms. Casey."

"You aren't kidding, Agent." This time any lightheartedness bled out of Cain's voice.

"Dominic, get the paperwork, then get my attorney on the phone," Vincent ordered. With a sneer, he looked at Annabel like a shark regarding a wounded fish. "How do you feel about Anchorage, Agent Hicks? Because once I'm done with you, you'll be investigating bear shit for the rest of your career."

"Is that a threat, Mr. Carlotti?"

"It's an invitation to meet me in court, and unless Lou over there says otherwise, I don't think I'll be alone in my complaint." He held his liquor as well as other license information up, but she didn't even bother to look at it. She and the other agents had seen what they'd come for.

"Tell me again, Agent Curtis, how this isn't personal," Cain said as the agent started to leave. "At least this time you all bothered to get a warrant and not shoot me at the first given chance. I thought you would've learned your lesson after paying some stupid flunky to bug my hospital room," she said, taking a chance that she was right.

Anthony pulled away from Hicks by shrugging her restraining hand off his shoulder, his face red. "You think you're smart enough to never get caught, but no one's that fucking smart. I'm going to love the day we bring you down, no matter how we do it, and I'm going to be the one who drags you there."

While Cain's comment was meant to bait, no one in the restaurant heard it, though Anthony's booming voice was hard to miss.

"Agent Curtis, stand down," his superior ordered. "My apologies, Ms. Casey."

"You can apologize from across the street, Agent Hicks." Muriel arrived dressed in a tuxedo, like most of the group that had been called away from the private dinner. "Sorry I'm late, but I was just finishing up with a bit of business." She gave a copy of something to Cain before addressing the group gathered in the main dining room. "The Fifth Circuit just issued an emergency protection order on my client's behalf, stating there must be five hundred yards between the agents listed here and Derby Cain Casey and her family." With a smile she handed over the brief as she pointed her date in the direction of the private dining room and away from the agents standing behind Annabel. "That includes everyone present, so please vacate the property or I'll involve the police, and we both know they'd love nothing better."

"There's no way the court sanctioned this."

The paperwork Annabel was examining looked authentic, though.

"Ordinarily no, but this was extreme circumstances, and neither I nor the court was willing to take a chance with my client's life again. If there was one rogue agent, who's to say there aren't more?"

The order wouldn't be in place long, but Muriel decided to have a little fun while she could. Anthony had been the weak link, and Cain had exploited it well.

As Annabel stood and read, none of her people moving, Muriel pulled out her phone. "Commissioner Albert, Muriel Casey."

The fact that she had his direct number snapped Annabel's head up.

"About that paperwork we filed, I might need some assistance." She paused to listen to something, never losing eye contact with Cain. "Carlotti's Italian Restaurant, and please bring as many units as you see fit."

"This isn't over, Ms. Casey." Annabel handed back the papers and signaled for everyone to pull back. No way in hell was she letting the New Orleans Police Department escort her anywhere.

"I bought you a night, cousin," Muriel whispered in Cain's ear when they embraced. "Use it wisely."

"I use them all wisely, Muriel, but thank you. Emma doesn't need any stress right now, so this should simplify matters."

"It sounds like you've got a lot to look forward to, then, so I want you to be careful as well."

Cain held out her hand out to Emma, who immediately took it. "I have everything to look forward to, cousin."

And every reason to fight for what's mine, she thought, and Emma read the sentiment clearly in her face.

❖

As they rode in silence to their new club after dinner, Emma enjoyed the feel of Cain's arms around her and her lips against her neck. Their afternoon had left them both in the mood to touch, and they didn't waste even that short span of alone time.

"Thanks for bringing me with you tonight, baby." Emma looked into Cain's blue eyes. She smiled easily when Cain's hand went to her middle. "Do you think it'll be a boy or a girl?"

"It'll be what I want most. A Casey with a lot of Verde mixed in. We're going to love it no matter what, so it isn't important to me what it is."

The excitement from the restaurant as well as having Emma this close in a very tight black dress was fueling Cain's libido. She felt Emma's nipple harden under the material as she squeezed her breast. "Tonight was about all our futures—mine, Vincent's, and Ramon's—and the futures of our families, so it was important for you to be there."

"Just remember that I belong to you and it's my job to make your dreams come true for the rest of our lives." Emma pressed Cain's hand harder against her chest as she brought their lips together. "Tell me we're almost done? I miss the kids and want us to be a family again."

"One dance, darlin'. Then we'll finish this."

The car stopped, and the noise coming from the line waiting to get into the new club was just audible through the thick glass. After another long kiss Cain knocked on the privacy window, and Merrick opened the door.

Their dinner companions were already at Cain and Emma's private table, and the others they'd invited were dancing and taking advantage of the open bar. Cain hadn't thrown a party like this in a while, and the crowd seemed happy to be there now that she felt the need to celebrate something.

When they paused at the top of the stairs that led down to the bar, the music didn't stop, but the DJ lowered the volume considerably, making people look up.

"They look stunning together," Muriel said to her date as they both stood up. "And I didn't realize till just now that I missed seeing them together." She glanced across the place as people started to clap, spotting Claire and Shelby not far from where Cain and Emma were standing. Since the agents' names weren't on the list, they weren't supposed to be there. Before she could do anything about it, Cain nodded in her direction, then motioned for her to forget it.

"The place looks great, honey."

Cain put her arm around Emma's waist as they descended the stairs. "Let's hope it isn't the explosive success the last place was."

"Not funny, darling."

The techno beat changed to something slow and sexy, and Emma pulled Cain to the middle of the dance floor. "Dance with me?"

"Forever and a day, my love."

The two agents scanned the room as the Caseys shared a dance, but they didn't see anything out of the ordinary. They'd been a little surprised when Cain had nodded to them on their way in, giving the bouncer the false impression of permission to enter. It was a chance, but it was worth taking, even if they did end up in jail.

Once the dance was over, the rhythm picked up again and Emma followed Cain's lead as they continued to dance. Emma's would only have one opening night, and they looked like they were prepared to enjoy it.

Before long, Remi and her date and Mano and Sylvia joined them, making Shelby and Claire relax a little more. From their vantage point Cain knew they were there and didn't care, and apparently all Cain had planned was a great party.

Forty minutes later, Cain and Emma made their way through the crowd to the back of the room and disappeared behind a door that Merrick opened for them.

"Joe?" Shelby whispered into her mike.

Claire ran to keep up as Shelby rushed toward the exit.

"What's wrong?" Joe responded.

"Does Cain's new real estate have a helipad?"

Lionel hacked into the city's building permits department and started scanning. "Yep. Nothing to accommodate anything big, but it does have one."

"Scramble something. Anthony was right. She's got something planned. Probably something remote." When Shelby got to the front door she could see the bird coming from the direction of the heliport next to the New Orleans Superdome. "Move it, Joe."

Instead of heading to the car, Shelby and Claire ran toward the building next door, which was one floor higher than the one they'd just left. Their badges got them in and worked again when they knocked on the door of a young physician just getting home from a double shift. When they reached the large windows facing Cain's building, they saw Cain leading Emma to the helicopter. Again Cain had her arm around Emma's waist, and Emma was pressed up to her side.

Relief flooded Shelby when she saw another helicopter coming from the west. Unlike the night Cain had lost the agents in Wisconsin with the same trick, tonight they would know exactly where she was going and what she'd be doing once she got there.

"Make sure they stay five hundred yards away. We wouldn't want to break a court order," Shelby said.

"Stop making jokes and get your ass on the roof," Joe ordered. He was driving as Lionel was busy looking at the fueling records for all the private planes in the vicinity, along with any flight plans they might have filed. "We need you airborne before we lose them again."

"Not going to happen again."

"Got something," Lionel said as he tried to keep his seat and ignore the fact that Joe was driving and watching the helicopter more than the road. "Carlotti fueled his plane this afternoon, but the pilot said they wouldn't have the flight plans until they were ready for takeoff."

"Hear that?" Joe asked Shelby as he directed them to the nearest interstate entrance ramp. "I'll call ahead and arrange something, and we'll meet you there in less than ten."

Shelby listened, and from their direction, Joe was right. Wherever Cain was headed, she would have to take a plane. Shelby couldn't understand why she'd pulled such a stunt, but at the moment all the speculation in the world wasn't as important as keeping up with Cain and, no matter how much she liked her, finally catching her at something so they could shut her down.

The blackness of Lake Pontchartrain came into view, as did the runways of the airport located on the south shore. "What's your ETA, Joe?"

"If we're lucky, in about five." He never let off the accelerator as they arrived at their exit. "Even if they're twenty minutes ahead of us, we won't have a problem. A Coast Guard plane's waiting for us, and she's fully fueled. Wherever they go, we'll be five hundred yards behind them."

Lionel was calling Hicks and giving her an update. They'd need help from the State Department if Cain was traveling someplace they didn't have jurisdiction. They pulled up as Cain and Emma were landing close to their ride. Again the couple stayed close together as they boarded and never looked back, even though they had to know they were being followed.

"What are you up to, Cain?" Shelby whispered into the noise of the rotor blades as she and Claire landed.

Chapter Forty-eight

The blinds in Muriel's private office were down, assuring Cain she was the only one enjoying the vision in the strapless black bra and thong. The extremely revealing undergarments had been necessary for the dress Emma had just taken off.

"What's all that leering for?"

Cain's deep chuckle hardened Emma's nipples noticeably.

"You stand there looking like that, and you wonder why I'm leering? I'm only human, darlin'."

"Think you'll still be leering when I'm as big as a house?"

Cain laughed again, but this time she stood up so she could inspect more closely. "I remember a bit of my leering and what happened after it sent you into labor with Hayden."

She traced a path from the presently flat stomach up to cup Emma's breast. "You're in my blood, lass, so I'll always desire you, no matter what."

"Are you planning to finish what you're starting now?" The starch of Cain's shirt felt good against Emma's back as she leaned farther into the strong body.

"We have a flight to catch," Cain said, but didn't let go.

"Then stop making me crazy or we'll be late." She pressed her hand into Cain's crotch. "Very late."

"Cruel, sweetling." Cain didn't want to, but she stepped back and unbuttoned her shirt. They *did* have a plane to catch, and she wanted to get business out of the way so she could leisurely finish what they'd started. "Now, please put something on before I forget what my name is."

"Did the men sweep tonight?" Emma stepped into an old pair of jeans and zipped them up before changing the bra and putting on a sweater.

"Thoroughly, why?" Cain settled for a pair of chinos, a fresh white shirt, and a dark sweater. The couple looked more like models for a Gap ad than a part of an organized crime family.

"Just curious as to what's going to happen next."

In the interest of time Cain gave her the quick version before escorting her to the elevator. When they reached the first floor of the club, their bodyguards were waiting, dressed very much like Emma.

"How did our fishing expedition go?" Cain asked.

"I believe the term is 'they fell for it hook, line, and sinker,' so I hope they dressed appropriately," Lou joked. He blushed when Emma walked up and pressed her hand to the side of his face that wasn't burned. "I'm all right, Mrs. Casey, really."

"Then take a stroll outside and see if we still have company," Cain said with a wink.

The back alley appeared empty except for the vehicle parked close to the door.

Though Vincent's plane was in the air heading south, Remi Jatibon's was sitting in the family hangar waiting for a trip north. Ten minutes after the Coast Guard jet had hit twenty thousand feet, the fuel truck pulled up at Jatibon's hangar.

The Caseys drove straight in and took their time boarding, since the hangar doors were closed and the building was windowless. Ramon had never cared for prying eyes, even when what he was doing was innocent.

"Welcome aboard, folks," the pilot said. "Ms. Casey, according to Mr. Jatibon and Remi, the extra cargo is in the small private office waiting for you." He pointed in the appropriate direction. "And the other cargo you sent ahead is in the bedroom."

Cain nodded and took a seat on the sofa.

"Cargo?" Emma asked, sitting next to her. They had to kill about thirty minutes before takeoff.

"Tonight is about repaying favors and settling debts. To accomplish that, you always need a little baggage, so to speak."

"Then I look forward to the morning."

Everything Emma had prayed for in the past four years was just beyond her reach, and that was what worried her the most—wanting too much always resulted in huge disappointment when it didn't pan out.

CHAPTER FORTY-NINE

The deserted airstrip was lit only by the headlights of the vehicles below, but the pilot still made a smooth landing. Once on the ground, as Emma kissed Cain one last time before following Merrick to one of the waiting vehicles, Lou carried a large bag from the plane and threw it into the back of another vehicle.

As they rode over the rough Wisconsin terrain, Cain closed her eyes and rested her head on the neck support. The bundle she held against her chest was still, oblivious to the rocking. Aside from Mook, who was driving, she'd brought along only Lou and Katlin. Emma and Merrick were already well on their way to Maddie's.

For once, she wished Hayden were a little older so she could've included him. Someday she'd tell him the whole story as part of his lessons for his future responsibilities, which included keeping the Casey secrets as well as their legacy.

They stopped next to a pitch-dark wooded area. After they entered the old stand of trees and walked about half a mile in, Cain noticed that the stars were barely visible, even though the trees were still bare. She had to give Mook credit for accomplishing what she'd asked. From the thickness of the roots, it couldn't have been easy.

"I owe you a bonus, man," Cain said. She now sat in the portable chair Katlin had carried for her, a lantern at her feet, and clutched her still-achy side. She could forget about it for long stretches now, but in the cold night air after a long walk she knew she still wasn't a hundred percent.

"It took me two weeks because I only worked at night, so I'm thinking fifty-yard-line tickets for a couple of games next year for

Hayden and me." The hole they were staring at was deep and more than worth what Mook was requesting.

Carelessly, Lou dropped his load onto the mud near the hole, and in the stillness of the night Cain heard a moan. Giovanni Bracato's eyes didn't open after Lou slit the bag apart, and they stayed closed until Katlin slapped him hard across the face, which woke him up from the sedative Vincent's men had given him.

Blinking rapidly, he tried to focus on where he was. He was sure he would wake from this nightmare and find himself in bed next to the young woman he'd hired for the night. The process by which he'd gone from her bed to a cold night on his knees had to be a dream.

"Personally," Cain's voice was low as she adjusted the lamp by her feet, "I like the city, but this place is starting to grow on me." She waved to the surrounding area. "It really is more suited for nights like tonight than the sprawl of New Orleans."

"You let me go now, and I might consider letting your family live."

"You shut your mouth now, and I'll let you live that many more minutes longer."

Cain's matter-of-fact tone made Giovanni stop talking.

"If you want a quick death, though, I'll be happy to accommodate you."

"Cut the shit, Casey. You aren't going to kill me."

Her chuckle came close to making Giovanni lose his temper, but he pressed his lips together and stopped talking again.

"Why do you think that?"

"You need me."

She raised her eyebrow at that statement, so Giovanni rushed ahead. "For balance, you need me. Besides, my sons will never rest until they avenge me, and you don't want that kind of shit." The urge to take a shot was more important to him than his immediate safety, so Giovanni took it. "It's less time for you to fuck that little piece—"

Lou hit him in the back of the head, pitching him forward and giving him a mouth full of mud for his words.

"Careful, Big Gino. I wouldn't want you to die on me before we're through."

"Sorry, boss," Lou said, even though he sounded less than sincere.

"No need. You just saved me the trouble." Cain pulled her coat tighter around her. "Are you done, or do we leave you with Lou a little while till we kill all that spunk?"

"What do you want?"

"What do I want?" She put her hand on her chin as if to think of a good answer. "Not too much, really. I just wanted to have a talk."

"That would've taken a phone call, so why all this?" Even though his hands were tied behind him, Giovanni could feel goose bumps rising on his arms. "Your father would've never tried anything like this. He understood the ways things were done."

"Like having a coward kill him from a moving car? You're right. I guess he underestimated how dishonorable you are."

Had there been more light, Giovanni was sure Cain would've seen the vein in his neck pulsate. "Dalton was careless, but that had nothing to do with me."

Cain's head fell back a little as she closed her eyes and took a deep breath. "I should start by saying that I told my wife this wouldn't take long."

Giovanni shrank back from her glare when she opened her eyes again.

"You wouldn't want to make a liar out of me, would you?" Leaning in his direction, she balled her fist, and the blow knocked him back so far, Lou had to jump to catch him before he tumbled into the hole.

"Why the fuck did you do that?" Giovanni shook his head, trying to clear the blood out of his nose.

"Call it incentive to pay attention." From her coat pocket Cain pulled a small pouch.

Giovanni spat, trying to get the copper taste out of his mouth, and almost hit Cain's boot. "What do you hope to gain here? Aside from me making it my mission in life to kill you."

"I gain knowing the truth of what happened. That's all, really, and in a way, so will you." Cain untied the drawstring on the pouch. "Actually, your new mission should be to ask for forgiveness."

The clink of whatever landed in her palm made Giovanni crane his neck to see.

"I have all the truth I need, so there's no reason to lie."

"You do, huh?" Giovanni laughed and shifted in an attempt to get the circulation going in his legs again. "You're a lot like Dalton." He needed to tip the scales back in his favor. "Do you realize that? A taste for cheap whiskey and cheaper women, but weak for everything else."

When he saw the first ring in Cain's hand, any other words died in his throat.

"If I'm lucky"—the next ring came out of the bag—"at the end of my life, people will compare me to my father." The third ring rolled out into Cain's palm, but she didn't look up until the last one came out and she returned the bag to her jacket.

"What have you done?"

"I observed your offspring, Giovanni. I watched them and how they lived." She stretched out her hand so he could see the four signet rings clearly. "Your sons were very much like you. Do *you* realize that?"

"*Were*?" The possibilities of what Cain had said were almost too much for Giovanni to handle, but he fought back the bile in his throat.

"Did you think I'm so weak that I'd ignore your attacks on my family?" The laugh that followed had nothing to do with mirth. "No, Giovanni, you now have to atone for every action you ordered."

Giovanni had always avoided tears, but they now flowed freely down his cheeks. "Please, not my sons. Anything but that."

Cain raised the first ring and held it to the light to read the inscription inside. "For my brother Billy, you paid with Stephano's life." With a quiet thud it landed in the mud in front of Giovanni. "For my mother's life, Michael's sacrifice seemed to fall short, but it'll have to do." The next ring fell next to the first. "Marie, my sister, was an innocent soul, but your boys couldn't respect that, and they gave her the most miserable of deaths."

At the word "innocent," Giovanni knew what name would come next, and the totality of his sins landed on his shoulders. His youngest, Francis, was too kindhearted to ever get far in his world, and Giovanni had kept him close so the vultures wouldn't get near him. He was doing better after Giovanni had started to spend a lot of time showing him the business, but he still had a lot to learn. Through his tears he recognized Francis's ring in Cain's hand. A car accident had caused the ding on the side that his youngest son had never had repaired.

"Francis was your sacrifice for Marie's death."

Cain's words confirmed his fears.

"That leaves us with one."

"Even if you kill me tonight, Gino will be my salvation. He won't rest until he avenges all of us." He spit again after the outburst, and again he landed on his face after Lou hit him.

As Lou lifted him, he sobbed when he saw the last ring in Cain's hand.

"Tonight I wanted you to know the pain of losing your entire family." The last ring landed in the dirt. "That was your price for my father's death. Every one of them is dead, and the Bracato name will die with them."

"No, I still have my grandson, and even you aren't coldhearted enough to kill an infant." He tilted his head to the side, trying to wipe his face on his shirt. "If you are, then you'll have a special place in hell."

With a nod Cain signaled Mook to come forward and hand over his bundle. Seemingly happy, Gino's infant son gurgled and smiled up at her.

"Your eldest son died thinking I'd done just that. He spent his last moments believing his stupidity had cost him the one good thing in his life."

Giovanni wanted nothing more than to break the bindings and rip Cain apart with his bare hands. "What, you're leaving that pleasure for me?"

"There's more than one way to kill something dear."

A deep breath did nothing to calm Giovanni's frustration. "What the fuck does that mean?"

"That after tonight, Giovanni Bracato III will cease to exist. Your family name will be forgotten within the week." She handed the baby back and Mook walked away, the outline of his body rapidly becoming nothing more than a shadow. "It ends tonight, Giovanni, and there's nothing left to say."

"Funny, I still have plenty to say."

Cain pushed, and Giovanni fell back into the hole Mook had

worked so diligently on, breaking his arm as he landed. The silence and miles of solitude swallowed his scream.

"Get me out of here." He imagined that every bug in the state of Wisconsin was crawling on him, and the sides of the space were closing in on him. "Casey, I fucking mean it."

Cain waved Lou off, then picked up a shovel and started filling.

Giovanni screamed louder when he felt the first load hit his chest, crystalizing what Cain had in mind.

She kept moving dirt until Giovanni could no longer be heard and she'd worked up a sweat despite the weather. Lou took over so Cain could get back to her loved ones.

At the car she took the baby back from Mook and kissed his forehead. "I didn't know your mama, little man, but from what I learned about her, I think she'd be happy for you. Because no matter what, you're going to be loved, and that starts now. I just buried your past, so you should have a good head start."

❖

"Cain told us the news."

Emma wasn't listening to Maddie, hadn't listened to her for the past hour. As much as she'd wanted to wake the kids earlier, Emma had told her to wait. She'd said she missed them but wanted Cain with her when she saw them again.

Emma tapped her nail against the front windowpane and tried to break through her fog of concern for Cain. "What news?"

"Cain bought the old Jones place, and she's going to let Jerry and your dad share it. We're planning on doubling our herd by the summer."

When the headlights of a vehicle appeared in the distance, Emma almost ripped the curtain off its rod. She didn't know why, but she'd been a nervous wreck since Cain had left her side. Things were probably fine, but now that everything she wanted was in her grasp, the thought of losing it was unbearable.

"Hi, darlin'." Cain's deep voice vibrated though Emma's chest as Emma practically jumped off the porch into her lover's arms. "Come on and let's get our present inside."

Mook handed her the baby and waved good night as he started for the stairs.

Maddie was the first to come up out of her seat when Cain walked in. She smiled when the little guy put his head down on Cain's shoulder and blinked big brown eyes her way.

"First, I want to thank you for taking our children in and keeping them safe." Cain couldn't stand Maddie's longing anymore, so she handed her the baby. "And if it's not too late, I want to talk to you two about something."

"We're set to take the day off tomorrow, so sure," Jerry answered. When he touched the baby, his hand covered the back of the child's head.

Cain winked in Emma's direction before sitting back and watching the bonding begin. "You two have been so kind to us, especially to Emma and Hannah while we were apart. Emma has told me how well you both treated our little girl, and I believe that kind of friendship should be rewarded."

"You don't owe us anything, Cain. Maddie and I were happy to help." The tough farmer held his finger up and laughed when the tiny fingers grasped it.

"I'll be honest, guys, if God has blessed me with anything despite the things I've done in my life, it's the love of my wife."

Emma linked their fingers together and smiled.

"No word can describe what came because of that blessing. When you hold your child for the first time, you believe your life has infinite possibilities and your heart fills with infinite love. The responsibility is sometimes daunting, but very worth it."

"We can't…" Jerry stopped. "I appreciate what you're saying, but Maddie and I can't have children."

Cain dropped a kiss on Emma's forehead before approaching the couple. "May I?" She held out her arms for the baby.

"My father always told me that your children are yours, but only for a short time. It's what you do with and for them in that time that will make them good people. Your time with him starts now."

Jerry's hands were shaking so much he almost dropped the baby when Cain handed him over. "Use it wisely, but only if you want."

"Do you mean it?" Jerry asked, as Maddie jumped to her feet.

"I mean it, and I can't think of two better people to care for him." Cain pulled adoption papers out of her coat pocket.

"Oh, my God." Maddie flung her hands to her mouth as tears rolled down her cheeks. "We can't thank you enough."

"There's only one thing I want you to remember." Cain took the papers and pressed them into Maddie's hand. "On here it says Baby Rath came from a Russian orphanage. He should never hear any other story about his origin."

"Why would we think differently?"

The baby sighed as Jerry kissed his forehead again. "We're going to love him and tell him this is his home. The way I see it, the rest isn't important."

"Then congratulations." Cain gently slapped his back and accepted a long hug from Maddie, who was still crying as she clung to Cain, watching Jerry cradle their new son.

"No one deserves this more than you do, Maddie. My cousin prepared the initial papers, the ones you're holding, in conjunction with one of her law-school pals who's currently practicing in Wisconsin. Once you and Jerry pick a name, give her a call. It's better all around, though, if you pick one before we leave."

"We won't ever have to give him back, right? I don't think I could bear that…the disappointment would kill me."

"It would take breaking me, darlin'."

Before Cain could finish, Emma walked up and placed her hand on Maddie's back. "Cain will often bend on some things, but breaking isn't in her makeup. Her word is her oath, and nothing will ever change it."

"Oh, Emma, you of all people know what this means to me." Maddie laid her head on Cain's chest like she would never let go. "Thank you, Cain. Tonight you've given me the only other thing aside from Jerry I've always wanted."

Merrick walked in carrying a few bags and put them down in the doorway. "Sorry, boss, I thought you were done." Outside a few doors closed quietly, but in the stillness the group still heard them. "The guys are back and turning in for the night, unless you need something else."

"I think we've accomplished enough for one night, don't you? Let's leave the Rath family to get acquainted."

Cain carried the bags in and gave them to Jerry, since he'd relinquished their new son to his mother. They contained enough diapers and supplies to last them a couple of weeks, which was more than enough time to lay the groundwork to make their story work.

"Enjoy, and we'll see you in the morning."

❖

"All set?" Katlin asked as soon as Merrick quietly clicked the door shut.

"Seems like it." Merrick gazed out at the yard and the men heading into the bunkhouse close to the fence line. "When was the last time you took a girl parking?"

"Does it entail driving? Because I have to warn you about getting lost out here in the middle of flat hell," Katlin said as she pushed Merrick up against the front of the house and pressed her lips against the side of Merrick's neck.

"The car you were in should still be warm. If not, you have the key, don't you?"

"Don't you worry, darling girl." Katlin offered her hand readily. "I'll keep you warm."

When the back door of the vehicle closed, Merrick climbed willingly onto Katlin's lap. They'd been doing so much for Cain that their time together had been severely limited. It had been so long since Merrick had wanted to be intimate with someone that now she wanted to rush and feel Katlin's skin pressed to hers and study more closely the tattoos that were seared into her memory.

"Make sure you tell me if I do something you don't like," Katlin said as she tugged Merrick's sweater over her head.

She bit down softly on a dark nipple, and Merrick hissed. "I don't do this often with a woman who's got a gun and knows how to use it."

"Shut up and get going before I shoot you just for incentive." Merrick pulled on Katlin's hair when she bit down a little harder on her other nipple.

"Oh, fuck."

"Now you're getting it, darlin'."

Merrick ignored the laughter as Katlin unbuttoned her jeans.

"Only this is going to mean so much more than just a roll in the back of a car. I hope you've come to realize that too."

Merrick kissed her and unbuttoned Katlin's shirt, wanting to feel the warmth of her skin. "I realize lots of things, but right now I want you to touch me." She sat up enough to take her pants off, then went right back to Katlin's lap. As she wove her fingers into Katlin's dark hair again, intending to entice her lips back to her breasts, she saw something at the fence line that didn't belong there. "What the hell?"

CHAPTER FIFTY

The course is set for Cozumel," the pilot reported. They were about twenty minutes into the flight and had been monitoring the target's radio transmissions. "With this headwind, it'll be another hour or so before we're on the ground. I called ahead and arranged for some local law enforcement, as well as some of our guys, to meet us when we land."

"Thanks a lot," Shelby replied. She'd been looking out the window all night, and when there was a break in the clouds she could see Carlotti's plane. The sight made her think of the night she'd met Cain and how truly afraid she'd been staring down death. "What business could she have in Mexico?"

"Maybe Anthony had something with those photos of Casey with Rodolfo Luis." Joe sipped on a Coke. "Wouldn't that just chap my ass?"

"From the time we started watching Cain, we haven't seen any hint of drugs," Shelby said.

"It's where the money is these days." Lionel was also looking out the window as he tapped his fist on the armrest. "Most of the big guys dealing that crap on the streets make more in a month than the three of us will in our lifetime. The temptation of all that cash might've been too much for her."

A strand of hair fell into Shelby's face when she shook her head. "I don't buy it. Casey's worth that now from just her legitimate businesses. Trust me, the IRS goes over every penny every year, and it's all accounted for."

"What you don't get, though, is that her type never gets enough. There's no magic number."

Shelby let Joe have the last word and stared out the window again. For once she felt as if they held the upper hand, and when Cain and Emma committed to their final destination, the surveillance would be in place. This time Cain wouldn't have any clandestine meetings in the middle of nowhere with no one watching, like the night she'd met Vincent Carlotti in a deserted field just over the border into Illinois. Shelby still carried the guilt of not telling anyone about that first night she'd met Cain, but she'd struck a deal for her life that she intended to keep.

They flew over the dark Gulf for another hour and twenty minutes, the pilot in the lead plane clearly in no hurry to land. When they started their descent, they were assured Cozumel was indeed the plane's destination. Quickly scanning their databases, Lionel discovered that Rodolfo Luis had a large vacation home in the area. The confirmation reminded Shelby again that no matter how much she liked Cain, Cain was in the business of breaking the laws she fought so hard to uphold.

As they stepped off the Coast Guard plane, the team caught only a glimpse of the couple as they entered the customs building and were out of the airport fast, presumably because it was so late.

The team wasn't in a hurry, since the DEA had agents outside in case they weren't quick enough.

As soon as the Mexican authorities verified their credentials, they hopped into a waiting car. "Relax and enjoy the weather, guys," the DEA agent who met them said. "Your targets are headed for the Hilton."

"How can you predict no detours?" Joe asked.

"I can't, but I thought it was a safe enough bet since the Hilton's car picked them up. My men will call if there's a change."

As the DEA guy relaxed into the driver's seat and turned onto the main drag, his radio came to life, and his partner reported that the two women in question had arrived at the resort and been escorted to one of the waterfront suites.

"You heard him. Now it's hurry up and wait."

Chapter Fifty-one

Emma lay with her eyes open, amazed at the silence. The house settled every so often, but that was the only sound. When she'd moved back home, she'd hated nights like this. With her head pillowed on Cain's shoulder, though, Emma wouldn't have minded if it went on forever.

"What wheels are turning in that pretty head?" The burr of Cain's voice sent a pleasant chill through Emma's body, and Cain pulled her closer.

"Thinking of how blessed I am."

They'd looked in on the sleeping children and then retired to the room Maddie had given them on their previous visit and locked the door behind them. After the kiss they'd shared at the top of the stairs, Emma needed to feel Cain's skin. She scratched along Cain's chest and smiled when her fingernails caused a shiver. "I'm thinking about what our next baby will be like." She shifted so she could see Cain's face in the moonlight. "I'm thinking about you roaming the aisles at the toy store."

"I've been visualizing that myself. I've got a lot of catching up to do when it comes to our little girl."

Even though Cain's comment was light, Emma teared up. "I'm sorry."

"What's wrong?" Cain rolled over and cupped Emma's cheek.

"Hannah's not going to know what hit her when we settle into a normal routine."

"Is that a bad thing?"

"No, love, it's just that for all her short life, presents have been of a practical nature. Just one more thing I caved in to my mother about. Toys aren't practical." Emma imitated Carol Verde's pinched voice. "I not only stole time from you, but I stole all those Christmas mornings and birthdays from Hannah."

"Listen to me." Cain placed her fingers over Emma's mouth. "I want you to forgive yourself. We can't change the past, just improve upon it. Hannah will know true happiness for the rest of her days not because of the things she's missed out on, but because we'll both love her. That alone will make even the heartaches that come along bearable."

"See, I told you I was blessed." Emma pulled Cain down, wanting to feel the weight of her. The sensation always made her feel safe.

"Let our love for each other see you through when you doubt your decisions, lass. None of us, no matter how much we'd like to think so, is perfect. In my eyes, though, you're about as close as they come."

"Flatterer." The sad feelings drained away as Emma nipped along Cain's neck.

"I'm more of a lover, really, but if it's flattery you're after, I can lie here and think of some."

"Honey, as much as I love the sound of your voice, talking is the last thing I want you to be doing right about now."

Cain worked her hand slowly between them and continued down until she found what she was hoping would be at the end of her journey. Emma was wet, and her hips jerked when Cain ran her fingers ran along the length of her sex. "What can I interest you in, then?"

"Shut up and make love to me." Emma pinched Cain's butt, but just as quickly she caressed it.

Their lovemaking was faster than either of them wanted, but it was satisfying. After they finished, Cain stayed awake enjoying the flush of Emma's skin and the way her breathing returned to a normal rate after all the exertion. The passion between them had left Emma lethargic, and she went immediately to sleep.

Running her hand slowly down Emma's back, Cain imagined their new life now that Giovanni and his pack of goons were gone.

Before she could get too far into her train of thought, the phone on the nightstand buzzed, and she grabbed it before it could wake Emma. As she listened to Merrick, she heard Emma moan softly when she tensed at the guard's words. "Don't make a move." Pulling Emma closer, she whispered, "Shh, lass, it's all right."

"She's making her way to the house from the field, Cain, and you don't want me to do anything? Believe me, I'd love to use my gun."

"If you stop her, then we'll never know what exactly she had in mind, will we?" Slowly Cain pulled away from Emma and picked her boxers off the floor. Emma seemed content for now, hugging Cain's pillow to her chest as Cain put her shirt back on and padded barefoot out of the room.

She leaned against the wall at the end of the hall and waited. Soon the front door creaked open and closed just as softly. The wood of the stairs barely made a sound as the intruder made her way up and headed to the room across from where Cain was standing in the shadows. Cain doubted that the woman would notice her at all unless she was looking directly at her, and she seemed focused on the closed door leading into Hannah's room.

With her hand on the knob, Carol Verde felt her heart run cold when she heard the floorboard groan ever so slightly behind her. Standing perfectly still as if that would make her invisible, she waited to see if it was just the house shuddering from the breeze outside.

"What do you suppose would happen if I were to kill you now and claim I thought you were a burglar? Not only that, but a burglar poised to harm or, better yet, take my daughter?"

"Your daughter? What a laugh that is." Carol was shocked at how close Cain had gotten without her hearing her. The floorboard evidently wasn't an accident; it was the one noise Cain had meant for her to hear. "Hannah is still pure, not like that abomination you call a son."

Cain whipped her hand up, wanting to choke the life out of the bitter old woman, but stopped at the last second and grabbed Carol's hand instead. Perhaps Carol's hearing wasn't all that great, but Cain's was keen.

"Please, don't stop on my account."

Wearing only the sweater Cain had discarded when they'd gone to bed, Emma stood in the doorway with her arms folded over her chest.

"Why, you ungrateful little…" Carol's anger made her shake as she glared at her daughter. "After all I've done for you, trying to save you from yourself."

The fact that Cain hadn't dropped Carol's hand hadn't escaped Emma's notice as she moved closer, not wanting to wake Hannah or Hayden. "It's not ungrateful of me to long for a life that makes me happy. As for saving me from myself, you obviously felt I needed it, but you never bothered to ask me."

Emma closed the gap between them and took Cain's hand, lowering it and kissing the palm. "I've made mistakes in my life, Mother, but my biggest was walking away from the only happiness I've known. Those are the things I have to live with, but my family has forgiven me. Perhaps it's time for you to resolve the hurts or bad feelings you have because of your poor decisions because, frankly, the people around you are tired of paying the price for you."

Cain stayed still and silent, knowing Emma had to fight this battle on her own. She watched closely as Carol opened her mouth for what Cain was sure was another barrage of hurtful comments, but the new player who was about to join the fun distracted her. She was almost sure it wasn't anyone who worked for her, since they all seemed to have finally learned to follow orders.

"Not another word, Carol."

Ross Verde had hastily dressed and rushed over when Emma had called him.

"This isn't your business, and I'm tired of kowtowing to you on this issue. For God's sake, Ross, Hannah lived with us. Don't you think her soul deserves saving?"

"It's a sin to lie, isn't that what you're always telling me? When have you ever kowtowed to anyone in your life, woman?" He ran his hand through his thinning hair and sighed tiredly. "I believe Hannah deserves to live her life with the people who love her, and if, for her own good, you're never a part of her life, then that's how it has to be. But I can't speak for Cain and Emma."

"What do you know? You've been sneaking over here turning that little girl against me."

"I've been spending time playing with both of them because I'm their grandfather and I love them. And I've seen how well adjusted Hayden is. He's a confident boy who'll become an extraordinary man. But it's late. We should go home and discuss this situation in private."

Instead of moving to leave, Carol put her hand on the knob of the door to Hannah's room.

Before she could open it, Cain curled long fingers around her wrist and squeezed just to the point of being painful. "If I were you, I'd listen to what my husband is telling me. Because you'll be going in this room and taking my little girl anywhere over my dead body."

Ross stepped closer and closed his hand around Carol's bicep. "Come on, we're going." He pulled her to him, obviously relieved when Cain let her go. "Kids, I'm sorry about this. I'll call you in the morning."

"Drive safe, Daddy, and let us know if you need anything."

They heard the heated muttering all the way out of the house, knowing the argument that would ensue would be monumental.

Once the front door closed, Emma fell against Cain in a silent plea to be held.

Ignoring the pain in her side, Cain bent, picked her up, and carried her back to their room.

"Why does she hate me so much?" The insecure little girl that still existed inside Emma wasn't allowed out very often, but Cain heard her clearly in the question.

"I don't think it has anything to do with you, my love. People like your mother just find it easier to hate people who are different for whatever reason they conjure up in their head, instead of trying to figure out what they hate about themselves."

Emma squeezed her eyes shut, not crying yet. "You sound like a therapist."

"Well, I'd love to get you on my couch at every given opportunity, but can you afford my fee?" The joke had its intended effect, and Emma ended up laughing against Cain's chest.

"If I ask really nicely, maybe you'll give me a job. Then I'll be able to pay up. Because if you ask my mother, I'm really screwed together in the worst possible way."

With little effort, Cain lifted Emma until she was draped over her. "You listen to me, Emma Casey. You're a beautiful woman inside and out. That doesn't happen overnight, so that means you were also a beautiful little girl. A beautiful and giving little girl who was wasted on your mother, so stop trying to figure out what you could've done differently to change Carol's heart."

CHAPTER FIFTY-TWO

The sky became a brilliant pink as the first fingers of light broke through the night. A rooster puffed his chest with air before letting out his first cry to greet the new day, and a tourist with her legs stretched out on the chair wearing a robe laughed at the little guy with such a loud voice. Her face was shrouded in shadows, but the interested sets of eyes looking on could see her bare feet clearly.

"Ms. Casey, there's a message for you." One of the resort workers handed her a folded piece of paper. "Could I get you coffee and breakfast?"

"Just the coffee, thanks. I'll order when my companion gets up. If she misses out on the hot bread you're known for, there might be bloodshed."

He laughed, as did the others listening in. "We try to not let that happen, since stains on the white sand is no good for the tourists."

"You know what the shame of putting this one in jail will be?" Lionel asked. They were sitting in the empty bar next to the beach with a very small mike pointed at the suite, and their new DEA friends were camped outside the front in case Cain decided to go somewhere without them.

"That she'll never date you?" Claire asked in return.

"I was thinking that she's amusing in a gangster, sarcastic sort of way and vacations in some really cool places."

When the others looked at him as if he'd grown horns, he shook with silent laughter. "Come on, you have to admit this place beats being stuck in the back of a van somewhere in New Orleans. And our next assignment will probably be some old guy who eats peanuts all day."

"The man's got a point, Joe, so leave him alone." Shelby scanned the grounds of the resort, trying to find their next post. Once the sun came up, Cain would see them if she as much as glanced toward the bar, and Shelby wanted to maintain the element of surprise as long as possible. "What do you two think of that stand of palms over there?"

❖

Above the band of pink appeared a band of blue sky, assuring those enjoying the sunrise of another perfect day without a cloud to mar their tanning time. With one more look at the shoreline, Muriel strolled back inside to grab a shower, leaving the message the man had delivered on the small table where the coffeepot sat.

Joe hopped off his bar stool and flagged down the server who was on his way to clean up the suite's patio, offering him a twenty to also bring back the note. Without hesitation, the man stuffed the money into his shirt pocket and soon returned with the light pink piece of paper.

The Blue Mayan at seven. Try not to be late.

The Blue Mayan was the hotel's restaurant—that was the easy part. But was the intended time morning or night? Leaving Claire, Lionel, and Joe on guard, Shelby went to check out the layout of Cain's meeting place.

In keeping with the rest of the resort, the restaurant was tastefully decorated. The tables were far enough apart to give the diners some privacy, and the large windows at the back provided a spectacular view of the Gulf. Surprising to Shelby, people were already arriving for breakfast, probably to try and make some tour off-site. But she was totally shocked when the elderly host approached her and smiled.

"Miss Daniels, would you like to freshen up before I escort you to you table? You are welcome to use our private facilities. You can brush you teeth and fix you hair, if you like."

"How do you know my name?"

"Ms. Casey, she call ahead and tell me to expect you. She here for the game fishing and said you share the same passion, but it's better with a full stomach."

Shelby laughed until she cried, as she had a tendency to do when she was tired, and followed compliantly, looking forward to freshening up. What she didn't expect was her favorite perfume, a sundress, and a pair of sandals in her size.

"There is also a shower, miss, if you like to use it before you try the lovely dress."

"Pretty sure of herself, isn't she?"

She didn't really mean the question for the man helping her, but he smiled and said as he began to leave, "Ms. Casey, she come here at least twice a year to enjoy the sport fishing, so I've gotten to know her well. If there's one thing she no lack, it's confidence."

Shelby thought about returning to telling the others what she was doing but knew that they'd eventually come looking. The helpful gentleman was waiting for her outside when she was done and escorted her to the only table located outside.

It was a rather romantic setting, secluded from the sides by a thick stand of palm trees, but with a clear view of the water. The breeze stirred her freshly washed hair as she sat down and waited, wanting to know what Cain had in mind with this meeting in this particular place. She was especially curious because the reconciliation with Emma seemed genuine.

The back door of the suite opened again, and Lionel elbowed Joe so he would look up. They had just been discussing going after Shelby when their target took precedence. The occupant stopped to say something to someone in the room, her face still indiscernible in the shadow of the patio. With a wave she stepped out into the sunlight, and both men came close to falling off their perches.

"Fuck," both men said simultaneously. Claire was already off her stool and heading for the restaurant.

"If *she's* here, then where's Cain?" Lionel asked. He felt like an idiot when Muriel smiled and waved as she passed. "Shit, I'm beginning to feel like we're hanging around for these people's entertainment."

They didn't hide as they followed Muriel closely to see where she was going. The host showed them to a table inside and handed them a menu. Claire was already seated and craning her neck to get a glimpse of the table outside.

Shelby had leaned her head back and closed her eyes, clearly enjoying the peacefulness of the spot. Before stepping out the door, Muriel stopped and admired the serenity of her face. Had they picked different paths in life, she could have easily fallen for Shelby.

"This is a great spot, isn't it?" She put her hands out in front of her when Shelby jumped and spun around. "I'm sorry. I didn't mean to startle you."

"When did you get here?"

"Last night, right before you did." The cast-iron chair scraped against the flagstone as Muriel took a seat and unfurled her napkin.

"Helping Cain find new ways to break the law?" Shelby asked as she swept a lock of hair behind her ear. "Or are you a fan of sport fishing too?"

"My cousin and I've never discussed her fishing preferences, but it's one of my favorite activities." The juice glass in front to her was filled without Muriel requesting it. "When you're a paid mouthpiece, as it were, it's nice to enjoy the quiet of the Gulf whenever possible."

"But I thought the gentleman said…" Shelby stopped as if going over her prior conversation. "He said Ms. Casey liked to fish."

Muriel poured the next round of juice herself as she shook her head. "Ms. Casey *does* like to fish. If you recall, I'm Ms. Casey too. I can show you my driver's license."

The word never vocalized, but Muriel clearly saw the "fuck" that formed on Shelby's lips.

"How'd you get here?"

"Vincent was nice enough to let me borrow his plane." A small part of Muriel felt bad for the agents who spent their lives chasing their tails trying to enclose what they considered rats like Cain and her in small cages. "It's so much better than flying commercial."

"She's not with you, then?"

"Cain, do you mean?" She laughed out loud at the contemptuous look Shelby gave her for even daring to ask the question. "No, she decided to sit this trip out."

"Who's the blonde with you, then?"

The look became murderous when Muriel laughed even louder.

"My, Agent Daniels, why would you care?"

"I don't, but I can't believe you would've brought someone who so resembles Emma without a reason."

"I'll be sure and let my secretary know that you think she's cute." Muriel curled her lips up slightly. "Since I do presume that you think so?"

Shelby ignored Muriel's comments. "Where's Cain, Muriel?"

"Not here, so how about we enjoy breakfast and, if you're free, a trip out to do some fishing?"

Muriel rose from her chair a second after Shelby sprang from hers and gently grasped her shoulders before she got two feet from the table. "I'm sorry. I don't mean to be so flip. There's nothing you can do about Cain right now, so stay. Stay and have breakfast with me, and we can pretend your three shadows aren't on the other side of that door."

"What about the blonde in your bed?"

Muriel eased her hands down until they rested on Shelby's hips, and she used the position to rotate her. "You could've asked the front desk when you got here. It's a two-bedroom suite. The blonde has her own bed and is typing files as we speak. She really is just my secretary and is here to catch up on some work that we fell behind on after our office was bombed."

Shelby missed the warmth of Muriel's body the moment she backed away and stood behind Shelby's chair. "If I stay, does that mean we can declare a truce, if only for a little while?"

"Perhaps that gulf between us isn't so wide after all." Muriel's hands strayed to Shelby's shoulders again after she took her seat.

Chapter Fifty-three

"You know something, lass?" The skin of Cain's back felt warm and comfortable as Emma worked her hands under her shirt. "I know I love you more than I thought I could love anyone."

"Thank you." Cain claimed her first kiss of the morning. "That was very sweet of you to say, but do you want to know what I know?"

"Will you put your lips to better use once you've told me?" She reached the band of Cain's shorts.

"My lips, my hands, and just about anything else I can think of." When Emma pulled her down as if to remind her of that promise, Cain shifted so she was more fully on Emma. "I know that our lives are sometimes hectic, but when I was lying here watching you sleep, something occurred to me."

"What's that?"

"That right now I'm blissfully happy, and I'm looking forward to whatever comes next."

Emma's tears came again at the sentiment in Cain's voice, and she pulled the large hand up and kissed each knuckle before sucking the thumb into her mouth. "I may not be able to predict exactly what'll happen next, but I can predict what'll happen right this second." Emma pushed past Cain's boxers, but stopped when she heard the creak of the door opening.

"You were saying?" Cain asked as she glanced over her shoulder.

"Don't blame me, mobster. You were supposed to lock it last night," Emma said, seeing Hannah standing there looking unsure of herself. She kissed Cain's jaw and lifted her hands above the blankets. "Come see us, honey."

A squeal accompanied the run to the bed, and Hannah landed on Cain's back when she made it on the bed. "Mom, you came back and brought Mama."

"I came back for you and your brother. It's time to go home." She laughed at the other kid standing in the door when he pumped his fist in agreement. "Did you two have fun?"

"Yeah, but I wanna go to the zoo," Hannah whined. "Haygen said there's one at home."

"There is, and an aquarium too," Emma added. She crooked her finger at their son, not comfortable getting up in her state of undress. "And a Mom and a Hayden, so it's the best place on earth."

"Feeling a little sappy this morning, huh?" He kissed them both hello and fell into Emma's arms for a long hug. "Come on, squirt. I heard Miss Maddie down in the kitchen making breakfast. We'll let our moms get back to their mushiness."

"What's mushy something?" Hannah asked as she climbed onto her big brother's back.

"Something we'll both be really lucky to find when we get big like them." With a wink for the grown-ups, he walked slowly out of the room.

Both of them laughed when he locked the door.

"Remind me to buy him a car when we get home," Cain said as she returned to where she was before they were interrupted.

"Whatever he wants. Just stop talking."

❖

By late that afternoon Cain sat on the front porch with their luggage, waiting for it to be loaded. She watched as Ross told the kids good-bye and talked to them near the fence line of Jerry's property. He was planning to come for a visit before the month was out.

Cain shifted her eyes to the door when she heard it open and smiled at Jerry. He looked tired, but she remembered what it was like to stay up with a baby at night. Even when Hayden was sleeping through the night, sometimes she would go into his room and just watch him.

"Happy?"

"I sure am, and ah…I…I wanted to talk to you alone before you left." Jerry shifted from foot to foot as if not knowing where to begin.

"No need to be nervous. Contrary to what the world thinks, I really don't bite." Cain sat on the banister and smiled.

"Cain, I can't begin to tell you how happy you've made Maddie and me. I've prayed all my life for a son, and I'd given up asking because I thought it would never happen." He paced, then finally stopped and looked at her. "I cried like a baby myself last night when Maddie laid him down between us. And before you left, I wanted to give you these papers back 'cause we picked a name and wanted to make it legal. Since your cousin and her friend are taking care of it, I thought you could take them with you and send them back whenever you can."

He handed them over, and Cain wondered if he was acting a little off kilter because he was tired.

"Just to be on the safe side, I'll send them to you with one of my men."

"Maddie and I hope you don't mind, but we thought his name was the best way to repay a little of what you've given us."

Cain unfolded the form Muriel had enclosed for them to fill out. "Jeremiah Cain Rath?"

"He deserves to be his own man, so he doesn't need all of mine. But he also deserves to know that he carries the name of a person his mother and I respect. The name of our friend Cain."

When Emma walked out holding the baby, she found them embracing. Maddie had just found out how far a kid could spit something out when he didn't particularly care for it. "You might want to scratch beets off his list of favorite foods, Dad." She handed him to Jerry and smiled when she saw him wipe his eyes before taking him.

"I don't much care for beets myself, son, so don't worry about it."

What sounded like a giggle escaped Jerry's mouth, and Emma knew he'd just realized that the word "son" was now part of his vocabulary.

"It's a wonderful thing, isn't it?" Emma touched his arm and laughed along with him.

"JC is the best thing we could've been blessed with."

"Found a name you like, huh?" Emma shook her head and laughed. "You don't have to tell me. Maddie's already filled me in this morning, and if you ask me, I think you made a great choice."

"Ready, lass?"

"Can I have a minute?" Emma inhaled deeply when she pressed her face to the softness of the sweater Cain was wearing, loving how quickly Cain's arms rose to encircle her. When she felt the gentle kiss placed on the top of her head, she smiled.

"Take all the time you need, and tell your father I'm holding him to that visit."

The wind was still carrying the cold air down from Canada, and Emma stopped at the top step and closed her eyes. As a child she'd loved walking in the big empty fields when the weather was like this and feeling the grass crunch beneath her feet. Even though everything looked dead and withered, in a few weeks the land would undergo another miraculous transformation, bringing with it the varying greens of spring and summer.

When she studied her father, she suddenly realized how much Ross had aged. The thick blond hair she remembered him combing back as he'd lift his cap when he was returning from the fields had thinned and gradually been replaced with more white. His smile, though, had remained the same.

"Thanks for not forgetting your ole dad before you flew off," he joked. His arms opened, and he hugged her like he hadn't in a while.

"I wanted to thank you for last night."

Ross put his fingers over her lips to get her to stop talking before dropping his hands to his side and using the fence for support. "The fact you're thanking me for that tells me how much I've failed you." He put his hands up again when she began to protest. "No, don't defend me when it comes to your mother. I shouldn't have let her be so hard on you all those years and let her have her way with what happened when Cain first came back to you."

"I had a little to do with that myself, Daddy." She glanced back to the porch and watched as Cain swung Hannah around over her head. "If you look over there, you'll see everything worked out just fine."

"That's what I wanted to tell you. I've spent time with your Cain, and even though I'm years late, you have my blessing when it comes to your marriage. It may not be legal in the eyes of the law, but she loves you and those children more than her own life."

"Thank you for saying that, and it's not too late." She stood next to him at the fence and pointed to the field. "I'm glad we came here to start over, because in a way all this land reminds me of what my life has been for the last couple of years, and it was no one's fault but mine. The winter's over, though, and I'm ready to start again."

"I'm glad, sweetheart, but just remember that if you ever need anything to give me a call."

"What about you and Mom? Are you going to be all right?"

"Your mom's going to spend some more time with her brother and his wife. I hope that doesn't bother you too much, but I'd like to try some of that happiness you keep talking about, and I'm more apt to find it on my own."

"In that case, give me a call if you need any pointers, and we'll be waiting for you at the end of April."

He put his arm around her and started them strolling back to the house. "You're going to be fine. We both will."

Before they made it too far, Cain came out to meet them.

"Ross, you want to take the kids out to the airfield for us?"

He nodded before kissing Emma's forehead and kept on going without her.

"Up for a little walk before we go?"

"I thought you wanted to get going."

"Oh, I do, but we have time for a little something first. I don't want to miss getting back to the city before Muriel and her new group of friends, but taking my girl on a walk takes precedence over that."

Without hesitation Emma took the offered hand, and they started off in silence. After a short distance, Emma guessed where they were going. When they stopped, they were back under the tree they'd sat under when Emma had introduced Cain to the lake between the properties.

"I told you once that life with me would never be boring." Cain uttered the words softly since there was nothing to talk over but the wind. "And I told you that I was going to love you above all others." Cain faced Emma and took her hands in her own. "Because I do, I'm going to do my best to keep you safe."

"You've done a wonderful job, love."

"We're here not for you to thank me, but for me to start trying to give you as much as you've brought into my life." Cain pointed to the area. "I didn't forget what you told me about the wishes you made here when you were a little girl, so I made a little deal with your father and Jerry."

"Tell me, devil, did you include any of your own brand of gentle persuasion in that conversation?"

Cain laughed and pulled gently on her hair. "I bought another farm adjacent to these so they could play with more cows if they deeded me this little bit of land in return."

"You *are* interested in cow races, I knew it."

"I can't guarantee you won't find a couple of bovines in your flowers in the morning, but I bought it to build a cabin here so we'd have a place to stay when we come to visit. A place with a bench under this tree so you can sit here and look at the water and make all the wishes you want."

Emma stood in silent shock, then finally shook her head. "Thank you for doing that and for understanding me so well. There's something special about this place that I've never been able to put into words, but you understood it anyway. I'll love sitting out here, but I don't have any wishes left to make."

"Sure you do. I'm certain you want something."

"I have two wonderful children and hopefully a third soon." She put her hands on Cain's chest and slid her left hand over her lover's heart. "I have a family of my choosing that loves me." With her right she cupped Cain's chin. "All those things were part of my secondary wishes."

"Secondary wishes?"

"Secondary, as in they came into play after I got what I wished for most of all." They fell into the kiss Cain started and pulled apart only after they needed air. "I wished most of all for someone to love me, keep me safe, and care about the person I am."

"Maybe the lake needs tuning, if all it could conjure up was me."

"The lake knew that my fondest desire in a mate lay in a pair of blue eyes, a tall sturdy frame, and a devilish heart. You talk all the time about the devil inside, Cain, and while that might be true, you're my salvation and my fondest wish."

Cain kissed her again as Emma slid her hands to the back of her neck.

"May you always think so, lass."

About the Author

Originally from Cuba, Ali now lives outside the New Orleans area with her partner. As a writer she couldn't ask for a better, more beautiful place, so full of real-life characters to fuel the imagination. When she isn't writing, remodeling, working in the yard, or cheering on the Tigers, Ali makes a living in the nonprofit sector.

Her novels include *The Devil Inside*, *Carly's Sound*, and *Second Season* (2007), all from Bold Strokes Books.

Books Available From Bold Strokes Books

The Devil Unleashed by Ali Vali. As the heat of violence rises, so does the passion. A Casey Clan crime saga. (1-933110-61-9)

Burning Dreams by Susan Smith. The chronicle of the challenges faced by a young drag king and an older woman who share a love "outside the bounds." (1-933110-62-7)

Fresh Tracks by Georgia Beers. Seven women, seven days. A lot can happen when old friends, lovers, and a new girl in town get together in the mountains. (1-933110-63-5)

The Empress and the Acolyte by Jane Fletcher. Jemeryl and Tevi fight to protect the very fabric of their world...time. Lyremouth Chronicles Book Three (1-933110-60-0)

First Instinct by JLee Meyer. When high-stakes security fraud leads to murder, one woman flees for her life while another risks her heart to protect her. (1-933110-59-7)

Erotic Interludes 4: Extreme Passions. Thirty of today's hottest erotica writers set the pages aflame with love, lust, and steamy liaisons. (1-933110-58-9)

Storms of Change by Radclyffe. In the continuing saga of the Provincetown Tales, duty and love are at odds as Reese and Tory face their greatest challenge. (1-933110-57-0)

Unexpected Ties by Gina L. Dartt. With death before dessert, Kate Shannon and Nikki Harris are swept up in another tale of danger and romance. (1-933110-56-2)

Sleep of Reason by Rose Beecham. While Detective Jude Devine searches for a lost boy, her rocky relationship with Dr. Mercy Westmoreland gets a lot harder. (1-933110-53-8)

Passion's Bright Fury by Radclyffe. Passion strikes without warning when a trauma surgeon and a filmmaker become reluctant allies. (1-933110-54-6)

Broken Wings by L-J Baker. When Rye Woods meets beautiful dryad Flora Withe, her libido, as hidden as her wings, reawakens along with her heart. (1-933110-55-4)

Combust the Sun by Andrews & Austin. A Richfield and Rivers mystery set in L.A. Murder among the stars. (1-933110-52-X)

Of Drag Kings and the Wheel of Fate by Susan Smith. A blind date in a drag club leads to an unlikely romance. (1-933110-51-1)

Tristaine Rises by Cate Culpepper. Brenna, Jesstin, and the Amazons of Tristaine face their greatest challenge for survival. (1-933110-50-3)

Too Close to Touch by Georgia Beers. Kylie O'Brien believes in true love and is willing to wait for it, even though Gretchen, her new boss, is off-limits. (1-933110-47-3)

100th Generation by Justine Saracen. Ancient curses, modern-day villains, and an intriguing woman lead archeologist Valerie Foret on the adventure of her life. (1-933110-48-1)

Battle for Tristaine by Cate Culpepper. While Brenna struggles to find her place in the clan, Tristaine is threatened with destruction. Second in the Tristaine series. (1-933110-49-X)

The Traitor and the Chalice by Jane Fletcher. Tevi and Jemeryl risk all in the race to uncover a traitor. The Lyremouth Chronicles Book Two. (1-933110-43-0)

Promising Hearts by Radclyffe. Dr. Vance Phelps arrives in New Hope, Montana, with no hope of happiness—until she meets Mae. (1-933110-44-9)

Carly's Sound by Ali Vali. Poppy Valente and Julia Johnson form a bond of friendship that becomes something far more. A poignant romance about love and renewal. (1-933110-45-7)

Unexpected Sparks by Gina L. Dartt. Kate Shannon's attraction to much younger Nikki Harris is complication enough without a fatal fire that Kate can't ignore. (1-933110-46-5)

Whitewater Rendezvous by Kim Baldwin. Two women on a wilderness kayak adventure discover that true love may be nothing at all like they imagined. (1-933110-38-4)

Erotic Interludes 3: Lessons in Love ed. by Radclyffe and Stacia Seaman. Sign on for a class in love…the best lesbian erotica writers take us to "school." (1-9331100-39-2)

Punk Like Me by JD Glass. Twenty-one-year-old Nina has a way with the girls, and she doesn't always play by the rules. (1-933110-40-6)

Coffee Sonata by Gun Brooke. Four women whose lives unexpectedly intersect in a small town by the sea share one thing in common—they all have secrets. (1-933110-41-4)

The Clinic: Tristaine Book One by Cate Culpepper. Brenna, a prison medic, finds herself drawn to Jesstin, a warrior reputed to be descended from ancient Amazons. (1-933110-42-2)

Forever Found by JLee Meyer. Can time, tragedy, and shattered trust destroy a love that seemed destined? Chance reunites childhood friends separated by tragedy. (1-933110-37-6)

Sword of the Guardian by Merry Shannon. Princess Shasta's bold new bodyguard has a secret that could change both of their lives. *He* is actually a *she*. (1-933110-36-8)

Wild Abandon by Ronica Black. Dr. Chandler Brogan and Officer Sarah Monroe are drawn together by their common obsessions—sex, speed, and danger. (1-933110-35-X)

Turn Back Time by Radclyffe. Pearce Rifkin and Wynter Thompson have nothing in common but a shared passion for surgery—and unexpected attraction. (1-933110-34-1)

Chance by Grace Lennox. A sexy, funny, touching story of two women who, in finding themselves, also find one another. (1-933110-31-7)

The Exile and the Sorcerer by Jane Fletcher. First in the Lyremouth Chronicles. Tevi and a shy young sorcerer face monsters, magic, and the challenge of loving. (1-933110-32-5)

A Matter of Trust by Radclyffe. When what should be just business turns into much more, two women struggle to trust the unexpected. (1-933110-33-3)

Sweet Creek by Lee Lynch. A celebration of the enduring nature of love, friendship, and community in the heart-warming lesbian community of Waterfall Falls. (1-933110-29-5)

The Devil Inside by Ali Vali. The head of a New Orleans crime organization falls for a woman who turns her world upside down. (1-933110-30-9)

Grave Silence by Rose Beecham. Detective Jude Devine's investigation of ritual murders is complicated by her torrid affair with pathologist Dr. Mercy Westmoreland. (1-933110-25-2)

Honor Reclaimed by Radclyffe. Secret Service Agent Cameron Roberts and Blair Powell close ranks to find the would-be assassins who nearly claimed Blair's life. (1-933110-18-X)

Honor Bound by Radclyffe. Secret Service Agent Cameron Roberts and Blair Powell face political intrigue, a clandestine threat to Blair's safety, and the seemingly irreconcilable differences that force them ever further apart. (1-933110-20-1)

Innocent Hearts by Radclyffe. In a wild and unforgiving land, two women learn about love, passion, and the wonders of the heart. (1-933110-21-X)

The Temple at Landfall by Jane Fletcher. An imprinter, one of Celaeno's most revered servants of the Goddess, is also a prisoner to the faith—until a Ranger frees her by claiming her heart. The Celaeno series. (1-933110-27-9)

Protector of the Realm: Supreme Constellations Book One by Gun Brooke. A space adventure filled with suspense and a daring intergalactic romance. (1-933110-26-0)

Force of Nature by Kim Baldwin. From tornados to forest fires, the forces of nature conspire to bring Gable McCoy and Erin Richards close to danger, and closer to each other. (1-933110-23-6)

In Too Deep by Ronica Black. Undercover homicide cop Erin McKenzie tracks a femme fatale who just might be a real killer...with love and danger hot on her heels. (1-933110-17-1)

Stolen Moments: Erotic Interludes 2 ed. by Stacia Seaman and Radclyffe. Love on the run, in the office, in the shadows...Fast, furious, and almost too hot to handle. (1-933110-16-3)

Course of Action by Gun Brooke. Actress Carolyn Black desperately wants the starring role in an upcoming film produced by Annelie Peterson. Just how far will she go for the dream part of a lifetime? (1-933110-22-8)

Rangers at Roadsend by Jane Fletcher. Sergeant Chip Coppelli has learned to spot trouble coming, and that is exactly what she sees in her new recruit, Katryn Nagata. The Celaeno series. (1-933110-28-7)

Justice Served by Radclyffe. Lieutenant Rebecca Frye and her lover, Dr. Catherine Rawlings, embark on a deadly game of hide-and-seek with an underworld kingpin who traffics in human souls. (1-933110-15-5)

Distant Shores, Silent Thunder by Radclyffe. Dr. Tory King—along with the women who love her—is forced to examine the boundaries of love, friendship, and the ties that transcend time. (1-933110-08-2)

Hunter's Pursuit by Kim Baldwin. A raging blizzard, a mountain hideaway, and a killer-for-hire set a scene for disaster—or desire—when Katarzyna Demetrious rescues a beautiful stranger. (1-933110-09-0)

The Walls of Westernfort by Jane Fletcher. All Temple Guard Natasha Ionadis wants is to serve the Goddess—until she falls in love with one of the rebels she is sworn to destroy. The Celaeno series. (1-933110-24-4)

Change Of Pace: Erotic Interludes by Radclyffe. Twenty-five hot-wired encounters guaranteed to spark more than just your imagination. Erotica as you've always dreamed of it. (1-933110-07-4)

Honor Guards by Radclyffe. In a wild flight for their lives, the president's daughter and those who are sworn to protect her wage a desperate struggle for survival. (1-933110-01-5)

Fated Love by Radclyffe. Amidst the chaos and drama of a busy emergency room, two women must contend not only with the fragile nature of life, but also with the irresistible forces of fate. (1-933110-05-8)

Justice in the Shadows by Radclyffe. In a shadow world of secrets and lies, Detective Sergeant Rebecca Frye and her lover, Dr. Catherine Rawlings, join forces in the elusive search for justice. (1-933110-03-1)

shadowland by Radclyffe. In a world on the far edge of desire, two women are drawn together by power, passion, and dark pleasures. An erotic romance. (1-933110-11-2)

Love's Masquerade by Radclyffe. Plunged into the indistinguishable realms of fiction, fantasy, and hidden desires, Auden Frost is forced to question all she believes about the nature of love. (1-933110-14-7)

Love & Honor by Radclyffe. The president's daughter and her lover are faced with difficult choices as they battle a tangled web of Washington intrigue for...love and honor. (1-933110-10-4)

Beyond the Breakwater by Radclyffe. One Provincetown summer, three women learn the true meaning of love, friendship, and family. (1-933110-06-6)

Tomorrow's Promise by Radclyffe. One timeless summer, two very different women discover the power of passion to heal and the promise of hope that only love can bestow. (1-933110-12-0)

Love's Tender Warriors by Radclyffe. Two women who have accepted loneliness as a way of life learn that love is worth fighting for and a battle they cannot afford to lose. (1-933110-02-3)

Love's Melody Lost by Radclyffe. A secretive artist with a haunted past and a young woman escaping a life that has proved to be a lie find their destinies entwined. (1-933110-00-7)

Safe Harbor by Radclyffe. A mysterious newcomer, a reclusive doctor, and a troubled gay teenager learn about love, friendship, and trust during one tumultuous summer in Provincetown. (1-933110-13-9)

Above All, Honor by Radclyffe. Secret Service Agent Cameron Roberts fights her desire for the one woman she can't have—Blair Powell, the daughter of the president of the United States. (1-933110-04-X)